Operation: Bayou Angel

Shepherd Security Book #6

Margaret Kay

This book is dedicated to those involved in an organization by the name of Imerman Angels. It is a one-on-one cancer support community, matching up volunteer Angel Mentors who have survived cancer or been the caregiver for someone with cancer with those in the process of fighting this horrible disease as the patient or as a caregiver. Find out more about this amazing organization at www.imermanangels.org.
Margaret

Shepherd Security Organizational Chart
Classified: Top Secret

Colonel Samuel 'Big Bear' Shepherd, Retired U.S. Army

<u>Alpha Team</u>
John 'Coop' Cooper
Alexander 'Doc' Williams
Anthony 'Razor' Garcia
Ethan 'Jax' Jackson
Madison 'Xena' Miller

<u>Delta Team</u>
Landon 'Lambchop' Johnson
Danny 'Mother' Trio
Gary 'the Undertaker' Sloan
Brian 'the Birdman' Sherman

<u>Charlie Team</u>
Jimmy 'Taco' Wilson
Mike 'Powder' Rogers
Rich 'Handsome' Burke
Carter 'Moe' Tessman

<u>Bravo Team</u>
Tommy 'Louisa' Flores
Eddie 'Needles' Winston
Kenny 'Ducky' Gallup
Elijah 'Kegger' Robinson

<u>Operations Center Analysts</u>
Yvette 'Control' Donaldson
Brody 'BT' Templeton
Anthony 'Wang' Miraldi
Caleb 'Hound dog' Smith

<u>Other Agency Staff</u>
Michaela Karras – TechLab Manager
Requisition Ryan Grant – Supply Chain Manager
Angel Jackson – Office Manager

Elizabeth Williams – Receptionist (PT)
Dr. Joe Lassiter – Team Mental Health Professional

Alpha

eyond the dense canopy of tree branches and hanging moss, the light from the moon and the stars in the cloudless night shone brightly. It filtered through the trees, illuminating random sections. The surrounding calls from the bullfrogs harmonized with the choir of crickets and cicadas, creating a sweet symphony that filled the still night air. The concert also covered the sound of twigs cracking and foliage rustling as the lone figure made her way up to the edge of the twelve-foot high chain-link fence that surrounded the old fish cannery plant that had been refurbished into the new BioDynamix facility.

She wore black combat boots, to help to protect her feet and ankles from possible snake bites, heavy-weight long pants, to help protect from the same as well as from insect bites. She wore a large black hoodie over her smaller frame and a black nylon face mask that revealed only alert brown eyes, eyes that cautiously scanned the area. Black gloved hands produced a set of wire cutters. She quickly cut an opening and pressed her five-foot-seven-inch frame through it.

Moving through the tall grass that edged the inside of the fence, she was careful to stay in the corner that she knew was shrouded in shadows. There were surveillance cameras everywhere at this plant. She'd be caught on one feed or another, she was sure. It was more a matter if she could gain entry into the warehouse to get a quick look at what was there and get out before she was seen, and guards arrived.

This was breaking and entering, most likely criminal trespass, and could possibly even be called industrial espionage. She knew if she got caught inside, it would be a trip to the local jail. She banished those thoughts from her mind, a bit too late to think about that. She crossed the open, manicured lawn and pressed her back against the metal wall of the building. She'd made it this far with no alarms, no spotlights, and no people invading this corner of the plant grounds.

She crept along the wall until she reached the door that she knew led within the warehouse. She tried the knob. Locked. She listened at the door, straining her ears to hear any possible sounds from within or from around her. Nothing. It was past midnight, but she knew this plant had activity twenty-four hours a day, seven days a week. She took a deep breath to summon her courage and fortify her will, and then she withdrew the lockpicking tools from her pocket. She'd never done this for real before.

She inserted the tension wrench into the bottom of the keyhole. Then the pick into the top. Her hands trembled slightly as she maneuvered the tools within the lock, tripping one pin set at a time. It seemed to take forever to unlock the door, when in reality it was less than three minutes, just like she'd practiced.

She cracked the door open, her heart pounding. Through the narrow slit she saw racks of empty shelves in front of her. The lighting was low. The area in front of the shelves was cavernous and filled with shadows. She heard nothing from within, heard only her own racing heartbeat. She slipped through the door and soundlessly reclosed it. She paused there, her back pressed against the metal wall. Still no alarms, no lights clicking on, no sounds of running feet converging on her location.

She moved further inside, following the line of tall black metal shelving racks towards the two massive garage doors. The last shelf was piled high, from the floor to the top shelf ten feet in the air with flattened boxes of all sizes, packaging material, bubble wrap, peanuts, and rolls of clear shipping tape. Otherwise, all the other shelves were empty.

Peeking around the end of the shelf, she was shocked to see no boxes at all on the warehouse floor. Nor were there any stacked along any of the walls. She hurried back to the door she came in, cracked it open and peered back into the quiet night. She half expected to find guards waiting for her. But no one was there. She rushed out, soundlessly closing the door, and then she retraced her steps back towards the southeast corner of the building. She quickly crossed the distance to the far corner and slipped back through the cut fence, disappearing into the dense undergrowth beneath the gnarled branches of the cypress and oak trees.

Even though it was sixty-two degrees out, the sweat poured down her body. The nylon facemask was soaked and clung to her face. But she didn't dare remove it yet. She followed the route back the way she'd come. Besides the snakes, coming across a gator was always a possibility too. She kept her eyes alert.

Five minutes later, she made it back to the dilapidated one-room shack that hung over the edge of the bayou. The pirogue, the small flat bottom wood boat, was tied up there, waiting for her. She glanced around and listened. There were no sounds to indicate anyone had followed her. But then she heard the engine of a car echo from the road to the east. Shit!

She was startled when a figure emerged from the shadows of the porch.

"Quick, give me the hoodie. The cops are just arriving," his whispered voice said.

She tore the hoodie over her head, revealing a black long-sleeved shirt beneath. It too was drenched with sweat. She pulled the wet black nylon mask from over her head, revealing thick, long black hair secured in a ponytail. She handed the hoodie to Bobby, her best friend and accomplice. She shoved the facemask into her pants pocket.

Bobby pulled the earplug from his left ear and handed it and the radio to her. He'd been tuned to the police channel.

"You're sure about this?" She asked in a whisper, guilt already gnawing at her.

"Just go, Brielle," he said. "I'll be fine. Hide out as planned and I should be there within forty-eight hours, seventy-two tops."

"Be safe. I love you, Bobby." She pressed a kiss to his cheek and then crossed the shack's porch and climbed into the pirogue, making sure to check for snakes. She grabbed the pole and pushed herself away from the bank as Bobby unfolded the piece of paper. She heard his inhale through his right nostril as he snorted the line of coke. Then he walked in the direction towards the road and where the police cruiser had just pulled up.

Upon reaching the far bank, she steered the small boat into one of the many finger streams that ran away from the main channel of the bayou. She quickly disappeared from view behind the trees and brush. Once she was a good distance down it, she placed the wire cutters and the gloves into the mask and dropped it into the middle of the channel, watching it instantly disappear below the dark water.

Further downstream, she pulled the boat over to the porch of another shack, tied the boat up, and climbed out. Then she made her way through the trees two-hundred yards east to the dirt path that led to the main road, to where the parked car, her escape vehicle, waited for her. By this time, she was chilled, the cool night air and the damp clothes a bad combination.

She pulled the keys from her pocket and unlocked the door with a shaking hand. After turning the engine over, she pulled her damp shirt from her and then grabbed the white fleece shirt that sat on the passenger side seat, pulling it over the lacy red bra she wore. She hoped the car would heat up quickly.

She was careful to drive the speed limit. Getting pulled over by the Parish Sheriff's Office was not part of the plan and would not be good.

Bobby heard the rustling of the underbrush before he saw the lights of the approaching searchers. They were heading in his direction. Showtime! He could feel the coke energizing him. He was mentally very alert. He had the black hoodie thrown over one shoulder, his skin beneath it was on fire, the rest of him was heating up. He slowed his gait, wanting to give the drug a few more minutes to fully dilate his eyes before he crossed paths with those searching. The question was, who would be searching? Would it be just the Parish Sheriff's Office or would the guards from BioDynamix be there too?

The dots of light appeared in the brush, getting larger as they got closer, until Bobby could clearly identify five separate flashlights. He purposefully walked into their line of sight.

"Freeze, Sheriff's Department!" A male voice called.

"Oh, hi," Bobby replied with a smile and a wave.

"Boy, I said freeze! And get your hands up!" The voice with a distinct Jersey accent repeated.

"Sure," Bobby said, raising his hands into the air. He kept a smile plastered on his face.

The five lights came in close. They were bright, blinding. Bobby dropped one of his hands to cover his eyes.

"I said hands up!" The voice yelled.

"Dude, you're right beside me. Do you seriously have to yell? And those lights are so bright," Bobby complained.

Someone pulled his hand away from his eyes. "Bobby Sherman. What the hell are you doing way out here?"

He recognized the voice. "Delroy, buddy, hi man, I don't know where I am. I'm just wandering."

"You're high. Damn it, Bobby, you stayed clean for so long," the baritone voice of Deputy Delroy Hebert said.

"We haven't arrested him in a while, we don't know if he's been clean," another voice said.

"You got any weapons on you, Bobby?" Deputy Hebert asked.

"No, man, you know I don't carry weapons."

Bobby felt hands patting him down. He felt the pipe and a small bag of crack get pulled from his pocket. "And what do we have here?" Another voice asked. "Looks like a trip to jail."

"You're lucky you didn't walk into a gator or into the bayou," Hebert said. "Damn it, Bobby, you trying to get yourself killed?"

"No, man, just, hum," he said blissfully, pretending to be higher than he was.

"Where is she?" The Jersey accented voice he knew was the new Sherriff asked.

"Her who?" Bobby asked, laughing euphorically, exaggerating the effects of the drugs.

"You know who. Your friend, Miss Jarboe."

"Don't know, haven't talked to her in a few days."

"Uh-huh," the Sheriff said skeptically. "Get him in cuffs and read him his rights."

Brian 'the Birdman' Sherman felt his phone vibrate in his pocket. Checking the display, he saw the number he didn't want to see. The phone number from Thibodaux and the Lafourche Parish lockup could only mean one thing. His brother Bobby got himself into trouble again. "Oh fuck, man," he swore beneath his breath. The timing couldn't be worse. His team was in the garage subbasement level of their headquarters packing up their SUVs, getting ready to head out on another DEA Partner Mission. He'd be gone a week. Bobby would have to cool his jets in the lockup. "This is Sherman," he said into his phone.

"We have a collect call from Bobby Sherman, will you accept the charges?" The electronic voice on the phone asked.

"Yes, I accept," Brian stated clearly.

"Brian, thank you for picking up," Bobby's panicked voice came across the line a second later.

"What is it this time?" Brian asked.

"I need you down here, Brian. It's bad this time, criminal trespass. But I didn't. I was high, and I just wandered onto this property, didn't have no criminal intentions," Bobby whined.

"Did you have drugs on you they recovered?"

"Just a pipe and a tiny amount of crack."

"Crack! Jesus Christ, Bobby! What the hell?" He swore under his breath. "When's the arraignment?" Brian asked.

His boss, Landon 'Lambchop' Johnson stood nearby. His eyebrows raised hearing Sherman's question into his phone.

"My PD can get it postponed till tomorrow if you can get down here."

PD, public defender. Brian Sherman knew that Bobby was already as good as incarcerated with one of the back-bayou public defenders as his counsel. "This is really bad timing, Bobby. I was just packing up for a mission. My boss is gonna be none too happy about this." He locked eyes with Lambchop. He moved the mouthpiece away from his mouth. "My dumb-shit brother got arrested again," he whispered to Lambchop.

"Your boat is hooked up at the marina. I left the AC running. It needs tending. I got no one else to call, Brian. No one I can trust. I just need to get back into rehab. I don't deserve jail and they're talking real jail time, state lockup. I can't go up state, Brian. Please, you gotta come down here and help me." Bobby actually cried.

"Fuck," Sherman moaned. The bill he'd get for power to his boat for even a week of the AC running full blast would be ridiculous. "Okay, I'll come," Sherman agreed. His eyes went back to Lambchop. He moved the mouthpiece away again. "I have to go," he whispered to his boss. "Can someone cover?"

Lambchop nodded. He immediately took his phone from his pocket and called Shepherd, Colonel Sam Shepherd, the head of the agency, his boss. He knew

Shepherd would be very unhappy about this, especially because there had just been another last-minute change of personnel to the mission. Lambchop had just been notified that Gary 'the Undertaker' Sloan, another teammate, had just gotten pulled from this mission and replaced with Doc, another medic, as Sloan was suddenly slated to cover a different mission in Cleveland. These kinds of changes, he knew, bothered the shit out of Shepherd. Too many moving pieces.

"Shepherd," he answered.

Lambchop relayed the issue. "Sherman is requesting emergency leave and I think it should be granted."

"I'll notify Jackson he's on your mission now and you'll be dropping Sloan and Kaylee in Cleveland on your way. Sherman will have to fly commercial. I'll get Angel on booking him a ticket," Shepherd said.

"Thanks, Shepherd," Lambchop said.

Sherman watched Lambchop carefully, listening to Lambchop's conversation as he also spoke with his brother. Bobby was babbling on about the boat some more, but not really apologizing, which annoyed the hell out of Sherman. Bobby wasn't supposed to be using his boat. "I've got it, you were high, and you left the AC on. The bill for even two days is going to suck," Sherman groused.

Just then, Sherman's best friend and partner, Gary Sloan, came into the garage. Sherman wished he would have a minute to talk with Sloan about him diverting to Cleveland. This wasn't going to be pleasant for him or his girlfriend, Kaylee. But there wasn't time to talk too much with him now. He closed the distance quickly, coming up to Sloan.

"What's up?" Sloan asked him.

"My little brother's gotten himself arrested again, drugs. If I don't go back and flash my badge to get him into rehab, again, it's a long stint in the state lock up this time. He also told me my boat needs tending, it's hooked up to power at the marina, running the AC. I'll get a hell of a bill for that if I don't go shut it down. He's got no one else to call. I've never heard him sound so desperate."

"Go ahead and take off," Lambchop told Sherman. "Jackson has been assigned to this mission to cover for you. Angel will have your boarding pass sent through to your phone before you reach O'Hare and Shepherd will have the ATF notified of the armed agent clearance they'll need to pass through to the TSA."

"Thanks, man," Sherman said to Lambchop, giving him a hug.

"Prayers for your brother's healing. Maybe this time the rehab will stick."

Sherman shook his head. "I sure hope so. The dumbass just can't stay away from the shit."

"Good luck, man," Sloan said, embracing him.

Then Mother, Delta Team's fourth and final teammate, embraced Sherman as well. "You need to tell him that he needs to get his shit together. Pretty soon it's going to be time for some tough love."

"Oh, believe me, we are way past the time for tough love. He's going to get my size twelve up his ass if he doesn't straighten up and fly right. Good luck with the mission. Be safe." Sherman grabbed his backpack and headed to his car.

All the way to O'Hare, Sherman couldn't help but feel bad for letting the team down. He owed Jackson, having to go on this mission last minute in his place, which meant he owed Angel, Jackson's wife. His thoughts drifted to Sloan, his best friend, who now also had a woman in his life. Not that he wanted what they both had, but, hell, he didn't know where his thoughts were going. He was just pissed at his brother, that's all this was, he decided.

He parked his car, a red pearl coat Dodge Challenger SRT Hellcat Redeye, his baby, in the garage, not his first choice to leave it at O'Hare International Airport. Then he proceeded to the terminal. He stepped up to the TSA Agent at the entry to the Security Checkpoint and identified himself as an armed law enforcement officer requiring the special security screening process. He was escorted to a side room where he declared his weapon, presented his credentials and the backup notification from DC permitting him to fly armed on this flight.

Angel had gotten him a direct flight into New Orleans, which left in less than an hour. He parked himself on a barstool at a bar near his gate and had a beer. He placed a call to Angel.

"Hi Brian," she answered on the second ring.

"Hi Angel, thanks for taking care of my ticket and everything."

"No problem. I'm sorry your brother is in a bind."

Sherman could tell Angel's attention was diverted. He heard clicking on the keyboard. "Hey, I really need a favor. I just parked my car in the short-term parking garage. Do you think someone from the office can come get it and park it at HQ? I don't want to leave my baby here. I'm sure it won't be here when I get back."

Angel chuckled. "I can send Requisition Ryan up right away. You probably should have taken an Uber to the airport and left your baby here."

Yeah, Sherman knew that. He wasn't thinking clearly when he got the call from Bobby, that was for sure. "Thanks, Angel, and thank Ryan too. Tell him I'll bring him some pralines or something from New Orleans." He gave her the location of the car. The office kept spare keys for everyone's vehicles. They'd have no problem getting his car for him, he was sure.

That was one load off his mind. He finished his beer and boarded his flight, seated in the center seat and wedged uncomfortably between two large men. Just his luck. Why couldn't it have been between two hot women? Because his day wasn't going that way, that was why. No, he wouldn't enjoy female conversation on the flight to New Orleans, he'd endure silence and cramped conditions. Everything about this trip sucked. He was really going to lay into Bobby when he saw him.

It was late afternoon when he touched down at Louis Armstrong International Airport, New Orleans. He got his rental car, a red Mustang GT convertible, thank you Angel! She knew him well.

He drove south through acreage he hadn't seen in at least a year, maybe longer. The heat up north had subsided with the coming of fall, but down here, it was still hot and sticky. Even so, he left the top down, enjoying the hot breeze blowing his dark brown locks around his head. He felt the wind blow through his beard and over his unshaven neck. He felt free and at peace. The unforgettable smells from the bayou to his left invaded his senses. He was home.

He pulled up in front of the Lafourche Parish Sheriff's office in the city of Thibodaux, what was considered a big city in these parts, and put the car in park. He had been able to sweet talk old Sheriff Claude Broussard every other time Bobby had been arrested, but old Claude was no longer Sheriff. He'd been beaten out a year earlier, losing the election to a northerner who had only lived in the Parish for a year, a businessman who promised to partner with the community and the small town mayors in the Parish to turn the economy around with new business and development. He doubted this new Sheriff would be as easy to sway as old Claude.

He passed through the front doors of the Sheriff's office and saw only a few familiar faces. Delroy Hebert, an old friend of his from elementary school and high school, sat at the duty desk. That meant he had some rank. "Del," Sherman greeted him with a smile as he headed in his direction. "How the hell are you, you old coonass?"

Delroy Hebert presented his hand as he leaned over his desk. "I told Bobby he's one lucky son-of-a-bitch that you'd come down here to bail him out, again."

"I understand it may not be as easy this time," Sherman said quietly, glancing around at the mostly new faces in the Sheriff's office.

"He had crack on him, not a huge amount, but enough. And he's facing criminal trespass. There was damage done to property, though not as much money as the owner is claiming. I suspect it's inflated."

"Thanks," Sherman said, knowing that Delroy didn't have to tell him anything.

"Do yourself a favor and don't identify yourself, as of yet," Delroy said in a whisper. "Save the federal creds for court tomorrow."

"The new Sheriff's not around?" Sherman asked, his curiosity more than piqued.

"Nah," Delroy Hebert replied. "I'll get you back to see Bobby. It's probably best you're in and out before Sheriff Henderson comes back."

Sherman had to think about what that could mean. First off, the fact that Del thought it important spoke volumes to him. Why though? That was the question. It was protocol and courtesy that any armed law enforcement officer coming into another jurisdiction identify themselves to the local law enforcement. This new Sheriff Henderson didn't know him from Adam. He owed the man an introduction and declaration.

"Sure, whatever you think best," Sherman replied.

He followed Del back through a new locked door that sectioned off the office. He found himself sitting in an interview room waiting for Bobby to be brought in. It occurred to him that he shouldn't be in an interview room with an undeclared weapon, but Del must have known he'd be carrying. Unlike in days past, Bobby wore orange prison pajamas when he was escorted into the room by a deputy, another face Sherman didn't know.

"Oh, man, thank you for coming," Bobby said, reaching to embrace his brother.

"No physical contact," the deputy said, halting Bobby and making him sit in the chair across from where Sherman now stood.

Sherman was put off by Bobby's appearance. He looked haggard. His hair was unbrushed, practically matted. His face had a bruise on it. His eyes went to the deputy. "How'd he get the bruise?"

The deputy's eyes went to Del and then back to Sherman. "He fell."

Sherman shook his head. He doubted that.

"Have you been out to your boat yet?" Bobby asked.

"No, I came right here as soon as I landed." Sherman watched his brother carefully. Bobby was trying to tell him something without telling him in front of the deputy. "But I'm headed there next to cut that AC."

"You haven't taken her out in a long time," Bobby remarked a bit too casually.

"I'm sure you have," Sherman threw back. "Is there something wrong with my boat? Did you damage her?"

"No," Bobby said quickly, his hands in a surrendering gesture. "I may have left the keys in the ignition. I'm sure it wasn't running though."

Sherman moaned and ran his hand over his beard. Great, so there was a chance the boat might not even be there. Might as well put a neon sign over the boat inviting any swinging dick or his brother to come take his boat out.

"So, you'll be in court tomorrow and help me get rehab?"

"I'll do my damnedest," Sherman said.

"That'll be more up to the execs at BioDynamix," the other deputy said.

Sherman's eyes swept over his name on the chest of his uniform. "Deputy Downey, is it?"

The man nodded. He was also a northerner.

Sherman couldn't figure that one out. How had so many Yankees gotten positions within the Sheriff's office? "What's BioDynamix?"

"The property he trespassed on and did damage to one of their fences is at the BioDynamix facility out off old Snake Road just south of Galliano."

Sherman's eyes went to Del.

"The old fish cannery," Delroy said. "It opened up earlier this year, some kind of biotech company, not sure exactly what they do out there except keep mostly to themselves."

"And they're the ones charging Bobby with criminal trespass?"

Del nodded again.

"Good to know," Sherman said. Then his eyes settled back on his brother. "Just try to relax and go with the flow till tomorrow." His eyes flashed to Deputy Downey. "And try not to take any more falls, that would look mighty suspicious."

The deputy wasn't fazed. But Sherman knew he got his message across. If anymore marks appeared on his brother in the next twenty-four hours, he'd be asking questions and this deputy had no idea who those questions would be coming through.

"Thanks for coming, Brian. I know you were busy."

"Just make sure your PD knows you won't cop a plea. If I can't get you out, demand a jury trial. You have to agree to a plea in front of a judge. Don't do that. You got it?" Sherman ordered.

"I understand," Bobby said. "I'll get my shit together this time. I promise."

Sherman had heard it all before. "Sure, you will, Bobby."

Bravo

From the Sheriff's office, Sherman drove southeast down Highway One towards Galliano. Normally an hour drive, Sherman made it in forty minutes, got to love the speed of a Mustang. As he drove, he found himself becoming more anxious, not relaxed as should have been the case. A visit to the BioDynamix building was in order, but first, his boat. He was sure there was something wrong with it, due to the focus Bobby gave it. If Bobby damaged it severely, he would be really pissed!

He pulled up to the little marina on the one hundred ninety-six-thousand-acre Catfish Lake, where he'd always kept his boat. True, he hadn't stepped foot on the Mighty Vulture in over a year, but it was still his boat. It was tied up in its slip, floating. That was a good indication that there couldn't be too much damage. He heard the AC running as he approached. Bobby hadn't been wrong about that. He had left it on, damn it.

He stepped on, a new feeling of bliss coming over him from the tipping of the boat in response to his presence. He climbed the ladder to first check over the controls on the flybridge. Everything looked fine. The key wasn't in the ignition. He wondered where the keys were. If they had been with Bobby's personal effects, he was sure Del would have spoken up.

Then he descended the ladder and tried the door to the interior. It was locked and all the curtains were drawn. He hoped to God he didn't find a mess. He'd have to kill Bobby if he'd trashed the inside of his boat. He pulled his keys from his pocket and unlocked and opened the door. A blast of cool air hit him. It felt refreshing as he'd already broken a sweat, just climbing the ladder. It had to be in the upper eighties and at least eighty percent humidity. His blue jeans clung to his legs. For a few seconds he contemplated changing into a pair of shorts and taking her out.

He entered the cabin and reclosed the door to keep the AC inside. Looking around, he was surprised to find that the interior of the cabin was neat and orderly. The only thing sitting out was a half-eaten sandwich and a can of soda on the table.

Bobby must have wandered away during his meal. He picked the can of soda up to place it in the sink and heard the fizzing of the carbonated beverage as he moved it.

It hadn't been sitting open as long as it should have. Bobby was arrested early that morning. He set the can down and drew his Sig P320, 9 mm, from the small of his back where it was nestled. His gaze took in the interior of the cabin with a new focus. Both the doors to the master sleeping cabin and the head were closed. Behind him, he noticed the three-foot by three-foot access panel to the aft storage area was open. Fuck, someone was on his boat! They were either in the storage compartment or behind one of the two closed doors.

He crept up to the open panel. He knew a closet-like space that could easily conceal a person or two lay within the bulkhead. He kept spare life vests and some fishing tackle equipment in the storage area, but it was not filled, by any means.

"I know you're in there. Come out with your hands up," he said loudly, his gaze on the two closed doors, his ears straining to hear any indication of movement anywhere on the boat. He waited a few beats. Nothing. "I'm armed and I won't hesitate to shoot." He again waited.

An apple was on the counter. He grabbed it and came up to the open panel. In one movement, he reached in and threw it as hard as he could into the opening. He heard it hit something and heard a startled gasp, followed by a string of curses from a raspy female voice. "Shit, that hurt! What the fuck asshole?"

"Come out of there," he ordered.

"If you want me out, you're going to have to come in and get me, but you may not be the only one armed on this boat, just saying. You might want to leave now. You are trespassing on private property," she called out.

The corners of Sherman's lips tipped up. Whoever this was, she was mistaken. "No, I'm the owner of this boat. You're the one trespassing, momma, a situation you're going to want to rectify. Now come out of there." She still didn't move. Sherman had just about enough of this. He grabbed the flashlight from inside the cabinet and dropped himself to the floor beside the opened panel. He rolled in, flashlight and gun in hand, aimed in at the space.

Within was a young lady, seated on a few orange life-vests, pressed against the far wall of the closet. She had long dark hair, and she gasped out when she was captured in the beam of light. He knew she couldn't see the gun pointed at her with the light blinding her. "I have a nine-millimeter pointed at your head. Now come out of there." His voice was calm. No reason to add more drama to this situation. He could see she had no weapon, at least not in her hand.

"You want me out, you're going to have to pull me out," she said defiantly.

Sherman considered it for a second. From her accent, she was a local girl, probably a friend of Bobby's. "Bobby's still in the lockup."

"He is? I thought they'd let him go once he was sober," she said with her raspy, sultry voice.

Sherman couldn't help but smile. "Nope, not this time. Now come out of there so we can talk."

He pulled himself out of the access panel when she moved, inching her way towards the opening. When she crawled out, he was on his feet beside the opening. He'd already re-holstered his weapon. He pulled her to her feet, all one hundred sixty-five pounds of her and then, while holding her wrists, pulled her over to the booth-like seating of the table. He pushed her firmly into the seat and then fastened her left wrist to the towel bar with a zip tie.

She pulled at it, her face showing outrage. "Cut this off, you asshole!"

"Stop fussing. You're going to cut your wrist up doing that." He stood back; arms crossed over his broad chest. She was cute, long black hair, big brown eyes, a medium complexion, looked to have some Indian and African in her, Creole, for sure. She was a few years younger than him, probably near Bobby's age. Bobby had good taste. He couldn't contain the smile that spread over his lips.

"Asshole! I'm talking to you," she said, still pulling her wrist, trying to free her hand. "Get this off me."

"Cool your jets, momma," he said.

"And what are you smiling about?"

He couldn't help but laugh. "You, all pulling at the zip tie, like you can break it. I know that towel bar is on tight, installed it myself. You're not breaking it either. Now talk. What are you doing on my boat?"

"It's my friend's boat," she argued.

"Bobby?"

"Yes," she said, like she'd somehow proven him wrong.

Sherman laughed. "If you know Bobby, then you know he doesn't have a pot to piss in. He can't afford this boat, not the monthly slip fee, not the power to run the AC. Who do you think pays for this?"

He watched as her eyes cast downward. When she looked up at him again, it was from beneath long, thick eyelashes, he noticed. She was cute! Way to go, Bobby.

"It doesn't matter who pays for it. Possession is nine-tenths of the law. The owner hasn't set foot on this boat for over a year."

"Until now," Sherman said. He reached his right hand towards her. "Brian Sherman, Bobby's brother, owner of this boat," he introduced himself. She gazed back at him with a look he couldn't decipher. It was almost antagonism.

Yeah, she knew who he was, and she wasn't impressed. She knew all about Brian Sherman and wasn't a fan, unlike many in the area who still considered him some kind of damned local hero. Finally, she took his hand and shook it. "Hello, Brian Sherman," she said.

Sherman smiled wider. She wasn't giving anything up. "And you are?"

"I guess I'm a trespasser on your boat."

Sherman chuckled. "Normally, when two people meet, they introduce themselves. Is there a reason you don't want me to know your name?"

"It just doesn't matter," she said.

"You are infuriating, you know that? Look, I had to drop everything and fly down here to help Bobby out. What are you doing on my boat? I just left Bobby at the lockup and he didn't tell me you were aboard, just that I had to come tend her. Why is that? And why do I get the feeling he called me down here to help you, rather than him?"

"Her?"

"The Vulture, this boat. Now, I want answers. What are you doing on my boat?"

"Mostly hiding," she said, which surprised Sherman. "You're not going to be very happy with me, but Bobby is in trouble because of me."

He waited. She didn't continue. He sighed out loud. "This is going to take a lot longer than it has to if you don't just come out with it."

She sighed too. "Bobby is a good friend, been my best friend for as long as I can remember. I feel bad that I let him help me, but I'd be the one sitting in lockup, or worse, if he hadn't."

"Worse?" Sherman asked.

"There is something illegal going on out at that BioDynamix plant. I can't prove it, yet, but I know there is. Something is just off. I'm a freelance reporter. I write a blog on Parish happenings and I've addressed the issues with that business, which has drawn heat to me. The Sheriff is on their payroll, I'm sure of it. Ever since my first post, the Sheriff's Office has been all over my ass. I've gotten pulled over and ticketed when there hasn't been cause. The Sheriff and his deputy, Downey, have been inside my house so many times, my neighbors think I'm doing them both."

A grin spread over Sherman's face at her statement. He wasn't sure who this chick was, but he liked her. "I'm sure Bobby likes that, his girlfriend rumored to be doing two other men."

Her face twisted into a grin. "I'm not Bobby's girlfriend, just his gal-pal."

Sherman laughed. "Then Bobby's stupid, going out on a limb for a girl who isn't his."

"I'm not his girlfriend because Bobby's gay, dumb-fuck," she said. She watched the disbelief wash over him. "Wait. You don't know that your brother is gay." She laughed aloud, a deep full-belly laugh. "Seriously, how do you not know?"

Sherman watched her closely. She was smiling wide. She had a beautiful smile. Could it be? Could Bobby be gay, and he didn't know? Why wouldn't Bobby tell him? Certainly, Bobby would know it wouldn't matter to him. He couldn't recall ever seeing him with a girl, didn't recall that Bobby had ever told him about a girlfriend. "Maybe," he agreed.

She laughed again. "Anyway, I was poking around that place the other night and Bobby was my diversion. He played the high man wandering so I could get away when I tripped their security. I felt bad, knowing he'd get arrested, and I'd be here hiding."

"What's your name?" Sherman asked.

She glanced up from beneath those thick eyelashes again. "Brielle," she said, extending her right hand towards him.

"We've got ourselves a problem here, Brielle," he said as he shook her hand.

"Yeah, I know." She agreed. She twisted the wrist that was fastened to the towel bar. "Want to let me loose now? I promise I won't do whatever it is you thought I'd do when you tied me to it."

Sherman chuckled. He really liked this girl's style. He leaned over her and snipped the zip tie, releasing her. Then he leaned his rear against the counter and crossed his arms over his chest again. "What do you think is going on out at that plant?"

She shook her head. "I'm not sure. They were given all kinds of tax incentives to move into that building. Galliano's new mayor, a good buddy of Sheriff Henderson, promoted them coming in as good for the Parish, they'd hire hundreds of locals, transfer in another hundred of its own staff, would be a boost for the local economy. That hasn't happened. They brought in over a hundred of their own workers, alright, and they house them in FEMA trailers in the main parking lot, ship in all their food and supplies too. None of them come into town for anything, not to eat at our restaurants, not to shop at our stores. As far as local hires, yep, they hired on just over fifty of our people from the Parish, but even that, something's wrong."

"How so?" Sherman asked.

"One of my friends was hired. They've all signed Non-Disclosure Agreements. Tina can't tell me anything at all, not what she does there, not even who else works there. She acts scared to death whenever I ask her anything about it."

"Is she normally a nervous type?" Sherman asked already discounting what Brielle was telling him.

"No, not at all," Brielle replied dead serious. "This girl normally has nerves of steel. I also work as a bayou guide. Tina worked with me till she got the job at BioDynamix. I've seen her handle gators and snakes. Even spiders don't phase her. But whatever is going on out at that plant has her spooked."

"NDAs are not that unusual, especially in the biomed field," Sherman said. "Just because your friend is acting all skittish doesn't mean there is something illegal going on."

Brielle felt angry with him, playing devil's advocate. Damn it, she knew something wasn't right. Why didn't he believe her? "All the local employees have to park offsite and get bussed into the facility. They don't want the employee's cars on the property. I've watched the grounds and the employees come and go, from atop the water tower. They're practically searched on their way in and out. I'm telling you, there is something very wrong."

Sherman felt the telltale shifting of the boat. Someone stepped onto it from the pier. He held his finger up, shushing her. His gaze flashed to the door. He hadn't locked it. He pointed to the opening to the storage panel and then he moved in front of the door and drew his pistol.

Brielle dropped to the floor and crawled into the space on her hands and knees, unaware her movement drew Sherman's gaze to her behind. The sudden opening of the door brought his attention back to the sights of his Sig. He stared at Deputy Downey, who was behind the long barrel of a Remington 870 12-gauge pump-action shotgun. Another man stood beside him. Sherman recognized the Sheriff's insignia on the badge pinned to his chest.

"Drop it, boy," the Sheriff said in a northern accent, New Jersey, Sherman would guess.

The corners of Sherman's lips tipped up. The Sheriff had just called him 'boy'. "Let's nobody lose their heads. I'm just going to reach into my back pocket and get my credentials." He kept the Sig aimed at the Deputy in his right hand but reached his left to his back pocket to retrieve his creds. He flipped it open, displaying his badge. "Agent Brian Sherman, ATF."

Deputy Downey's eyes flashed to Sheriff Henderson.

"A federal agent in my Parish and you didn't come identify yourself to me?" Henderson said after several silent moments.

"I tried when I came to the Sheriff's office, but you weren't there. I had come to see my brother. I'm here as a private citizen, not working a case."

"Your brother got himself into deep shit, this time. I'm well acquainted with that brother of yours," Henderson said.

"What do you say? Should we put our weapons away?" Sherman asked. When neither of them moved or spoke, Sherman continued. "You came on my boat, weapon drawn, unprovoked. Just what the hell is going on?"

The Sheriff motioned to his deputy, who dropped his weapon to his side.

Sherman nodded and lowered his as well. But he didn't put it away. He stared hard at the Sheriff. "Now, that's better. Why are you on my boat, Sheriff?"

"I thought it was Bobby's boat, and we were just conducting a search for more drugs."

"It's my boat, not Bobby's and I don't authorize a search. Just so we're clear, Sheriff, I plan to ask the court tomorrow that Bobby be remanded into a rehab facility and my choice would be a facility up north where I can keep an eye on him."

"You are aware that the owner of the land he was trespassing on is pressing criminal charges. He damaged their fence," the Sheriff said.

"I am aware, and I plan to make it right with them. Certainly, they prefer restitution to incarceration, that's if they don't want to create a hostile environment down here. People in these parts are a community that doesn't appreciate outsiders harassing the less fortunate of them, something I don't think all Yankees understand."

The Sheriff's lips twisted into a scowl. "Times are changing. Even the bayou has to come into the twenty-first century of lawfulness."

"The Creole and Cajun cultures are something I don't think you understand, Sheriff. We protect our own. It's been that way a long time before you got here, and it'll be that way a long time after you're gone."

The Sheriff's lips tipped into a grin. "I don't plan on going anywhere, boy, and from where I'm standing, you're more a northerner now than I am."

"I have deep roots in this community, something this community isn't likely to forget. If you have any sway with that BioDynamix plant, you may want to remind them of that. If this goes to trial, a jury of Bobby's peers isn't going to take too kindly to them refusing restitution in favor of prosecution and incarceration. They need to understand the landscape going in."

"I'll pass that on," the Sheriff said. "Sorry for the inconvenience and misunderstanding." He nodded his head and then motioned to the deputy who stepped back away from the door.

Sherman watched the two back away from the door and then he felt the boat's movement, indicating the two had stepped back off and onto the pier. He followed them with his eyes, watching them retreat back to the parking lot. He remained in the doorway until their car pulled out of sight.

He stepped back within the cabin, closed and locked the door. "They're gone."

"They were here looking for me," Brielle said, poking her head back out of the panel.

"I know. It's not safe for you to stay here while I'm gone," Sherman said, thinking aloud.

"Where are you going?"

"Out to that BioDynamix plant. I don't trust the Sheriff to deliver my message to its execs. I think a personal visit before court tomorrow is in order."

Brielle took a seat back at the eating area and took a bite of her sandwich. She watched him closely. "Are you really an ATF agent?"

Sherman nodded. "I sure am." Well, officially anyway.

She forced a small smile. Wow, well, Bobby had sure called someone who could help her. She pointed to the small refrigerator. "There's food in the fridge if you're hungry. It's dinnertime, that plant is wrapping up operations for the day. They do run a Saturday shift, so you may be able to have that meeting tomorrow morning before court."

Brian Sherman forgot it was Friday and nearly six p.m. The sun was setting as he'd watched the Sheriff and his deputy walk up the pier, the long shadows cast in front of them from the setting sun at their backs. He opened the refrigerator and pulled several containers of lunchmeat and cheese from it, as well as a half a loaf of bread. He looked inside the fridge again. There wasn't any beer, just soda pop. He found that odd. Last he knew, Bobby liked his beer, the cheap piss-water that was brewed up near Metairie.

Brielle pointed to the cabinet behind him. "There's chips in there."

"You seem to know where everything is kept on this boat. Where's the beer?"

"Bobby isn't drinking anymore. He's cleaned his act up, only smokes socially."

Sherman knew that meant weed. "What about the harder stuff? He wasn't just high on pot when he was arrested."

"Bobby knows he can handle his coke; knew he wouldn't go off on a tangent telling them anything about me with some coke in him. He had just enough on him that they'd arrest him, but it wouldn't carry with it a long sentence. It gave me the chance to get away."

Sherman shook his head. "He had crack on him, not coke, Brielle."

"The crack was the cover drug, just to have enough to look like a user. He snorted a quick line of coke to be high and throw them off."

He didn't like it one bit. Bobby had set himself up as the sacrificial lamb. But why? Why was he protecting this woman? "You must be special to Bobby, if he'd do that for you."

"I told you, we've been best friends forever." Her voice held an edge.

Sherman wondered why he didn't know who she was, if that was the case. He took a bite of his sandwich, suddenly realizing he was hungry. For a second, his mind wandered to his team. They'd be on the ground in New York, meeting with the DEA. Another pang of guilt hit him that he wasn't there with them. He was down here, dealing with this bullshit.

Then his mind went to his buddy, Sloan. Had he met with Kennedy's parent's yet? He was sent there alone with his girlfriend to try to get intel from her parents who had participated in an illegal adoption. He knew Kennedy wasn't ready to see her parents yet. He made a mental note to shoot Sloan a text later, to see how it went.

Sherman devoured his sandwich, got a can of soda pop, and then grabbed the chips. "Are those cabins still out on Moss Island in the channel?"

"Yes," Brielle answered, reaching into the bag and grabbing a handful of chips.

"I think it would be safer to stash you out there until I can get this sorted out. We'll cast off in a few minutes."

Brielle didn't like it, but she remained silent. She wasn't safe here, that was clear. She was sure the Sheriff would keep this boat under surveillance and board it again the second Brian Sherman left tomorrow morning to go to the BioDynamix plant and to court. She only hoped he could get Bobby off.

Sherman changed into a pair of shorts he found amongst the many clothes stored in the master bedroom. They weren't his things. It looked like Bobby was living on the boat, something else he'd have to address with his brother. He chuckled to himself. The shorts fit. Either Bobby had lost a little weight, or he'd gained some. He'd have to take a closer look at Bobby tomorrow. He hadn't noticed much about his body in the oversized prison jumpsuit he wore.

Coming back into the main cabin area, he noticed for the first time, Brielle's generous and alluring figure. She stood with her back to him, still munching on chips. She wore jean shorts over her nice round backside and a form fitting dark blue girly t-shirt, that he had noticed earlier dipped to reveal ample cleavage that looked natural. Her legs looked muscular and strong. A smile came to his face as he viewed her thighs, almost imagining them wrapped around his waist. Yes, Brielle was one fine looking woman.

She turned as though she sensed him watching her. The look on her face wasn't friendly. Did she somehow know what thoughts his mind had been having? "So, you stay inside. I'm going to take her out now and we'll get you hidden on Moss Island."

She nodded.

Sherman took the boat out, piloting it into the quickly setting sun. It was a beautiful evening. The clouds were long, transparent wisps in the sky of rich pinks and deep purples, which darkened by the second. The air was still warm, up near seventy-eight degrees, heading for a low of sixty-seven. The lake was a smooth sheet of glass, serene and nearly vacant. Only a few other boats dotted the horizon, mostly fishing boats, charters, heading in after a day on the lake.

Brielle stayed in the cabin, hidden. She ran the events of the past few days over in her mind. If Brian Sherman could get Bobby off and take him back up north with him, that would solve one problem. It wouldn't help her personally though. And she was sure that once Brian Sherman had his brother safe, he wouldn't give a rat's ass about her. She would be on her own. She was no better off with Brian-the-wonder-boy here than she was before he showed up. As she sat in the cabin, her mood became more foul. And, she was pretty sure he had been ogling her too, great.

Sherman opened the boat up, enjoying the speed of the Vulture and the wind whipping through his hair. He pulled up near a channel marker and tied a line off to it after he'd traveled a good hour out onto the lake. Before he dropped Brielle off on

Moss Island, he wanted a few more answers from her. He figured she knew enough people in this area that she very well may not be there when he went back to get her.

"Why did you stop?" She asked as he came back into the cabin. She'd been peeking out the windows and she knew they were not at Moss Island.

He leaned against the inside of the door; arms crossed over his chest. "I think there is more to your story than you've told me, and I want it all."

"I have been up front with you. I didn't have to tell you anything, but Bobby trusts you, so I guess I have to as well." She knew her tone was snide and clipped.

"But it's not your first choice, to trust me? I've picked up on an underlying antagonism you seem to have towards me. What the fuck, Brielle? I'm the guy that's helping you."

Her lips twisted into a scowl. "I'm sorry. I know most people around these parts love you, Brian Sherman, local hero, Navy SEAL, brought our little football team to state as quarterback your senior year, the first and last time that's happened. You saunter into town once every year or so and your admiring masses fall at your feet, women offer themselves up, willing sacrifices to your very manly, sexual prowess. I'm sorry I'm not one of your adoring fans."

"Whoa," Sherman gasped, stunned. Then a small smile tugged at his lips. She had stated that all so elegantly, almost poetically. He'd have to read one of her blog posts. "Just what did I do to you to garner such harsh thoughts from you?"

She stared at him in outrage. "You really don't know?"

Sherman shook his head. "No. I've never laid eyes on you before today, so how could I have done anything to you?"

"You made me scream, peaking in my window when I was twelve years old."

Sherman's mind searched his memories. Nope, blank. He had no recollection of peeping in windows at preteens. He shook his head.

"You sat at my family's kitchen table, pretending to be the faithful boyfriend, when you were just waiting to take my sister's virginity so you could then break up with her and break her heart."

"What?" Sherman demanded.

"You were the lowest of the lowest, one of those guys who sleeps with every girl he can get into bed."

"What the fuck?" He demanded. He had no idea where any of this was coming from. He hadn't been that guy. Sure, he had many girlfriends when he was in high school and yes, he slept with them. What teenaged boy wouldn't if it was offered? It continued to be offered all throughout his high school years. "Who was your sister?"

"Dahlia, Dahlia Jarboe," she replied. "She was in love with you and you broke her heart when you broke up with her. She only slept with you because she thought you two would get married."

"Married? I was seventeen years old. I wasn't about to marry anyone."

"It's too bad you never told her that."

"I was up front with all my high school girlfriends. The Navy and out of the bayou were always my destinations, not the altar."

"She thought you'd take her with you."

"She thought wrong. Look, I'm sorry your sister was delusional, but we were seventeen years old. It was a high school fling." They stared each other down. "And I don't saunter," he added after a lengthy pause.

"Oh, you saunter, alright," Brielle argued.

Then he remembered the bedroom window incident she had mentioned. "Now I remember. I came to pick Dahlia up for a date and saw movement in the window. I peeked in, thinking it was her window, but there was a little girl inside and she screamed like she was on fire when she saw me."

"Yes, that was me," Brielle confirmed.

Sherman laughed. "Brielle Jarboe, now I remember you. Look, I'm sorry your sister thought we were more than we were. I promise you, I never let on to her that I would marry her or anyone else. What's she up to these days, anyway?"

Sherman heard a motor near and then cut. He peeked out the window on the port side. It was a boat, coming up alongside his. Fuck.

"What is it?" Brielle asked.

"More like, who, is it?" Sherman replied, already suspecting he knew.

The boat rocked; someone was getting onboard. He pointed to the access panel to the storage area, still open. Then he pulled his phone from his pocket, holding it in his left hand, as he drew his weapon with his right. He waited. The handle jiggled on the door.

"There's a nine-millimeter pointed at that door," he called. "I highly recommend you identify yourself. I'm well within my rights to defend my property."

"It's Sheriff Henderson," his familiar voice called. "Just out for our nightly patrol and want to make sure all is okay with you. Boats don't normally tie up to the channel markers."

Sherman put his gun away. He unlocked the door and opened it. The Sheriff and two of his deputies came into the cabin, uninvited. The men all looked around. The Sheriff's eyes went from the open access panel to Sherman.

"There's no drugs on this boat. I did a thorough search."

"Who were you talking to?" The Sheriff asked. "Heard voices as we boarded."

Sherman hit dial on his phone. He knew Madison was manning Ops tonight. He doubted she'd be too busy with the team on the ground in New York. He brought the phone to his ear. "Madison, sweetheart, sorry I had to hang up on you so fast. It was just the Sheriff boarding my boat, again," he said into the phone when she answered. He'd dialed her personal phone line.

"Oh, okay," she replied casually.

"Here, let me put you on a visual feed." He waited a few seconds, to give her time to get the appropriate background behind her, and then he switched over and held the phone up, so she could see the Sheriff and his two deputies. "Sheriff Henderson, meet my girlfriend, FBI Special Agent, Madison Miller. Madison, this here is the Parish's highest law enforcement officer, Sheriff Henderson, who is making me feel real welcome and protected with two visits today."

Madison laughed. "Now don't go making him feel too special, Sheriff Henderson," Madison said sweetly. "I don't want Brian thinking he's all that. He'll be impossible to live with. Did you get your brother's problems sorted out, honey?" She asked.

"I'm still working on that," Sherman said.

"Sheriff, certainly you can help him, a professional courtesy," Madison suggested.

"I'll see what I can do, ma'am," the Sheriff said, not at all thrilled with this turn of events.

Sherman smiled at him, knowing the Sheriff knew exactly what he'd done and why. There was no way he could disappear now that his FBI girlfriend had seen the Sheriff and his crew on the boat. "Have you gotten your vacation approved to come down here tomorrow morning?" Sherman asked her. "The lake is beautiful. You should bring your brother, John, and come down for the weekend. He'd love the fishing out here, I guarantee."

Madison had to laugh. Yeah, Cooper fishing? That wasn't something she could even envision. "I'm still waiting to hear from my director if I can be off till Monday. And John, yes, I'm sure he would love a few days out on the lake."

"Okay, well, I hope your vacation gets approved. I miss you already, sweetheart," Sherman said. "I'll call you back later tonight, before bed."

"I'll talk to you later, Brian," Madison said with a smile. "Sheriff, it was nice to meet you."

"You too, ma'am," Sheriff Henderson said in a forced pleasant voice. Everyone knew it was forced.

"I'll walk you out," Sherman said to the Sheriff. "It's never been illegal to hook up to a channel marker. Has something changed I'm not aware of?"

"No, it's just normally not done and as I said, we wanted to make sure all was okay."

Out on the deck Sherman smiled at the Sheriff. "As you can see all is okay, but thanks for dropping by, Sheriff." He was sure the Sheriff and his deputies wanted to pummel him as they got back into their boat. He watched them motor away.

Then he went back into the cabin. "Damn but he's persistent," he said. "You can come out now."

Brielle crawled back out of the open access panel. She pulled herself to her feet and pointed back within the space. "It's a good thing I'm not claustrophobic."

"I know they'll be watching. We don't dare drop you at Moss Island. They'll be all over it after I pull away."

"Might be good if they are, as long as I'm not there."

Sherman pulled his phone back out and redialed Madison.

"Yes, Brian, honey?" She answered.

"He's gone," Sherman said.

"Cooper is here now," Madison reported, turning all business-like. "I have you on speaker."

Sherman brought them up to date on the situation. He switched back over to visual and moved beside Brielle. He introduced her. "I need the digital unit to find out all they can on the Sheriff, Deputy Downey, the new mayor of Galliano, and the BioDynamix company and its executives. I'll text correct spellings of the names to you." He knew they would run Brielle to ground too. That was a given.

"We're on it," Madison said. "I'll also reach out to Shepherd. Do you really want Cooper and me down there tomorrow morning?"

Sherman hated to put more stress on the agency. "I think so. I'm not sure what will happen in court tomorrow and I need to get Bobby out of that jail before he has another accident and takes another fall. Plus, I need to protect Brielle. The Sheriff can't get his hands on her. She's sure there's something less than kosher going on, and based on the Sheriff's attention, I'd say it warrants a closer look."

Brielle was surprised that Brian Sherman was taking her side and asking his FBI girlfriend to come help. Of course, he'd have a beautiful blond with blue eyes as his girlfriend. She looked thin too. She was sure this Madison was the whole package, looks, brains, body.

Madison and Cooper assured him they'd be down and meet him at the marina in the morning. Then she signed off.

"Thank you. It was nice of you to ask your girlfriend to come down and help me too," Brielle said.

Sherman laughed. "Madison's not my girlfriend, she's one of my coworkers, but I knew she'd play along and know something was up when I called, calling her sweetheart. That man who was on the call, Cooper, that's her husband and a fellow agent."

Brielle was surprised. They'd been so convincing. "Really?"

Sherman focused his smiling eyes on her. "You were jealous for a second, weren't you?"

Brielle got flustered. When she spoke, her words were harsher than she meant them to be. "Jealous, no, never. I just didn't think you could land a beautiful blond like her."

Brielle's words were hurtful. She really did think he was a piece of shit. "You never answered my earlier question. Whatever happened to your sister?"

"Nothing, she eventually got over you. Sorry, Mr. Ego, she's not crying in her sleep, waiting for the great Brian Sherman to come back to her."

"That isn't what I meant," Sherman corrected her, his voice just as cutting. "What's she doing now?"

"She's a shaman at the reservation, embraced our Coushatta roots. She and my dad both live there, up near Acadia."

"What about your mom? I always liked her."

"My mom died about a year after yours, a drunk driving accident."

"I'm sorry," Sherman said.

"Yeah, me too," Brielle answered. "I was real sorry about your mom. I spent a lot of time at your house with Bobby after you were gone to the Navy. She was always so kind to me. I helped Bobby take care of her. She fought, no matter how sick she was."

Sherman nodded numbly. His mother had died of cancer seven years earlier. He had no idea that this girl had known his momma or that she'd helped take care of her. Though he should have figured someone had. That had been a lot on Bobby, who became her primary caregiver. His father, he knew, hadn't handled it well. He'd crawled inside a bottle, unable to deal with the fact that Helene Sherman was dying.

"We should probably go back to the marina and get some sleep. I don't think the Sheriff will call again tonight, and he'd be less likely to show up there, with witnesses."

Brielle nodded. A part of her was glad. She did feel she was safer with Brian Sherman than she'd be alone on Moss Island. She watched him leave through the cabin, once again leaving her alone. She'd love to be up on deck or up on the flybridge with him. It looked like a beautiful night. Her thoughts went to Bobby, alone in his jail cell and that guilt hit her again. *Hopefully, Brian will get him out tomorrow*, she thought. If not, she contemplated turning herself in.

By the time Sherman pulled the boat back into the marina, it was nearly twenty-two hundred hours. He sent that text to Madison, also providing the correct spelling of Brielle's name and the few details he knew about her, including her Parish Blog, The Lafourche Letter. He Googled it on his phone and read a few of her posts on the way back into the marina. Her writing was good, her style catchy and original, and the content was hardcore news, no fluff. She had several articles on the BioDynamix plant, questioning why the Parish gave them tax breaks to set up shop and also questioning exactly what they did, what their business was. The articles were inflammatory, there was no doubt about that.

He tied the boat up and came back into the cabin, startling her as he entered. "Sorry," she apologized. "I guess I'm still jumpy. When you stepped onto this boat earlier, while I was eating, I nearly jumped out of my own skin," she admitted. "I couldn't get into that storage space fast enough."

Sherman was surprised. She seemed cool, confident, and collected, defiant even as she argued with him about coming out when he found her. He wondered for a second if this supposed uneasiness was manufactured on her part. "I've got you now and you're safe. I really don't think that Sheriff will be back tonight."

"If you hadn't brought that woman onto the phone to see Sheriff Henderson do you think anything bad would have gone down?"

Sherman breathed out hard and ran his hand over his scruffy jawline. He didn't like that she had thought that was a possibility too. "I didn't want to take any chances. I agree with you that something isn't right down here, but would the Sheriff had done me physical harm? I don't know. That's a hell of a leap." Though he knew it wasn't out of the realm of possibilities and he surely had felt threatened, but he wouldn't admit that to her.

He pointed towards the master cabin. "We should probably get some sleep."

She stood and moved towards the open doorway; the queen-sized bed lay within. She was not happy when he followed. "You're not sleeping in there with me."

Sherman had to chuckle at her and the stern look that was across her face. "I'm not sleeping on the fold down," he said, motioning towards the kitchen table and booth area that folded down into the other bed. "I'm over six foot. I don't fit on it."

She turned around and scooted past him, going back to the kitchen table area. "Well I'm not lying in the same bed as you, so I guess I'm taking it. If you were a gentleman, you'd give the lady the comfortable bed though."

Sherman laughed aloud. "On my own boat? Give the trespasser the more comfortable bed? Momma, you're whacked if you think I'm going to curl up on that little, uncomfortable space when a perfectly good, big bed is available for us. It's big enough to share."

"Yeah, you'd like that, wouldn't you? You haven't changed at all over the years, still trying to get a girl into bed any way you can!"

"Do not flatter yourself, thinking I have ulterior motives. But I would prefer you be in with me, so I can protect you, if need be. And if the Sheriff does come back, the folded down bed would be mighty hard to explain."

She thought about it for a second. She hated to admit it, but he was right about that. Why would the spare bed be folded down with only one person on the boat? She flashed a glare at him as she brushed past him, returning to the master cabin. "Just keep your hands to yourself."

Her voice definitely held warning, which made Sherman smile at her back, or rather at her ample backside that his eyes were focused on as she retreated deeper within the cabin. He had to admit, her butt was about perfect to his liking. He wouldn't turn her down if some under the cover's moves were on her mind. Hell, he'd be happy just to feel over that exquisite ass of hers.

She pulled the covers back on the right side of the bed as he came into the cabin. He closed the door and locked it. He watched her drop onto the mattress. "You are leaving all your clothes on?"

Her glare at him was one of outrage. "This is nothing but sleep, you got that?"

Sherman laughed again. "Yes, but that doesn't mean you can't be comfortable. I know no woman wants to sleep in her bra."

"Well this woman doesn't want to invite your thoughts or your hands to go anywhere they shouldn't."

Sherman smiled wide and pealed his shirt off. He set his gun within the top drawer of the built-in bedside table and set his phone atop it. His eyes never left her as he pulled the covers back on his side.

"Put your shirt back on and don't you even think about taking those shorts off," she warned.

Sherman didn't answer, he just crawled into bed. He received a text message from Caleb Smith with the digital unit, verifying the spelling of Brielle's name. Sherman responded. Then Smith messaged back that he'd be on it all night and hoped to have some intel by morning. Sherman thanked him and then set his phone back down.

It vibrated again. Another text message. This time, it was a text from Sloan. He'd proposed to Kennedy, who now went by the name Kaylee. A smile drew up the corners of Sherman's lips. Son-of-a-bitch! Sloan had really done it. He knew Sloan had bought the ring weeks earlier. Sloan had shown it to him and promised to tell him whenever he popped the question. Sherman knew he'd be best man at their wedding whenever that would be. Sloan had hinted at a long engagement.

"Congrats, I assume she said yes," he texted back.

A picture of a very happy Kaylee, with the ring on her finger held up in front of her face to the camera, was the reply. The grin on Sherman's face spread wider.

"That's great. I'm happy for you both," he replied.

Then he turned the light off, plunging the cabin into darkness. He pulled the covers over himself. He laid on his back, keenly aware of the still form that reclined just out of touch range beside him. He couldn't remember the last time he was in bed with a woman who wasn't snuggling up to him. He bet Sloan wasn't lying on his back with Kaylee not touching him right now. He would bet his left nut that 'we just got engaged' sex, would be hot. There sure were perks to being in a relationship.

Charlie

When Sherman woke the next morning, the sun that streamed through the light-diffusing blinds on the cabin windows greeted his eyes. He held a butt cheek in each hand. Brielle was nearly atop him, her face nuzzled against his chest. He felt her soft breasts pressing into him, just below his pecs. Her bra was off. He wondered when that had happened, and if he had done it in his sleep. She'd really be pissed if that was the case.

Since his hands were there, he couldn't help himself from kneading and massaging her cheeks. They were firm, muscular, the perfect size. He unconsciously moaned in pleasure from the sensation.

"Get your hands off my ass," Brielle's raspy voice warned.

"You're the one on top of me," he said. He noted she hadn't moved yet.

"I'm just snuggling, that doesn't mean I've invited your hands onto my ass."

She still hadn't moved. "Just snuggling with a man in the morning sure as hell invites it and a whole lot more."

"Look, there's snuggling and there's inviting sex, two very different things. Can you honestly tell me you sometimes don't want to just snuggle and feel another human being against you without thoughts of sex coming into your mind?"

"Yeah, I can honestly tell you I've never once thought I'd rather just cuddle than have sex."

"I think you may have mistaken the feeling of wanting a connection to wanting sex."

Sherman rolled her to her back and came atop her, pressing his morning wood between her legs. "I don't think there's mistaking this as wanting to snuggle. My cock sure as hell wants to snuggle inside of you, but momma, that's called sex."

Her big brown eyes, now open, gazed into his with amusement. It was not what he expected. "Bobby is not like you at all. He and I lie in the same bed often, and just snuggle with each other. Everyone needs a physical connection with another human being that they care about. It doesn't mean it is anything sexual. It's just a human need."

"So, let me get this straight. You and my brother often lay in bed holding each other like this and nothing sexual ever happens?"

She smiled like she'd proven her point, and she nodded.

"Well, then that proves Bobby's gay as fuck, because Brielle, there ain't no way any straight man could lay in bed with you and not want to be inside you. I think you've been hanging out with too many gay men if you think that's normal."

She laughed. Then she angled her face up towards his and he was sure she was going to kiss him, but his phone vibrated a new text message, drawing his attention to it. He retrieved his phone. Madison. She and Cooper were on the dock, approaching his boat.

"Madison and Cooper are here," he said.

He went to roll off her, but returned to where he'd been, making a point of settling in with meaning. He took her jaw, cupped in his hand. He raised it as his face approached. His lips very softly brushed against hers. He pressed a few light kisses slowly to her lips, his lips parting just enough that she'd feel the heat and moisture from the inside of his mouth, but he didn't penetrate her lips. If he knew how to do anything, it was how to kiss a woman to make her want more. If any more was going to happen between them, it would be her initiating it.

"Good morning," he whispered, and then he rolled off her.

She laid dazed from his kiss, gazing at the large tattoo across his upper back as he grabbed his gun out of the drawer. It was of an eagle with an anchor, a rifle, and a pitchfork clasped in its talons, with an American flag behind it. It was detailed and beautiful. She watched as he then left the room, leaving her lying there, wondering what had just happened. No one had ever kissed her like he just did, and his tongue didn't even penetrate her lips. She hadn't even really returned his kiss. She'd been too shocked to.

Sherman opened the back door as Cooper and Madison reached the boat. "Hi, glad you could come," he greeted.

Madison came aboard first, embracing him and pressing a kiss to his lips. "Good morning, sweetheart," she said with a smile.

Sherman had to chuckle. He figured they'd already reconned the parking lot and saw they were being observed. He stayed in part. "Did you have a good flight, baby?" He pressed another kiss to her lips before his grin met Cooper's less than friendly stare. He shook Cooper's hand. "Welcome aboard the Vulture. Come on down into the cabin, I'll get some coffee on."

He led them into the cabin. The door to the master bedroom area was closed. He figured Brielle was getting redressed. "It's safe to come out," he said, coming up alongside the door. "Were there eyes up in the parking lot?"

"Yeah, Barney Fife in his uniform," Cooper said. "I thought of asking him if he'd like us to go get him a cup of coffee, you know, one LEO to another." He chuckled.

Sherman grabbed the coffee pot and filled the carafe. Then he dumped the water into the reservoir and spooned grounds into the filter. He figured the supplies on the Vulture had to be Brielle's doing. Bobby sure as hell was never that together to actually plan ahead to what his needs may be. He'd have to thank her later.

"Thanks for coming," he said, gazing at Cooper and Madison. "I know something is dead wrong here, and I needed the backup."

"No problem," Cooper said. "Just don't ever enjoy kissing my wife that much again." A smile lit his face.

Sherman laughed as the bedroom door opened. Brielle stood there, looking uncharacteristically shy. She forced a small smile. "Hi."

"Hi Brielle," Madison said, reaching her right hand around Sherman, who stood between them. "I'm Madison. It's nice to meet you." The women shook.

Brielle sized her up. She was five-eight, fit, and her blue eyes were even more vibrant in person. She didn't wear much makeup, didn't need to. She had flawless, radiant skin. And like she had guessed, she had the perfect body. "It's nice to meet you too."

When their hands separated, Cooper thrust his forward. "And I'm Cooper."

After they shook hands, Brielle tucked a thick section of her long hair behind her ear. "Thank you for coming. The harassment the Sheriff's office has been giving me is one thing, but I didn't think they'd be all over Brian the way they have. I honestly think something bad could have happened to him last night had he not called you, Madison. The Sheriff was really pissed that he had you on Skype and you saw him."

"That was good thinking, by the way," Cooper congratulated Sherman.

"Yeah, thanks," Sherman said. He motioned to the table seating area. He slid in beside Brielle. "A buddy of mine down at the Sheriff's Office warned me right away that I didn't want to declare my badge. Told me to save it for court today. The Sheriff wasn't there when I went to see Bobby, so I didn't have to, but he sure as hell was not happy to see it the first time he came onto this boat." Sherman paused and shook his head. "He had no right to be on this boat and I know he would have broken in and searched the place had I not been here."

"And he would have found me," Brielle said. "I feel guilty, knowing Bobby is in jail because he helped me. Even after he's out, I don't know what to do, where I'll go. I haven't been in town, I've been here, hiding. The Sheriff isn't going to leave me alone. I know he knows I'm the one who broke into BioDynamix."

"Then maybe you need to come up north with Bobby and me," Sherman said.

Brielle shook her head. "I'm not going to leave my home. I belong here. They don't."

"We need to build you an alibi," Madison said. "I checked local happenings. There was an environmental protest in New Orleans on Thursday and Friday, and it wraps up today. We can hack into a hotel and backdate a reservation and proof of check-in. We could even doctor some social media posts to show you there. Do you think that would be a good enough alibi for the Sheriff?"

Brielle nodded. "Yes, and if I write a blog post about it, that could do it." Her eyes went to the side of Brian's head. "So, you're really leaving and going back up north after you get Bobby out of jail?"

Sherman nodded. "I feel I have to get Bobby out of here, for his own protection."

"What if they won't let him out and into rehab?" Brielle asked.

"Then I have a federal warrant and will take him into FBI custody," Madison replied before Sherman could even think about what his next move would be. "One way or the other, Bobby is getting out of jail today."

Sherman smiled at her and nodded. "Thanks."

"Thank Shepherd," Cooper said.

Brielle sat back, feeling defeated. "So, you're all going home today?"

"Tomorrow," Madison said. "We'll give the digital unit another twenty-four hours to dig up what they can on everyone involved and help lay down your cover story." The digital unit and Garcia in New York were working on this, on the New York Partner Mission, and even working on leads from Sloan's mission in Cleveland. They were spread thin.

Brielle nodded. At least she'd have them here for another twenty-four hours. She'd managed alone up till now, she'd be just fine without them, she told herself, not believing it. She had Bobby before, and he'd be gone too.

"Why did you break into that plant, Brielle?" Cooper asked. "What did you hope to find?"

"At the very least, exactly what they're making."

"Do they have camera surveillance? Were you caught on it?" Madison asked.

Brielle nodded. "They do. I wore a big black hoodie, black jeans and a face mask. They'd never be able to identify the intruder as me. Bobby had on similar clothing. I left the hoodie with him."

"Did you do any damage within the facility that they will pin on Bobby?" Sherman asked.

"No, I just looked around the warehouse. It was empty, packing material but no boxes with anything in them."

"That's suspicious in itself," Sherman noted.

"I've been watching that plant for two weeks. Nothing but supplies for the employees who live onsite has come in or been shipped out during that time period. And they supposedly only run a first shift, with Saturday overtime, at least with people from the Parish, but the employees who live onsite are on for twelve-hour shifts around the clock, seven days a week."

That too was suspicious as far as Sherman was concerned. "Did anyone see you staked out, watching the place?"

"I wasn't staked out. I planted a camera atop the plant water tower."

Sherman sighed out loud and ran his hand over his forehead. "You have illegal surveillance going on that plant."

Brielle shrugged. "It's only illegal if someone finds it. No one knows I was up there. And even if they find it, no one can trace it to me."

Now Madison moaned. She reached into the back pocket of her jeans and withdrew her phone. She placed a call to Caleb Smith. She wished her teammate Garcia, the best digital guy they had, had been at HQ, but he was with the team in New York on the DEA Partner Mission and chasing down info on their suspects. She certainly hoped Caleb Smith was up to the task.

"Smith," he answered.

"I have a situation I need you to remedy." She relayed the facts. She listened while Caleb Smith clicked away on his keyboard. After a few minutes, he gave her the news she didn't want. He had easily traced the feed to Brielle's home IP address. Her eyes met Brielle's. "Our guy is going to divert the feed, so it doesn't lead back to you. Right now, it's clearly pointing to your IP address." Her eyes swept over Sherman and Cooper. "HQ will monitor the feed for now."

Brielle shrugged. "I guess I don't know as much about that stuff as I thought I did."

Anger rose inside of Sherman. What other risks had she exposed herself to? "Let me get this straight. Getting info on this isn't your official job. You're not employed as a reporter for the Gazette or any other news agency."

Brielle's defenses went up. It showed on her face. "That's right, but there is freelance work I've gotten paid for. I've had articles and blogs picked up by official news outlets. Journalism isn't like it used to be. Most of us work freelance these days, investigating things and then selling the stories to the markets."

The coffee was done, Sherman got up to pour cups as a diversion. He wished his teammate Mother was here. Mother would know what to say to diffuse the tension and phrase his thoughts in a different way. All he could think of to say was, you have got to be fucking kidding me! She would risk her life and his brother's for what? A chance to sell a story to a news outlet? He knew, of course, that he couldn't say that to her. She'd clam right up.

He set cups in front of Madison and Brielle first.

Brielle pointed to the cabinet above the coffee maker. "There's a bowl of sugar up there, can you get it down please?"

It really annoyed him that Brielle was more at home on his boat than he was. He wondered how much time she and his brother spent on this boat all curled up, snuggling in his bed, doing nothing sexual. He shook his head at that thought and swore under his breath. "Son-of-a-bitch!"

He handed her the sugar bowl and a spoon and then placed a cup in front of Cooper, before retaking his seat with his own cup. He took another second to calm his thoughts and his anger. "Brielle, no one doubts your sincere desire to figure out what is going on down there at that plant. I think we are all just worried about you, exposing yourself to risks." Mother would have been proud of him. "I've got Bobby, so it's not even about him. Do you have any idea how much trouble you could get yourself in, legally? And if there is something illegal going on in that plant, I'm sure they won't hesitate to hurt you to keep you quiet."

She gazed at him with outrage. "They're not going to kill me and throw me to the gators in the bayou."

Yes, that's exactly what could happen. The gazes he exchanged with Cooper and Madison proved they thought it was a possibility too. Cooper rubbed his fingers over his forehead. Sherman knew Cooper well enough to know that he was considering their next move. He kept his eyes focused on Cooper.

"Okay," Cooper said. "So, you're going to go down to that plant this morning before court and talk with their execs or their head of security to get the criminal charges dropped."

Sherman nodded.

"I'll go with you. Then you should come back here and pick Madison up. Your adoring girlfriend needs to go to court with you, warrant in hand, in case your brother doesn't get released to you. I'll stay here with Brielle while you're gone and if that Sheriff comes back, he'll be greeted with my badge and surely won't know what the fuck is going on." He chuckled at the thought of it. He carried CIA creds. "And in the meantime, Brielle, you need to do some work to back up your cover story of being at that protest in New Orleans. We'll sneak you out somehow tomorrow morning and drop you in New Orleans."

"Please tell me you turned off your cell phone and any other devices you have," Madison said.

"Yes. It's been off since before I left my apartment to come here, so Bobby and I could plan my little visit to the BioDynamix facility. To create my story, I need to do some research on this protest, online research."

"I'll loan you my phone," Madison said.

Brielle nodded her head. "Thanks."

"I highly recommend you rethink staying here. You can come back with us, would be a hell of a lot safer for you," Cooper said.

"I'm not leaving," she said. Her voice was firm.

"Oh hell, then I'm not leaving either," Sherman said. "It's not safe for you here, Brielle. Why don't you understand that?"

"Nothing is going to happen to me," she argued. "Do you really think those guys came over here all the way from China just to hurt me?"

"China?" Sherman demanded. "What the hell? This is the first time you've mentioned they're Chinese."

"What does it matter what their nationality is? Yeah, most of the workers living in those FEMA trailers are Chinese or Chinese American's. I don't know which."

Sherman's head was about to explode. This was a whole different ballgame now. "Do you have any clue what all the Chinese are in to? And that just ratchetted up the danger level for you. Those people in Beijing have no regard for human life, not their own people's and not yours."

Just then, Cooper's phone rang. It was Shepherd. He stood and paced near the door as he answered. "Hey Shep. I think I know why you're calling."

"What the fuck, Coop?" Were Shepherd's clipped words in greeting. "Smith just notified me the workers he is seeing on the feed from that plant in Louisiana are mostly Chinese. Why am I hearing this from him?"

"We just found out, ourselves." His gaze shot daggers at Brielle.

"The principals who are on the corporate filings are all American names, headquartered in New Jersey, but Smith was reviewing footage and just notified me we have trailers full of Chinese on that property."

"Our girl just informed us of that fact and that she broke into that warehouse the other night when Bobby Sherman was arrested to take the fall for her. There is no product at all in that warehouse, nothing coming in or going out."

"I'm going to loop in the FBI, Homeland, and the CIA. This just became a high priority case. Sloan is getting back from Cleveland tonight. I'll send him down. I may pull the rest of Delta Team from the DEA Partner Mission to check out the names and addresses in Jersey or send them down your way if they're needed."

Cooper glanced around at the interior of the boat. "We're going to need to find a new base of operations, a safehouse."

"And you need to get your witness secured," Shepherd ordered.

"We still need to get Bobby Sherman out of here," Cooper said. "We could send them both up on the plane that brings Sloan in."

Sherman's eyebrows raised. Good, Sloan was coming down. He'd feel a lot better with his partner, onsite. He wished the remainder of Delta Team would come down too.

"I'm not going anywhere," Brielle argued, picking up on Cooper's statement of sending them both up. "I have valuable information on this, local contacts. I can be helpful."

Cooper shot her a glare of warning.

When her eyes met Brian's, he too regarded her sternly. She glanced at Madison, who looked worried, not mad. "I can help. I'm from here. I know people. I work as a bayou guide. I have resources available to get you in and out unnoticed."

"You are also in more danger than you realize," Madison said gently.

"That's where all of you come in. You'll keep me safe." Her eyes went to Brian. "I trust you."

"At this point it's not about trust. The Chinese are dangerous. The Chinese mafia runs drugs, human trafficking, illegal gambling, all sorts of bad shit. The PRC is the biggest sponsor of cybercrime in the world, initiating attacks on systems here in the U.S. and all over the world. I'm not sure who these people are, but they aren't up to anything good, that's for sure," Sherman replied.

"The Chinese don't have to be on our soil to commit cybercrimes," Madison said. "I'd cross that off the list."

"All right, we'll be in touch after court," Cooper said, and then he ended his call with Shepherd. He turned back to the table. "Shepherd is bringing the FBI, CIA, and Homeland in on this."

Brielle huffed a sarcastic laugh. "Isn't that overkill? We still don't even know who they are or what exactly they are doing."

All three of the gazes back at her, told her they didn't think it was. They were so serious; a chill went through her.

"We need to find a new place to stay. This is too exposed," Cooper said.

"So, Sloan is coming in tonight?" Sherman asked.

"Yeah, he gets back from Cleveland this evening and Shepherd will send him right down," Cooper said. "He may even send the rest of Alpha and Delta."

Brielle wasn't sure what that meant, but the one thing she was sure it did mean was that these three people would be sticking around to investigate BioDynamix. And they'd be sticking around to protect her, as well. That was good.

"Highway one runs all the way to Port Fourchon. That area has a lot of oil coming into the port, so I'm sure the government has a facility or two down that way we can take over as our base. It's only a half hour away. That would be the perfect place," Sherman suggested.

Cooper tapped out a text to Shepherd to ask about that port and a possible safehouse for them there. "You'll more than likely have to check Bobby into a rehab facility within twenty-four hours if he's released to you."

"I want it up north. I already did some research. There is a highly rated facility near the office. They work with the courts and Bobby won't be able to just walk out of there."

"Bobby doesn't have a drug problem. It was faked for me to get away," Brielle argued. "You can't seriously be planning to put him into rehab, are you?"

"If the court remands him to rehab, he has to be in a locked down residential treatment center for a minimum of thirty days or until that facility deems him adequately recovered," Sherman said. This would be a three-peat for him. He knew the laws well.

"That's not fair! He doesn't need to be there."

"Brielle, the court doesn't know he faked it. This is how it works. Because of the charges against him, it's going to be either prison time or rehab and you can bet the court will check up on him," Sherman said. Personally, he didn't think another thirty days would hurt Bobby any.

Brielle grabbed her forehead with both hands and massaged it. "God, I feel so bad about this. Bobby was just helping me. What if we discover something very illegal is going on at that BioDynamix plant? Will that be enough to overturn the court decision?" She watched the three of them exchange glances that she couldn't read.

"We'll figure that out when we get there," Cooper said.

Brielle wasn't sure what that meant, but it didn't sound like it would be enough to get Bobby released. She never should have let him be the diversion, her cover. If anything bad happened to Bobby because of her, she'd never forgive herself.

Delta

Sherman and Cooper were both dressed in blue jeans and short-sleeved polo shirts. Sherman drove the Mustang convertible with the top down to the BioDynamix facility. On the drive there, Cooper considered their options. The main purpose of this visit was to get them to drop the charges against Bobby. But they also needed to do a little recon to try to figure out what was going on at that plant. This may be their only opportunity to legally step foot inside that facility.

"The way I see it, we've got two options," Cooper said. "We declare ourselves as federal agents right away in hopes that will make them more cooperative towards dropping the charges against your brother, or we keep that info to ourselves and you go in as just the brother wanting to make restitution."

Sherman nodded. "I've been thinking the same thing, evaluating how each scenario will help to achieve our mission objectives. We do need to see if we can get any intel on exactly what's going on out there, too. That's as important as getting the charges against Bobby dropped."

"As soon as we say federal agent, their guard will be up," Cooper said.

"It'll already be up. If the Sheriff is on their payroll as Brielle thinks, they're already going to know I'm a federal agent. I say we walk in there with our badges and guns on our hips, in full view."

"Bobby's your brother, so it's your call."

"Thanks, Coop, I appreciate that. Yeah, that's how I want to play it. Getting Bobby off is primary. We can dig into that business other ways after Bobby is safely up north."

"And Brielle?" Cooper asked.

Sherman laughed out loud. "Now that is one young lady that I don't know what to do with. There's no doubt she has a lot of great local contacts that could be beneficial in figuring this out, but she's reckless. Pulling a stunt like breaking into that place and getting Bobby arrested because of it." He shook his head.

"Not to mention the illegal camera surveillance," Cooper added, "that led right back to her."

"Why do reporters always think they're invincible, that the bad guys aren't going to kill them to keep them quiet? That girl put herself in more danger than she is aware of, and that's without the Sheriff's focus on her." Sherman paused and shook his head again. "The fucking Chinese," he swore.

"Smith and the digital team are looking hard at the Chinese at that plant. So far, there are no links to Beijing, so Shepherd is thinking Chinese Mafia. He's trying to pinpoint which Triad they might be."

"I wish Garcia was at HQ. It's not that I don't trust Smith, it's just that I know how tenacious Garcia is."

"Smith and the rest of the team need to have opportunities to take the lead and prove themselves. We can't rely on Garcia for everything. The man is going to be a father and needs to step back and work only fifty or sixty hours a week." He chuckled.

Sherman laughed at that, as well. It was true. Many of the team members worked more hours than having a family would accommodate. Both Jackson and Doc had reduced their hours to fifty a week when they were at HQ, and they'd both reduced their field time. Garcia would, too. Alpha Team was becoming a part-time field team. Cooper had taken on a lot of the administrative functions at HQ. And Madison pulled more shifts in Ops because of Alpha Team's reduced schedule, which wasn't a bad thing. She was very effective there.

They rolled up on the twelve-foot high chain-link fence that surrounded the large BioDynamix facility. This fence was new. It hadn't been here when this place was the old fish cannery. Very little of that old building remained, just the two-story brick office building portion. The majority of the large plant structure was new construction, Sherman noted.

Both men pulled their badges from their pockets and held them up to the guard within the little bus stop structure on the outside of the closed gate. "Federal agents to see your chief of security or your CEO, in regard to the break-in the other night," Sherman said.

The gate guard got on the phone. After several lengthy minutes of him waiting silently with the phone pressed to his ear, he acknowledged whoever he spoke with, hung up the phone, and turned back to Sherman and Cooper. "Please drive forward to the brick building and go within. Mr. Spencer, our Chief of Security, will meet you at the reception desk."

"Thank you," Sherman acknowledged. After they'd passed through the gate, he whispered to Cooper. "He's not a local."

"Not from Jersey, either," Cooper added.

The car drove up the long, winding drive that wove its way through the oak trees. Coming onto the straightaway, the rows of FEMA-type trailers were seen in the main parking lot. Cooper counted the rows, eight across and five deep. Forty trailers. He would bet that three to four Chinese slept within each trailer. He wouldn't call it living in them because if they were working twelve-hour shifts, seven days a week, that wasn't living.

Sherman parked in front of the brick office building. Both men affixed their badges and guns onto their hips. They passed through the double entry doors and came up to the reception desk where a young woman, who appeared to be in her late twenties, sat. She seemed surprised to see them enter.

"Hi, sorry, didn't mean to startle you," Sherman said, making sure his accent was thick. "I'm Special Agent Brian Sherman and this here is Special Agent John Cooper. We're supposed to meet a Mr. Spencer here." He flashed his credentials in front of her face for a brief second.

The receptionist's eyes darted between the two of them. "I'm sure Mr. Spencer will be here shortly."

Both men's eyes casually glanced around the lobby and reception area. There was no signage whatsoever, no company directory of names, the company name wasn't even displayed within the building. Then Sherman's eyes discreetly viewed the receptionist's desk. There weren't any papers on the desk. There was not even a name plate in front of her, just her computer.

She was a local girl; Sherman knew right away. Her Cajun accent was heavy. "And you are?"

"Tina Landry."

"Ah, Tina," Sherman said with a smile. "I think we may have a mutual friend." He paused and dropped his voice down low as he leaned over her reception desk. "Miss Brielle Jarboe." He stared hard at her.

All the color drained out of Tina Landry's face. Her eyes went wide, and Sherman swore if she could have hopped up out of her chair and ran away, she would have.

"Not really a friend, more of an acquaintance, someone I used to know, a long time ago," Tina stammered.

Sherman pulled one of his cards from his wallet. It had only his name and phone number, no title, nothing else on it. He handed it to her. "In case you ever need anything, anything at all."

She politely took the card from him and set it on her desk. Sherman was sure she'd hand it over to the Chief of Security the second they left, but just maybe she wouldn't. She was scared, so it was worth a try. Just then the sound of heavy footsteps quickly approaching was heard. From their left, a large man barreled down the linoleum floor, his eyes fixed on them.

Sherman stepped forward with a smile, producing his credentials. "Special Agent Brian Sherman, ATF," he said.

The man's dark eyes studied the credentials. Then his gaze met Sherman's. "You any relation to Robert Sherman?" He had a New Jersey accent.

"Yes, sir," Sherman said. "Bobby's my little brother. I'm here to ask you to drop the criminal charges. I'm prepared to make full restitution on his behalf."

Cooper presented his hand. "I'm Special Agent John Cooper," he said, without mentioning that his badge and credentials said CIA.

"Mike Spencer," the man said, shaking Cooper's hand. "Chief of Security here at BioDynamix."

"What exactly is it that BioDynamix does?" Cooper asked.

"Cancer research," Spencer replied. "Bio-identicals, a targeted way to fight the strongest cancer cells in the worst cases." He paused and chuckled. "That's the extent of my knowledge on what our scientists do."

Both Cooper and Sherman chuckled along with him.

"I'm sorry my brother trespassed and caused damage to property and I surely do hope he didn't interfere with any of the important work y'all are doing here," Sherman said, laying his accent on heavy. "But he was just high and wandering around. He didn't mean no harm."

"We're always on guard for others trying to rip off our research," Spencer said. "We can agree that wasn't the case with your brother. Even the Sheriff doesn't think Bobby was working for anyone, trying to steal our secrets."

"He wasn't," Sherman guaranteed. "If I offer restitution in court this afternoon, will y'all accept it and drop the charges? Prosecution and incarceration aren't going to get my brother off the drugs, but remand into a drug treatment facility will."

"If we decline?" Spencer asked.

"Then Bobby will plead not guilty and demand a jury trial. The pool of jurors from this Parish will have sympathy for a local over a corporation from up north that is new to the Parish. That I can guarantee you. Roots in the community are everything down here in the bayou. The Cajun and Creole cultures are strong, and in case you haven't been out in the community to notice, they stick together. You won't win a jury trial down here."

"Well, I appreciate you coming to tell me that," Spencer said with an edge to his voice. "You plan to take your brother up north with you?"

That was when both Cooper and Sherman knew for sure that the Sheriff had spoken with this man.

"That's correct. If the judge will allow me, I plan to bring Bobby to a highly rated drug treatment facility in my home area and keep him up there with me after he has completed the program. He's done drug rehab down here and been released right back into the same environment with the same people and triggers to use. I believe a change of scenery is needed to finally get him off the shit."

Spencer nodded. "The damage to the fence is in the amount of eight-hundred-fifty dollars."

Sherman knew that was inflated, but he wouldn't argue. "I'll cover that if you agree to drop all charges."

"BioDynamix will agree to that provided you remove your brother from this area."

Sherman and Cooper both found that an odd statement. Certainly, this man knew that the Sheriff suspected Brielle of the break-in. Brielle was the one who had written several inflammatory articles. She was the one poking around and asking questions.

"Agreed," Sherman said.

Spencer thrust his hand towards Sherman.

Sherman shook it, a gentlemen's agreement. Interesting. "Thank you. I'll see you later then, at court."

Spencer nodded. He shook Cooper's hand next. "Agent Cooper," he acknowledged.

"I don't suppose you'd want to give us a tour of your facility? I'm just fascinated with the important work you are doing here," Cooper said. "My parent's both died from cancer. I am in awe of all the new treatments available."

"I'm sorry for your loss, Agent Cooper," Spencer said. "But I'm sure you understand, we don't give tours. Our work is closely guarded."

"Of course," Cooper said.

The two men left. They remained silent until they had driven off the grounds.

"Cancer, huh?" Sherman said with a smile. "Was that the Mack or Peterbuilt type of cancer that killed your parents?"

Cooper laughed. "It was indeed a Peterbuilt, model three-seventy-nine."

"Well, my mom did die of cancer, so if they are not doing research and using that as a cover for something illegal that is going to really piss me off."

Sherman and Cooper parked in the marina parking lot and made their way down the dock and back to the boat. Both men kept a sharp eye out. They didn't see any deputies, but they didn't think the Sheriff had pulled his surveillance of them. Madison sat on the lounge chair on the flybridge of the boat in the sun. She had on a tank top, and a pair of jean shorts.

She stood and made her way down the ladder when they boarded. She came up to Sherman and pressed a kiss to his lips. "I'm glad you're back, baby. And I hope you had luck."

Cooper and Sherman exchanged glances. So, the recon on them remained. They wondered where he was at.

"Let's go below," Cooper said.

They entered to find Brielle lying on her stomach facing the open door within the open master cabin.

"She's doing research on the protest she's supposedly at so she can make a blog post," Madison said. Brielle had Madison's computer tablet in front of her.

"Where was Barney? We didn't see him," Cooper asked.

"Inside the cabin of the boat two over, towards the parking lot. The dumb-shit took his uniform shirt off, but who wears a plain white t-shirt and black work pants on a boat?" Madison said.

"But it was all quiet? He didn't approach?"

"No, he's just been watching me."

Cooper's lips tipped up. Of course, the deputy was. His wife was hot. Any man would watch her if given the opportunity. "I'm sure you gave him a nice show too."

Madison smiled and nodded her head.

"So, what happened at the BioDynamix facility?" Brielle asked, pulling herself up from the mattress.

"In exchange for eight-hundred-fifty dollars to repair their fence, highway robbery, and me taking Bobby up north, they will drop all charges against Bobby."

"So, the Sheriff had talked to them?" Brielle asked.

"Yep, sure did. But more importantly, the Chief of Security was very specific that I get Bobby out of the area. That's significant and shows they believe he was in on it. Given your different sizes, there is no way they believe it was Bobby who entered their grounds or their warehouse that they saw on their surveillance footage, but they still want him gone."

Brielle wasn't sure why that was significant to Brian. "Did you get a look around at what they do there?"

"No, we were not invited past the lobby, which was pretty nondescript, no indication of what they do there based on the lobby. No signage at all," Cooper said.

"They say they are doing cancer research," Sherman told Brielle, watching her closely for a reaction.

Brielle felt anger flare inside her. "Like hell they are!"

Sherman and Cooper exchanged glances.

"What was that?" Brielle said, pointing between them.

"We met your friend, Tina. She's the front desk receptionist," Cooper said.

"She turned ghost-white at the mention of your name, claimed you were close once, but that you're really just acquaintances now," Sherman told her.

Really? Just acquaintances? Brielle knew she shouldn't be surprised. She and Tina had been friends for a long time. Friends, not just acquaintances.

Sherman watched Brielle's lips turn down. He knew her friend's statement hurt her. "You're a lot more than acquaintances, aren't you?"

"I guess not," Brielle remarked. "Never mind that I'm her son's Godmother."

"She's afraid," Sherman said. "That reinforces that there is something illegal going on out there. If they were doing groundbreaking cancer research, she'd be proud to work there. I'd like to get the chance to question her away from work."

"I tried, she quotes her NDA and won't say a word."

"Maybe we'll have better luck," Madison said. "If she knows we will protect her, maybe she'll give something up."

"So, you're planning to stay longer than twenty-four hours?" Brielle asked.

"Yes. We'll be here until we're done looking into BioDynamix," Cooper said. "We agree with you, something isn't right there."

Oh, thank God! Brielle thought. She relaxed a bit.

"I'm going to go change into an appropriate outfit for court," Madison said. She grabbed her backpack and sealed herself inside the master cabin. When she reemerged, she wore a nice pair of blue jeans and a button-down silk shirt.

"We'll have to declare ourselves as law enforcement to the police at the security checkpoint," Sherman said. He'd run this play a few times. "And then I'll identify myself to the judge and plead my case for Bobby."

"If it goes against you, I'll present the extradition warrant. Robert Sherman is wanted by the FBI in Chicago," she said and then giggled. "Bobby will just have to waive the extradition, thereby agreeing to it."

"I'm hoping for a few minutes to have a brief conversation with him before court," Sherman said.

Madison drove them in the SUV. They identified themselves and declared their weapons at the security checkpoint to enter the courthouse. Sherman couldn't believe he was back here, doing this again for his brother. Of course, this time, the circumstances were different. Though misguided, Bobby had thought he'd done the right thing to help Brielle.

Brielle, now there was an infuriating woman who he would like to get into bed. She hadn't been wrong about that. He hoped once they got Bobby out, that she'd go with the flow and do what they told her to. He was honestly concerned that she'd go rogue and not follow their game plan, especially if it didn't suit her or if she didn't agree with the approach. Cajun women were fiercely independent and stubborn. All Cajuns were known for their steadfast devotion to family, so her hatred of him for the supposed wrong he'd done to her sister didn't surprise him. His lips tipped up with that thought. Where in the hell had Dahlia gotten the notion that he would marry her?

He saw Bobby within the courtroom. There were three arrestees in orange prison pajamas seated to the side of the courtroom. He led Madison over.

"Brian, thanks for coming. This is my Public Defender, William Layton," Bobby introduced, pointing to the short man in the cheap suit who looked like he was about twelve years old. "This is my brother, Brian, who I told you about."

The PD came to his feet and thrust his hand out to Sherman. "It's nice to meet you, but I think you gave Bobby bad advice. They're offering a plea deal, will only get him a year in the state pen. If this goes to trial, and he's convicted, he could get eight years."

Sherman released his hand. "Do you know who I am?"

"Yes, Bobby told me you're a federal agent. But that doesn't matter regarding these charges."

"My brother is not pleading guilty or taking a plea deal." His eyes scanned over Bobby. "You okay? No more falls or anything?"

"Yeah, they've left me alone." His eyes were on Madison.

"This is my girlfriend, Special Agent Madison Miller," Sherman introduced.

Bobby shook her hand. "It's nice to meet you. Brian never did tell me nothing about you. Where are your manner's Brian, keeping the knowledge of a fine looking woman such as this from me?"

"Don't even," Sherman warned for show. Yes, he'd have to talk with his brother at a later time about women. He was convinced that Brielle had not been lying. After much consideration, he was sure Bobby was gay. How had he not seen it before?

"It's nice to meet you, Bobby," Madison said.

Sherman leaned in close to Bobby's ear and whispered. "Whatever I say, agree with me. You got it?"

Bobby nodded.

"If this doesn't go our way, we have a Hail Mary, so don't worry," Sherman added.

"All rise," the Bailiff announced as the door to the judge's chamber opened. "The honorable Basil Guidry presiding."

Everyone stood.

Good, he was a Cajun, Sherman thought. That was the first break. Now he'd just need a few more.

The judge took his seat on the bench. "You may be seated," he said with a strong Cajun accent. "We are arraigning three cases this afternoon."

Sherman had never been in his courtroom before. He could only hope the man was fair.

"Robert Sherman, please take the defendant's chair," the Bailiff called.

Sherman moved to the defense table with Bobby and his Public Defender. The PD was obviously annoyed with Sherman taking a spot at the defense table. He glanced between the judge and Sherman. All three men stood. Madison sat in the chair behind them in the gallery.

"In the people verses Robert Sherman, on the charges of criminal trespass, possession of drugs and drug paraphernalia, and public intoxication, how do you plead, Mr. Sherman?" The judge asked.

"William Layton, counsel to Mr. Sherman," the PD announced. "My client pleads not guilty."

The judge shuffled a few papers and didn't look happy. "In the matter of bail, what is the people's recommendation?"

"We request bail be denied, your Honor. Mr. Sherman has many priors, he's been remanded to drug rehab instead of jail on two previous occasions, and this time there was criminal damage to property. A fence was cut, and the owners claim that the damage exceeds eight-hundred dollars."

"Excuse me, your Honor," Sherman cut in. "If it pleases the court, I feel I need to identify myself to you. I am Brian Sherman, Robert Sherman's brother." He pulled his badge and credentials from his back pocket. "I am a former Navy SEAL, and currently serve our country as a special agent with the ATF, headquartered in the Chicago area. I have offered full restitution for the damage to the fence to the BioDynamic's facility in exchange for the dropping of those charges. I am prepared to make full restitution to them through the court cashier today." He made sure his Cajun accent was strong. "My brother is addicted to drugs, your Honor. Jail will not rehabilitate him. It more than likely will only feed his drug addiction. I request he be remanded one further time to drug rehab."

"Is a representative from BioDynamix present in this courtroom?" The judge asked.

"Yes, your Honor," Mike Spencer, from Biodynamix said as he stood.

"Do you have the authority to accept or decline Mr. Sherman's offer of full restitution?"

"I do your Honor," he said. "And Biodynamix does accept Mr. Sherman's offer to pay in full today the amount of eight-hundred fifty dollars to repair the damaged fence. And if he does, we will drop the charges."

"So decided," The judge said. "This court will remove the charges of criminal damage to property and criminal trespass. Mr. Sherman, you will pay the court cashier. Bailiff, please draw up the paperwork."

"Yes, your Honor," the Bailiff replied.

Sherman watched Sheriff Henderson's face. The man was not happy.

"And on the request for remand into a drug treatment facility rather than jail, your Honor?" The PD asked.

"If Mr. Sherman pleads guilty to the drug possession charges, the court will consider it," the judge said.

The PD leaned in and whispered to Bobby and Sherman his advice that Bobby plead guilty.

"No," Sherman replied. "He only pleads guilty to the charges if drug rehab is approved."

"I can't tell the judge that," the PD said.

"Well, I can," Sherman said. He turned to face the judge. "Your Honor, if the court approves an in-patient drug treatment facility, my brother will plead guilty. However, if it will not, he requests a jury trial and pleads not guilty."

The judge looked pissed. Sherman guessed he'd pushed too far.

"While I agree that Mr. Sherman had no criminal intent," the judge said, "his repeated and habitual drug use borders on criminal." He leaned forward and glared at Bobby. "Mr. Sherman, you have been remanded to rehab on two previous occasions. Why am I to believe that the outcome this time will be any different?"

"If I may, your Honor," Sherman spoke up. "This time I intend, with your permission, to take Bobby back up north with me and check him into a top-rated facility. After the mandated thirty days as an in-patient, I will keep him with me for his out-patient treatment to ensure he is staying on track. It is my hope that my brother will find gainful employment in my home area and remain with me so that I can monitor him and be sure he does not backslide this time."

"This court does not have any payment agreements for remand with any drug treatment facilities outside of this area," the judge said.

"I plan to pay cash in full for the treatment at the facility I have chosen. It does work with the courts in the Chicago area, and I have already spoken to the court liaison at that facility, who indicated that they will work with this court and provide status updates. He will be housed in the remand wing and will not be able to check himself out or leave the facility before the thirty-day mark."

The judge read back through his papers and then looked pensive. He breathed out a heavy sigh. "Mr. Sherman, do you share your brother's optimism that the third time can be the charm?"

"I do your Honor," Bobby said. "I stayed clean for a long time after the last rehab. It's hard coming out of rehab to your old life, your friends, being around other people who use, triggers. I think up north with my brother I have the best chance that I've ever had to stay clean. I don't want to use drugs, your Honor. I want to be sober. I want to work. I want to contribute to society, but mostly I want my brother to be proud of me. I don't want to be a burden to him."

The judge nodded. He had listened intently to every word, and more importantly, he'd watched Bobby's face as he spoke, just as Sherman had. Bobby wasn't blowing smoke up anyone's ass. He legitimately wanted Brian to be proud of him. "Okay, this is your last chance, Mr. Sherman. I will be making notes that you have been advised of such. If you ever appear back in this Parish, before any judge, you will not be given the option for drug treatment rather than jail. This is your last chance."

"Thank you, your Honor," Bobby said.

"Thank you," Sherman echoed.

The judge glanced between the two Sherman men. "Pay the cashier and you may take Bobby with you. I'm releasing him to your custody as a federal lawman. There will be paperwork for you to sign accepting him into your custody. You must have him checked into the facility within twenty-four hours. All the contact information for that facility must be left with my Bailiff. Do you understand these instructions, Agent Sherman?"

"I do. Thank you, your Honor."

The Bailiff followed them out of the courtroom. "Mr. Sherman, you are to stay with me while your brother completes the paperwork and pays the cashier." He pointed Sherman in the direction of the cashier, handing him the piece of paper to submit with it. "We'll be in this holding room, waiting for you. I have the paperwork you will fill out before I release Bobby to you. Please join us with the receipt after you've made payment."

"Thank you," Sherman said.

He watched the Bailiff lead Bobby, the PD, and Madison into the room. Then he went to the court cashier. He paid the eight-hundred-fifty dollars on his credit card, a way over-inflated price to repair a cut fence. Then he returned with the receipt to the holding room. There he filled out the paperwork accepting Bobby into his custody. If he failed to check Bobby into the named drug rehab facility within twenty-four hours, there would be arrest warrants for both Bobby and him.

Echo

Sherman could see the questions all over Bobby's face as they walked out of the courthouse. Bobby could barely contain himself from asking about Brielle. As soon as they were in the car, Sherman turned to gaze at Bobby, who sat in the backseat. "She's fine. We're taking you there now."

"Oh, thank God!" Bobby said. "I've been so worried about her."

Madison turned the engine over. "She's been worried about you. If you really care about that girl, you'd never have agreed to let her break into that place."

"There's no stopping Brielle from doing anything she wants to do, and I do care about her. She's been my best friend forever."

Madison gave Sherman a sideways glance. He could read the question that flashed through her eyes, just a friend?

"That's right, even Miss Jarboe says that she is just Bobby's gal-pal, nothing more. That wouldn't happen to be because you're gay, would it Bobby?"

Bobby shot Sherman a scowl. "No, just because she's only a gal-pal doesn't mean I'm not doing her, doesn't mean I'm gay."

Sherman laughed out loud. "Come on, Bobby, like I'd care? You're my brother and I love you, no matter what. I just want you to clean your act up and be happy. That's it."

"Didn't Brielle tell you? I haven't used in months. I don't even drink no more. That was all a diversion to help Brielle get away."

"Yeah, she did tell me all that and also that you're gay. It's not a big deal, Bobby. And I should have known. You've never spoken with me about a girlfriend and I've never seen you with a girl before, not even Brielle. She says you two have been best friends forever. How come I didn't know anything about her?"

"How come I didn't know anything about your girlfriend?" Bobby demanded, pointing at Madison.

"Oh, I'm not Sherman's girlfriend," Madison said.

"Yeah, that was a cover story for the Sheriff, long story. Madison is just a coworker."

"Oh, that's too bad," Bobby said.

Madison chuckled, but said no more.

Sherman let the topic of Bobby's sexual persuasion go. The car was quiet for a few minutes. "What were you thinking? Setting yourself up to get arrested again?"

"It just seemed like the best way to protect Brielle. She was going in to snoop around that place, if I helped her or not."

"And calling me down was to help her, not you."

"Well, us both, but I figured she could use your help. Brian, the Sheriff has been all over her shit. It's blatant harassment. If she wasn't right, he wouldn't be targeting her like he is."

"Yeah, well, I'm no fan of the new Sheriff down here. He boarded my boat twice since I got here. I know he was looking for Brielle."

"You kept her hidden, didn't you?"

"Of course, I did," Sherman said. "As soon as I found her and figured out what was going on, I knew I had to hide her."

"You're not really sending me up north and into drug rehab, are you?"

"Bobby, yeah, duh, of course I am. It is court mandated. You have to be checked in within twenty-four hours."

"I won't go and leave Brielle. Plus, I don't need drug rehab. I'm clean, Brian."

Sherman blew out a loud breath. "Bobby, I am a law enforcement officer. I have to obey a court ruling so yes, you have to go to drug rehab. I'm going to pay cash for it, and the place I picked isn't cheap. But it's out of the Parish and you'll be safe there, which I can honestly say I don't think you will be down here."

"I don't have a drug problem no more."

"Then think of it as a vacation," Sherman said. He was losing his patience. "What don't you get? You set yourself up and now you have to pay the piper."

"And you can't get me out of it?"

"Not yet. Maybe if we prove there's something illegal going on and we explain to the court the circumstances, but there's no guarantee."

"Well, fuck, thirty more days in rehab."

"I think you're getting off pretty easy," Madison spoke up. "You should have called Brian before pulling this stunt. He maybe could have helped you on the front end of this."

"Like you'd have taken me seriously and come down if I told you what we were going to do?"

"If you'd told me they have trailers full of Chinese out there and that Brielle has been harassed for writing articles about BioDynamix, yeah, you damned-well better believe, me and my coworkers would have come down. My boss has brought in the FBI, CIA, and Homeland Security. We're taking this pretty damn serious."

Bobby shifted in his seat. He didn't know what to say to that, so he said nothing. A deep frown set on his face and he gazed out the window.

They arrived at the marina and went to the boat. Cooper sat in the sun on the seating area at the back of the boat. Bobby was startled seeing him there. "He's one of my teammates," Sherman whispered to him. "I wouldn't leave her unprotected while Madison and I were at court."

Bobby nodded.

"Cooper, my brother, Bobby," Sherman introduced.

Cooper presented his hand. The two men shook. Sherman opened the door to the cabin and motioned Bobby inside.

"Brielle," Bobby said, the relief apparent in that one word. They swallowed each other up in an emotional embrace. "I was so worried about you."

As they pulled apart, Brielle ran her fingertips over the bruise by his eye. "Sheriff Henderson or Deputy Downey?"

"Does it matter?" Bobby said. "The questions about you never stopped." Then he made eye contact with Sherman. "Thank you for coming, Brian. I'm sorry I didn't reach out to you for help before."

Sherman nodded. "Me too, could have saved you a trip to jail. But we're here now and we'll get to the bottom of this."

Bobby embraced Brielle again. He held her tightly.

"Can you two give us a few minutes?" Cooper asked, his eyes on the embracing pair.

"Sure," Brielle said. She pointed at the master cabin. "I'm working on a blog post about a protest I'm going to use as a cover for where I've been," she told Bobby as she led him that way. "You can read it and let me know what you think." Bobby often read her work before she posted it.

Once the cabin door was closed, Cooper spoke. "We have a tight timetable, less than twenty-four hours to get Bobby up north and checked into rehab. And we need to decide if we'll allow Brielle to be involved going forward, that's after we sneak her off this boat." Cooper spoke in whispers.

"She does have the local contacts and knows the area even better than I do," Sherman pointed out. "The bayou changes from season to season. She works as a tour guide and is a better local resource than I am. It's been too many years since I've lived here." He told himself it was only for that reason that he wanted the lady to remain with them.

"We get her to New Orleans as planned," Madison said. "Then figure it out."

"I'd sure like to solidify a cover for her for the next few weeks," Sherman said. "Even if she is down here with us."

"I think we can do that," Madison said. She tapped out a text message to the digital team. "We can establish a cover for her up north, near Bobby for the duration of his rehab."

"I like it," Sherman said.

"What aren't we thinking of?" Cooper asked.

"Nothing. We're on hold until Sloan gets down here. We have to keep Brielle covered, can't sneak her off until he's here to take her," Sherman said.

"Moving under the cover of darkness is preferred, anyway," Cooper said. "We can't do anything until Shepherd gets back to us, so I say let's take this boat out and cruise around the lake." He smiled. "You did invite me down for a boat ride."

Sherman moved to the master cabin door. He rapped once and then opened it. His mood instantly turned sour. On the bed, Bobby and Brielle were snuggled up, reading the computer tablet screen together, practically cheek to cheek. Upon closer inspection, Bobby was reading, Brielle was wrapped around him like a snake constricting its prey.

"Hey, we're going to take the boat out." He pointed to the shorts he'd worn the previous afternoon, which were folded and on the shelf near the bed. "I'm wearing those. I want you up top with me, Bobby. Sorry, Brielle, you have to stay hidden down here."

She rolled off Bobby and sat up. "I'd sure love to be topside if even for a minute."

"Too risky," Sherman said.

"He's right," Bobby told her, coming to his feet. He kissed the top of her head.

"Give me a minute with Brielle, will you?" Sherman asked Bobby.

Bobby nodded and left the cabin, closing the door behind himself.

Sherman took a seat beside Brielle. He had an irrational anger surging through him, seeing her and Bobby all snuggled up. He knew it was irrational. "We're working on a long-term cover for you, so the Sheriff won't be looking for you down here anytime soon. Know that everything we're doing is to keep you safe."

She smiled and nodded. Then she placed a chaste kiss on his cheek. "Thank you, Brian, for everything."

Sherman's hand was drawn to push back the section of hair that hung over her cheek. He tucked it behind her ear and then lightly caressed her exposed jawline with the back of his fingers. "My brother is very lucky to have you as his friend."

"Yeah, he got arrested helping me, very lucky." When she and Bobby had closed the door, he nearly broke down, worried about her, worried about himself and stressing about this trip up north into rehab. She didn't feel like a very good friend.

"He wanted to help you because he's so loyal to you. There aren't many people who'd get arrested to help a friend. That's a strong friendship."

"Bobby's fragile, more than you'd think. You need to go easy on him, Brian. Him walking into rehab is gonna take its toll on him."

That was when Sherman realized that the cozy little scene, he'd interrupted, was Brielle giving Bobby what he needed, physical comfort. If Bobby was gay or not, there was a strong relationship between Bobby and Brielle. He wasn't sure how he felt about that. "I will, don't worry." Sherman came to his feet. He nodded at the door. "Go on and let me get changed into these shorts."

Brielle rose and left the room, rejoining the others in the main cabin area. Madison came out of the bathroom a second later. She'd changed back into her shorts and tank top. When Sherman rejoined them, Cooper's phone rang.

"It's Shepherd," he announced before answering it. He stood by the glass door, gazing out as he listened. "Very good," he said after a lengthy pause while Shepherd spoke. "Thanks. I agree." He disconnected the call and then turned back to the others. "Shepherd secured us a safehouse down at Port Fourchon. He's sped up the timetable. Sloan is in the air right now, headed into Golf-Alpha-Oscar. After he deplanes, our bird will fly into Mike-Sierra-Yankee and wait for you there." His eyes were focused on Sherman. "Sloan will pick up a rental car at GAO and then call for instructions."

"Good," Sherman said. "There is a spot he can meet us at, south of here, where we'll transfer Brielle to him."

"What do you mean transfer me to him?" She demanded.

"Sneak you off this boat, so the Sheriff won't see. The man flying in, Sloan, is my best friend. I trust him to protect you, Brielle."

She nodded. That was good enough for her and truth be told, she was anxious to get off this boat.

"And you will fly out with Sherman and Bobby this evening. We'll establish a cover for you that you are up north near Bobby for the duration of his treatment," Cooper said.

"Fly out? I'm not leaving," Brielle insisted.

"It's just for twenty-four hours to get Bobby checked into rehab and establish a cover for you. It's best if the Sheriff thinks you are up north for the next month." Sherman knew that it would be up to Shepherd if she would be allowed to return or not.

"How exactly will this work?" Brielle asked, skeptical.

"We'll take the boat out and meet Sloan on the south side of the lake. We'll sneak you off the boat, and he'll take you to New Orleans. Our digital team has already secured your cover at a hotel. You'll get dropped there in time to do your blog post with pictures and video, and you will check out of the hotel. You'll want to mention in your blog that you'll be going up north for the next month," Madison said.

"Once we get back to the marina, I'll button the boat up and the four of us will drive to New Orleans. Bobby and I will pick you up on the way to the airport," Sherman said.

"And Cooper and I will check into a hotel to enjoy the sights in New Orleans as our cover, but we'll drive to the safehouse our boss has established for us at Port Fourchon." She paused, and her eyes shifted to Sherman. "Kaylee is on the plane, so Sloan will fly back out with you to get her home and get her settled. Then Cooper and I will set up recon on that BioDynamix facility," Madison said.

"You're going to want to get a bayou view of that place. I was thinking, since nothing is coming in or going out through the front doors, maybe they're using the bayou as cover."

"HQ is trying to get a satellite dedicated to the area," Cooper said. "Shepherd's pulling Alpha and Delta back in. Garcia and probably Jackson will stay at Ops. He'll deploy the remainder of the team to help with this case."

Even though Sherman felt relieved that his team would be on the ground, he knew pulling them early from the DEA Partner Mission was not good. They had a contract with the DEA that they were breaking by cancelling this mission. Sure, mission priorities dictated coverage, and with trailers full of Chinese, that ratchetted the priority on this one way up, over a suspected meth lab.

"You can't be out in the bayou without a guide. It's dangerous out there," Brielle said.

"I'm sure we'll be fine," Cooper replied.

Brielle's face instantly showed she was annoyed with her advice being discounted the way it was.

"You know, she's probably right," Sherman said. "There are seven different venomous types of snakes in this area, venomous spiders, and the gators to watch out for."

"I'm a bayou and swamp guide," Brielle said. "Another reason I shouldn't go up north, even for twenty-four hours if y'all are planning to venture out into the bayou."

"We won't go wandering around too much without you," Cooper said.

"Brian, who's paying for this airline ticket. I can't afford a last-minute flight," Brielle said. "Hell, the hotel charge alone will max out my credit card."

"We've got it, don't worry," Sherman assured her. He wouldn't go into the company Lear. She assumed they'd be flying out on a commercial airliner. He didn't need to correct that right now. Nor would he tell her the cost of the hotel room was covered. He could see the wheels in her head turning. "Are there any other objections or reasons you can't go that you want to throw out?"

Brielle looked away. She didn't realize that she was that transparent.

"Brielle come up north with me. I need you there to willingly walk into rehab again." Bobby wrapped his arms around her.

She placed a kiss on Bobby's cheek. Then she nodded her head yes.

"Okay, now let's run through the script for the phone call between you two once you're in New Orleans and your phone is turned back on," Cooper said.

"Is this all really necessary?" Brielle asked.

"Very," Sherman said.

Foxtrot

herman's phone vibrated and rang softly. Sloan. "Are you on the ground?" He asked as he answered.

"Yep, just taxiing to the hangar. I should be off in the next fifteen minutes. The DEA maintains a hangar here. I guess there is a lot of DEA activity at Port Fourchon."

Made sense to Sherman. With all the oil and other things that came in down there, he bet multiple agencies had a heavy presence at that port. They'd see when they got down there. "Take the road out of the airport west and head south on Highway One. Go west on Oakridge Lane till you come to Oakridge Boat Launch. We'll meet you there."

"I'll text you when I get there," Sloan said. He disconnected the call and then squeezed Kaylee's hand. He gazed into her beautiful blue eyes. "I shouldn't be more than a couple of hours." Kaylee ran her fingers through her rich auburn hair. Sloan's eyes tracked her movements. Then his eyes focused on her ring finger and the ring he'd put there the previous night. "I love you."

Kaylee smiled wide. "I love you too. I'll be fine. Don't worry about me."

"I'm sorry we had to leave Cleveland early."

"Don't be. It's your job. I understand." Though it had been jarring. One second they were planning on dinner at Gary's brother and sister-in-law's home, the next second his boss, Shepherd, called and ordered them to the airport right away. The company Lear was en route, and they'd be flying to Louisiana. She'd been with him long enough to understand that it was some sort of emergency, and she knew not to ask too many questions.

He kissed her as the plane pulled up in front of the hangar. He saw multiple cars and two aircraft within. "The pilot will be around the whole time you're in the hangar in New Orleans. Let him know if you need anything."

"I'll be fine," she reiterated. She picked the paperback book up from her lap. "It's nice to have some time to read for pleasure."

Sloan kissed her again and then exited the plane, realizing that she fit into his life perfectly. The Lear took back off within twenty minutes after it had landed, the destination, Louis Armstrong International Airport, New Orleans.

"Brielle we'll all be up top while we cruise over to the south side of the lake. Don't come out of this cabin till one of us comes to get you," Sherman said.

"I know. I've got it," she assured him. How she'd really love to be able to be up top in the sun.

Madison handed her a ballcap. "Hide your hair and wear your sunglasses when you get off the boat."

Brielle took the hat from her.

As Sherman went topside to prepare to cast off, he glanced at the boat two over where he could see the deputy, still staked out within the main cabin. He slid his sunglasses on and then hopped from his boat and crossed the short distance on the pier. He stepped onto the Windsor, a thirty-two-foot Bayliner, and made eye contact with the man. He went right up to the glass door and opened it.

The deputy was startled.

"Hey, just wanted to let you know that we're going to take the Vulture out for an hour or so. I promised my girlfriend and her brother a ride. You can tell the Sheriff I'm flying my brother out of New Orleans this evening to get him checked into rehab. Are you gonna follow? Because if so, I'll just invite you to come on board with us."

The man obviously didn't know what to say. His face contorted into a scowl. "Um, no, that's all right," he stammered.

"Okay, we'll see you in about an hour or so then." Sherman smiled to himself as he stepped off the other boat and returned to his own. By this time, Cooper, Madison, and Bobby were out of the cabin.

Cooper chuckled at him. "You had to poke the bear, didn't you?"

Sherman laughed. He climbed the ladder to the fly bridge. "Bobby, are my binoculars still up in that compartment?"

"Sure are. I haven't moved or touched any of your things, Brian."

Brian rolled his eyes. Sure, he had. From what it looked like; Bobby was living on his boat. He'd have to ask him about that at some point. He figured Bobby had lost his apartment and had nowhere else to go, so he just moved in here. After all, it was free.

The afternoon sun shone brightly as the Vulture cut through the water. The lake was busy. There were a lot of charters out as well as personal fishing boats and some pleasure craft. Cooper kept his eyes trained through the binoculars, watching the nearby boats. After thirty minutes of Sherman pushing the boat's top speed, it didn't appear anyone followed, but he couldn't be sure. Hell, they couldn't be sure there wasn't a tracker some place on the boat. They'd have to be fast, cutting into the inlet that led to the boat launch after they knew Sloan was there, drop Brielle, and then get the hell out of there even faster.

Sherman circled the area, staying as close to shore as he could until he got the text message from Sloan. He stood on the boat launch. Sherman navigated into the channel. It was just deep enough here for him to nose up to the furthermost pier before he'd bottom out.

"Coop, go out on the bow and keep watch for me. And Madison, get our girl and tell her to go out on the bow too," Sherman said.

Both moved right away. Bobby sat back, watching.

Brielle peeked out of the windows. They were in the channel. It wouldn't be long now. She stuffed her hair in the ballcap, not an easy feat as her hair was so thick. The door opened, and Madison poked her head in. "Time to move. When we get into position, you need to move fast. No conversation, just go with our man and do what he says."

Brielle shook her head and grinned an amused smile. Jeez, these people were so serious. You'd think they were in Russia or China spying on our enemies. She grabbed her backpack and followed Madison out. Madison pointed to Cooper on the bow. Brielle could see they were creeping towards the dock. She put her backpack on and carefully moved forward.

By the time she came up beside Cooper, the nose of the boat was within a foot of the narrow pier where another man stood. She felt the telltale vibration from below, indicating the boat had made contact with the sandy bottom. This was the closest the boat would get to the pier.

She grabbed onto the railing and swung a leg over it. "Help to steady me," she said to Cooper. Then she reached her hand to the man on the pier. He took her hand and helped to muscle her over. When both of her feet were on the narrow piece of wood, she gazed at the stranger's sunglass covered eyes. He stood the same height as her. "You're Sloan?"

He nodded at her, glanced at Cooper, and then took hold of her upper arm and led her at a quick pace up the pier and towards land. "Don't say another word till we're in the car."

Brielle hurried to keep up with him. He had long strides. He brought her to the passenger side of a black SUV, closed the door once she was within, and then hurried to the driver's door. He turned the engine over and drove away at a normal speed. She'd half expected he would tear out of the parking lot.

"Keep the hat and glasses on until I drop you at the hotel," he said.

"Sure." She gazed at this man. He wore a t-shirt and blue jeans. His hair was on the longer side, like Brian's. She assumed he was an ATF agent too. "You're Sloan, right?"

His eyes flickered to her. His lips cracked a small smile. "Gary. And you're Brielle." He presented his right hand. "It's nice to meet you."

She shook his hand, feeling a bit more relaxed. "You too."

Once Sloan turned onto Highway One north, he set the cruise control for the posted speed limit. They had plenty of time to make it into New Orleans before Sherman would arrive, and there was no reason to draw any attention from law enforcement to them.

Sloan pulled the SUV up in front of the hotel. "Power your phone up and I'll give you my phone number in case you need anything before Sherman gets here."

Once she had his number programmed in, she gazed at him, waiting for further instructions.

"Go inside and do your posts but stay in the lobby in view at all times. I'll let Sherman know you're set, and he'll have Bobby call you."

"Do you really think someone could be monitoring Bobby's or my phone?"

"We're taking nothing for granted. Trust us, Brielle. This is what we do, and we do it better than just about anyone else out there. I've known Sherman for over a decade. He's my best friend and my partner. If he's worried, there must be a good reason. He's not a man that worries easily."

Brielle nodded as she processed that. What occurred to her was that she was probably safer now than she had been in the last few months. She was definitely much safer now than she had been since she broke into the BioDynamix facility, before Brian found her. Why was it that she felt more afraid than she ever had?

"Go on," Sloan said with a nod towards the hotel. "I'll be out here watching until Sherman gets here. You have my phone number. Call me if you need me."

Brielle nodded and forced a smile. Sloan knew it was forced. He could see the fear in her features, in the choppiness of her movements as she grabbed her backpack from between her feet and got out of the car. She didn't look back as she walked to the front door to the hotel and entered, disappearing into the crowd of people who came and went through the glass double doors.

The lobby was crowded. She managed to find a seat at the counter in the bistro area to the left of the main doors. She laid her phone onto the counter beside her and waited for it to ring. Two minutes later, the ringtone startled her. "Hey, Bobby. How's it going?"

"Not so good, Brielle. I, um, I got arrested a few nights ago."

"What? Why didn't you call me before now?" She asked.

"I did, your phone went right to voicemail."

"Oh, my battery was dead. I forgot to bring my charger with me. I borrowed some guy's earlier. I'm still in the Quarter, at that demonstration I told you about. I wish you'd come with me. Why'd you get arrested?"

"Long story, but I have a favor to ask."

"Of course. Anything."

"Where are you right now?"

"At my hotel."

"In the Quarter?"

"Yes. Now what do you need, Bobby? If you need me to come home, I can. I'll check out and," she began, but he interrupted.

"No, stay there. I'll be there in about an hour. Which hotel are you at?"

As planned, she gave him the name of the hotel and which street it was on.

"Check out and I'll call you when we arrive. My brother Brian is here."

"Okay," Brielle agreed. "But what is going on, Bobby?"

"I'll tell you when I get there," Bobby said as scripted.

"Bye," she said, feeling foolish. That whole call had been stupid, as far as she was concerned. She didn't believe that anyone had access to listen in on their phone calls.

Sherman reached to Bobby's phone and hit the end button. "Good."

"I still think that was stupid. I doubt anyone has hacked into either of our phones."

Sherman shot Bobby a glare. "It happens more than you'd believe." He wouldn't tell his brother his team did it on a regular basis.

"Let's roll," Cooper said. Both he and Madison stood by the door, backpacks in hand.

The four of them left the boat. Sherman had it all buttoned up, with the power and AC disengaged. "Do we need to stop at your apartment and get you more of your things? You'll be up north a month," Sherman said to Bobby.

"I kind of don't have an apartment no more. I lost my lease a few months ago and have been staying on the boat. I have my warmer clothes in this bag," Bobby replied, swinging his backpack onto his shoulder. "Some of my stuff is in boxes at Brielle's. I'll probably have to borrow some of your clothes, if that's okay."

"Like the way you borrowed my boat," Sherman said as he unlocked the Mustang.

"We'll catch you guys later," Cooper said from near the SUV he and Madison had rented.

Madison came up beside Sherman. "Bye baby." She pressed a kiss to his cheek.

Sherman pulled his little red rental car onto Highway One and pointed it north. It was still warm, a seasonable seventy-seven. The top was down. He figured they'd reach New Orleans just before sunset. He felt relieved to be leaving the Parish and Sheriff Henderson behind. Knowing that Sloan had Brielle, brought him peace of mind.

"About Brielle," Bobby said from nowhere. "She's not a casual sex kind of girl, believes in relationships and commitment."

Sherman's head snapped to view his brother. "Why would you tell me that?"

"Come on, Brian. I've seen how you look at her. And even though I am not attracted to women, even I can appreciate that she's beautiful and has all the right curves in all the right places."

"Oh, so you finally admit to me that you're gay. Thank God!" Sherman said. "Bobby, you have to know I love you and accept you for whoever you are and only want the best for you."

"Maybe, I just never knew how to tell you." The truth was, his brother had quite a reputation with the girls. He'd been a Navy SEAL, was a real man in every way. Bobby never felt like he measured up to Brian. Add in that he liked men instead of women, plus all the trouble with drugs he'd gotten into, and he was sure his brother would be disappointed in him if he knew he was gay.

"Just like that." There was a silence for a few moments. "So, do you have anyone special in your life?"

Bobby chuckled. "You mean like a boyfriend? No. I had a guy I really liked, thought we had a future together, but the last time I got sober, he didn't, and he wasn't going to. He wasn't healthy for me to be around."

"Wow, I'm sorry, Bobby. But that sounds like it was a very mature decision, choosing your health over him."

"Yeah, it wasn't easy," Bobby admitted. "But back to Brielle. Her last two boyfriends really did her wrong, hurt her bad. They both cheated on her. She doesn't need anyone who isn't looking for a committed relationship, who won't be faithful to her. She deserves that and more. So, if you can't be that person, don't go there with her. That would really piss me off and I don't think I'd ever forgive you."

"You really care about her."

"I love her like a sister," Bobby said.

"I'd say. Don't worry, Bobby, I don't plan to hurt Brielle." Even as he said it, he evaluated his motives. He was attracted to her. There was no doubt about that. And if he could get her into bed for more than just snuggling, hell yeah, he'd definitely go there, but a committed relationship? He knew that was not a destination he'd planned on. He wouldn't purposely hurt her, or anyone for that matter. Well, fuck. This conversation definitely changed things. He just wasn't sure how.

The remainder of the drive was mostly in silence. Occasionally, one of them would throw out a memory about some place they passed on the route. Sherman's mind was stuck on what Bobby had said about Brielle though.

They crossed over the Mississippi, pulled into the Quarter, and up in front of the hotel at eighteen-twenty hours. The sun was just setting. They'd made it in just over an hour. Sherman wasn't known for going the speed limit. Bobby sent Brielle a text message that they waited out front. Sherman glanced around. He didn't see Sloan, but he knew he was there, covering Brielle.

A few minutes later Brielle came out of the hotel, backpack slung over her shoulder. She'd changed into blue jeans and she wore them quite well, Sherman noticed. Yes, there was something about Miss Brielle Jarboe that captured his attention. Had it been a few years earlier, the agency protocol of not getting involved with anyone related to a case would have been enough, but hell, all of Alpha Team had broken that protocol as did Sloan. He hardly considered it a protocol any longer.

Bobby got out of the car and gave her a hug. He followed the script and introduced her to Sherman. They shook hands. Then Sherman handed her several bills. "Do me a favor and go into that sandwich shop. Get five footlongs and bags of chips. We're going to need to eat." Bobby took her backpack and threw it into the backseat with theirs. Then he began to step away from the car to follow her. "Not you. You're in my custody and cannot be out of my sight."

"Are you kidding me?" Bobby exclaimed. "I'm not going to go nowhere."

"I have to follow the law, Bobby. Now get back into this car."

"Fucking jagoff," Bobby murmured below his breath as he got back into the passenger seat.

Sherman heard him, but let it go. He looked away, his lips curving into a grin.

Ten minutes later, Brielle rejoined them, a large bag in her hand. Bobby opened the door, intending to fold his seat forward for her to get into the back, but she climbed over the side of the car and dropped herself into the backseat. She slid in gracefully, Sherman thought.

Sherman wasn't even on the highway yet when Sloan called. "Brielle had a tail. I got a picture of him taking pictures of you guys. He didn't follow after you pulled away from the curb. I'm eight cars back. No one's following you that I can see. Unless they're further back and have a tracker on your car."

"Thanks," Sherman said.

"Remind me to tell you about our adventures in Cleveland. The two hitmen that killed Melody showed up, arrested their asses. They planted a tracker on my rental car when we were in her parent's house, followed us to my nephew's football game."

"Damn," Sherman swore. "Yeah, after we are in the air you and I will have to chat."

Sherman drove to Louis Armstrong International Airport to the private jet hangars that were far from the main passenger terminal. Sloan pulled up beside Sherman's rental car in the parking area in front of the hangar. They all got out of the vehicles and grabbed their bags.

"This is my brother, Bobby. Bobby, my partner and best friend, Gary Sloan, known him since BUDS, were deployed to the Sandbox together."

Sloan presented his hand. "Nice to meet you, Bobby, heard a lot about you."

"Just believe the good," Bobby said as he shook Sloan's hand.

The four of them passed through the front door and into the hangar. There was an armed guard at a desk in the small front office. "Credentials, please," he said.

Both Sloan and Sherman pulled their ATF badges.

The guard checked them carefully and then handed them back. "I was told you would have two rental cars that need to be returned. May I have the keys?"

They both handed the keys to him. He waved them through the door behind him. As they passed him, they noticed the display on the computer screen in front of him. There were a dozen camera feeds queued up of all angles outside of the building and many interior shots, including several that showed their plane.

They passed through the door that the guard unlocked electronically and into the large hangar. The Shepherd Security Lear was the only aircraft within. Another armed guard stood by the stairs that led into their aircraft.

"What is this place?" Brielle whispered to Brian. "What kind of facility is this?"

"It's a government hangar," Sherman said. "Most major airports have them."

"How come nobody knows about them?" Brielle asked.

"Those of us who use them know and we're the only ones who need to know. Civilians don't need to know what kinds of facilities the government and military use." His voice held warning.

Brielle's eyes flashed to Bobby. He looked equally as in shock as she was as they approached the private jet. "Who owns this jet?" She asked.

Sherman glanced at her. "The agency we work for. Look, Brielle, you're going to have a lot of questions. I won't have answers for all of them. A lot of what we do is classified."

They reached the guard at the foot of the stairs into the plane. "Credentials please," he prompted.

Brielle couldn't help but stare at the assault rifle he held in his hands, but she did see that both Brian and Gary flashed their badges at him too. Certainly, he knew the man in the office would have asked. He nodded and relaxed his posture after inspecting their credentials.

"Is the pilot and female passenger on board?" Sloan asked the guard.

"Yes, sir," he acknowledged.

"Thanks," Sloan replied and then went up the stairs first.

Sherman waved Brielle to board ahead of him, and then Bobby. He boarded last and closed the door behind himself. He stuck his head into the cockpit. Two pilots were on board. "We're good to go whenever we have clearance."

"We've got a takeoff window open at the top of the hour. You're all going to want to settle in fast."

"Great. I'll make sure we do." Sherman closed the cockpit door and headed aft. Sloan was already introducing Brielle and Bobby to Kaylee. He smiled, watching the scene as he approached. Kaylee was showing off her engagement ring already. Yeah, she looked pretty damned happy. "Kaylee, congrats!" He gave her a big hug.

"Thanks, Brian. I was so surprised." She presented her hand.

"It looks good on you. I saw it when Sloan bought it. It's been sitting in his locker for a while."

Her eyes went to Sloan. "You did?" She slapped his shoulder. "You're such a sneak."

Sloan laughed and gave her an affectionate hug.

"We better all take our seats and buckle in. The pilot says our takeoff window is coming up fast."

Just then the engines engaged. Sherman let Brielle and Bobby sit across from Kaylee and Sloan. He knew Kaylee needed to hold his hand during the takeoff and landing. He wondered how Brielle handled flying. She'd have Bobby beside her if needed, which kind of pissed him off. He'd like to be there for her. He shook that thought off and seated himself by the computer equipment. He always liked to check the weather forecast for wherever they were headed, especially when heading north from a warmer climate.

As the plane rolled forward out of the hangar and travelled along the taxiway in front of all the cargo hangars, Sherman watched the four of them seated towards the rear of the plane. They continued to chat. He couldn't hear what they were saying though. The Shepherd Security Lear lined up behind several other planes on the noncommercial waiting lane leading to the runway.

He saw Sloan take hold of Kaylee's hand when their plane turned onto the active runway. Bobby and Brielle sat with their backs to him. He couldn't see if Bobby held her hand or not. He wasn't sure why he was so fixated on the thought, but he was.

After they reached cruising altitude and leveled off, Sloan got up and made his way forward. He took a seat beside Sherman. "Is Brielle Bobby's girlfriend?" Sloan asked.

"No, just his gal-pal," Sherman replied. "So, it turns out my little brother is gay." He shook his head. "I don't know why I never knew. It took that little brunette to tell me for me to know, kind of pisses me off."

Sloan laughed. "Are you sure? They seem pretty cozy."

"They lay in bed and snuggle all the time because it's just a human need to have a physical closeness with another person, and nothing sexual ever takes place," Sherman said in an animated tone.

"He must be gay," Sloan concurred with a laugh.

"Yeah," Sherman agreed. "So, tell me about Cleveland."

Sloan ran his fingers through his hair. "Oh, man, I don't want to see that look on Kaylee's face ever again. She saw the two men who'd killed Melody and looked terrified, hid her face in my chest and whispered who they were."

"You said they put a tracker on your rental car?"

"Yeah, while Kaylee and I were in her parent's house, which went very well by the way. Phil Lewenski had been communicating with the two of them. Sent them back to Cleveland to watch the parent's house. I guess after she paid Lewenski that little visit, he started to wonder if she was Melody or Kennedy. They'd been there staked out since Lewenski was let out of prison and on house arrest. When presented with a deal, they both rolled on all of those L.A. scumbags we busted. Lewenski's back in jail where he belongs."

"Damn," Sherman swore. He'd been with Sloan since he'd gotten the phone call that his ex-fiancé was found murdered in her parent's house, was with him when he viewed the body and knew it wasn't her. And he was with Sloan when they found her half dead in the attic above the funeral home. That seemed like it was ages ago, not just two-and-a-half months ago. "It went well, Kaylee seeing her parents?"

Sherman knew she hadn't wanted to ever talk with them again. Kaylee, the name she chose to go by now instead of Kennedy, had also found out that she'd been adopted and that Melody, the girl who was killed, was in fact her twin sister. The whole situation had been pretty fucked up. He didn't blame her for not wanting to talk to her parents, who had never told her the truth about her adoption.

"Yes. She broke down and cried as she hugged them. I'm glad she was forced to see them. She needed that. Now I feel we're really free from everything from the past so we can move forward."

"So, when's the wedding?"

Sloan smiled wide. "We haven't really decided. Both of our families will be invited, which will add complication. I guess whenever operationally it will work. We're in no hurry. Everything is great the way it is. We're back together and that's all that matters."

Sherman smiled and nodded. "I'm glad for you both." His eyes went to the back of the plane and the back of Brielle's head. Bobby's words of not going there, if he wasn't interested in a committed relationship, replayed through his head. Well, damn.

"So, Shepherd is pulling the rest of the team back. Garcia was already pulled from active surveillance on the DEA mission to help the digital team out. Between that partner mission with the DEA in New York, my excitement in Cleveland, and your shit down in the bayou, they needed the help. After we get dropped in Chicago, the pilots are flying into Teterboro to pick them up and bring them home tonight. We all have a briefing at zero six-hundred tomorrow at HQ."

"Yeah, Shepherd texted me about it. He want's Brielle there too."

"He was really pissed she hadn't said anything about the Chinese to you before she did. I wouldn't be surprised if he gave her the third degree about what else she might know but isn't saying."

Sherman shook his head. "She didn't think their nationality was a big deal." He smiled at that thought. "There aren't many people out there who don't see nationality or color when they look at people."

"She's getting to you?"

"How so?" Sherman asked, downplaying Sloan's question.

Sloan smiled a knowing grin. "Yeah, that little brunette is getting to you. It's a good thing she's not Bobby's girlfriend, huh?"

"I have no idea what you're getting at," Sherman said.

Sloan knew it was a bullshit comment. He knew his friend well enough to see that Sherman had a thing for her. He let it go though. "Before I forget." He pulled his phone from his pocket. "Here are the pics of the man who was taking pictures of Brielle with you and Bobby. I don't know which of you he was following." He brought the pictures up and handed his phone to Sherman.

Sherman viewed the pictures. It was a man in his late twenties to early thirties. He had longish blonde hair spiked up in the front, kind of messy looking, with dark roots. His face was narrow, his clothes trendy. And Sherman was sure he'd never seen him before. He shook his head. "I know I'd remember that hair. I am sure I haven't seen this guy anywhere."

They brought the phone to the rear of the plane and showed the pictures to Bobby and Brielle. Neither of them had ever seen him before either. "His hair is dyed," Bobby said. "Look at his dark eyebrows."

"Yeah, I noticed that too," Sherman said. "As well as his roots."

"I've already sent the pics to HQ to see if they can get an ID on the guy," Sloan said.

"So, you didn't notice this guy before we pulled up?"

"No, but he didn't follow Brielle out of the hotel. He was on the street, appeared from nowhere when you pulled up."

"Well, blond-boy wasn't trying to be inconspicuous, not with that hair," Sherman said. He motioned Sloan forward and only spoke again when they were at the front of the plane. "It wouldn't be a stretch that someone put a tracker on my rental car, just like yours in Cleveland. It wouldn't be a bad idea to give Cooper and Madison a heads up, so they check their car over too." He turned to the console in front of him and sent off a message to them both. Ops was automatically copied in as well.

Sloan shook his head, deep in thought. "You've got the Chinese, links to New Jersey, and the Sheriff of your Parish all tied together, unlikely alliances."

"Let's not forget the new mayor of Galliano too. He seems to have a role in this mess," Sherman added. "Cancer research, very unlikely. I'd say more likely drugs or something to do with oil as close as that plant is to Port Fourchon and Galliano Airport. I hope we can figure this out sooner rather than later. I don't think Miss

Brielle Jarboe is going to want to sit on this story for too long." And with that thought, he typed out a message to Shepherd.

Golf

The plane descended through the turbulent night sky into Chicago Executive Airport. The winds were blowing from the west at thirty miles per hour with occasional gusts up to forty. It was the bumpiest landing that Brielle had ever experienced. She guessed it was for Kaylee, as her hands gripped the armrests with white knuckles. She didn't realize that her own hands did, too. Sweet Bobby had his hand on top of hers.

The plane taxied to the Shepherd Security Hangar. Both Sherman and Sloan took their phones off airplane mode. There were no new messages. That was a good sign to indicate that nothing had gone sideways while they were in the air.

Sherman popped the cabin door open and was immediately reminded he was back in Chicago. The air was cool, forty-five degrees, which felt like twenty-eight degrees with the wind that whipped through the open hangar door. He had a base-layer shirt in his backpack. It would have to do. Brielle already wore the black hoodie as she'd gotten cold on the flight. The hoodie would have to do it for her until they got to his place and he could loan her some warmer clothes.

Four of the Shepherd Security cars were parked in the hangar. They said goodbye to Sloan and Kaylee and watched them drive out first. Sherman secured the hangar door after the jet pulled back out on its continued flight into Teterboro. Then he joined Brielle and Bobby in the warmed-up SUV that sat idling beside the hangar.

Sherman drove straight to the rehab facility to check Bobby in. They met the evening manager in her office. She had everything ready. Sherman presented the court paperwork. The manager would be sure the court liaison received it first thing in the morning. Sherman mandated that Bobby may call only himself or Brielle.

"And I want to be notified right away if he receives any calls or visits from anyone, including other law enforcement."

The manager nodded. She'd been advised this was a special case with special handling required. She assured Sherman his requests would be followed. "Last order of business, I need both your signatures." She handed them the admission forms.

Sherman signed and then turned the clipboard to Bobby, who blew out a deep breath. His eyes went to Brielle. "Only for you."

She pressed a soft kiss to his cheek. "I love you, Bobby."

He signed his name and handed the clipboard back to the manager. He couldn't believe he was back in a locked-down rehab facility.

Then the manager took them on a tour. It was a luxury facility with a pool, hot tub, full gym, and a lobby and dining room that looked like a five-star hotel. Everywhere there were comfortable couches and chairs, some with other residents sitting and quietly talking, reading, or just enjoying the quiet. There were plants and fountains everywhere. It was beautiful.

Then the manager took them to the hallway that was lined with doors. "This is the residence portion of the facility. Each room has its own bathroom." She slid a cardkey through the lock on door number two-ten. "This is your room." She swung the door wide to reveal a room that rivaled the best hotel rooms. It had a queen-sized bed, nightstands, a wall-mounted television, desk, chair, and couch in calming shades of blue.

"Wow, this is nice," Bobby said. He noticed the plush down comforter on the bed. Peeking into the bathroom, he noted it was equally luxurious. "This sure as hell isn't the Jefferson Parish rehab center."

"Told you," Sherman said.

"It's still court-mandated rehab," Bobby said.

"Think of this as a vacation at a spa," Sherman replied.

"Yeah, one I'm locked in at," Bobby complained.

"As long as you remain in your room during room hours, your door won't be locked. You have the key and can come and go throughout the facility as long as you obey the rules and participate in your scheduled sessions with the counsellors." The manager handed him a folder. "All the rules, hours, and expectations are in this packet. You will need to read through it all this evening."

Bobby opened the folder. The first page listed his counselling session times. "Three sessions a day? Are you kidding me?"

"Hey, you're the dumb-shit that got yourself arrested," Sherman reminded him. "They've got my boss' number. If there are any problems, they'll call him if they can't get a hold of me. Don't embarrass me, Bobby."

Brielle embraced Bobby. "Just go with the flow. Please, promise me you'll behave and stay out of trouble."

Bobby kissed the top of her head. "I'm going to behave. I promise you."

Sherman locked eyes with Bobby. "Call or text me if you need anything and I'll have someone from the office bring it to you if I'm away. I'll talk to you soon. Enjoy your vacay."

Bobby forced a smile. He watched Brian and Brielle leave with the manager. He stared at the closed door for quite a while after they left. Then he sat down on the bed. It was very comfortable. He flipped through the packet. He'd have to play along until hopefully Brian could spring him.

Brielle had tears in her eyes when they exited the building and the cool Chicago October night air smacked her face. She shivered against the brisk breeze. She felt Brian wrap his arm around her. He pulled her into his body as they walked to the SUV. He opened her door and closed it after she climbed in.

"He's going to be okay. You saw that place, it's nicer than most hotels."

Brielle glanced out her side window and tried to calm her emotions. She wasn't one who cried often or easily. "I know."

"Hopefully he'll swim, use the gym, get into shape. The food they serve is healthy, cooked by a top chef. If he has to stay the full thirty days, you may not even recognize him when he walks out of there."

"Promise me you'll try to get him out sooner," Brielle pled, her eyes still gazing out of the side window.

Sherman reached over and took hold of her hand. "Once this is over, if I can, I promise you I will."

She turned her head, so she viewed the side of Brian's face. There was ample lighting from all the streetlights to see his attractive features. She studied his profile. He and Bobby shared many physical characteristics, a strong jawline, the same hair color. They even had the same nose.

But their personalities were worlds apart. Bobby was fun to be around, loyal, and would do anything for anyone, like get arrested to provide a cover. She loved Bobby like a brother. She had spent so many years hating Brian for what he did to her sister. This Brian and that person were two different people though. This Brian was strong and capable. She felt she could trust him. That was hard for her to reconcile.

"Thank you."

Sherman's eyes flickered to her. "Are you okay?"

"Yes. It was just hard to leave Bobby, knowing he's only there because he helped me." She felt Brian squeeze her hand and only then realized he still held it.

"He wanted to, and I know he doesn't regret it for one second. Bobby will be fine."

Sherman drove to his condo. He parked in the driveway in front of his two-car garage. He led her to the front door and unlocked it with his code. Once inside, he disarmed the alarm. He turned the light on to reveal the small main room.

Brielle glanced around. The kitchen, eating area and a small living room area were in the main room. Through the doors at the rear of the room she saw a bathroom and doorway into the bedroom. A third door was on the wall that butted up against the garage. The walls were beige, the furniture brown. She judged the living space to be smaller than the garage, but it was bigger than her apartment.

"This is nice," she said, still glancing around.

She noticed a grouping of pictures on the top of a table up against the wall between the doors to the bedroom and bathroom. A cross hung above them, the only thing on any of the walls. She crossed the room and studied the eight pictures in frames, his family. She recognized his mother and father. There was even a picture of him and Bobby as children taken in front of their childhood home.

"Do you have a washer and dryer I can use? I'm out of clean clothes."

"Yeah, in the bathroom. I need to wash a few things too. We can throw our stuff in together and do one big load."

Brielle chuckled that sultry laugh of hers in response, bringing a smile to Sherman's face. He really liked her raspy voice and how her laugh sounded. He liked a lot of things about her. "What, is that too intimate for you? Letting our underclothing comingle and rub against each other?"

She laughed again. "Yeah, it's just weird and yes, there is something intimate about it."

"As we tend the load, I promise I won't try to picture you in your panties, a sight that I'm sure I'd enjoy very much."

"Stop," she reprimanded him, but the smile on her face was anything but harsh.

Sherman laughed harder. "Let me get you something to put on so you can wash what you're wearing too."

She followed him into the bedroom. His bed was queen-sized, the comforter white, his furniture black. He set his backpack on the bed and pulled his dirty clothes out. He disappeared into the closet for a second then returned carrying a laundry basket full of wadded up clothes, and a long-sleeved Henley shirt draped over his arm. It was dark blue.

He handed the shirt her way. She held it up in front of herself. It was long and hung halfway down her thighs. "Thank you. This will work."

"Let me know if you want a pair of pants and I'll find something that will fit you."

She glanced at his hips. She doubted he'd have anything. Her hips and butt were a lot wider than his.

He dumped the basket of clothes onto the bed. "Put what you need washed in first, then I'll add to it to make a full load."

"Do you have a blow dryer? I'd like to shower and wash my hair." She unloaded all her dirty clothes into the basket, self-conscious of her underclothing. Even though she dressed mostly in jeans and girly t-shirts, her panties and bras were lacy or satiny in bright colors. They made her feel good, feminine, desirable. Kind of a joke, she thought, given that she hadn't had a boyfriend, let alone a date in over a year.

Sherman thought about it as he gazed at her underclothing in the basket. Yeah, he could totally envision Brielle's curvy figure in the sexy items in front of him. He shook his head. "Sorry, no, I don't have one, probably don't have a good enough shampoo and conditioner for you either."

This was the perfect opportunity for Brielle to ask him the question she had been dying too, without coming out and asking him directly. "Doesn't your girlfriend keep that kind of stuff here?"

Sherman froze. No, not only did he not have a girlfriend, he never had women at his place. He had two women he dialed up for casual sex when he had the need, but he never had them here. He went to their places so he could control when the encounter was over by leaving. He rarely stayed the night with either of them. He thought for a long second about that. Brielle would sleep with him, snuggled against him in his bed all night. Well, damn.

"I don't have a girlfriend. I'm away for work most of the time so one really doesn't fit into my life."

"Doesn't Gary have the same schedule as you? He has a fiancé. It looks like it can work."

Sherman nodded his head. "It can, when the people and the timing is right. A few of the guys are married and have a kid. It's rough though, a lot of time away and a lot on the wife to take care of."

"I'm sure if they love each other enough it's worth it to them," Brielle said. "Anyway, I'm not sure what I'm going to do without a blow dryer. My hair is so thick that it will still be damp in the morning."

Sherman thought about that for a second. "We have to go to HQ first thing tomorrow to meet with my boss and the rest of the team. There is an apartment that our office manager keeps stocked. I know there is good shampoo and conditioner there as well as a blow dryer. Let me text her and make sure no one is using it. We could go early, and you can catch your shower there."

"That would be great, thanks," Brielle said.

He typed out a message to Angel. Then he carried the basket of clothes to the bathroom while Brielle changed into his shirt and her last pair of clean panties from her backpack behind the closed bedroom door. He threw the clothes into the washer and waited for Brielle to bring the clothes she was wearing to be washed.

Brielle slid on the long shirt, wrestling with it to pull it over her hips. She looked down, and then over her shoulder at her butt. Great, it hugged her like a pair of leggings, which she never wore because she hated the look on her. She had her father's build. Her sister, Dahlia, had been blessed to have inherited her mother's slender frame. She wished in that moment that she had too.

She carried her clothes into the bathroom. She was greeted by Brian's gaze obviously wandering over her body. She noticed he had a small smile on his lips. "Stop. And my eyes are up here." She pointed to them with her left hand. Her right held her clothes.

Sherman chuckled. "Momma, no red-blooded American man would be able to keep his eyes off your curves. I'm sorry for being a pig and letting my appreciation of you be so noticeable."

"Yeah, because it would be better if you were sneakier," she said with a laugh. "That really is not okay, you know."

"I do think you have been hanging out with too many gay men, because every straight guy would surely be checking you out like I just did."

She pushed her clothes into the washer. "I seriously doubt that." Her voice was a bit more bitter sounding than she had intended.

Sherman didn't like the tone of her voice or what he realized was the fact that she had, on several occasions, disagreed with him on how fine she looked. And he didn't think that it was because she was offended by his comments. Brielle doubted his sincerity, didn't see herself as attractive. Bobby's statement about her last two boyfriends cheating on her came back to him. He was sure that kind of thing would hit a woman's ego hard. It made him angry that she doubted her attractiveness because of the two weasels who had cheated on her.

He took hold of her by the shoulders and spun her to face him. He gazed intently into her eyes as he spoke. "Let's get one thing straight. You, Brielle Jarboe, are a fine-looking woman. I am very attracted to you. It is going to be very hard for me to lay in my bed with you tonight and just hold you, nothing else. And, the only reason I will just hold you and not try to talk you into making love with me is because I respect you. You behaved recklessly by breaking into that plant, but it took courage. I read several of your blog posts, and you are a good writer. You called the Mayor of Galliano out, the Sheriff out, and raised questions about that BioDynamix facility, holding nothing back. That too took courage and I respect courage."

Brielle was surprised by Brian's words. She stared into his eyes, only noticing now how the brown depths sparkled with life. He had sincere eyes, comforting eyes. "You really read a few of my blog posts?" She asked after a lengthy silence.

Sherman nodded his head yes. "They were good."

A smile curved Brielle's lips. "Thank you." She took her writing very seriously. She wanted so badly to get a job as a full-time journalist. It was her dream since college.

Sherman placed a soft kiss on her forehead. He hadn't been lying when he said it was going to be hard to lie in his bed holding her without making love to her. Even now, he was yearning to kiss her deeply, to caress over every wonderful curve on her body. His body was surging with the need to pull her frame up against his and feel the incredible sensation of her softness against every inch of him.

Luckily, his phone vibrated on the bathroom counter, where he'd set it. He stepped back and grabbed it. It was a text back from Angel. It was okay to use the apartment on nine. He typed out a quick message of thanks. Then he stepped in front of the washer and turned it on. "That was Angel, we can use the apartment tomorrow morning."

"Who's Angel?"

"The office manager and wife of one of our guys. You'll meet them tomorrow. We have an early meeting at the office and will fly back out, I assume by mid-morning. My boss is deploying a few more men to Port Fourchon with us to carry out the surveillance."

A chill gripped her. She shivered.

"You cold?"

"Yes," she said with a small smile. She wouldn't tell him it was not temperature related. The fact that his boss thought more men were needed in the bayou showed how seriously they were taking this. She had thought about it and realized that these people were professionals. If they thought there was something to worry about, it must be serious.

"Let's go to bed and snuggle under the covers. I'll warm you up."

She followed him from the room. He pulled the covers back and motioned her to slide in first. She pulled the back of the shirt down over her butt as she climbed in. The sheets were cold. The chill that invaded her this time was temperature related.

Sherman set his badge, gun, and phone onto the nightstand. He watched Brielle. She watched his every movement. Then he kicked his shoes off and dropped his jeans to the floor. Her eyes remained on him. Then he pulled his shirt over his head and dropped it beside his jeans. He flashed her a provocative smile. "Don't worry, I won't remove anything else." He moved to slide into bed beside her.

"You need to put something else on, sleeping pants, a t-shirt, anything. Besides, these sheets are cold."

"Nope," he said with a grin as he covered himself with the bedcovers. "My bed and I'll sleep how I'm comfortable. And we'll warm those sheets up real fast."

He had a devilish smile on his face, Brielle noted. His cockiness and flirtiness should have pissed her off. It didn't. If anything, it made him more attractive to her.

He wrapped his arms around her and nestled in close. She laid reclined but propped up on her elbow. He pulled on her, causing her to roll into him. She readjusted her position so that her head was on his chest. She was distracted by his hand, resting on her hip.

"Woah," she said when his hand traveled over her hip and landed on her butt.

"Damn, your ass is cold," Sherman said.

He rubbed his hand over her bottom, getting way too close to intimate parts. "Please stop that."

Sherman chuckled. "Brielle, this isn't me trying anything, just trying to help warm you." But he knew his words were lies. The sensation of running his hand over her panties, her nicely shaped ass cheeks below them, filled his thoughts with images that were very sexual.

"Brian, please don't," she repeated. She was very aware of every inch of his skin that was in contact with hers. His legs were pressed to hers. His other arm was wrapped around her, below her shoulders, and he held her around her waist. Her cheek was pressed against his warm chest. She could hear his heart beating. And his pelvis was pressed to hers. She could feel his excitement growing against her.

He rolled her to her back and hung his face over hers, being careful to keep his erect penis to the side of her, though he was sure she had already felt it. "Brielle, my apologies." His voice was a whisper. "No woman should have to ask a man twice to stop. I'm trying to control myself. I did tell you I am attracted to you and I know I just acted on my feelings, against your wishes." He smiled a guilty grin. "I really do like your butt though."

His words surprised her. Brian Sherman was a man of honor. If he had been before or not, was irrelevant. She knew she had previously judged him on the actions of a seventeen-year-old kid, not the man he was. "Thank you." It was all that she could say out loud.

"Goodnight," he said softly. And then his lips brushed hers.

They shared a lengthy kiss, without him ever parting her lips. Like before, she felt the warmth and the moisture from his mouth on his lips. She wanted to deepen the kiss, to take it to the next level, but she knew she didn't want to do anything more with him and that would have signaled him that she did. She wasn't a tease and tried hard to not send mixed messages.

Sherman enjoyed that she kissed him back but was confused that she didn't initiate more into the kiss. Women always did. Withholding his tongue always made them push theirs into his mouth. She was one tough cookie. From how she'd acted, he was sure she was as attracted to him as he was to her.

When he pulled his lips away and opened his eyes, he gazed into her beautiful brown eyes that were dilated with desire. The expression on her face said she enjoyed the kiss and wanted more. He couldn't figure her out. Was this more of her insecurity because her last two boyfriends cheated on her? Or was it her suspicion that he wouldn't be faithful?

"We do that well," he whispered as he rearranged her hair off her face. He caressed her cheek with the back of one hand. "I'd never hurt you, Brielle."

She gazed at him with uncertainty. Her heart pounded in her chest and her body bristled with energy from that kiss. She dragged a breath in after realizing that she wasn't breathing. "You said you wouldn't pressure me to have sex."

"And I'm not. That was just a kiss goodnight." His lips pulled into a grin. "But you're thinking about it."

"I'm not on birth control," she confessed.

"Why not?"

"Because I'm not having sex with anyone. My last relationship ended over a year ago and when I do meet someone, I plan to take it slow and allow plenty of time to get to know him before I sleep with him. I'll have a lot of time to know it may happen before it does."

"Hum, now that sounds like you have it all planned out. There isn't much room for any spontaneity in there. You're discounting that you may find yourself laying with someone who you just can't resist wanting more with."

"I'm Catholic. I don't do that, Brian."

"I'm Catholic too, but I'm also a realist. I know that there are just some things we can't control, and nor should we. Life is too short to deprive ourselves of things we want, or people we want for that matter. Tomorrow is not guaranteed for any of us. I've been shot twice and have seen buddies die. My momma died of cancer at the age of forty-seven, way too young. I'm sure the only regrets the people I've known who died too young was of the things they never did, not the things they did do."

Brielle was shocked by his words. It took her a few seconds to process what all he'd said. "I'm sure," she agreed. "Have you really been shot twice?"

Sherman nodded. He hadn't moved. He still hung his head over hers.

"Where?"

"The first one hit my upper thigh on my right leg. I was lucky. It hit on the outside edge, didn't fuck up too much muscle and hit no bone. The second time I was shot, it was in the arm." He moved his left arm forward and his eyes led hers to a spot on his upper arm where a scar marred his skin. "That one did a little more damage."

Brielle's eyes focused on the scar. Then she reached her hand up to it and ran her fingers over the flesh. "What does it feel like when your shot?"

"It hurts like hell. It burns and throbs."

"How long did you have to wait for a doctor to treat it and give you pain killers?"

Sherman's eyes angled away from hers and he stared at the pillow beside her head. "It felt like forever, but it was only a matter of seconds each time. Sloan, my partner, is our unit's medic. He got pain killers in me within minutes both times and bandaged me up." He felt her fingers trace his jawline. Then they slid down his neck.

"I'd sure like to kiss you, and I mean really kiss you. And if you want it to end there, I promise you, you won't have to tell me twice," Sherman whispered.

Brielle knew she wanted that real kiss, she knew she wanted more. Her body throbbed with desire. But she wasn't ever going to be that girl again who slept with a guy too soon. If a man really wanted her for who she was, he'd have no problem waiting till she was ready. Without thinking more about it, she nodded her head yes, and reached her lips up towards his.

She felt his lips press to hers, just as softly as they had before. He gave her a few of those same kisses with his lips slightly parted before she felt his tongue nudge her lips. She instantly responded, opening her mouth and entwining her tongue with his. He deepened the kiss, and she felt overwhelmed by the desire that washed over her. The kiss was lengthy, vigorous, left her breathless, and made her want more.

"May I make love to you, Brielle Jarboe?" He asked with a raspy, soft voice.

Brielle breathed out heavily, trying to catch her breath. She knew she wanted that, but she couldn't. "I can't Brian. I'm sorry." Her words were soft, apologetic, and pleading.

Sherman was disappointed but not surprised. He pressed a kiss to her forehead. "Then turn over onto your side, snuggle with me, and press your cold ass to me so I can warm it up. Let's try to get some sleep."

"Thank you, Brian." She felt a deep appreciation for him. He was a true gentleman, probably the first gentleman she'd ever been with. She turned onto her side, facing away from him.

"Just so we're clear. I want you. I will ask you again at some point in the future, but not tonight." He reached up to the bedside lamp and turned it off. Then he snuggled in close to her.

When Sherman heard the buzzer indicating the washer was through its cycle, he reluctantly pulled himself from beneath Brielle. She had rolled over and half her torso as well as her head and one leg laid across him.

"Where are you going?" She was surprised she'd already fallen asleep.

"Washer's done. I'm going to throw our clothes into the dryer. I'll be right back." He pressed a kiss to the top of her head.

She felt the heat leave the bed with him. She remained with her head on his pillow, watching the open bedroom door while he was gone. She really liked snuggling with him, and she was very attracted to him. He was handsome, sexy, and capable. She felt safe with him. She knew he wasn't relationship material, but still, she thought about what it would be like to make love with him. She bet he'd be giving, not selfish like her last boyfriend who didn't seem to put much effort into pleasuring her. Of course, while they were together, she gave him the benefit of the doubt, that maybe he didn't know how to.

If she was to ever have sex with someone she wasn't in a relationship with, it would be with Brian or someone like him, though she doubted there were many men like him out there. She certainly had never met anyone like him before. It would be hard for her though to have an intimate encounter with him and not want a relationship with him. She knew she'd be setting herself up to be hurt, and she didn't need any more of that in her life.

She watched Brian reenter the room. He slid back into bed with her. She readjusted her position to give him his spot back, but she nestled in close. "I really like snuggling with you, Brian."

"I guarantee you'd like naked snuggling even more."

Brielle chuckled.

Sherman loved her sultry laugh. He admitted to himself that he was quite enamored with her. The fact that she had refused him did make her more attractive, he'd admit that. It was a challenge, and he always loved a good challenge. But it was more than the chase. He hadn't lied when he told her he respected her. He did, and not just for her courage to go after BioDynamix. She was a loyal friend to Bobby, loved him like a brother. And Bobby was loyal to her, loved her like a sister. He was sure him wanting to sleep with her somehow bordered on incestuous because of that. He laughed to himself with that thought as his hands caressed over her hips and lower back.

He let his hands wander over her butt. Her cheeks were finally warmed up. He gave them a gentle squeeze and then returned them to her lower back. He wouldn't make her tell him to stop again. He kissed the top of her head, which again rested on his shoulder. He could get used to falling asleep like this.

Hotel

The morning was hectic. The alarm he set went off at zero four-thirty. He left Brielle lying in his bed while he took a quick shower. She was back asleep when he reentered his bedroom eight minutes later. He turned the bedside light on, earning a moan and a few choice curses from her. She pulled the covers over her head.

"Come on, get up and get dressed. We need to roll in fifteen minutes. I have the dryer on heating the wrinkles out of our clothes. We need to pack up fast and get to the office so you can take your shower."

"What time is it?"

"Nearly quarter to five. The meeting with my boss is at zero six hundred."

"How long will it take to get to the office?"

"About fifteen minutes," he replied as he pulled a pair of boxer briefs on and then a pair of blue jeans.

"I have fifteen more minutes to sleep," she moaned.

After he zipped his fly, he pulled the bedcovers back.

She grabbed them and tried to pull them back over herself. "Oh, come on!"

"Get up. You can dress as we pull our clothes from the dryer." He pulled on her arm. "Up!"

"Too fucking early," she swore below her breath, but she complied and got up.

Sherman disappeared into his closet and returned with two base layer shirts. He handed her one and then pulled the other over his head. He also had a light gray hoodie with the words US Navy across the front. He handed it to her. "Here, you'll probably need a hoodie at night while we're back home, and I don't think you should wear the black one that you wore during the break-in to that BioDynamix plant. Wear this one. You'll need it. It's only thirty-nine degrees outside."

"Jeez it gets cold early up here."

He followed her out of the room and into the bathroom. They folded the clothes together, shoving them into their backpacks. He left her to use the facilities and get dressed. They left his condo at five minutes to five.

Brielle was glad the car had a passenger-side seat heater. She was cold. The car was cold, the air was colder. They passed a coffee shop with a drive through. It was open. "Coffee, please?" She pointed it out.

"There's coffee at the office. I'll make you a nice big cup while you're in the shower."

"I hate you," she said in an animated voice.

Sherman chuckled. It was obvious that she wasn't a morning person. He hoped she would wake up in the shower. This meeting with Shepherd and the team was not one they could be late for. Little did she know that her return to Louisiana was up to Shepherd. He also knew that she'd have to be locked in some place if it was decided that she would not return. She would not take it well.

Brielle was surprised how much traffic was on the streets at this early hour. She paid attention to the route he took and was surprised when he turned into a parking garage that was attached to a building that was ten stories tall. She counted the floors to know. A lot of lights were on in the building. They went deep into the parking garage, to sub-basement level two.

She also watched with great fascination the security gate and two garage doors they passed through that Brian had to enter a code into a panel to open. They emerged into a brightly lit private garage. About a dozen cars were parked there. He pulled into a parking spot, turned the car off, and then turned to her.

"Inside, touch nothing and stay with me at all times. This is a secure building and you can't wander around unescorted."

"Okay," she agreed, wondering why he made such a big deal about it.

They got out of the car and crossed to the elevator and the door. She watched as he pressed his hand to a pad and then entered a code into the keypad. Twenty seconds later, the elevator arrived. They stepped in, and he pressed nine. The elevator ascended quickly. They stepped out when the door opened, and she followed him to a door with no markings.

He opened the door to the apartment and flipped the lights on. She entered behind him and closed the door. The main room looked like a small hotel room with a small kitchen with a table to eat at. It was cozy.

He pointed to the bathroom. "Get your shower. I'll make coffee and bring a cup in so it's on the counter when you get out."

She flashed him a stare of warning.

"The shower door is frosted. I won't see a thing."

"Don't be looking," she warned. Then she sealed herself within the bathroom. She set her backpack on the closed lid of the toilet and engaged the water. The shower door was heavily frosted. She reached her hand within the shower and noted that he was right. She really couldn't make out any detail. Only then did she disrobe, draping her clothes over the backpack.

Brian had been correct that there were bottles of shampoo, conditioner, and body wash in the shower stall. There was even a name brand face cleanser. She showered as quickly as she could, even though the hot downpour felt so good that she wanted to linger there for a long time.

"I'm just setting your coffee onto the counter," she heard Brian's voice.

"Is there any sugar?"

"Already in, one and a half teaspoons." He'd been watching when she added it the previous morning on the boat.

"You remembered?" She said, surprised. "Thank you."

"You're welcome, now hurry up." His eyes took in the sight of her distorted features behind the frosted glass. How he'd like to step into that shower with her!

Fifteen minutes later she opened the bathroom door. She wore her blue jeans and a dark green girly t-shirt. Her hair was wrapped in a towel. "I need to leave the door open while I blow dry or I'll sweat to death. And can I get another cup of coffee?"

"Sure," Sherman said. He took her cup from her. He was already on his second cup.

She returned to the bathroom, and towel dried her hair for a few seconds. Then she fired up the blow dryer and hoped her hair wouldn't frizz out too badly. She blew it from all angles as she sipped the second cup of coffee that Brian brought her. When it was nearly dry, she ran the ends around her brush in an attempt to tame it. In the end, she gathered it into a high ponytail.

Before they left the room, she pulled the base layer shirt over her head. Then they carried their belongings out of the room. He led her to the stairs and repeated the palm-print and keypad routine. She wondered why the security. It wasn't like they were at a government installation that she could tell. This looked like any other office building.

He led her down to the fifth floor and they exited the stairs. She heard voices coming from a room to the right, its door open. She pulled her phone from her back pocket, five-fifty-five. She took a deep breath to steady her nerves, which were suddenly jumpy. She wished she'd asked Brian more about this meeting before now.

Brian motioned her to enter in front of him. She stepped in, surprised by the number of men in the room. Seven, she counted seven. Some were standing over near the conference table, some sat at it. She stopped as she viewed them. They all looked strong and solid. A few looked downright dangerous. Gary was there, sitting beside the man in the wheelchair. She took a few more steps forward when Brian's hand pushed on her lower back.

"This is Brielle Jarboe," he introduced. "My brother's friend and the reporter who broke the story on the BioDynamics facility in her Parish Blog."

Brielle was stunned he introduced her as a reporter. No one had ever called her that out loud before. It brought a proud smile to her face, knowing he thought of her as one.

Sherman ushered her up to Shepherd, who sat in his wheelchair at the head of the table. "Brielle, this is our boss, Shepherd."

Brielle forced a small smile, suddenly feeling very intimidated. Even this man in the wheelchair had massive arms and looked strong. His face was lean and had sharp angles, making him look harsh. "Hello," she said, extending her hand to shake his.

"Good morning." He shook her hand. "You provided us with a lot to look into. For the record, we agree with you that something isn't right with that facility."

Her smile relaxed. "I'm so glad. Thank you."

"We're going to get started. Take a seat," Shepherd motioned to two chairs across the table.

Sherman noticed the monitor was on, a blue screen. As he led her to the designated chairs, he introduced her to Mother as they passed him and then to Lambchop. The monitor suddenly displayed Cooper and Madison. He pointed across the table. "That's Jackson and Garcia." Then he introduced her to Burke from Charlie Team, who took a seat beside him.

Doc entered last, closing the door behind himself. "Sorry I'm late, Shep."

Brielle pulled her phone out of her pocket and checked the time. It was one minute after six.

"Oh good, you have it on you," Garcia said. He stood and reached across the table, pointing at her phone. "I'll take that now."

Brielle instinctively pulled it closer to her body, and she stared at the man who was the most dangerous looking of them all. His eyes were dark, the expression on his face serious and stern.

"It's okay. He's our tech guy. He's going to forward everything on your phone to one of ours for you. That way, if anyone is monitoring your phone, it will ping in this area regardless where your phone data is transferring to. You can text, call, make blog posts through our phone and all of it will point back to yours, right here in the Chicago area," Sherman said.

"You can do that?" She asked the man whose hand still hung over the table.

"I can do a lot of things."

She reluctantly handed her phone over to him.

"Cooper, Madison, glad you made it on," Shepherd said. "You've gotten the site secured?"

"Yes, we took over a private area within a Coast Guard facility here at Port Fourchon. They have been most hospitable. They even have a fully stocked private galley for us, and they provided us access to rooms within their sleeping quarters. The coffee from the machine sucks. That's the only downside," Cooper reported.

"The oil companies ferry their workers on and off their rigs from the heliport here and over a hundred boats come and go from this port daily, loading and unloading supplies as well as oil. There's a lot of activity," Madison added. "We'll be able to come and go from this location with no one paying us any attention. Everything here is constantly in motion."

"Good. Glad you suggested that location, Sherman," Shepherd said. "You've all had the opportunity to read the briefing. Garcia and Jackson will support you from Ops. The digital team is still looking into the people involved. There are quite a few inconsistencies that we need to take a deeper dive into."

"So far, there is nothing suspicious in Sheriff Henderson or Dwayne Stuart, Galliano's Mayor's financials. If they've taken any bribes to open and protect that plant, the cash didn't go through their private U.S. based accounts. I'm still looking," Garcia said. "As far as the Chinese in those trailers, we don't have a single hit from facial recognition yet and we were able to capture some good pictures of at least a dozen of them from that surveillance camera you set up, Brielle. The satellite has just moved into place, we'll see what we can get from it."

Brielle was shocked that they had a satellite watching the area. Who were these people that they could make that happen? Brian was with the ATF. The ATF had satellites?

"Has the digital unit dug up anything on blonde-boy, who was taking pictures of Sherman, his brother, and Brielle out in front of the hotel? He didn't follow them when they left for the airport. I found that odd," Sloan asked, his eyes on Garcia.

"Not yet. We will though. It's just a matter of time."

"When you come down, you need to bring me some field Ops equipment so I can dial in," Madison said. "I want to be able to tap into that satellite feed on a bigger monitor than my tablet."

"Garcia send down some motion sensitive cameras too. I want to get some planted in the trees in the bayou surrounding the back of the plant. Since nothing has come or gone from the front of the building except what appears to be supplies for the Chinese living on-site, we need to watch the back of the facility. I'd bet you anything that is their means of transport," Cooper added. "I wasn't aware how wide that waterway is in spots. They could bring a damn big boat right up to the back of that plant."

"I've reached out to the appropriate governmental agencies. No one knows about any bio-identical cancer research. Bio-identicals are used in hormone replacement therapy. It sounds catchy and high tech, but isn't applicable to cancer care, is what I've been told," Shepherd added. "So, let's figure out what it is they are really doing."

"What involvement will the regular FBI, CIA, and Homeland have?" Cooper asked.

"We are running anything regarding the Chinese on-site through them and I will keep them updated. Otherwise, it's our show. We're sanctioned to continue as we see fit," Shepherd said. "Somehow, we need to get eyes inside that facility. Now that Garcia is back in Ops, we'll try to break past their firewall, but I'm not confident we'll breach their network from outside."

Garcia stared intently at Brielle while Shepherd spoke, unnerving her greatly. "Brielle, you have a friend that works there, Tina Landry," he said, looking down at his computer tablet's screen for a second, reading her name. "All we need is someone to insert this flash drive into any computer on their network and we're in." He held up a small flash drive. "Can you get her to do it for us?"

"I don't know. She's scared, won't even talk to me about BioDynamix, says she signed an NDA and will get fired."

"We might be able to change her mind on that," Sherman said. "If she knows the authorities are looking into that place, maybe she'll help us in exchange for protection."

"I'll try," Brielle said. "Anything you want me to do."

"Do you know anyone else who works at that plant?" Sherman asked.

"I know about five more well enough. I know where they live and what bar they spend their off hours in, but I wouldn't call any of them friends like I do Tina."

"Start with Tina. We'll go to others if needed, but I don't want too many people to know that place is being investigated," Shepherd said. He tossed a pad of paper and a pen to her. "Give us any and all info on those others who work there from the Parish. Our digital team will investigate them before we greenlight talking with any of them."

"Sure," Brielle said. She started to list names and addresses, anything she knew about them.

"And Brielle, this should go without saying, but your cover is that you are up here near where Bobby Sherman is in rehab, so no posts about BioDynamix. After we get to the bottom of this, you can report on it, but we get to review the piece first. You cannot mention us to anyone. We don't exist," Shepherd added.

"I'll be monitoring your digital footprint," Garcia said. "If you mention us in any way, you will be arrested."

Brielle stopped writing. She gazed up at Garcia. His face held warning. Her eyes shifted to Shepherd. He too wore a serious expression. "That's called censorship and harassment, you know."

"It's the terms. If you want to continue to follow this story and get rights to report on it, you follow our rules. There are certain things that the public is better off not knowing about. Our unit is one of those things. It has to be this way for us to be effective," Shepherd said.

"Agree to it, Brielle," Sherman whispered in her ear. "I'll explain it more to you later and answer any questions you have."

"You will get to solely report on it once this mission is concluded, as long as you follow our rules. You get the exclusive. I'm sure you will be able to sell the story to all the major news outlets. This story can be a big break for you if it turns out to be something," Shepherd said.

"Okay," Brielle agreed, but she didn't like it. And these guys and this organization was as much the story as what was going on at the BioDynamix facility. She'd have to figure out a way around this.

Shepherd handed a document across the table. It was a legal agreement to abide by what they'd laid out.

Brielle glanced through it. It was short, to the point, and written in plain English. "I don't sign anything that my attorney hasn't reviewed."

The corner of Shepherd's lips tipped up. "Ms. Jarboe, you either sign the agreement and abide by it or you do not accompany my team to Port Fourchon. Your continued involvement is at my discretion."

Her eyes went to Brian.

"This is how it has to be, Brielle. Agree to the terms. It's your story. Certainly, you want to be there to see it through and get the credit for the investigative reporting on it," Sherman said.

She thought about it for a few seconds. Brian was right about that. And if it turned out to be something big, this could catapult her career as a journalist. But she just really didn't like that they had the final say on what she could report. "Fine," she agreed and signed the form. She handed it back to Shepherd.

"Thank you, Ms. Jarboe," Shepherd said. "Okay, pack up your gear. You fly back out as soon as you're ready. You'll fly into Pensacola. A Coast Guard chopper will shuttle you into Port Fourchon. Let's get eyes in that facility and figure out what the hell they're up to. Be safe, people."

The men around the table stood. Brielle came to her feet a few seconds later. Garcia moved around to their side of the table. He handed the flash drive to Sherman. "Give me about a half hour with her phone and I'll have the agency phone ready for you to pick up. I'll be in my workroom."

Sherman nodded. "I'll be up to get it before we head out." Then he led her from the room, following the others. They took the stairs up two flights to Sherman's office.

She glanced around as he packed his computer tablet up. He had two pictures of the bayou in frames on each of the walls. A New Orleans Saints blanket was draped over the couch. "Just who are you guys? You're not an ATF agent, are you?"

"The short answer is not exactly, but I do carry ATF creds and authority. We are a multi-agency task force with ties to the government and our military. As Shepherd said, we don't exist."

"Black Ops," Brielle said as though it was a dirty word.

"Something like that," Sherman agreed, but Brielle knew that was exactly who they were. And Sherman knew she knew.

"When this is over who gets the credit for exposing what's going on?"

"That depends on what it's about. If it is drug related, the DEA will take the credit for the investigation and the bust. If its terrorism related, Homeland and NSA will most likely take it. Anything cyber and the FBI or CIA will take point. Once we figure it out, we'll call the appropriate agency in to help with the takedown. They get us warrants and provide us cover."

"So, you don't ever get the credit for the work you do?"

Sherman faced her with a serious expression on his face. "If anyone ever hears about us, then we haven't done our jobs, or something's gotten really fucked up. We don't exist and we operate outside of regular channels. It's how we are able to get things done that other units can't."

"Doesn't it make you mad that you never get the credit for what you do?"

"We do with the people who matter. It's not about the public knowing who really raided a drug house or who really rescued a hostage from terrorists. It's about protecting people and the U.S.' interests and getting the job done."

Brielle stared at him with wide eyes, having a small idea of the enormity of what these people did. "Does Bobby know what you really do?"

"No."

"What would have happened if I didn't agree to sign that NDA?"

"You would have been taken into custody by the NSA and kept locked away until this is over. Our names, this facility, our Lear you flew on. No one can ever know about any of those things. We won't be able to do our job the way we do if word got out about us. And believe me, if that was to happen, a lot of people would die."

Brielle stood wide-eyed. She didn't think he was being dramatic or stretching the importance of what his group did for her benefit. If anything, she thought he was being modest. "I understand. Don't worry, I'll never tell anyone about your group."

Sherman's lips cracked a smile. He leaned in and placed a kiss on her forehead. "Thank you."

He turned away, and she watched him pack up more equipment. Then he led her to the elevator, and he pushed 'sub-two rear' on the elevator panel. He led her into a locker room that was bustling with activity. Many of the others who'd been in the meeting were there, packing up weapons, bullet-proof vests, and other articles of clothing.

"Sit here. Touch nothing and don't move," he said to her, placing her on the bench, a locker down from his. They were enormous lockers, more like the size of a large chest of drawers.

She watched with fascination. He pulled a bag from his locker loaded with clothing, a bullet-proof vest that had the letters ATF on it, and a helmet. He checked the gear over and repacked it. Then he tossed the bag to the floor behind him. She noticed the others were making piles behind themselves with bags too. He pulled a rifle case from his locker next. He unzipped it, revealing an assault rifle. He checked it over and then rezipped the case. Several handguns came out of his locker next.

She glanced around at the others. They were all equally armed. There was more fire power in this room than the entire Lafourche Parish Sheriff's Department had, she was sure. They looked like they were packing up to go to war.

"Toss your bag with the others," he said, pointing to her backpack. "That way it'll get loaded with the rest of our gear."

She noticed his backpack was with the items he'd removed from his locker too. She sat her bag next to the rest.

"Lambchop, my gear is ready," Sherman yelled over to him. "I'm going to take Brielle with me to get her phone from Garcia."

"We've got it," Lambchop assured him. "Try to make it fast. Ryan's loading our ammo into the vehicles now. I want to be out of here ASAP."

Sherman led her back to the elevator. She was quiet and looked almost shell-shocked. "You okay?" He asked her with a squeeze to her hand.

"Yes," she said nervously with a forced smile. "I don't think I've seen that many guns in one room before, not to mention the SWAT clothing."

"It's all necessary, the body armor, the weapons. The people we are usually going after are armed to the teeth. We need to be too."

"It's just a little unnerving," she confessed. And she had to admit to herself that it changed how she felt about him. He did a dangerous job, protected people, went after criminals and terrorists. Brian Sherman was a hero.

Sherman smiled. "I guess it would be."

She glanced away. Not what he expected.

"What's the matter?" Sherman asked.

Brielle wouldn't admit to him how unsettled all this made her feel or how insecure she felt due to the presence of the others. When it was just her and Brian on the boat, she was okay. Even when Madison and Cooper came onto the boat, she was okay with that too. But now, after sitting in that meeting and knowing that all those men would be going back down to the bayou with them, well, it intimidated the hell out of her.

"Thank God you're the good guys," she finally said.

The elevator opened on eight and they stepped off. He halted her in the hallway. "We are, the good guys. You're not doubting that, are you?"

"No, not at all."

"Then what is it?" His eyes stared a hole through hers. She didn't answer. "I can see something is wrong. Now what is it?"

"Nothing," she lied.

"Brielle, you need to trust me."

"I do."

"Then tell me what's wrong."

She sighed out loud. "It's just all those men that will be going back down with us. It's not what I expected. I don't know them. I know I can trust you."

"Brielle you can trust them too. They're my teammates. Lambchop, Mother, and the Undertaker are my brothers. I trust them with my life."

"The Undertaker?"

Sherman laughed. "Sloan, Gary. That's his callsign."

"Okay, yeah, that name instills trust," she remarked sarcastically.

"Look, I know this isn't what you're used to, but we are. We operate in teams and we're really tight. I can tell you at any given time what any of those men are thinking. And every single one of those men are highly effective Operators, the best of the best or they wouldn't be on this team. You can trust them."

"That doesn't help put me at ease," she moaned. "If anything, it makes it worse."

"How so?"

"Brian, when I look at you, not only do I see the man I know you are now, but I see the teenager who dated Dahlia, so you don't intimidate the hell out of me."

"But the rest of them, they do, intimidate you," he concluded.

She nodded. "Yeah, the guns openly worn by everyone. The physical conditioning of each man. Hell, even your boss in the wheelchair is built like a brick shithouse. And this guy we're going to get my phone from. He threatened to have me arrested. Do you have any idea what sitting in that room was like for someone who isn't one of you?"

Sherman wrapped his arms around her and pulled her in close. "I'm sorry, Brielle, I would never know how you felt. What I can tell you is that they are all good guys. Even Garcia. I know he can be a little intense, but it's only because he does such a good job. He's so dedicated he can be scary, but he'd also lay down his life for you in a heartbeat."

"Most people aren't like you guys, you know."

Sherman chuckled. "Believe me. I know. But we will figure out what the hell is going on down there, get proof, and bust them if it's illegal. And we'll keep you protected while we're doing it. My team are just people that do a difficult job, that's all, human beings. Try to see them as just people when you look at them."

Brielle nodded. She took a step back, pulling away from him. "Thank you. You know, I've never felt intimidated like that around anyone."

"It can be overwhelming," Sherman agreed. "You're not the first person to be in the position you're in, that we're helping the way we are." He remembered how belligerent Kaylee was when she first encountered the team. In hindsight, and with Brielle's admission, he now figured that how she acted was probably due to how afraid or intimidated she felt by being confronted by all four of them. He wondered if Angel or Sienna had felt that way.

"I'll really try to keep that in mind and relax."

"If you feel like that again, trust me enough to talk to me," Sherman said.

"I will. I promise."

He brought her to Garcia's workroom. Garcia gave her the agency phone and explained how his programming worked to mirror her real phone's data. Her own phone, if being monitored, would alternately ping off cell towers near the rehab facility and Sherman's condo. He showed her how to access all her stuff from her own phone on the agency phone.

"You cannot download anything to this phone. Several of the game programs you had on your phone are not secure enough for our network, so I did not load them." He opened the games folder on the agency phone. "These are secure and permissible if you find you must play games." Then he opened the music folder. "Here is all the music from your phone." He handed a set of wireless earphones to her that he'd already paired to her phone. "I usually listen to music while we are en route, thought you may want to too. There will be a lot of downtime during the operation."

"Wow, thank you," she said.

"I listened to some of that Zydeco music you have on here. It's very interesting. I've never heard any before, but I know it's native to Cajuns and the Creole bayou folks. I have to admit, I don't understand the difference between Cajun and Creole and Googling it didn't help any."

"No, it's about as clear as the brackish water in the bayou," Sherman said. "Some go strictly by skin color; mixed race is Creole and white with French origins are Cajun. Others in New Orleans say that if fancy you're Creole, and Cajun means rustic."

"Others say Cajuns are those who live in the city and Creole are the swamp people," Brielle said. "Since I am so mixed with different cultures, American Indian, Caribbean, Spanish, probably even some African, I identify as Creole. My sister, Dahlia, proclaims she's American Indian, would never say she's Creole or Cajun for that matter."

"Yeah, that's all pretty confusing," Garcia said. "My parents came here from Mexico. I'm straight up Mexican, easy. Anyway, here's how to access the agency text messages. I have the members of the team that will be on the ground programed in as well as myself and Jackson." He pointed out the Ops contact. "This will get you to our Operations Center. Call it if there is an emergency. It's manned twenty-four-by-seven,"

"Wow, thanks," Brielle repeated, genuinely surprised by his thoroughness. She was sure though that she wouldn't need the contacts.

Indigo

hen Sherman and Brielle returned to the Team Room, it was empty. All the bags were gone, and no one remained. He led her through to the garage. The men milled around the two vehicles. Requisition Ryan was just wheeling his empty ammo cart back towards the elevator. Sherman greeted him as they passed.

"Good timing," Mother called. "Ryan just finished loading our ammo."

"We need to roll," Lambchop said, and then slid into the driver's side of one of the SUVs.

Mother climbed behind the wheel of the other. Sherman led Brielle over to the Suburban that Lambchop was in. Sloan was just settling himself in the passenger seat beside Lambchop. Sherman opened the back door and motioned for her to get in.

At the other SUV, Sherman watched Doc get in the front passenger seat as Burke climbed into the backseat. He hadn't had much of an opportunity to work with Burke. Delta normally worked with Alpha Team. He was sure Burke was competent, or Shepherd wouldn't have hired him, but he would have felt better if Garcia or Jackson had been on the detail.

Lambchop's eyes in the rearview mirror flickered to Brielle. "How are you holding up?"

She smiled at him, remembering what Brian had said. They were all just human beings doing a difficult job. Nothing to be intimidated by. "I'm fine. I feel like I just stepped into a Tom Cruise movie."

The men laughed.

"Those things are so fake," Sloan said. "Kaylee loves to watch those action flicks and I can't help but pick them apart."

"What do you like to watch?" Brielle asked.

Sherman laughed. "And don't say porn." He reached forward and smacked Sloan on the shoulder.

Sloan laughed. "As little as I'm home, I don't want to watch anything when I'm alone with my fiancé. That's all I'll say."

The men laughed again. Brielle smiled. She pictured Kaylee, remembering how cute she and Sloan were together. He held her hand while she was obviously nervous about the takeoff and landing. Well, with the turbulence they'd hit, she too had been nervous. Bobby held her hand, but he'd been as afraid as she was. She glanced at Brian. She wondered if he would sit beside her on the plane this time and if he would hold her hand in front of his coworkers if she was nervous. He hadn't been physical at all with her when they were around the others.

As they drove, it started to rain. By the time they arrived back at the same hangar at the same airport they'd arrived at, it was pouring. Within, the cars pulled up to the same jet. They all got out of the cars. Brielle shivered against the cold in the hangar. The dampness made it feel a lot colder and the Navy hoodie she wore wasn't warm enough.

"Go into the plane and sit as far back as you can. I'll join you after we're loaded," Sherman said to her.

She felt bad boarding the plane empty handed when she saw how full both SUVs were with supplies. When working as a bayou guide, the heavy lifting was on her. She was just as much one of the boys as the actual boys were.

From her seat at the back of the plane, she watched them load the bags. It went remarkably fast. They had a system, a rhythm. She suspected that they worked that well together under all circumstances. Her respect for this group of people increased with that realization.

The man introduced as Mother made his way back. He sat himself across from her.

"Have you warmed up? I can get you a blanket," Mother offered.

She was still just a little chilled. "That would be nice, thank you."

She watched him go to a cabinet. He brought her a pillow and a blanket. Then he settled back into his seat. By then, the big black man who had been introduced as Lambchop made his way back to them too. Although Brian had not specifically said, she guessed that he was the one in charge of the team.

"Sherman will be on board in a minute. Do you need anything before we take off?" Lambchop asked.

"That's very nice of you, thank you." She held the pillow and the blanket up. "He," she said pointing to Mother, "got me these. I think I'm set."

"My name's Mother," the Hispanic man who was seated reminded her.

"I know. I just feel silly calling you Mother."

His lips pulled into a grin. "Almost everyone calls me that. I go by Danny too, if you prefer."

Brielle smiled. "Danny, it's nice to meet you."

"And my name is Landon," the black man said.

"Thank you. So, you all have nicknames?" The men both nodded. "What's Brian's?"

Sloan was within earshot. He laughed. "Brian hasn't told you his callsign yet?"

She shook her head no. All the men laughed. She didn't know why.

"The Birdman," Sloan said.

"What?" Sherman said from behind him.

"Your callsign," Sloan said. "Brielle asked what your callsign was."

"Oh, looking to talk bad about me, are you?" He made eye contact with Brielle and smiled a cocky grin. "It's because I have no fear of heights. I'll climb up anywhere and hang out where the birds land."

The men laughed again. Yeah, they all knew his callsign wasn't earned by brave climbing feats.

"As I remember it, it was because you couldn't stop yourself from flipping people the bird, mostly at our training officers who then PT'd us to death because you flipped them off during a one-finger salute, or while you held your hand by your side," Sloan said.

Sherman shrugged. "You remember it how you want to; and I'll remember it how I want to. You can't deny though, that I did climb up where most others wouldn't."

"That's because the rest of us didn't have a death wish," Sloan said.

The three men still stood between him and Brielle. Sherman pointed to the seat beside her. "And that seat is mine. One of you needs to back off."

Lambchop flashed a knowing smile at him. "I'm sitting up near the front. I was just making sure Brielle had everything she needs."

Sherman noticed she already had a pillow and a blanket. He was a little annoyed. He wanted to get her what she needed. He wanted to take care of her. He went to the small refrigerator and got four water bottles. Lambchop had already moved forward when he returned. Mother and Sloan were settled into the chairs that faced Brielle. He handed them each a water bottle. At the front of the plane, he noticed the door was secure. Doc and Burke were settled in across from Lambchop. The team was loaded and ready to go.

He took the seat beside her as the engines started. He felt the craft vibrate. He checked her lap. Her seatbelt was already on. He secured his own after handing her a water bottle. He reached over and massaged over her shoulder. "Are you still cold?" She had the blanket draped over her legs.

She yawned and then locked eyes with him. "I'm warming up. When I'm allowed to, I would like to recline my seat and try to sleep all wrapped up in this blanket. I'm still tired."

He leaned his head in close to her ear. "Didn't you sleep good last night?"

"I slept great," she said with a knowing smile that struck him as flirty. "But someone's alarm woke me up way too early, four-fucking-thirty!" She rolled her eyes.

Sherman laughed. "I'll see if tomorrow we can let you sleep into at least five-fucking-thirty," he teased her.

"Then I guess I better get that nap." She flashed him a smile.

The plane rolled forward. Brielle watched out the small window as it pulled out of the hangar. Rain pelted the aircraft as it taxied. It turned onto the active runway and paused only a second before the pilot throttled up and the Lear sped down the pavement, slicing through the sheets of rain.

Sherman watched Brielle closely during takeoff. She was relaxed, her eyes fixed on the cabin window. Once they leveled off, he glanced across the aisle at Mother and Sloan. They both watched him. Shit, he was sure they both knew that Brielle meant something to him. He wasn't sure why that bothered him, but it did. Fuck it, he decided. So, his teammates knew that she meant something to him, big deal. It wasn't like he was going to put a ring on her finger too. He leaned in close to her, lips to her ear. "You can recline and try to sleep now, if you want."

She turned her head into him, her nose tapping his, their lips but centimeters apart. He smiled and everything else and everyone else on the plane faded away from her view. She couldn't help but gaze over his face, his eyes, his lips. She wanted another of those real kisses from him.

An instant of turbulence shook the plane, and she snapped out of it. "Oh, I hope it's not that bumpy all the way down to Louisiana," she said, recovering from nearly kissing him.

Sherman pulled away from Brielle when the plane shook. Damn, he'd nearly kissed her. Or she'd nearly kissed him, he wasn't sure which. "No, we should be out of it soon. It's safe to go ahead and lay back." He took hold of the blanket. "I'll wrap you up in it and tuck you in snug after you recline."

Brielle put her hood up, reclined her seat and got comfortable on the pillow. Brian did indeed lay the blanket over her, and he tucked it in all around her. She closed her eyes and willed herself to go to sleep. Her thoughts would not quiet though. Her brain was fixated on the fact that she almost kissed Brian. She knew she wanted him, but the problem was, she wanted a relationship with him, not a 'whatever happens' with him. She couldn't accept that, wouldn't accept that with him or anyone else.

After the turbulence stopped, Sherman moved forward. Mother and Sloan followed. Lambchop advised there were no updates. Sherman hadn't expected any yet. The six members of Shepherd Security went over the facts of the mission, knowing they couldn't fill in any of the gaps without the info that only the digital team could dig up.

"The fact that the Sheriff has been all over Brielle since she started her blog attack of BioDynamix, and he got all over my ass as soon as I got into town, proves to me that he's in on something. His actions have not been those of a normal Sheriff," Sherman said. "I say we continue to focus on him, maybe even do our own active surveillance."

Lambchop nodded. "How threatened did you feel by him?"

"If I hadn't gotten Madison on the video call to see him, I'm not so sure there wouldn't have been an accident involving my boat. There was no reason for him to board me twice, especially the second time after I'd already identified myself as a federal agent."

"One thing we absolutely do is keep Brielle safe from him. We'll have to take her with, to talk to Tina Landry, but she has to otherwise remain unseen," Lambchop said.

"Yeah," Sherman said, glancing towards the back of the plane at her. "She's not going to like it, but the less she leaves that Coast Guard building, the better."

Sloan stood beside him. "Don't worry, we'll have your girl covered," he whispered in Sherman's ear.

Sherman shot him a caustic stare, to which Sloan just smiled a crooked, knowing grin. Mother smiled and nodded too. Who did Sherman think he was fooling?

The Lear descended through the sunny Florida sky over Pensacola Naval Air Station. It was a beautiful eighty degrees out when they deplaned. Everyone immediately shed their warmer shirts and jackets. Brielle tied the Navy sweatshirt around her waist. When this was over, she wanted to keep it if Brian would let her.

A transport sat nearby to take them and their gear to the Coast Guard Chopper, the Sikorsky MH-60T Jayhawk. This time, Brielle helped to unload the bags. She insisted on it. "Look, I normally load the tour boats with supplies. I'm not some fragile female who can't do any physical work," she told Brian. Besides, she'd feel more a part of the team if she could pitch in and help.

"Fine," Sherman relented.

Before she knew it, Brielle was seated deep within the big orange and white painted Coast Guard helicopter. There wasn't even a window to look out of except the large front window that showed her only sky. Brian handed her a ballcap. "Hide your identity as best you can when we get off this bird."

She took it from him. The ballcap also said U.S. Navy. She wondered if he was still considered active duty. She still didn't have a good idea of exactly what their unit was besides Black Ops. She knew that could be military or government. Given that she'd never be able to write a story on them, she figured it didn't matter which they were, but she would like to know just to satisfy her own curiosity.

The Coast Guard chopper landed on the helipad painted cement. The doors opened, and they all exited. They were parked near three other Coast Guard helicopters. About a hundred yards away was the back entrance to the Coast Guard Building. One of the men who'd been in the back of the helicopter with the Shepherd Security Team went to the building to get a cart to help transport their equipment.

"We've got your team set up in our vacated north wing," an officer who came from within the building said as he approached. "I'll show you."

Sherman turned back to Lambchop. "We're going ahead, I'll be back out in a minute."

Lambchop nodded. Yes, best to get Brielle inside right away. The man returned with the cart. Lambchop and the rest of the team unloaded their bags and supplies. It would take two trips.

Brielle followed Brian and the officer into the building. They went through a door immediately within the entry to the right. It led them into a hallway which emptied into an exterior room with all the blinds drawn where Madison and Cooper were. It was a lounge, but they had added a few tables up against one wall to transform it into their on-site command center. They had two computer tablets open on one of the tables.

Cooper rose from his seat as they entered. "I thought that was your chopper coming in." He glanced at Brielle. "Stay here with Madison. The Birdman and I will go help with the equipment."

Brielle had to smile at Brian being called the Birdman. It again reminded her just who he was, and the smile left her face as fast as it had appeared. The job he did was dangerous. She watched the two men leave. Madison came to her feet as well. She pointed to a space beside the tables. "We'll have them stack the equipment here, personal bags can be brought to the sleeping quarters." She pointed at a door that led out of the room.

A few minutes later, the men entered, carrying bags. Madison directed the positioning of them. Brielle stood back, watching. It again struck her how there was an order, a rhythm in how they interacted. The ammo was lined up on one of the tables, the rifle bags set immediately beside the table. The personal backpacks were sat on one of the couches. It didn't take long for all the bags and equipment to be brought in and organized under Madison's assertive direction.

The room was suddenly crowded with the gear and the eight members of the Shepherd Security Team. She watched them greet Madison and Cooper with hand clasps, shoulder bumps, smiles, and many overlapping conversations. The reporter in her closely observed the interactions. She was sure she was seeing relationships between these people that few others ever got to see. They were as tight of a unit as Brian had said, that was obvious.

"Sleeping quarters are through here," Cooper said, pointing to the doorway across the room.

Sherman handed Brielle her backpack before picking up his own.

Cooper led them through the door and into a hallway. "Unisex bathroom." He pointed at the first door to the left. It was propped open. Within, four sinks were visible from the door. "Madison has already called the first stall on the right as the girl's stall. Unless you guys want to endure Xena's wrath, I suggest you remember that. And it goes without saying, but I'll point it out anyway, the urinals are closed."

Brielle poked her head in. There were four toilet stalls and further in, she saw shower stalls. She wasn't sure how sharing a bathroom would work. She'd have to ask Brian later.

"Madison and I took this first room." He pointed to the door across from the bathroom. "There are four more double rooms." He pointed to the four doors like a flight attendant on a commercial aircraft pointing out the exit doors during the safety briefing. "And the galley is there." He pointed to the open door at the far end of the hall. "Brielle, you get your own room."

Brielle nodded. She watched the men open the doors and enter the rooms. She stood still, waiting for what, she wasn't sure. Her eyes found their way to Brian's. He hadn't entered a room either. They soon found that they were the only ones left in the hallway.

They stared at each other in silence. Brielle knew she wanted him in with her. Through the open doorways, she could see that two twin beds sat in each room. They wouldn't be able to sleep in the same bed but being in the same room would satisfy her. She didn't know how to tell him that was what she wanted though. He'd been different since they were with his team. She didn't want to embarrass herself by saying anything, and she especially didn't want to embarrass him with his teammates by implying there was a relationship that didn't exist.

Lambchop exited his and Mother's room, bags left on the bed. He opened the one door that no one had entered that laid beside his room. "Looks like this is your room, Brielle."

Sherman watched Brielle bring her backpack into the room. He stepped up to Lambchop and motioned him to the end of the hallway, near the galley. "I think it's a mistake to have Brielle in there alone. We still don't know that she won't take off on us. I should be in there to watch her."

A knowing grin spread over Lambchop's face. "Where exactly did she sleep last night?"

"Same as the night before on the boat, in my bed with me,"

Lambchop sighed out and closed his eyes for a moment. That's what he suspected. At least Sherman didn't lie about it. He respected that.

"It was just sleep, nothing more," Sherman guaranteed him. "Brielle just likes to snuggle up against someone when she's going to sleep." Yeah, even as he said it, it sounded lame and he wouldn't believe him either.

"Since when do you just snuggle with a woman?" Lambchop whispered in an accusatory tone.

Sherman smiled wide. "Since Brielle demanded it and would allow no more."

Lambchop stared hard at him. Could it be that Sherman had met his match? He smiled inside at that thought. Sherman was known to play around, somehow always managed to hook up with any woman of his choosing. "You know there are protocols," he began, but Sherman interrupted him.

"Don't quote a protocol that practically doesn't exist any longer, not since Jackson broke it and then Cooper and Miller, with each other. Let me now mention Garcia and Doc, and Sloan also breaking that particular protocol. Shit, Lambchop, I'm waiting for you and Michaela to break it too. Anyone with eyes can see how close the two of you are."

"Michaela and I are just friends, and this isn't about me. It's about you, being in bed with a woman associated with this mission."

Michaela, the master of many inventions that kept them safe, was a coworker and a good friend, nothing more. Could Lambchop have feelings for her if he allowed himself? Not that he'd admit to anyone. It pissed him off that Sherman brought her up, but he knew that Sherman was clutching at anything he could to justify his actions with Brielle. Lambchop smiled at Sherman, realizing that this was the first time that he knew of that Sherman had real feelings for a woman, not just a sexual intent. Maybe this wasn't so bad.

"Unless the lady objects, I'm taking the other bed in her room. I really don't care what anyone thinks about it. Let Cooper lecture me on why it's a bad idea."

"She seems like a nice girl, one looking for a relationship, not a fling. I can always tell. Don't hurt that girl, Sherman," Lambchop warned, not that he thought Sherman knowingly would.

Sherman flashed a lopsided grin at him. He'd just been given permission to carry on. "I'd never hurt her or anyone else."

As he stepped into the room, closing the door behind himself, he was well aware that a relationship was the only destination that Brielle was headed for. The question was, how far was he willing to go to get this girl? Unfortunately, he didn't have an answer for himself. But he knew he didn't want to risk losing her either by not being there for her. Her pleading eyes when they'd stood in the hallway communicated quite clearly that she wanted him in here with her. He wouldn't let her down.

He pointed to the second bed. "Mind if I take that one?"

Brielle smiled at him. "Not at all. I was kind of hoping you would."

Sherman dropped his bags on the bed and then he walked over to Brielle and took her into his arms. "Just kind of?"

"Okay, more than kind of."

Sherman pressed a kiss to her forehead. "Good."

Her smile turned more hesitant. "I'm not sure what this means though."

Sherman dropped his forehead against hers. "I don't know either. I can't make you any promises, but what I can tell you, is that I like you a lot and I want to see where this can go, on your terms. I went out on a limb with Lambchop to be in here with you. I have to know you're on the same page that I'm on."

A warmth spread throughout Brielle like she'd never felt. She closed her eyes. If this was a dream, she didn't want to ever wake up from it. "I'm on the same page," was all she could force out from her strangled vocal cords. She held onto his waist tightly as though it was her only connection to this reality.

Sherman wasn't sure why Brielle's response was so short. He expected more from her. But she did hold on to him with what he perceived as trust and affection. "We need to get back out there, for a briefing."

"Sure," she replied, taking a step back from him.

Sherman stopped her. He slid his hand up her arm, over her shoulder, and up her neck to her jaw. He gently angled her face as his lips approached hers. His kiss was soft and unhurried. His tongue danced with hers in a slow waltz. He needed her to know that he meant what he'd said. He needed the physical connection to her for just that moment.

When the kiss ended and Brielle's eyes opened, he saw what he was looking for. Her eyes sparkled with life and lust. She gazed at him with trust, affection, and desire. He knew in that moment it wasn't the thrill of the chase or the challenge that was driving him. For some inexplicable reason, this woman captivated him, and he wasn't going to be foolish enough to let his intentions go unsaid. Not too long ago, he had watched as Sloan nearly lost Kaylee by not declaring his feelings. He was not going to make that same mistake. But a relationship? Yeah, he could be making an entirely different mistake by going there.

"I'm not a man that plays games," he said. "Life is too short and unpredictable not to lay it out there."

"Agreed," she said with a smile.

"In here, I'll hold you. But out there with the others," Sherman began.

"I understand," she interrupted.

He pressed another kiss to her lips and then led her out of the room.

Juliette

he fact that Sherman and Brielle reentered the room together went unnoticed by no one. Everyone else already was in the room. "Good, we can get started," Cooper said. "We'll go up the bayou after dark and plant the cameras to monitor the back of the BioDynamix facility using NVGs. Forecast is for overcast skies. All of Delta Team plus Burke will go in. Madison and I will monitor from here. Doc, will you take the first overnight monitoring shift?"

"I'd prefer that," Doc said. "Olivia had us up half the night. I could easily fall asleep right now."

"Olivia is his baby girl, just about three months old now," Sherman whispered to Brielle.

Brielle gazed at Doc, trying to envision this man with a little baby in his arms. He wore a gun on his hip, in open view. He was older than the others, his face serious with sharp angles. She remembered that Brian had said a few of them had wives and kids. She wondered who else in the room did. That was a story in itself, the men who did this job and had a family. That was another story she'd never be able to tell.

Cooper clasped Doc on the shoulder. "We'll only wake you for an emergency. Set your alarm, you're on at twenty-two hundred. I'll catch a nap this afternoon and be up for the first half of the night."

"I'll take over for you at zero-three-hundred and stay on till the team returns," Madison volunteered.

Sherman liked how Madison and Cooper were a cohesive team, always. They stepped up and made sure operationally that everything went smoothly, even when that meant working opposite shifts. He respected them, and he felt a pang of guilt for offering them up as an example of the nonfraternization protocol not being followed. When on duty, no one would ever guess that they were married. He'd been on many missions with them and it was a nonissue, their relationship.

"When do I go talk to Tina?" Brielle asked.

"Not for a few days. We want to watch and see what shakes out before we reach out to her. If we're lucky, we may figure out what's going on without involving her," Cooper said. "Brielle, we will want you at the monitors with us when the team heads up the bayou tonight to plant those cameras."

"I should be with them. I know that bayou like the back of my hand."

"Yep, and that's exactly why I want you sitting at our control center when the team goes in," Cooper said. "You'll be on comms and can give them direction."

She nodded. "Besides the gators, there are venomous snakes and spiders to watch out for."

"Before we head out, we'll Google the nasty ones they'll have to look out for," Sherman said. "We're going to want to keep the cameras accessible when we mount them. There's a lot of movement in the bayou. I expect we'll expend battery power every other day, maybe even daily, even with the cameras on standby until motion activates them."

"Great, so we can expect to have to go out nightly to replenish the batteries?" Mother asked. "I have to say, this bayou of yours is sounding less hospitable to me by the moment."

Both Brielle and Sherman laughed.

"The bayou is an acquired taste," Sherman said with a smile.

"It's beautiful, vibrant, thriving with life, both animal and plant. I've always found it to be magical, the Spanish Moss hanging from the trees, the morning fog hovering close to the ground in the still air," Brielle said. "But you have to respect the animals who call the bayou home. It's theirs, we are merely intruders in their ecosystem."

Sherman's lips curved into a smile. She had no idea how poetic she sounded, how beautifully and eloquently she spoke about a place that obviously meant a great deal to her. If he wasn't already completely enamored with her, that statement right there would have done it.

"Sherman, you and Brielle take the lead on the mission plan. Figure it out and we'll reconvene at nineteen-thirty hours," Cooper said.

The briefing ended. Doc headed to his room to sleep. The crowd in the room thinned. Sherman led Brielle over to the tables. He grabbed his own computer tablet from one of his bags and brought up a map of the bayou to plan the mission.

"I should be out there with you, and you know it," she said.

Sherman's lips pulled into a grin. "And I'm feeling a whole lot better about this, knowing you'll be here monitoring the mission. Camera feeds from each man will display on a couple monitors. You'll see what we all see, the big picture. You're more valuable overseeing the entire operation than you'd be out with us."

"And safer," she remarked. "Look, I know you're going to do whatever you can to protect me."

Sherman looked her in the eyes. Hers beamed defiance and strength. A smile curved his lips. "Momma, you better believe I want you kept safe. That's my job, and I promised Bobby I would. That's what you do for people you care about."

Her gaze softened, as did her voice. "I care about you too."

"Then watch over the operation from here."

Brielle nodded, relenting.

They finished planning the details. Sherman left his tablet on the table beside the two others. He knew Madison would want at least four more computer monitors to bring up mission feed and maps on during the operation. Then they joined Lambchop, Mother, and Sloan in the galley for a bite to eat. Lunchmeat and cheese, bread and standard picnic sides were stocked in the refrigerator. They'd been purchased from a grocery store deli. They made themselves sandwiches and then joined the others at the table.

"Did Madison and Cooper go take naps too?" Sherman asked.

"Yes, and so did Burke. I'm almost done eating. I'll go monitor the equipment," Lambchop said. "We were just discussing initiating active surveillance on Sheriff Henderson. I'll speak with Cooper about it after we plant the cameras. I think we have enough manpower to pull that off while surveilling the BioDynamix facility."

"If we can at least get his phone paired and monitor all incoming and outgoing calls, that would be a good start. I know Garcia was going to dump his phone records, Mayor Stuart's too, but to hear content will give us a good picture of what's going on."

Brielle's attention was focused on him. "Isn't that illegal?" Slipped from her mouth.

She watched smirks form on all four men's faces.

"Not exactly," Sherman remarked. "If we find evidence, we'll get a warrant."

"We operate outside of normal channels," Mother added. "It's how we get the job done."

"Sometimes you have to skirt the law to get the bad guys, who remember, don't follow the rules. But we do dot our I's and cross our T's, so what we get sticks." Sloan said.

"So, let me get this straight. From what I've seen on television, when you pair a phone you get access to listen into someone's calls?"

Sherman nodded. "We see the number it came from or the number our subject dialed as well as hear the conversation. It's a very effective tool."

"And my phone or Bobby's phone could have been paired, and we'd never know?"

"That's right," Sherman said.

"That's why Bobby and I did that stupid phone call when I was at the hotel, for the benefit of anyone who may have been listening?"

Sherman nodded, though the call had not been stupid. He wouldn't argue that fact with her though.

Lambchop finished and left the room to go man their onsite Ops equipment. Soon after, Mother and Sloan announced that they were going to lie down and catch a few hours' sleep. They had a few hours until the nineteen-thirty briefing.

Brielle helped herself to another serving of the potato salad. "So, if we reconvene at seven-thirty, what time will y'all head into the bayou?"

"We'll discuss the mission for nearly a half hour and gear up. Cooper acquired us boats. I estimate it'll take close to four hours to make it up the channel to be within range of the BioDynamix facility, necessitating the cutting of the engines. Then maybe another half hour to paddle to our LZ."

"So, you probably won't get back here until around five a.m.?"

"At least," Sherman agreed.

"Wouldn't it be smarter to leave right away, so you can run at a higher speed in the daylight and only slow down when the sun sets? You'd be able to plant the cameras faster and get back here earlier."

"We don't want to encounter very much bayou traffic. The fewer people who see us, the better."

"Can't you blend in during daylight and don your tactical gear when you near the plant?"

Sherman smiled. She had well thought out arguments. "Do you really think my unit will blend in, in the bayou?"

Brielle giggled. "I suppose not." Most bayou people knew everyone on sight who belonged, and this group did not fit that category.

"And we don't want to be nosing around outside that plant too early in the evening. We do this kind of thing often. We know what works."

"You know, if the BioDynamix folks are using the bayou to transport product, the regulars in the area would have seen them. There's got to be a way for me to reach out to them, to check the comings and goings from the back of that plant. I can't believe I didn't think about that before now."

Sherman nodded. "That's a good idea. I'll run it by Cooper and Lambchop after the briefing."

"Why is Landon called Lambchop?"

Sherman chuckled. "It goes back to when he was a new SEAL and his teammates were picking his callsign. That's how it works, your team decides on your callsign. You know the Shari Lewis hand puppet, Lambchop?"

Brielle smiled and nodded.

"I never worked with him in the Teams. He was with the Pacific Fleet. Sloan and I were assigned to the Atlantic Fleet, but rumor has it that Lambchop excelled at everything he did, cruised right through BUDS, Hell Week was a cakewalk for him.

He was a SEAL's SEAL from day one. One of his instructors liked to try to get under his skin and break his mental concentration by calling him marshmallow, cream puff, and a variety of kid's cartoon or stuffed animal names. The only one that ever made the man crack a smile was Lambchop, so that stuck as his callsign."

Brielle chuckled that sultry laugh that Sherman loved. "And what about Mother?"

"He's everyone's Mother Hen."

"He did get me the pillow and blanket right away. He's a nice guy. Is he one of the married guys?"

Sherman laughed. "Mother," he paused as he shook his head. "No, he's too busy taking care of everyone else on the team to be bothered with taking care of himself. I'm not sure he could do this job if he had a woman. His desire to take care of her might overshadow him doing his job."

"Do you really believe it's an either-or situation?"

"It could be for him. I guess it depends on the man and the woman. I was worried when Sloan and Kaylee got together that she'd be too demanding of Sloan's time, but that didn't turn out to be the case. She understands the job we do, the importance, and how much of our time it consumes. She knows it's who Sloan is, not just the job he does."

Brielle thought about that for a long minute while she chewed another large forkful of food. She nodded. "Yeah, I can see that. I'd think any woman who is with one of you would have to be self-sufficient because of the amount of time you spend working, and she has to be understanding and accepting of last-minute changes in plans if you suddenly get sent someplace, like Madison and Cooper, coming down here with only a few hours' notice."

"I think if a woman truly understands the importance of the job, the rest comes with it. It's not a life for everyone."

Brielle's gaze was thoughtful. "I'll admit, this is all unlike anything I've experienced in my life. Without seeing what you do firsthand, I'm not sure any woman would be able to fully understand it."

Sherman wouldn't tell her that the wives had all seen it firsthand. That wasn't her business at this point. If she remained with him when this was over, and met them, then he'd tell her. Remain with him? Whoa! Where had that thought come from? Her remaining with him would most likely mean living with him. Was that what he wanted?

"I meant to ask you, about the unisex bathroom, how does that work?"

"Madison claimed one of the stalls for you two, so you don't have to worry about the seat being left up or peed on. We're all comfortable using the bathroom together, there are doors on the stalls, and no one will peak through the cracks, not that you can see much through them. Using the sinks beside the opposite sex, not an issue."

"What about showering?"

"There are private changing spaces outside of each shower stall with shower curtains and no nudity outside of the curtains will happen. Just make sure you have clothes to change into when you go in."

"Wow, you all must be really close if you're that comfortable with both males and females occupying a bathroom together."

"I trust my teammates. No one will violate your privacy. It's really just like using any other public bathroom, or gym shower facility."

Except that males and females would be using it together. She was skeptical. It showed on her face.

"Let me prove it to you. We probably should try to catch a few Z's ourselves. Let's go hit the head together before we lay down."

They dumped their paper plates in the trash, put the food away in the refrigerator, and then walked to the bathroom together. Lambchop was at the sink, washing his hands when they entered. Brielle glanced at him and then looked away. Yeah, she wasn't too sure how comfortable she could be with this.

"First stall on the right is yours," Sherman reminded her. Then he took the stall beside hers.

Brielle shut the door and locked it. Her eyes scrutinized the cracks to judge for herself how much someone peaking in would be able to see. Too much, she decided. Then her eyes went to Brian's boots in the stall beside her. He faced the toilet. Before she had her pants unbuttoned and dropped, she heard him peeing. She dropped her jeans and took a seat, but was unable to go. It wasn't until Brian flushed the toilet that she was able to. Then she heard him at the sink, washing his hands. Yes, this was way outside of her comfort zone.

"I'll be in the room," he called and then left.

She finished up, thankfully alone in the room, and then washed her hands. She checked out the shower stalls. Brian was right. There were private changing rooms in front of each shower. Then she returned to the room she and Brian had claimed as theirs.

"I have my alarm set for nineteen hundred. That'll give us two hours of sleep."

"Will that be enough sleep for you?" Brielle asked. "You'll be up most the night."

Sherman's lips quirked into a smirk. If only she knew how used to operating on little sleep, the entire team was. "Yeah, don't worry about me." The temperature in the room was comfortable. He wouldn't need a blanket. He grabbed the pillow from the second bed and tossed it onto the one she'd claimed. He pointed to the bed. "Lay on your side and leave room for me."

A big smiled came to Brielle's face that he just loved to see. Man, she had a beautiful smile that lit her whole face. He watched her crawl onto the bed, that lovely ass of hers in the air before she settled into her position. He dropped himself beside her, willing his arousal to subside. He snuggled in close. The two of them together barely fit on the bed. But that didn't stop him from drifting off into a deep sleep right away. He'd slept in many more uncomfortable places before.

Brielle drifted but didn't really sleep for long. It felt good to lie with Brian and snuggle. Their conversation in the galley about a woman being with a man who did the job he did, replayed through her mind. If this story opened doors to her as she hoped it would, she might have a similar job, leaving with little notice to chase assignments all over the globe. Any man in her life would have to be understanding of that, too. She was pretty sure Brian would be. As a matter of fact, he'd probably be the most understanding of any man that she would ever be with. This thought brought a smile to her face.

The alarm went off. Sherman silenced it within seconds. He came to his feet and grabbed the bag with his tactical gear. He unpacked his black fatigues, including his bullet-proof vest. He mounted the mission camera to the vest. He turned his back to Brielle as he changed clothes.

Brielle watched Brian disrobe. She was once again given a great view of the large tattoo across his upper back. She studied it closely. The big American flag struck her differently this time, now knowing what Brian's job really was. He was a true patriot, an American hero, and this flag professed who and what he was, just as the trident insignia proudly proclaimed that he was a SEAL, the best of the best. Her heart swelled with pride and admiration for the man he was.

After his pants were on, he turned to face her, pulling his shirt over his head. "Enjoying the view?" He asked in a cocky tone with a smile to match it on his lips.

Brielle smiled as well. "You better believe I am."

Sherman chuckled. He secured two handguns onto his pants, one holstered at his waist, the other holstered halfway down his thigh. Then he pulled his bullet-proof vest on. He grabbed the black patch to cover the white ATF letters and secured it to the front of the vest. He handed a second patch to her. "Here, cover the letters on the back for me."

She took it and pressed it to the back of the vest. It adhered with Velcro. It was sobering, seeing him dressed in his tactical gear, two guns holstered in sight, a bullet-proof vest on. When he turned back to face her, he took her into his arms. He pressed a kiss to her lips.

"This should be pretty routine tonight. I don't expect we'll engage with anyone from that plant. You don't have to wait up for us. After we plant the cameras and pull back out, I want you to go to bed. I'll try not to wake you when I come in."

"Stay safe," she muttered. "I do really care a lot about you. You know that, don't you?"

Sherman kissed her again. "I know. And you know I feel the same way about you." He embraced her a final time and then nodded to the door. "We better go. I want to swing by the galley and get a cup of coffee."

"Me too."

Danny and Gary were in the galley with coffee cups in their hands when they entered. They too were dressed in their tactical gear, complete with bullet-proof vests and sidearms. Brielle couldn't help but stare at them. Her eyes swept back to Brian as he handed her a cup of coffee. "Thanks." Then she watched him fill a cup for himself.

"I hope it's cooled off some outside," Mother remarked.

The sleeves of his shirt were pushed up his forearms. Brielle saw script letters tattooed on the underside of each arm. She couldn't make out what they said. She'd seen tattoos on most of these men. She didn't have any, but she suddenly thought about getting one when this was over, something that spoke to her Creole or Indian roots.

Sherman pulled his phone from its compartment in one of the many pockets of his cargo pants. He pulled up the weather app. "It's currently sixty-seven, going to a low of sixty-two, with an eighty percent chance of rain by twenty-two hundred."

Both Sloan and Mother smiled. Good, the rain would cover any sounds they may make.

Sherman nodded to the door. "We need to get to the briefing."

Burke, Landon and Cooper were already in the lounge when they entered. They each had coffee cups in their hands. Burke and Landon were dressed in the black tactical gear and armed as well; Brielle noticed. She also noticed several of the rifle cases were open, the weapons laying on the table the ammo was on, next to open ammo cases.

"Okay, let's get started," Cooper said. "Sherman, the show is yours."

Sherman grabbed his computer tablet from the table. Brielle noticed there were several more computers lining the table than there were earlier. He brought up the map of the bayou that they had looked at earlier. He zoomed in on the mouth of the bayou in the port area.

"The five of us will go up the bayou in two flat bottom boats and use the outboard motors. We enter the Bayou Lafourche here. The channel is wide and deep, but we still need to look out for wildlife in the water. We'll need to all the way up the bayou, so we won't exceed five knots. We'll use front facing lights to watch for anything in our path until we near the BioDynamix plant. I expect it will take us about four hours to reach it."

"How much boat traffic do you anticipate crossing our path during the trip upstream?" Lambchop asked.

"There shouldn't be too much this time of night," Brielle said. "Most of the bayou tours are done by sundown. Most fisherman are in by then too. As you get deeper into the bayou, you may come across some local traffic, folks who live on the bayou, but once the rain starts, you shouldn't encounter anyone. They all hunker down when the rain starts at night."

"When we reach this bend," Sherman pointed it out on the map. "Then we cut the engines and use paddles the remainder of the way. We'll cut our lights and go on NVGs at that point as well. We'll step onto the land here," he said as he pointed to the spot that he and Brielle had previously decided was a good location.

"Excuse me, Brian," Brielle spoke up. "Now that rain is due, it would actually be better if you land here." She pointed out a place about one hundred feet further than he'd designated. "It's not as cloaked from view from the BioDynamix facility as the spot we picked earlier, but the bank is more solid here. That area we picked earlier degraded during the rains last spring and it will be mighty slick in the rain."

Sherman smiled at her. "And that is why we have a bayou guide to help us. We land where Brielle said, and we make our way to these three points to mount our cameras." He pointed those three locations out. "We mount two cameras at each location. One pointed directly at our target facility, this one to the north pointed upstream, this one at the south end pointed downstream, and the one in the middle pointed behind the cameras. We'll try to mount them on hollowed out stumps drilling the camera head into the bark. That way, we can tuck the battery packs into the cavity."

"The Undertaker and Handsome will remain in the boats to recon the area as the others mount the cameras," Cooper ordered. "You may have to take a gator or a snake out if it gets too close to our men."

"No, you absolutely do not need to do that," Brielle argued in outrage. "Most encounters between snake and man or gator and man are accidental. They aren't looking to do us any harm. Remember, you're the intruders in their world, not the other way around. If you give them a wide berth, they normally leave you alone."

"I'll give them a very wide berth, but I'd prefer not to be bitten," Mother said. "So, please watch my six, gentlemen."

The men laughed. Brielle did not.

"Really, encounters are rare," Sherman said. "They want to avoid you as much as you want to avoid them." He opened a saved tab on his tablet. "Here are the nasty ones to avoid." He showed them several pictures of different poisonous snakes and spiders. "All these are venomous and live somewhere in the bayou. Some swim, many hang in the trees and they'll drop onto you in your boat if you get too close to the tree line that hangs over the water."

"The gators are most active at night, to feed. You'll see their glowing eyes first. You'll want to avoid them as much as possible," Brielle interjected.

"I'll avoid them entirely," Mother guaranteed, garnering him laughs from his teammates.

"Any questions?" Cooper asked.

No one had any.

"We need a callsign for Brielle for the evening. How does her initials, BJ sound?" Cooper asked.

"No fucking way," Sherman protested. "No one refers to Brielle as a sex act."

Several of the men laughed.

Cooper's lips tugged into a grin. "Sorry, didn't think that one out."

"Cleopatra," Lambchop said. "It fits."

Brielle smiled. "I like that better."

"Okay, Cleopatra it is," Cooper said. "I'll notify Ops. That's it. Go on comms, load your weapons, and take off," Cooper ordered. "Be safe, gentlemen."

Brielle watched as they all placed earplugs into their ears, their comms. Then they loaded their assault rifles with magazines. They also secured spare magazines to their uniforms and within pockets of their cargo pants. It was startling to see. It was not unlike how it was in the movies, but the fact didn't escape her that this was real, was dangerous.

Once they were all stocked with ammo, Lambchop's eyes swept his teammates. "Let's do our prayer here before we head out."

Brielle watched as the men came in close to each other. Each man bowed his head. She noticed that Cooper did as well.

"Dear Heavenly Father, protect us, your sons, on this mission. Let us not encounter anyone we must do battle with and let no civilians cross our path. Keep your creatures who make the bayou their home far from us as well, as we do not want to cause them any harm. We pray this in the name of your son, Jesus Christ. Amen."

"Amen," the others repeated.

Brielle was surprised by his prayer, especially that he acknowledged the animals who live in the bayou. She smiled at him with appreciation when he flashed her a grin. For such a large, menacing man, he had a gentleness.

Then she watched them file out of the room, their hands loaded down with weapons and the bags containing their night vision goggles and the cameras. Her eyes settled back on Cooper, suddenly feeling restless. "So now we just wait, huh?"

"We have some set up to do and I'll show you how to operate some of the equipment we'll use to monitor the team." He led her over to the table and motioned for her to have a seat. He sat beside her. He opened a case on the table and took out two sets of communication earplugs like the team wore. Theirs had a lip mic in addition to an earpiece. He turned them on and handed her one. "Listening mode is on, but you have to toggle this switch to talk. We'll leave that mode off for now. The team's comms are in both modes and will remain that way for the duration of the mission. Everything gets recorded, both visually and auditory. So, make sure if you address anyone, it's by their callsign only. We don't ever use real names."

Brielle nodded.

Cooper logged into the laptop that sat in the middle of the four others, the one with the large monitor. The silver case it came out of sat on the table behind it. Brielle recognized the case. They'd brought it with them from Illinois. He went through several menus and then the screen split and the visual feed from the cameras worn on the vests of the five men displayed. He tapped a few more keys and three of the feeds jumped to the screens of three of the other tablets sitting beside the large one which retained two of the displays. Only then did Brielle notice that the callsign name of the man wearing the camera displayed at the bottom of his feed.

"We see what they see, but we have the benefit of seeing what everyone sees at the same time. Gives us a bigger picture of what's going on than each individual man sees. Gives us an advantage," Cooper said.

Brielle nodded. She watched as the men walked the short distance to the Coast Guard dock at the rear of the building. They climbed down the ladder to the boat entry platform and boarded the two bayou boats that waited there for them. She heard their conversation through the comms.

"Damn, these things are smaller than I anticipated," Mother complained as the boat he was in got filled with Lambchop and Burke, as well as all their gear.

Lambchop was at the bow. He turned the front search light on. "We shouldn't encounter any waves to speak of once we enter the bayou."

"Yeah, it'll be like we are skating across ice," Sherman said.

"We have space in this boat if you want to throw some equipment over," Sloan volunteered. He too stood at the bow and turned the front search light on.

Lambchop handed several bags over to Sloan. That freed up quite a bit of space in their boat. The engines on the boats were started. Brielle was surprised how quiet they were. She watched through the feeds the boats pull away from the dock and motor out into the channel.

Then Cooper logged into the fourth computer. He pulled up a map. It showed the facility they were at and eight dots. Five of them were moving in a cluster, the men in the boats. He clicked a few more keys and the three stationary dots disappeared. He saw the questioning look she was giving him. "Trackers, we all have them." He watched her glance over him. "Injected in our shoulders."

"Why?"

"We always need to know exactly where our people are during a mission and if God forbid anyone is ever captured, we need to know where they are brought so we can rescue or recover them."

At first, she didn't understand the difference between rescue and recover. Then the realization dawned on her. You rescue those who were alive and recover those who are dead. This again reminded her how dangerous their job was.

"Besides the team, you may hear other voices during the mission. HQ is dialed in as well. Yvette, our lead analyst is in Ops tonight as is Garcia. She goes by Control and Garcia's callsign is Razor. And remember, we've given you the callsign of Cleopatra for the evening."

"Yeah, I like that a lot better than BJ."

Cooper chuckled. "Sorry about that."

Now Brielle laughed. "It's okay. I've been called worse."

"When this is over, I'm sure those people out at the BioDynamix plant and Sheriff Henderson will all be calling you a lot worse."

"As long as they're all behind bars I won't really care what they're calling me."

When the boats reached the mouth of the bayou, Sherman slowed his boat. "This here is the Bayou Lafourche. It runs one-hundred-six miles north. Respect it and the life that makes this place home, gentlemen. We'll stay to the right of the channel, within the channel markers."

Sherman quickly ran through his pre-mission ritual. He removed his dog tags from his shirt, kissed them three times and then tucked them away. He checked each weapon, and then he kissed his dog tags one last time, followed by making the sign of the cross in classic Catholic fashion, spectacles, testicles, wallet, watch. Sloan of course watched him, amused by the Cajun's superstitious ritual before every mission. Only when he was through did he increase the speed of his boat and pilot it into the bayou. The other boat followed.

At the Coast Guard facility Brielle watched the feed from the Undertaker's camera. "What was that Brian just did?"

Cooper laughed. "The Birdman, as do many, has a specific pre-mission ritual. That's what that was. He says kissing his dog tags ensures no one will use them to identify his body. He checks his weapons over to be sure they are locked and loaded, and of course he makes the sign of the cross as he says a final prayer for a successful mission."

"I'm surprised you wear dog tags. I thought black ops personnel didn't want anyone knowing who they were."

Cooper's lips quirked into a smirk. "Who said we were black ops?"

"Come on. I'm not stupid. You're neither regular military nor are you regular federal authorities. That leaves only black ops."

"We're a hybrid organization. That's all you need to know about us."

"I signed the NDA. It's not like I'm going to tell anyone anything."

Cooper nodded, a serious expression on his face. "That you did."

Her questioning gaze remained focused on him.

"We don't wear our military dog tags on specific, sensitive missions. Otherwise, when we go out, we do."

She appreciated that he answered her question.

As the boats made their way up the bayou, surrounded by trees on both sides rising up from the water and on the banks, the sounds of the bullfrogs, birds, and other creatures increased. In front of the boats, the lights showed insects of all sizes flying around in front of them, hundreds of them. The water below them looked green and murky. Tree stumps of all sizes poked from the water or were seen just below the surface, another hazard in the water to avoid.

"Whoa, look at that," Mother said, pointing to the left. "That gator is huge." It laid on the bank, sideways.

"That's a good ten-footer," Sherman replied. "Keep an eye out in front of the boat. Steer around any in the water. They won't move and we don't want to hit them."

They proceeded further, and they took a narrow side channel. It would meet back up with the main channel further up the bayou. This route would keep them better hidden from view. The animal sounds were deafening. Grunts and other loud calls joined the cacophony. It sounded otherworldly. And it was pitch black out, not that much sky would be visible through the dense canopy.

"Wild pigs," Sherman said. "They're nocturnal, of course most of the animals in the bayou except for the birds are."

At the control center at the Coast Guard facility, Brielle glanced at the monitor tracking the team. They were about halfway to the BioDynamix facility. "Looks like they are on schedule."

Cooper tapped a few keys on the keyboard. The view zoomed out, showing the mouth of bayou all the way up to the BioDynamix facility. The team was a little more than halfway. "When we're live on our mics only refer to it as our target. No names."

"Okay," she said. She knew she had a lot to learn about what to say and do. She was very grateful to be allowed to be present and participate at all.

Cooper clicked his mic on. "You're making good time. You're over halfway."

"Roger that, Coop," Lambchop's voice came through their comms. "Handheld GPS confirms."

"Radar shows the rain moving in. You can expect it to start within the hour," Cooper advised.

"Good, it should disperse some of these bugs. They're thick and everywhere." He brought his arm up in front of the camera. It was covered with bugs.

"It will," Brielle said to Cooper.

"Cleopatra confirms the rain will help."

Ten minutes later, the rain came down. It didn't start as sprinkles. It came down in sheets of big drops. The bugs instantly cleared and the sound of the rain pounding the leaves and the surface of the water drowned out the animal sounds. If it stayed this loud, they wouldn't have to cut their engines until much closer to the facility.

Doc entered the room, coffee cup in hand. He pulled a third chair over and sat on the other side of Cooper. "Did I miss anything?"

"No, the team is still en route. They've made excellent time. They should hit their LZ in about forty minutes." Cooper pointed to the monitors. "It started raining an hour ago."

Doc shook his head. "Let's hope it's still raining when they make their LZ."

"Yep," Cooper agreed.

"Why is that better?" Brielle asked.

"The rain covers noise and it'll make the foliage move, helping to conceal the team's presence," Doc answered.

The rain still came down in a deluge. The building was in sight before they cut the engines on the boats. They paddled the short distance to the bank. "Cleopatra, do you still advise a landing at your designated coordinates?" Sherman asked.

Cooper helped Brielle turn her comms to transmit. "You're live."

She pulled the mic up under her lips. "Affirmative, Birdman. But step as far inland as you can as you disembark. The edge will be fragile with this much rain washing over it."

"Roger that."

She watched the camera feeds. The boat with the three men in it went in close to the bank. Landon stepped off first. Danny handed him the bags in their boat. They all wore a single lensed, pair of goggles over their eyes and under their ballcaps, the NVGs. Then Danny stepped off. Brian's boat moved in close as soon as the other moved away. Brian handed the bags off to Danny and Landon. The two other men gave him a hand up as he stepped onto the bank which was all that kept him on his feet. The ground was saturated and slippery.

The men each took a pack with cameras and disappeared into the thick foliage. Lambchop remained there on the south side, closest to where they'd stepped off the boats. He quickly found the stump of an old hollowed out cypress tree that was chest high. He mounted the camera's, dropping the battery packs into the hollowed-out tree. He secured the camera's in place by drilling into the wood. The drill sound was not heard over the loud downpour of rain.

Mother cautiously made his way through the brush until he was directly across from the BioDynamix building, which could barely be seen through the heavy downpour. He found the perfect stump. It rose out of the water, leaning back over the land, topping out at nose height. He got ready to drill into the cypress to secure the camera that would face the building.

"Mother, freeze!" Brielle practically shouted, getting everyone's attention. "Now step back. That knot in the tree two inches up from where you were about to drill is a Carolina Wolf Spider's nest. You'd have them coming out at you like the insects in the light before the rain started if you disturbed their nest."

"Damn, thanks Cleopatra," Mother said. "I saw a couple snakes slithering out of this other stump." He pointed to a stump to the left.

"I saw them too. They're not poisonous and they wouldn't be hanging out with any venomous snakes. Go ahead and use that stump," Brielle advised.

Sherman, of course, heard the exchange. He couldn't help but smile. Brielle may have felt intimidated by his teammates, but she spoke up when it mattered. She fit in and understood what they did. He felt a pride wash through him. Yes, Brielle could be one of them, one of the women like Kaylee, Sienna, or Elizabeth, the other wives, who were a special breed of women to be with a man who did this job. Their conversation from earlier came back to him.

He had questioned his motives regarding her, but he knew now, that he wanted her in his life, whatever that could look like. Now, he'd just have to convince her, and he'd have to figure out how to be in a relationship. He knew it wasn't his strongpoint and the whole idea of a committed relationship and sex with only one person, were foreign concepts to him. But he'd told her he wanted to see where a relationship between them could go, while adhering to her terms, and he meant it.

As he mounted his two cameras, he thought about that. He wasn't sure how much longer he could lay with her and not make love to her. That would be one thing he'd have to work on, getting her to trust him enough to have sex with him.

Just then, a light came on at the back-dock area at the BioDynamix building. "Got activity at the target building." He hunkered down and didn't move a muscle. And he watched the movement at the target building.

Cooper and Doc immediately began clicking keys, zooming cameras in and scrutinizing footage. "Nothing is approaching from up or downstream," Doc said.

Brielle sat still, watching them.

"Got a single man out back, standing in the protected overhang of the building," Cooper said. "Well, his torso and head are protected. His feet and legs are getting drenched." He clicked his keyboard, sharpening the image. "Hell, I've got an ID on him. Will fill you in later off comms. Not sure what the fuck he's doing out there."

"Looks like having a smoke," Sherman broadcast. He could clearly see the man light up and the smoke billow around his stationary form. He too identified the man as Mike Spencer, the head of security that he and Cooper had met during their visit to the BioDynamix plant. A few seconds later a second person stepped through the back door. "He's got a smoke buddy." He focused on the second person, a Chinese male.

"We see him," Cooper replied.

"We need to get ears over there," Sherman spoke. "If that's the normal smoke break location I'm sure a lot is discussed out there that we will want to hear."

"That will be a bit more difficult," Lambchop chimed in.

"I agree, we need to try to pull that off," Cooper said. "We'll talk about it during our debrief."

"With this rain, there ain't no way those guys will see us moving around over here," Sherman said. "Let's finish mounting these things and get out of here."

Lambchop was done, without incident. Sherman finished up and made his way back towards Mother. Mother was having a few problems. The snakes from within the stump he was attempting to secure the camera to, kept slithering out and interfering with his efforts.

Sherman came up beside him. "There must be a hell of a nest in there."

Sherman looked around. He pointed out a tree stump that would work. He checked it over carefully. No spider nest, no snake activity. He got busy drilling on the backside of the large stump as Mother worked on the front. They finished up and headed back to the bank where Lambchop waited. Unfortunately, neither of the boats moved in. The head of an alligator was in the water right off the bank, blocking the boat from coming in to pick them up.

The light at the BioDynamix building turned off. Smoke break was over. Sherman focused through his NVGs. No one remained outside. He sure would like to get a listening device planted over there. To be so close and not be able to do so, was a bitch and a half.

The gator circled and approached the boat that the Undertaker was in. Handsome brought his boat up to the bank. Sherman helped Lambchop and Mother step aboard. There was a lot of water on the floor of the boat. Immediately, the men began bailing as Handsome piloted the boat away.

"Go around him and bring the boat in," Sherman told the Undertaker.

"Go around him? He isn't exactly cooperating," Sloan complained.

"Take it out into the channel a few feet. He'll follow and then you can circle back around."

Sloan did as Sherman had suggested and sure enough, the big gator followed him. He'd just as soon take it out, but he knew Brielle would be all over his shit when they got back if he did that. It followed him as he piloted the boat back to the bank, an unsettling feeling having such a lethal predator stalk you. He held a hand out and pulled Sherman back into the boat. Sherman's boots splashed into at least six inches of water. He too immediately began to bail.

As they made their way back down the bayou, the heavy sheets of rain still shrouded the area. The continuing torrent wasn't letting up. They were all drenched. Had been for hours. Sherman couldn't wait to get back, take a nice hot shower, and crawl into bed with Brielle.

Kilo

*B*rielle sat in the chair watching the boats retreat back down the bayou for a good half hour after they pulled away from the bank. The downpour hadn't let up any and the weather report didn't forecast it moving out of the area until daybreak. She knew there was nothing left for her to do, but she was fascinated with the activity that was set in motion by the identification of BioDynamix Chief Security Officer, Mike Spencer and the unknown Chinese man who took their smoke break at the back door.

Cooper was still talking with Garcia at headquarters through his comms, which Brielle listened into with interest. Doc solely had the team on his comms. Every once in a while, she heard him talk with the men in the boats. She glanced back at the mission feed captured from the cameras on their vests, which still displayed on the monitors. They ran in the dark, with their night vision goggles giving them a better view of the bayou in front of them, than the search lights would.

"So, here's the thing about Mike Spencer," Garcia's voice broke in on Brielle's focus on the monitors. "I've got nothing on him before twenty-three months ago when BioDynamix filed their articles of incorporation. At that time, boom, driver's license, activity on his Social Security number, a checking account opened."

"How can that be?" Brielle asked, forgetting her lip mic was still on.

"I found a legal birth certificate filed in New Jersey at the right time for him, but nothing from then on. That usually indicates an identity takeover of a deceased child. I'm searching for a death certificate now."

"That's disgusting and despicable that someone would do that," Brielle remarked. "Imagine being that poor parent and finding out someone took over your dead child's identity."

"That parent is likely in their sixties by now," Garcia said. "And they'll probably never even know, but I agree with you, I'd be plenty pissed if I were that parent and my kid isn't even born yet."

"How is Sienna feeling?" Cooper asked.

"Pretty good. She's just tired. I finally felt the baby move this morning. He's kicking up a storm!" You didn't have to know Garcia to hear the excitement and pride in his voice.

"He?" Cooper asked. "I thought you weren't going to find out the gender."

Garcia laughed. "Planned not to, but we had an ultrasound this morning and the stem was prominently displayed on the apple. There was no disputing what we saw."

Brielle saw Cooper's smile spread over his face.

"Congrats, man, that's great." He turned to Doc. "Garcia and Sienna found out it's a boy."

Doc smiled. "I know Elizabeth was kind of hoping for a girl to be best friends with Olivia, but yeah, a boy, that's great."

"Doc sends his congratulations," Cooper said.

"Oh, hello," Garcia's all business voice came through their comms. "I found a death certificate on Maribel Spencer, Michael's mom, dated October seventeenth, nineteen ninety. But interestingly enough, she's one of the officers on the Articles of Incorporation for the BioDynamix Corporation, with an address at an assisted living facility in Trenton."

"Aren't there safeguards in place that will alert someone if a dead person is filing legal documents?" Brielle asked.

"No, even with computerized records, databases aren't linked to crosscheck for those kinds of things," Cooper advised her.

"That seems like a no brainer, don't let a dead person get a driver's license or be the legal owner of a corporation," Brielle said.

"This is a sophisticated organization, pulling this much off," Garcia said. "There are inconsistencies with the other owners, as well. I'm diving into them too, but hitting a harder wall. I was lucky to find Maribel's death certificate. It was filed in Fort Lauderdale, Florida. I only found it because her obit was published in the local Trenton newspaper."

"Keep on it," Cooper said. His eyes met Brielle's. "How much longer are you planning to stay up? You're welcome to listen in as long as you want, but there is no need."

Brielle hadn't really thought about it. There was still activity and conversations taking place, and the journalist in her didn't want to miss any of the story. "The whole process fascinates me. Did Landon mention to you that we had discussed active surveillance on Sheriff Henderson?"

"No, he didn't," Cooper replied. "But I think it's a good idea."

"I think that should be extended to Deputy Downey too. That man gives me the creeps. If anyone laid his hands on Bobby, I bet it was him. I've felt threatened by him on multiple occasions."

"How so?"

"He's literally pushed his way into my house when I told him he couldn't come in. He stands close, way too close if you know what I mean, to intimidate."

"The digital team is already looking into him."

"He spends his off hours in this little dive bar in Cut Off. I've heard rumors from a female bartender there that he gets handsy after a few too many whiskeys."

Cooper's lips curved into a smirk. "Good to know if we need to scoop him up."

"I was also thinking. If they are moving anything down the bayou, the people who live near there or spend any time in the area, would have seen something. There are a couple of people in particular I can think of who I should talk to."

Cooper nodded. "We'll add that to our list. Local witnesses could be our best resource."

Brielle appreciated that Cooper was open to her suggestions. She was still up when Madison came into the room carrying a cup of coffee. Brielle checked the time on her phone. It was three a.m.

"Did everything go alright?" Madison asked.

"Yes, everything went as planned." Cooper clicked a few keys. He zoomed out on the map that showed the team's trackers. "The team should be back in about an hour." Then he came to his feet. "There's no activity in the bayou behind the BioDynamix facility, just the rain."

Madison took his seat. She glanced over at Brielle. "I'm surprised to see you still up."

"I slept on the flight down and I'll admit I was fascinated by all the activity since the guys planted the cameras. I got to listen in on the discussion between Cooper and Garcia and hear about what the digital team found so far."

Madison glanced back at Cooper.

"I'll fill you in, in the morning when we have a briefing with the entire team. I'm going to grab a few hours' sleep. We'll reconvene at nine hundred."

"Sounds good," Madison said as Cooper stepped towards the door across the room that led to the bathroom and bedrooms.

Brielle came to her feet as well. "I think I'm going to do the same."

She used the bathroom, alone, and then returned to the bedroom. She left her clothes on but crawled beneath the covers. She had a hard time falling asleep. She wished she could talk or text with Bobby. They usually text messaged every night if they weren't together. She missed him.

The team got back at zero four-twenty. The rain still fell. Sherman had already done the math. There were four shower stalls and five men. He wanted to be one of the first in so he could get to Brielle fast. With his new realization about Brielle fitting into his life, and the role he wanted her to fill in it, he couldn't wait to get to her.

"We've had no movement at the back of BioDynamix since you planted the camera's," Doc said as the men filed into the room.

"I hope we get something soon," Lambchop said. "The more I think about it, the more I think we should hold off talking to Tina Landry or any other civilian until the digital unit has resolved every inconsistency and have full dossiers on everyone on our radar including the Chinese involvement."

"We'll talk about that later. Cooper set a briefing at nine hundred hours. Get some sleep," Doc said.

Sherman had already been stowing his weapons as Lambchop spoke. He didn't need to be told twice. He made a beeline for the bathroom and the showers, beating everyone else in. He peeled off his wet clothes, hanging them to dry from anyplace available. He was sure there were laundry facilities they could use after they woke.

After a quick, hot shower, he wrapped a towel around himself and made his way to his room, hoping he wouldn't encounter Madison along the way. He entered the room and made out Brielle's form on her bed. He pulled a pair of skivvies on and then crowded in beside her.

Brielle came awake as Brian's warmth and the fresh scent of the soap wrapped around her. "Mm, you smell good."

Sherman pressed a kiss to her lips. "Scoot over and give me some room. He snuggled in and immediately drifted into a deep sleep, not realizing he had not set his alarm.

At zero-nine-zero-five, a loud pounding on the door woke them both. "Damn it, Sherman, you're late for the briefing," came Sloan's voice.

"Oh, fuck," Sherman swore, coming awake. "We'll be right there."

Brielle's eyes opened, and she rolled over.

"Why are you wearing your clothes?" Sherman asked her.

"Why aren't you wearing any?"

Sherman chuckled. He got up and pulled a shirt and a pair of jeans on. "We're late for the briefing."

Brielle jumped up. She finger-smoothed her hair and put it up in a ponytail as they quickly walked to the lounge.

"Nice of you to join us," Cooper said sarcastically.

"Sorry, Coop, forgot to set my alarm."

Sloan stood beside him. "Sorry if I interrupted anything," he whispered.

"Just sleep," Sherman guaranteed him.

Sloan wasn't so sure.

"You both look like hell. Go get yourselves coffee. We'll wait five more minutes to get started," Cooper offered.

The two of them went to the galley. The sun shone brightly through the window.

"Are you in trouble?" Brielle asked.

"No, Cooper's just busting my chops." He handed her a cup and then got his own, black, as she stirred sugar into hers.

They returned to the lounge and seated themselves in the two open chairs.

"Last night's mission was successful. We've got clear feed coming through the cameras," Cooper said.

"We need to get ears out by that smoking spot," Sherman spoke up.

Cooper nodded. "Agreed. We'll work with HQ on how we can achieve it."

"I also think we need to initiate active surveillance on Sheriff Henderson," Lambchop said.

"We definitely need to get his phone paired," Cooper agreed. "Lambchop, that'll be your and Handsome's assignment for the day. Come up with a mission plan and run it by me later."

Lambchop smiled and nodded.

Next, Madison gave updates on everything the digital unit had and had not discovered. She started out with what Garcia had dug up on Mike Spencer and his mother, Maribel. "And the three other officers on the corporate filings are suspicious as well. Shepherd has reached out to federal authorities to pay them visits at their declared addresses, all in the Trenton area."

"What the hell is it with New Jersey?" Sherman asked.

"Mayor Stuart is from Jersey too," Brielle added.

"Yes, he was a businessman, owned several gentleman's clubs there," Madison said.

Brielle laughed out loud. That laugh that Sherman loved. "I wonder if the good Christian folks in Galliano know they elected the owner of strip clubs as their mayor."

The team chuckled. "Here's the really interesting thing, Stuart's brother is listed as an officer on the corporate filings for BioDynamix with his address listed as one of those clubs. The FBI will determine if there is an apartment over it that he lives in, but his IRS records have him in California, so I'm going to guess not."

"So, he may not even know that his name was used." Doc said.

"I think I'd have to kill my brother if I discovered he used my name and Social Security number like that," Sloan said.

"And Garcia and the digital team hasn't had much luck tracing the money, either. Oddly, there doesn't appear to be any made from that plant. Garcia is still trying to figure out how they're making payroll for the local Parish workers. There were multiple fund transfers from a bank in Jersey into the plant fund when it opened, but no more infusions of cash," Madison reported.

"Well, I know Tina's check goes into her bank every week, no problems," Brielle said.

Madison nodded. "I'll notify Garcia her paycheck is direct deposited. Maybe he can back-trace the funds to see if it originated from a different account than he found."

"Hey, I mentioned it to Cooper last night. It occurred to me that if any strangers were using the bayou to move anything in or out of the back of the plant, that I know several locals who may have seen something. I need to talk to them."

Sherman wanted to say absolutely not, but he knew he couldn't. He sipped his coffee and watched Cooper and Lambchop.

"I think we add that to the list of resources a few days out," Cooper said. "The fewer people who know that plant is being investigated, the better."

"These are all local people, Cajun and Creole, swamp people who don't like BioDynamix any more than I do," Brielle argued.

"And we'll talk to them in a few days if our active surveillance doesn't bring us results," Lambchop said.

"We don't want to potentially put any civilians in danger," Mother said. "That's why we'll hold off on talking to your friend Tina, for as long as we can too."

"I'd feel a whole lot better about involving any civilians if we wait until after we get some answers on the Chinese. If they are part of one of the Triads, we don't want to put anyone in that kind of danger," Lambchop added.

"I'm not sure who's worse, the Mexican's, the Colombians, or the fucking Chinese. The DEA is struggling with them all," Sherman said.

"And they're all involved in human trafficking," Cooper said, "which may be what we're looking at with the Chinese in those trailers. If Brielle is right and they work twelve-hour shifts, seven days a week and never leave that property, that screams of slave or captive labor. HQ is watching the satellite feed carefully, monitoring their movements in and out of their trailers. If we can see images that back my assumption up, we'll know that most of those people in those trailers are not our enemies but are people in need of rescue. That will decrease the number of people we need to worry about if we breach that facility."

"Speaking of people who live in those trailers, is that where Mike Spencer lives?" Sherman asked.

"He must," Madison confirmed. "There are no records of him renting or buying anything in the area. And no footage of him leaving that facility on the video recording that was captured from Brielle's camera on the water tower."

"The same is true for the three men who rotate on as the gate guards. They return to the facility after their shifts," Cooper added.

Brielle wasn't sure how she had missed that or failed to think about where the gate guards lived. None of them were hired from the Parish. She of course didn't know this Mike Spencer even existed. She wondered how many more people worked inside the plant that she didn't know about.

"So, they probably live inside those trailers too," Doc concluded. "We need to know how many Tangos we'll be facing if we go into that building. It sounds to me like we need to talk with this Tina Landry sooner rather than later."

"Let's give the digital team and our surveillance at least another twenty-four hours," Cooper said. His eyes shifted to Lambchop. "Fast-track that plan to pair Sheriff Henderson's phone and let's initiate some active surveillance on him, as well. There is a car rental here at the port, get what you need."

"I'll need a third man to surveil him," Lambchop said. His eyes shifted to Mother.

"He's yours," Cooper confirmed. "Okay, we have our short-term plan. Doc will stay on overnights monitoring the equipment. Madison and I will take overlapping evening and overnight shifts with Doc as needed. We'll assist the digital team when we're not on. Sloan, Sherman, and Brielle, you're assigned to monitor the feeds from now through twenty-one hundred when Doc will take over. Come up with your own schedule for coverage, two of you on."

That must have been a known signal to the others that the briefing was over. Brielle watched them all get up. Doc left the room, she assumed to sleep. Landon, Danny, and Rich left together. She heard Landon prompt them with a desire to get coffee. They'd plan their mission in the galley.

"Cooper and I will go cook up some breakfast for everyone," Madison said.

Cooper grumbled but followed her from the room.

Brielle was excited that she'd get to be involved and monitor the camera feeds from the bayou and any other surveillance that was put in place. She would love to watch Sheriff Henderson's movements. She'd love to catch him doing something illegal, the bullying prick.

"Do you want to catch a shower, Brielle?" Sherman asked. "Sloan and I can take the first monitoring shift."

"That would be great, thanks."

"Don't forget to take everything in you'll need. There are towels stacked on a shelf in the far-left corner of the room and a bin beneath them for the dirty ones," Sherman said. "By the way, Sloan, do you know if anyone checked on laundry facilities so we can dry our clothes from last night?"

"Yeah, Mother already did. He gathered up everyone's clothes, and he's tending them."

A smile cracked Sherman's lips. He should have known Mother would already be taking care of it for them.

Brielle rushed back to their room, grabbed her backpack and entered the empty bathroom. She went to the shower stall to the far left and then she grabbed a couple towels. As she finished her shower and turned the water off, she heard two male voices enter the bathroom, Landon and Danny.

"I respect the hell out of him for speaking up," she heard Lambchop say.

"Charlie Team has been on the Power Grid Protection Project for what, well over a year?" Mother said. "It's only natural Handsome would feel his other skills have gotten rusty."

"We should have anticipated it. Well, we will with the other team members as we loop them back into traditional cases."

Brielle heard toilet stall doors close and then she heard what could only be the sound of the two men peeing. She remained perfectly still and didn't make a sound.

"Yeah, actively surveilling a Sheriff is high stakes, though from what Brielle and Sherman say about him, I don't think we're going up against someone with a great deal of training," Mother said. "Sounds like the perfect job to reintroduce Handsome to surveillance work."

"I'll talk with Cooper. We may want to take an inventory of his skills and come up with a partial retraining plan if any other required competences appear rusty," Lambchop said, thinking aloud.

The toilets flushed and Brielle heard the stall doors open. She heard water at the sinks turn on.

"We'll run this like a standard surveillance in all other regards, acquire the subject, pair his phone, and surveil his movements," she heard Landon say.

Then their voices grew quieter. She assumed they left the bathroom until she couldn't hear them any longer. She quickly toweled off and dressed. Then she brought her backpack back to the room where she towel-dried her hair more and combed it out. She left it loose so it could air dry. Hopefully at some point, she'd be able to go outside and sit in the sun for a half hour to allow it to dry completely.

When she reentered the lounge, she found Brian and Gary eating their breakfasts. A full plate sat in front of the empty third chair for her. Her heart swelled with gratitude, realizing how considerate that was for someone to think of her.

"That looks and smells amazing," she said as she approached.

"I got you a little of everything," Sherman said. "I'll eat whatever you don't want." He beamed a smile at her, appreciating how beautiful she looked without a trace of makeup on and her wet hair combed back from her face, hanging loosely.

"Thanks," she acknowledged with a smile of her own as she took her seat. "Any movement on the cameras so far?"

"Just a few boats coming and going. So far, no one has approached the dock by the target facility," Sloan reported. "And no one has taken a smoke break either."

"Spencer must be a hard-core smoker if he stepped out during last night's storm to have one," Sherman remarked.

"Yeah, I can't believe there isn't somewhere in that facility to sneak a few drags," Sloan chimed in. "And if they're making drugs with slave-labor, I can't believe they're that concerned with a healthy workplace."

Sherman nodded, deep in thought. "You're right. There may have been something more involved in those two men stepping outside last night."

Lima

The three of them manned the monitors from nine-thirty a.m. through nine p.m. Brielle stayed the majority of the day, letting Brian and Gary each go take five-hour naps. Besides her shower, she only stepped away to use the bathroom or to get herself and the guys food from the galley. By the time Doc headed over to the tables with a cup of coffee in his hands, she was beat.

"That's the fourth time in the last minute that you yawned, Brielle. I told you, go to bed," Sherman said.

Doc took the third seat. "I'm on now and Cooper is in the galley, heading this way. You're both relieved."

Brielle came to her feet.

"You go on," Brian said. "I'll brief Doc and be in shortly."

Brielle yawned deeply again. The lack of sleep the previous evening and sitting still watching the feed on the monitors nearly all day, had gotten to her. "Sounds good." She hit the bathroom on the way to the room, passing Cooper in the hallway. She was relieved no one was in the bathroom. She didn't like the coed bathroom thing one bit.

She laid on her back, on top of the covers in all her clothes, just waiting for Brian. He came into the room fifteen minutes later.

Sherman gazed at her stretched out on the bed. She looked very peaceful and relaxed. "You're not going to sleep in your clothes, again, are you?"

Brielle giggled. "And you're not going to sleep nearly naked again, are you?"

Sherman crossed the room and laid atop her, snuggling in close. "How about we both sleep nearly naked?" A beautiful smile curved her lips that instantly perked his cock up. Either that or it was because his pelvis was nestled against hers.

"Not happening," she said.

Sherman chuckled. He loved how tough she was. He kissed her as softly and gently as he could, given he wanted to rip her clothes off and bury himself deep inside her. After a lengthy and vigorous kiss, he pulled his lips back and hovered but an inch over hers. When she opened her eyes, they were dilated with an intensity that convinced him she wanted more.

He caressed her cheek and then slid his fingers gently down her neck as he stared into her beautiful brown eyes. He traced along the neckline of her t-shirt, dipping his fingers beneath. He felt the soft flesh of her breast beneath his touch and then slid his fingers under her bra. Her nipple hardened as his fingertips brushed over it.

"Brian," she gasped, grabbing his hand.

"What's it going to take for you to trust me?"

"Just more time."

"I'd never hurt you. If I'm with you, I'm with you and only you."

She pulled his hand out. Her eyes flashed a questioning and then a knowing gaze.

"Bobby told me how your last two boyfriends hurt you, Brielle. I'd never do that to you."

"He had no right to tell you anything."

Sherman saw the fire in her eyes. "He only did because he loves you. He was warning me away, told me he'd never forgive me if I hurt you."

"What else did he tell you?" She demanded, stunned they'd have that conversation, pissed that Bobby would have told Brian what he did.

"That you're not a fling kind of girl. You believe in relationships and commitment. He told me to stay away from you if I couldn't be that for you."

Brielle huffed out and her head snapped to the left, focusing on the door like she wanted to run out it. Sherman could see she was pissed. He hoped her anger was directed more at Bobby than him. "Brielle, look at me."

She kept her eyes focused on the door. "I can't believe you and Bobby had that conversation."

"Brielle, look at me," he repeated more forcefully. When she didn't, he pressed a kiss to her cheek. Her heated gaze instantly flew back to his. Her lips were twisted into a scowl. "What are we doing here? We both want to see where this can go, this thing between us. So, I know your last two boyfriends were scumbag assholes that cheated on you. If I knew who they were, I'd pay them a visit and give them both a beatdown for hurting you. I know we'd eventually get around to talking about our pasts and you'd tell me. Why is this an issue?"

She huffed out a disbelieving sigh. "You think I don't want to have sex with you because my last two boyfriends cheated on me? Is that it?"

"Partially has to be. I wouldn't be so eager to trust someone if that happened to me."

"Brian, what don't you understand about me just wanting to take it slow and really get to know you before we jump into a physical relationship? If we weren't together under these circumstances, if we were starting a normal relationship, we'd have a first date. Then a second, then a third. Things would move more slowly, a kiss goodnight, more kisses, making out. I wouldn't go to bed with you the first few nights I went out with you."

An amused grin curved over Sherman's lips. She wouldn't? What kind of Pollyanna world did she live in? "So, consider that first night and the morning on the boat our first date. The second night at my place was our second, with more kisses. Last night was our third, and this is our fourth. Aren't we to that making out point yet? Or that open conversation where we talk about what we really want in this relationship?"

She rolled her eyes. "It's not quite that easy, you know. I like you, Brian, a lot. But I need to take this slow for reasons you can't understand, and it's not just because I've been cheated on."

"But that is part of it, isn't it?"

She shrugged. She didn't want to admit that it was probably a big part of it.

"Answer me three questions," Sherman pressed.

She nodded.

"Do you like sex?"

Her facial expression showed her surprise he'd asked her that. "What kind of question is that?"

"An easy one to answer. Do you like sex?"

"Yes," she softly admitted.

A small grin formed on his lips. "Good. Do you like to kiss me?"

She couldn't help the smile that tugged at her lips. "Yes," she admitted, embarrassed.

Sherman's smile grew larger. "Do you believe me when I tell you that I would never hurt you?"

Her gaze wandered over his face. "You are probably the most honorable man I've ever been with. I have no reason to doubt you."

"So, that's another yes?"

She chuckled that laugh he loved to hear. "Yes, that's another yes."

"I told you I don't play games. I told you I am attracted to you and that I would ask you again to make love with me. I told you I would abide by your terms, and I have. But damn it, Brielle, we are both adults and just kissing you and holding you at night isn't enough. I want to feel over your body, over your skin, not just over your clothes, which I haven't even been able to do to my satisfaction. I want to enjoy you as a man enjoys a woman. I cannot be any clearer with my intentions."

"No, you have been clear," she conceded. "You've been honest."

"I'd say it's time for you to be honest with your intentions, too."

All past hurts clouded her thoughts. "Asking me that is asking for a lot of trust."

"No relationship can succeed without trust, Brielle. I trust you enough to be open about my intentions."

"I promised myself I would take it slow with the next man I was with. I didn't do that the last few times." She saw he was about to comment on that. "And before you tell me you're different from how those guys were, I already know that. This whole situation is different. How long will this investigation last? A week? Two weeks? A month? And then what happens after that? You go back up to Chicago and then what?"

"That's what this is about?" Sherman asked. "Son-of-a-bitch, momma. You think I'm just gonna say goodbye and go back up north when this mission is over and leave you?"

She shrugged again. Yes, that's exactly what she thought.

Sherman placed a tender kiss on her lips. "I said I wanted to see where this thing between us can go and that's not tied to this operation. I want to see how you can fit into my life, because I think you'll fit pretty damn well. I've got a hell of a lot of leave time saved up, time I'll take to see you. And I've got money saved to fly either one of us to see the other. This thing between us doesn't end when this mission ends."

Sherman kissed her again, this time holding nothing back. He burrowed his pelvis more intimately against hers, pulling on one of her thighs to give him better access. Then that hand tucked itself under her ass and he groped over her cheek. He kissed her and ground his pelvis into hers for at least five minutes. She kissed him back enthusiastically.

Heated, he removed his t-shirt, quickly pulling it over his head so that his lips were not off hers for too long. Her hands greedily felt over the flesh on his back. She wasn't holding back. His blue jeans became uncomfortably tight. Encouraged, he stood and dropped his jeans. He could see the wheels turning in her head. Was she ready for this yet? Taking her silence as consent, he reached down, unbuttoned and unzipped her jeans and then took hold of each pant leg and pulled them from her.

As he yanked her pants off, she stared at his manhood, amply displayed in his undershorts. Her gaze raked its way up his well-formed abs and chest. Her eyes locked onto his as he came back atop her. With their jeans off, a whole new awareness struck her as his hard length pressed between her legs. She gasped from the near invasion of him.

Things heated up and escalated quickly from there. His kisses sizzled. Her flesh tingled wherever his hands caressed, and they glided over her entire body. At some point, she realized both of his hands groped over her breasts. Her bra was unhooked and pushed aside. When had that happened? He rolled them, rearranging their position, so she was on top of him, her legs straddling him. He kept hold of her neck so that their lips did not part.

When she felt his hands tuck into her panties, and he freely fondled over both ass cheeks while he moaned his pleasure, grinding his cock up against her, she knew she was reaching her point of discomfort. His fingers dove deep, meeting her outer lips and she pulled her other lips from his. "Brian," was all she had to say, and he withdrew his roving hands from within her panties. He caressed over her back, his lips reaching back to hers.

A few minutes later, at the sensation of her t-shirt being pushed up, she again stopped him. "We need to slow this down," she pled.

"Oh, momma, no, we need to take this to the next level," he replied. He shoved her shirt up. "Let me take this off." His other hand pulled down on the back of her panties. "And these off."

"Brian." Her voice was soft.

Sherman moaned out his frustration. He knew she had reached the end of her comfort zone. But damn, did he want to make love to her. He knew she had been as into it as much as he had. He pulled her panties back up, pulled her shirt back down and then just embraced her.

He rearranged their position again, so that they each laid on their sides, facing each other. He kissed her lips one more time. "I respect that this is where it ends tonight. I don't like it, but I respect it." He gave her another kiss, and then he got up.

Brielle watched him pull his jeans back on and then he stepped towards the door. "Where are you going?"

"To take a shower." Then he left.

When Sherman reentered the room, Brielle laid in the middle of her bed, under the covers. Her eyes were open and staring at him. He shed his jeans and came back over to the bed. "Move over and give me some room."

She scooted over, keeping her face turned towards him. He slid into bed with her, taking her into his arms.

The clean scent wafted off Brian, filling Brielle's nose as his skin warmed hers. "Are you mad at me?"

She heard Brian sigh. "I'm not mad, just disappointed it ended where it did. I want to make love to you, Brielle, but I'll wait till you're ready."

"Did you jackoff in the shower?"

"Yeah, didn't want to get blue balls, don't need to be walking around here in pain."

"I'm sorry, Brian," was all Brielle could say.

"Don't be," he said. "We wait till you're ready."

Though in his head he couldn't come to terms with why she said she wasn't ready to make love with him. Nor could he understand why she needed to take it slow. They were both consenting adults, and it wasn't like she was a virgin, waiting for her Prince Charming to come sweep her off her feet. And hell, didn't she understand how mixed the messages were that she sent wanting to snuggle in bed?

She embraced him, pulling herself up against his strong form. "That felt good, and I did like it."

"Yeah, it did feel real good," Sherman confirmed. He stroked over her back and noted that her bra was off. She wore only her t-shirt and panties. Things were moving in the right direction, just too slowly for him. He embraced her more tightly. Then sleep overtook him.

When Brielle woke the next morning, she was alone in the bed. She glanced around the dorm-style room, not really expecting to see Brian. And she did not. She reached over and grabbed her phone from the table that sat between the two twin beds. It was nearly ten a.m. She jumped up and quickly dressed. She again secured her hair in a ponytail.

She entered the bathroom, encountering Danny and Rich within. She wasn't getting any more comfortable with this coed bathroom arrangement. She put on a pleasant smile and greeted them on her way into the designated female only stall. She joined Rich at the sinks and grabbed her toothbrush and toothpaste from the small shelf where everyone was keeping theirs.

"You slept late, must have been really tired," Rich remarked.

"Yes, I was surprised when I saw the time." She squeezed the toothpaste tube. "Is there much going on this morning?"

"No, just monitoring the surveillance equipment. This is the boring part, the downtime when we're just waiting. That's a lot of what surveillance work is, waiting and watching."

"I'm especially interested in the surveillance of Sheriff Henderson. After the bullying and all the other crap that he and Deputy Downey have pulled against me since I published that first article on BioDynamix, I so want something damning against him to come to light."

"Well, we put trackers on both their squad cars, we have Henderson's phone paired, and I know the digital team is diving so far into his background, there won't be much we don't know about him."

"I hope so," Brielle said. "Where is Brian this morning?"

"He's at the table in the lounge, monitoring feed. There's still some breakfast out in the galley. Doc prepared it this morning, so it's ultra-healthy. He ran to the local grocery store to get fruit, yogurt, and granola. And I'm pretty sure the omelets he made were made with only the egg whites." Burke chuckled.

Brielle went to the lounge first to see Brian. He and Gary sat in front of the equipment. "Good morning," she greeted as she approached.

Brian's smile as he gazed up at her set her worries that he was mad at her to rest. "Good morning."

Gary echoed the greeting.

"Anything interesting going on this morning?"

"No, just normal workday stuff. We watched the Parish employees arrive for work at BioDynamix. They parked in that far lot outside the fence and were bussed up to the building, just like you said they were. I've never seen a group of people act more like a herd of sheep," Sherman said. "Just watching them, anyone would agree something is very off."

Brielle felt almost vindicated that Brian agreed with her. She'd been virtually alone in her suspicion of that place for so long. To have the agreement of her assessments by this group gave her a sense of justification, confirming that she wasn't paranoid or crazy.

"And Sheriff Henderson finally showed up at the police station at nine-thirty. He left his house at seven but made a stop at a house outside of town belonging to a woman I don't remember, who's known as Bitsy Phillips. Tracker on the car had him there for an hour and a half. He took several calls from Downey while he was there, lied and said he was at home."

Brielle laughed. "Bitsy Phillips? Oh my God! Brothel Bitsy is screwing Sheriff Henderson. That explains a lot."

"Why don't I remember her?" Sherman asked.

"I'm glad you didn't know her. Back when we were coming up, only the lowest-life scum that paid for her services knew her. The last few years, probably because she aged, she became more of the Parish's madam, who helps arrange a higher-class network of female companionship aimed at the tourists who come in to fish. They get lonely, you know."

"Yeah, I imagine after handling their fishing rods all day, they want a lovely young lady to handle their personal rods," Sherman joked.

"The Parish has harsh anti-prostitution laws, but Sheriff Henderson doesn't enforce many of them, and this explains why," Brielle said.

"It's interesting, but it's not the proof we're looking for on him," Sloan said. "So, he's screwing a whore, big deal. I'd have preferred we recorded a call between him and Spencer at the BioDynamix plant discussing drugs or whatever it is they are up to out there."

Unfortunately, Brielle had to agree with him. "Has your digital unit dug up anything more?"

"We're due to have a briefing with them at thirteen hundred this afternoon," Sloan said. "We'll find out then. Cooper and Madison will be back by then, they're just grabbing a few hours nap."

"Where's everyone else?" Brielle asked.

"Doc was up all night. He went to bed too after he made breakfast. There's still some in the kitchen," Sherman said. "You should grab some."

"Lambchop, Mother, and Handsome were talking about reacquiring the Sheriff and surveilling him later today. They're in the galley," Sloan said.

Brielle was hungry, and she wanted a cup of coffee. "Can I get either of you anything from the galley?"

"Thanks, I'm good," Sherman said.

"Me too," Sloan agreed.

Brielle could hear the conversation of the men in the galley as she approached. They were talking about the Sheriff. Their conversation halted when she entered. Danny pointed out where the breakfast foods were in the refrigerator. She'd have to microwave it to reheat if for herself.

"You must have been tired. You slept late," Mother said.

"Yes, I guess I was," Brielle admitted.

Lambchop pointed to one of the empty chairs at the table as Brielle lifted her plate and coffee cup from the counter, her eyes on the door. "Join us. We have some questions about the Sheriff and we're hoping you can help."

"Sure," she replied, somewhat hesitantly. She took a sip of her coffee after she was seated.

"When he first started harassing you, did he ever warn you away from BioDynamix?" Mother asked.

"Not in so many words, and never directly. It was implied. He said things like people don't like you digging into things that are none of your business. If you know what's good for you, you'll stop. Downey was a little more threatening. He forced his way into my house one time and made a point of telling me how flimsy the door and locks were. He said he'd sure hate to get called to the scene and find me hurt or worse."

The three men exchanged glances. Lambchop shook his head. "Brielle, why didn't you file a report with state or federal authorities?"

Brielle shrugged. "I guess that never occurred to me. And I didn't think either one of them would actually hurt me. They've pulled me over and pushed their way into my house dozens of times. It got to the point of being more of an annoyance, than making me feel afraid. Besides, it would be my word against theirs."

"I think you've been very lucky that nothing else happened. I'm glad Sherman found you. If you'd been hiding anywhere other than his boat, we may not be here right now," Mother said.

"And you might not be either," Lambchop added.

By the serious looks on all their faces, Brielle knew that they all thought it had been a good possibility that she could have been hurt. "You just never think that someone known to you would hurt you, certainly not law enforcement officers."

"Statistically speaking, most murder victims are killed by people they know," Burke said. "Some statistics put it as high as eighty percent."

"Thanks, that's comforting," she said with much sarcasm.

Mike

$\mathcal{T}$he briefing at thirteen hundred brought some well-needed updates from the digital unit. Shepherd and Garcia were on the monitor. The team at Port Fourchon was seated in chairs pulled up and clustered near the largest of the monitors on the table.

"Here's what we dug up on the four owners of record on the Articles of Incorporation for BioDynamix. You all know about Maribel Spencer, the mother of Mike Spencer, both of whom are deceased. I finally found Michael Spencer's death certificate," Garcia said. "He drowned at an upstate New York summer camp when he was thirteen. We have no ID on the man who has taken over his identity, yet."

"FBI ran down Mayor Dwayne Stuart's brother, Donald. He has never lived or received any other mail at the apartment over the Trenton Gentleman's Club that Dwayne Stuart owns, until the articles were filed. As far as we can tell, he's been in California for over two decades, without a single trip back to Trenton. Dwayne Stuart did live and receive all his mail at that address, though, until he moved to Louisiana. There is nothing tying Donald Stuart to any of it," Shepherd reported. "We believe his name was used fraudulently."

"A third officer on the corporate filings is Jennifer Brubaker. This appears to be another deceased child identity take over from the Trenton area," Garcia said. The monitor switched over to display the New Jersey driver's license for Jennifer Brubaker. She was Asian. "Does she look familiar to any of you?"

They all agreed they had not seen her in the area, but they would remember her. Could she be the link to the Chinese?

"FBI visited the address this license has. She hasn't lived there in over a year. We're running her driver's license photo against the Asian women Brielle's camera captured. But so far, nothing," Garcia said.

"The last officer, Keith Louis, is a cousin of Sheriff Henderson, whose W-2's indicate he worked at one of Stuart's strip clubs up until the corporate filings. He's in the wind, don't have any current employment or housing info on him. The FBI visited his last known address. His landlord said he vacated the premises nearly two years ago," Shepherd said. His driver's license photo displayed, dark red hair, receding hairline, glasses over his round face.

"Finally, the first real piece of evidence tying Dwayne Stuart and Sheriff Henderson together," Sherman remarked aloud. It was what everyone else was thinking.

"The digital team will continue to dig into the finances. And we'll try to get more on these people we just discussed. Continue your surveillance. We'll touch bases again tomorrow at seventeen hundred if nothing develops before," Shepherd ordered. Then the monitor went to a blank blue screen when Shepherd cut the transmission from HQ.

Cooper stood and stretched. "I'm heading back to bed. I'll take an overnight shift with Doc." His gaze went to Lambchop. "Wake me if anything comes up."

Nothing came up. The team continued their surveillance. There was no activity on the cameras that focused on the back of the BioDynamix facility except Spencer taking a few smoke breaks with the Chinese man.

Brielle did enjoy that she and Brian made dinner for everyone that evening. It felt normal working in the kitchen together. Brielle loved to cook, just never had many people to cook for. She and Brian worked together well. They talked a lot about Bobby and Brian's childhood. Helene Sherman had told Brielle so many stories while she cared for her during her illness.

With so much downtime, Brielle's thoughts kept focusing on the fact that she'd nearly had sex with Brian the previous evening. She knew that Brian was honorable. She believed him when he said he would make a commitment and stick to it. She wanted to let it go further, but she also knew that her past was holding her back. She decided that she'd really try to let it go a little further and see how comfortable she felt. Brian was a good guy. It wasn't fair to Brian that the action of two jagoffs were stopping her from trusting him.

That night when they went to bed, Brielle had a headache. No, she really had a headache. Probably because she had spent so much time obsessively thinking about having sex with him. Brian went to Gary and got Tylenol for her. He got her a water bottle and brought them to her in the room. Then he held her and they both fell asleep.

The next morning when Brielle woke, she was again alone in the room. It was ten a.m. She hadn't slept till ten since college. She ran into Cooper in the bathroom. He was heading to bed. After, she got a cup of coffee and joined Brian and Madison in the lounge.

"Where is everyone?" She asked as she approached.

"Good morning, sleepy head!" Sherman greeted with a crooked smile.

"You shouldn't let me sleep that long," she replied.

Madison's gaze flickered back at her and then reaffixed on the monitors. "You've obviously needed it. Don't feel bad. There's not much going on here. This is the boring part of surveillance, waiting for something to happen."

"Mother, Lambchop, and Burke left early to surveil the Sheriff again. They should be back early this afternoon. Doc and Cooper are sleeping, and Sloan went to the store to get us more food. See, you missed nothing," Sherman said. "Did your headache go away?"

Brielle sipped her coffee. "Yes. It's gone this morning."

After she finished her coffee, she took a shower. Then she helped Gary put the groceries away. The others returned after lunch with plans for the three of them to go back out that night to surveil the Sheriff. A call was recorded on his phone that morning to a burner phone that was traced back to a store in New Jersey. He told whoever he spoke with that he'd see them at midnight.

Shortly thereafter, Brielle headed back into the galley to get another cup of coffee. She glanced out the window and her breath caught in her chest when she saw the man who stood less than seventeen feet from the window talking with one of the Coast Guard people. Brielle crouched down fast, so that she was no longer visible in the window. Her shaking hand removed her phone from her back pocket. She dialed Brian. Thankfully, he answered on the first ring.

"What's the matter?"

"He's here, that man that Gary took the picture of, who was watching us in New Orleans. He's right outside this galley window, talking with one of the Coast Guard people."

"You're hidden?"

"Of course, I am."

"We're on it. Stay where you are." He disconnected the call and then relayed the issue to the others in the room.

"He hasn't seen those of us who were in New York," Lambchop said. "Mother and Handsome, you both go outside and get eyes on this guy. Watch him and follow him, but do not engage if you can avoid it. I'll go to the galley and get Brielle out when it's safe to."

Sherman didn't like that he couldn't do anything to help, but Lambchop was right, it was best that anyone who had been in Louisiana and had been seen, stay out of sight. "Madison, do we have any surveillance that could have this fucker on it?" Sherman asked.

Madison clicked over her keyboard. "The Coast Guard gave me access to their exterior security cams. Let's see if I can get him on a camera or two." She clicked through several camera feeds before the one that showed their mystery man and the Coast Guard officer displayed on her monitor. "Got him."

Through their comms they heard Mother's voice. "We've got him in sight. Handsome passed and is about fifty yards ahead of them, sitting in one of the vehicles, watching. I can't hear the conversation, but we can get that from the Coast Guard personnel once they separate."

"I don't like this. He could be spilling everything he knows about us," Sherman said nervously. "Lambchop, is Brielle okay?" He hadn't brought her back yet. Sherman was getting antsy.

"Affirmative, she's hidden. Our man is in a position to see right in this window. I don't dare move her yet."

"The conversation ended. Coast Guard man is heading back around the building towards the entrance. Someone needs to intercept him," Mother said.

"I've got him," Sherman said. At least he could do this to help. He hated standing around doing nothing. He headed to the door from their secure area that led into the entryway into the facility. The man in a coast guard flight suit that he had observed on the monitor, talking with blond-boy, was just entering from outside. "Hey, were you just talking to a civilian with spiked up blond hair around the corner, in front of the windows to the galley."

"Yes, nice guy, had a lot of questions about our search and rescue operations."

"I'm with the group using the north wing. Did he ask any questions about us, or about any other groups that use your facilities?"

The man looked thoughtful for a moment. "Not specifically, but now that you mention it, he did ask if any federal agencies had a presence at the port."

"And what was your reply?" Sherman asked.

"I told him I wasn't at liberty to discuss U.S. assets that may or not be located at the port. Then he said, oh, come on, I can't believe the DEA doesn't have a permanent presence here and at every other seaport coming into the United States. We laughed together about it, but no more was said."

"The conversation went on for longer than that. What else was said? This is important." Sherman pushed.

"Not much more."

"Did he say who he was or what he was doing here at the port and over here near your facilities?"

"No, and I didn't think to ask. We get a lot of people just nosing around, taking a look at our helicopters, fascinated by the search and rescue we do. Hey, there was one more thing, he did ask if we ever fly over inland waterways, the bayous, the lakes. I told him that we do conduct search and rescue up as far as Lake Pontchartrain when we are called in for an assist."

Sherman immediately thought that question significant. "One last thing. Did he have any sort of accent?"

"Yes, New York or New Jersey," the Coastguard man replied.

"Thanks," Sherman said, and then he slipped back through the door into the north wing.

"He's on the move, Handsome and I will trade off, but I could use you outside, Lambchop," Mother broadcasted.

Lambchop had just gotten Brielle back into their main room. He'd given her the okay to get off the floor as soon as their suspect passed the window. "On my way."

He met Sherman in the short hallway leading back to the building's main entrance.

"Is Brielle okay?"

"Yes, she's in with Madison."

"Get this guy and let me interrogate him. I'll find out why he's tailing us."

Lambchop laid his hand to Sherman's shoulder. "Easy there. Let us see what he does next and where he goes." Then he passed through the outer door.

Sherman immediately returned to their control room. Brielle looked shaken. He looped an arm around her. "Are you okay?"

"Yeah, just startled. It was a shock, seeing him outside the window."

"Do you think he saw you?" Sherman asked.

"I don't think so. I turned and dropped to the floor as soon as it registered who he was."

"Good thinking and I'm glad you called me right away. The team is on him."

"How did he find us here?" Brielle asked.

"We'll find out. Don't you worry."

His confidence helped to put her at ease.

"He approached from the south side of the building," Madison said. "I've got some good pics of him. I'm forwarding them to Ops at HQ now. He can't be a professional. A professional would have avoided the cameras."

"So, who the hell is this fucker then?" Sherman demanded. He was frustrated that he was sidelined. He'd feel a whole lot better if he could be out there, going after this guy.

Madison knew it was a rhetorical question, and that Sherman was blowing off steam. She kept her eyes on the camera feed until blond-boy and the rest of the team were out of camera view.

"Shit," Lambchop's voice came over everyone's comms. "He's gone. A car just pulled up, and he got in." Lambchop recited the make, model, and license plate number.

Madison typed it into a message to the digital team. Then she got up and went to her room. She woke Cooper up. She filled him in as they walked back to the lounge. They arrived as the three men entered the room.

"Do you think you were made by blond-boy?" Cooper asked.

"Hard to say. I don't think so," Lambchop replied.

"I say no," Mother added. "I think his pickup was pre-arranged, not in response to us following him."

"How did he find us?" Brielle asked.

"I don't think he necessarily did," Sherman answered. "From what he was asking the Coast Guard personnel, it sounds like he was checking to see how far north they went."

"If the Sheriff is in on what's going on, certainly he knows the operation radius and criteria for Coast Guard involvement," Madison said.

"We're missing something," Cooper said.

"Let's back up to the Sheriff. How did he win the election?" Sherman asked.

"He had the backing of several of the mayors of the towns in the Parish, Galliano, Cut Off, Golden Meadow, Thibodaux," Brielle said. "There's no doubt in my mind that there were some payoffs involved. Galliano's mayor is from up north, but not the others. Old man Delafosse up in Thibodaux has been mayor for longer than I've been alive. He's Creole, got no reason to throw in with the likes of any Yankee," Brielle said.

"We start there, with the election," Cooper said. "I'll get this info to our digital unit and have them look into the mayors and why they threw their support behind Henderson."

"You suspect something more illegal than payoffs, don't you, Cooper?" Lambchop asked.

"Yeah, I have to wonder if Henderson and his New Jersey cronies got some dirt on the mayors that they didn't want to get out."

"Blackmail?" Brielle asked.

Cooper nodded. "As you said, Thibodaux's mayor had no reason to align himself with Henderson. Greed is always a motive, but protecting a secret always trumps greed."

"How long after Dwayne Stuart got elected as Galliano's mayor did the BioDynamix plant get announced?" Lambchop asked.

"It was in the works for at least six months before, the lawyers for it negotiating with the prior administration. It was after Stuart got elected that all the tax incentives got put on the table and the deal went through," Brielle said. "And it moved really fast after that. The work crews came in practically the next day and tore down the old cannery structure. The warehouse is new. It went up fast."

Sherman shook his head. "Nothing moves that fast in the bayou. They had to have the work crews under contract just waiting for the go ahead to demolish that old structure, architectural plans had to be drawn up, building permits already in the works."

"Dwayne Stuart fast tracked everything," Brielle said. "BioDynamix held a job fair in the gymnasium of the Galliano High School. Hundreds applied for jobs less than a month after Stuart took office."

"Even that takes coordination and planning," Madison said. "Sherman's right, these things don't just happen without a lot of development and preparation going into it."

"Was it a surprise that Dwayne Stuart won the election?" Cooper asked.

"To some," Brielle said. "Look, the rural Parishes of Louisiana are well known for political corruption, the boy's network, nepotism, and political favors ruling appointments. It's a tight community. The fact that several Yankees won elections at all is mind boggling. Dwayne Stuart ran on a platform of changing the status quo, of getting new industry and new money into Galliano, something many didn't think the prior mayor was interested in doing. The airport brings in a lot of revenue as does the tourism, but a lot of people bought into Dwayne Stuart's vision that Galliano could be more of a commercial hub."

"Besides BioDynamix, is any other new industry in the works?" Lambchop asked.

"No. That all kind of fell off everyone's radar," Brielle said. "Until I started writing about it. Not only did I attack BioDynamix in my posts, I questioned what more Dwayne Stuart would do for Galliano."

"How do you think any of that ties into blond-boy and his visit here?" Sherman asked.

"I'm not sure. But I agree with Madison. The Sheriff would know when he or someone else could call the Coast Guard in. We've assumed a cohesive group of criminals up to this point. Maybe that isn't the case. Maybe they aren't all chummy and sharing information." Cooper ran his hand over his scruffy jaw. "Okay, add watching the exterior cameras of this facility to your surveillance in case he comes back. I'm going back to bed."

Before Cooper left the room, Lambchop filled him in on the phone call the Sheriff made that morning and his plans to go back out and surveil him that evening to see who he was meeting. Cooper approved the mission.

Brielle returned to her room too. She closed her eyes and did some deep breathing to try to calm herself. Blond-boy's presence really rocked her. She wasn't so sure that Brian was right about why he was there. How had he known where they were in New Orleans? She didn't like that this guy had shown up twice. That was too much of a coincidence.

"Are you okay?" Sherman asked coming into the room. He closed the door behind himself.

"Yes. I just needed a few minutes. Do you really think that guy being down here could have nothing to do with us?"

"I do." Sherman turned his back to her and unzipped his bag. He heard the bed creak. His lips curved into a smile as Brielle wrapped her arms around him from behind. Gazing down and seeing her hands on his abdomen spiked his excitement. He grew hard instantly. "I swear you're trying to kill me, woman."

"How so? I'm just snuggling up to you," she replied in her raspy voice. She dropped her head against his back.

"You have no idea what effect you have on a man, or you do and you're just teasing me."

"I am no tease, Brian Sherman. I just like to feel you against me."

"I'd sure like to feel more of you against me, more than I felt last night," he said, his voice sounding strangled, even to him. He grabbed one of her hands and slid it down below his belt. "This is what you do to me, just snuggling up to me." He rubbed her hand over his hard-as-steel member.

"I know you want more, Brian."

"What are we doing, Brielle?" Sherman asked, turning her to face him. He wrapped his arms around her and pulled her in close. "We're both adults and we both want a physical closeness. Last night felt great to both of us. It shouldn't be this hard."

He kissed her more passionately than he'd ever kissed anyone. He pulled her pelvis close to his and held her tightly to himself. She returned his kisses just as enthusiastically. He felt her body completely meld into his, her soft breasts pressed beneath his hard pecs, her pelvis fitting perfectly against his.

He pressed hot, wet kisses down her neck, over her clavicle and across the exposed skin on her chest. He loved these V-necked t-shirts she wore. She held onto him with a tight grasp, holding him in place, not pushing him away. Below her shirt, he could see her hard nipples poking through the thin fabric of her bra. He angled his mouth over her right breast and gently bit down, blowing a hot pulse of air out as he did. He was rewarded with a deep moan from her.

The sensation of Brian's pelvis against hers, pressing his hard cock into her and that of his lips on her were overwhelming. Brielle didn't think she'd ever been as sexually excited as she was in that moment. Her mind raced with thoughts of what making love with him would feel like. She knew that she was ready to jump off that cliff.

"I want to make love to you, Brielle Jarboe," Sherman whispered in her ear. "I need to make love to you. Let me make you feel incredible."

"I'm not on birth control," she said in a breathy voice.

"I've got a condom," he whispered.

He kissed her again, and she kissed him back. He grabbed her at her hips and walked her back towards the bed, their lips never parting. He ran his hands up her ribcage, inside her shirt. His fingers coming in contact with the satiny fabric of her bra intensified his desire. He reached behind her and unhooked it. Then he pulled her shirt and her bra over her head.

He didn't see the startled expression on her face. His eyes were affixed on her breasts. Then his lips took her left nipple while his hand felt over the other breast. "Heaven," he murmured.

Brielle laid her hands onto his shoulders. "Brian," her voice squeaked.

"Do not tell me to stop," he said, his mouth hovering over her breast. He nestled his head against her chest, both hands now caressing her breasts. "These are beautiful. You're beautiful. You have no idea how badly I want you."

"I do, because I want you too," she admitted.

Her words filled Sherman with heat and exhilaration. Euphoria surged through him. His hands went to work on unfastening her pants. As he pushed her jeans down her legs, he trailed kisses down her abdomen. He dropped to his knees to continue to peel her jeans off.

Brielle felt like she was on the edge of an orgasm just from his touch, his kisses. She wasn't sure how she'd last when he actually touched her intimately. It had been so long since she'd made love with a man. She felt him working her jeans off. She became self-conscious about her hips, her thick thighs, the fat that clung to her abdomen no matter how much she worked out.

She felt Brian wrap his arms around her hips, his hands gripping her ass cheeks. Then she felt the heat of his kiss at the apex between her legs. She sighed out loud, a breathy moan that accompanied wetness flooding her. She trembled. It wouldn't take much for her to explode. Then she felt him press open mouth kisses on her upper, inner thighs. She wanted to scream. She wanted to feel his tongue and his fingers touch her most intimate parts.

Sherman helped her step out of her blue jeans and dark green panties. His eyes viewed her dark green t-shirt and satiny bra beside them. Damn if that wasn't the best sight he'd seen in a long time, her clothes off her and on the floor. Then his eyes scanned up her body, and he knew that her body was the best sight he'd seen in a really long time.

He allowed his hands to feel over her flesh, over her muscular calves and thighs, over her ass, finally bare in all its glory for his hands and eyes to behold. He spent a few extra seconds kneading her cheeks, then he pulled himself to his feet, his eyes taking in every square inch of her torso. He felt over her breasts again. They were everything he imagined they would be. Soft, perky, her nipples the perfect shade of dusty rose.

Brielle gazed into Brian's eyes after he pulled himself to his feet. His eyes were dilated, desire beaming from them. There was no mistaking what his eyes conveyed.

"Damned, but you are the most beautiful woman I've ever been with," he whispered.

Brielle was sure she blushed deep red. Her hands shook as she pushed his t-shirt up his torso. He helped her to take it all the way off. His hands beat her to his belt. He undid his pants and pushed them down his legs, his eyes raking over her body the entire time, the thrill in him building by the second.

When he pulled her naked body against his. His flesh bristled with energy and exhilaration everywhere it touched her. He kissed her, undulating against her. His anxious cock wanted inside her, poked her lower abdomen with determination. He knew all it would take would be to bend his knees just a little and he could slide right into her. He suddenly didn't want a condom between them. He wanted nothing between them.

Brielle grasped his upper arms with determination. Her knees were weak, and her insides had turned to jelly. She kissed Brian with as much eagerness as he kissed her, the sensation of skin against skin searing her and numbing her brain.

She felt his shaft glide between her legs. It didn't penetrate her, but it rubbed against her clit. She gasped out, overpowered by the incredible desire that flooded her from it just touching her. "Condom," she moaned.

His lips pressed kisses to her neck. "Is your cycle pretty regular? Know when you're ovulating?" He whispered.

"Yes," she gasped.

"And you're not ovulating now?"

"No," she replied in a long drawn out grunt as the length of his cock slid over her clit again.

He guided her to lay on the bed, her ass hanging over the edge. He pressed an intimate kiss to her and then made love to her with his mouth until he could taste that she was reaching her peak. Just as she emitted a throaty growl, he pulled away and maneuvered between her legs, raising her pelvis to meet his, and pressing his length into her slowly. He groaned, the vise grip hot and wet around his member.

He thrust into her slowly until he was buried all the way inside her. He transferred her cheeks onto one arm and then reached up to her clit with his thumb and circled her as he drove into her repeatedly. It didn't take long for him to feel her clamp down on him, a tortuous force that made him see stars. When he felt a deluge of wetness coat his cock accompanying an agonized cry from her throat, he exploded, an orgasm so powerful he fell atop her, his knees giving out.

Brielle floated in the after bliss of their coupling, trying to catch her breath and force her eyes open. She felt him deep inside of her, throbbing. She was in no hurry to break the connection. It felt right. It felt wonderful. She felt him shift and his weight was lifted from her chest. She opened her eyes to gaze into his beautiful brown irises that were focused on her with affection.

He kissed her just as passionately as he had when their clothes were on, with hopes of getting them off. "Thank you for trusting me," he said in a soft voice. "I'll never hurt you, Brielle."

And she believed him. She wrapped her hand around his neck and pulled him in for another kiss. "You were right. I like naked snuggling even more than snuggling with you with our clothes on."

"Told you," Sherman said. He kissed her again and circled his hips, driving his still hard cock deeper within her. "I might just have to do that again. You got another of those orgasms in you?"

Brielle smiled wide. "Women always do, the question is, do you?"

"Wrap your legs around my waist," he said with a sexy grin.

She immediately did.

"Oh, yeah, that feels good," he murmured.

He knew it could go either way. His cock could calm down, but if he thrust it in and out of her enough, he could come again and satisfy both of them. He face-planted in the mattress beside her head and grabbed both of her ass cheeks in his hands. He lifted them from the mattress and kneaded them like he'd never get to touch them again. He immediately felt the anticipation of another orgasm build. He turned himself loose and drove into her with such a fury that he feared he would scare her, but he couldn't stop. It felt too good, painfully good. He knew the sounds that forced their way from his strangled throat sounded inhuman.

This time, the explosion in his brain was dizzying, flipped his whole world upside-down. He clung to her to bring himself back to consciousness. Wow. That had been the most powerful orgasm he'd ever experienced. He had no perception though if Brielle had orgasmed too or not. He was sure had she yelled for him to stop, he would have heard her, so she must not have.

He wrestled to pull himself onto his forearms. Brielle's eyes were still closed. He kissed the tip of her nose. A smile pulled at her lips. He kissed her cheek and then brought his lips to her ear. "That was so good, I think I passed out," he whispered. He watched her smile spread wider.

"I know I did," she said softly.

He noticed her chest heaved with every word.

"So, you'd maybe want to do that again sometime?"

She giggled. "Oh yeah, I would."

A warmth spread through Sherman. An image of her in his bed in his condo flashed through his mind. He wanted to make love to her in his bed just like that until neither one of them had any strength left, and then he wanted to hold her and fall asleep with her in his arms. He wanted to sit her butt-naked onto his kitchen counter and orally pleasure her until she couldn't take any more. He wanted her there with him is what became apparent to him.

"Let's shift onto this bed and let me just hold you for a little bit," Sherman said.

She pulled herself onto the bed as he withdrew from inside of her. She watched his penis come out, his unsheathed penis. "The condom? Where's the condom?"

"I didn't use one," Brian admitted. "Didn't want anything between us."

"What?" She demanded.

"I'm clean, I promise." He reclined beside her, but she sat straight up.

"Brian, you didn't pull out. You came inside me twice." She was horrified.

"If anything happens, I'll be right here with you," he offered.

"If anything happens? Like you mean if I get pregnant?" She glared at him. "Shit, I can't believe you'd do that."

"It wouldn't have felt anywhere near that good to either one of us if I'd put the condom on," Sherman said. "Besides, you said your cycle is pretty regular."

She stared at him in a panic. "I'm Catholic, Brian. If I get pregnant, I'm having a kid and I'm not ready for that yet. I just turned thirty and have only a few years to try to get my journalism career off the ground. A kid doesn't fit into that plan right now. You had no right," she said, but her words halted when Brian sat up and pinned her to the mattress in one fluid movement.

"I'm here, whatever happens. I've slept with women who mean nothing to me and always have worn a condom. I didn't want that with you because you mean something to me. You mean a lot to me. I made love to you. I didn't have sex with you."

"And if I get pregnant?"

"I'll marry you and be the best damn daddy any kid has ever had. I wouldn't be like Tina's baby daddy and not be a part of my kids' life. Hell, if you want me to, I'll marry you right now. Lambchop is our team pastor. He's married all the guys. I'll call him in here right now to officiate a ceremony."

"Right now, with us both lying here naked as the day we were born?"

A smile spread on Sherman's face. "That's right. I'm sure it would be a first for him though."

"I want a career in journalism, Brian. This story could propel me into the big leagues. I want to travel the world and write about real news stories, stories that matter. I've dreamed about it for so long."

"Then I want that for you too. Move up north with me when this is over. Chicago is a major news outlet. If this story breaks like we think it will, you can get a job with any of the networks in Chicago, I'm sure. I want you with me, Brielle."

"Leave the bayou? I always thought this would be my home base, where I'd come back to in between stories."

"I'm going to convince Bobby to stay up north with me. Come stay with us."

"I have to think about it, Brian. I can't just give you an answer to something this big without thinking about it."

"Tell me one thing. Do you want to be with me? Do you want to see where a relationship between us can go?"

A smile pulled at her lips. "Of course, I do."

"Then that's all that matters. The rest will work itself out." He pressed a kiss to her lips.

November

Sherman pulled himself from the bed. Brielle dozed. Sloan was waiting for him in the bathroom when he pulled himself out from beneath the hot downpour of the shower. "Use it now if you need to. Brielle's going to take a shower when I'm done in here. She's not quite on board with the unisex bathroom while showering."

"I imagine she needs to," Sloan said.

"What's that supposed to mean?" Sherman replied.

"FYI, the cold air return vent in your room is connected to Lambchop and Mother's room."

"Is it now?" Sherman asked, knowing they'd been heard.

"Yep, and Lambchop just got up from a nap, or rather was woken up during it."

A boyish grin pulled at Sherman's lips. "I can explain."

"You're going to have to take that up with Lambchop. He's not happy with you," Sloan said.

"Where is he?" Sherman asked. He was never one to dodge the consequences of his actions, and he didn't like the idea that he had disappointed Lambchop.

"The galley."

Sherman clasped Sloan on the shoulder. "Thanks." He dressed quickly and then he walked down the hall, heading for the door that led into the galley. Within, Lambchop stood, sipping coffee and staring out the window. "Any of that horrible coffee left?"

Lambchop turned to face him, and he could see the disapproval in Lambchop's eyes. It bothered Sherman, knowing he'd let Lambchop down. He respected his team lead immensely, both as an Operator and as a moral human being. He often wondered how Lambchop, a devout man of God, reconciled the job they did with his deep religious beliefs.

"You know where the coffee is. Go ahead and take what you want. You know how to do that well."

"It's not what you think. I'm going to marry that girl," Sherman said. "So, you better get your bible ready, maybe Sloan and I will have a double ceremony."

Lambchop's lips tugged into a grin. He never thought he'd see the day that Brian Sherman declared he was going to marry someone. "You were out of line, sleeping with her here."

Sherman's lips twisted into a frown. "Probably, but she wanted the connection as much as I did, needed it. She's tough, but not used to any of this. Seeing that guy out the window really rocked her."

Lambchop drew in a gulp of his coffee. "You find a different way to comfort her going forward. You're celibate the remainder of this mission. You got that?"

Sherman beamed a smile at Lambchop. "Yes, sir." He knew that things were okay between him and his boss.

Just before Lambchop, Mother, and Handsome headed out to surveil the Sheriff, Lambchop called Sherman out of the lounge where everyone was gathered. Cooper had just gotten up. Sloan and Madison were primary with Cooper on surveillance for the next few hours.

"You can use my tablet," Lambchop said as Sherman's was in use in the lounge. "You have a video chat with Lassiter in ten minutes."

"I do?" Sherman asked, shaking his head. "I thought we were okay."

Lambchop laid his hand on Sherman's shoulder. "We are. Just talk with Lassiter."

Brielle came into the hallway. "I'm heading to bed. Are you coming, Brian?"

Sherman's eyes flickered to Lambchop. "Not yet. Give me about a half hour then I'll be in." He'd make his video call from Sloan's room.

Brielle glanced at them both, not sure what was going on. "Okay. I'll probably be awake still."

"Remember, you're celibate going forward," Lambchop whispered.

"Yeah, I got it."

Once inside Sloan's room, Sherman activated the link to enable the video chat with Lassiter. He wasn't clear on why he had to talk with the good doctor, but Lambchop said he had to, and he had the rank to order it.

"Hi Joe," Sherman greeted him when Lassiter's scarred face appeared.

Joe nodded and smiled. "Sherman, creating a few issues for Lambchop, are you?"

Sherman shrugged. "Not intentionally." He beamed a smile at Lassiter. "I can't help that this woman got to me like she did."

"You're going to marry her, huh?"

"Trust me, I'm more surprised than anyone," Sherman replied. "But I'm not about to make the same mistake Sloan almost did. I like this girl and am not going to let her get away without exploring what a relationship with her would be like. I've already asked her to move in with me when this is over."

"And is she going to?"

"She said she had to think about it, but I think she will. She's on the same page as me."

"You also have your brother to consider."

"As far as Brielle is concerned, as long as I'm good to her, he's fine with me pursuing her."

"That's not what I meant," Lassiter said. "You've also taken his recovery on as your responsibility, emotionally and financially."

"The way I see it, I have no other choice. He's family, Joe, and where I come from family is everything. It doesn't matter what it costs. I have plenty put away and earn a good paycheck doing this job."

"And if Brielle moves in with you, you're taking on getting her established in a new town, too. That's a lot for a man who's had no responsibilities to anyone besides his team."

Sherman laughed. "I don't see it that way, as a responsibility. I see it more as a gift I am able to give, a hand up for Bobby. He's a smart kid, capable of doing a lot more than he has so far in life. I think getting him out of the bayou is the best thing for him. He can get a job up there far easier than he can in the Parish with his reputation and history down here."

"And Brielle?"

"If this story gives her the big break she's looking for in journalism, Chicago is a better market to pursue it in. I just want the opportunity with her to see if we can work out. I don't understand why any of this bothers Lambchop or Cooper."

"They care about you, Sherman, just want to be sure you're not getting buried beneath responsibilities and demands on you that could cripple you."

Sherman laughed. "Then neither of them knows me well at all, if they'd think that. And I thought this was because Lambchop was pissed that I slept with Brielle here, during the mission."

"Not pissed, concerned. I don't need to tell you that you have a reputation with the ladies, but you've never let that side show itself during a mission. The fact you went there with this woman caused Lambchop to be very concerned about you."

"Is he doubting my professionalism, doing the job?"

"He's worried you're emotionally involved and will lose your edge."

Sherman laughed aloud. "Yes, you better believe I'm emotionally involved, but if anything, that will keep me sharp. This bastard Sheriff has been harassing Brielle for months. He or his deputy laid hands on my brother while he was in custody, and I was harassed from the second the Sheriff met me. This guy is as dirty as they come, and he's going down. And I'll make sure of it."

Lassiter nodded. "Okay, it doesn't get any more personal or emotional than that."

"Lassiter, you have to understand. This asshole came into the bayou, my home. He's not from down here. He doesn't get to do what he's been doing. Not him, not the mayor of Galliano, not the fuckers out at that BioDynamix facility, especially not them, using cancer research as a cover. None of those people are from the bayou. They are outsiders who came down here to take advantage, to commit a crime, or do whatever the hell it is they are up to."

Lassiter considered Brian Sherman's words and the emotion that was evident as he said them. He knew Sherman's mother died from cancer. He had a very personal reason for being so incensed that cancer research was being used as the cover for something that they were all sure was illegal. "Fair enough. Keep your emotions in check and be cognizant of what you're feeling. It can be a help to keep your edge or a hinderance that will interfere with your effectiveness in doing the job. That's all up to you."

"I understand, Joe. You'll sanction me to continue?"

Lassiter's lips twisted into a grin. "I see no reason to stop you. And I look forward to meeting your lady when this is over."

Sherman smiled wide. "I will gladly introduce you to her. She's something special."

Lassiter nodded. "She must be."

When Sherman entered his and Brielle's room, she was already asleep. He slid in beside her and reveled in the sensation of holding her. She was his girl, and that realization was powerful. He hadn't been lying when he told Lambchop and Lassiter that he was going to marry her. He'd never thought that about any other woman, ever.

The next two days, the team monitored their surveillance equipment on rotating shifts. A trip was made up the bayou to change the batteries in their cameras across from the BioDynamix building. Sherman along with Mother and Handsome made that happen without incident.

They continued to watch the Sheriff as well. His meeting had been at the Galliano Airport. Photos of the man he met with were sent to HQ. That man flew out on a Cessna immediately after the meeting. Photos of the plane were also sent to HQ, but so far, there was no info on either the man or the plane. The number on the plane wasn't registered to that model plane. It had been altered.

The digital team at HQ were busy and made some real progress. As Garcia always said, follow the money. They did and found the origin of the money that biweekly deposited into a New Jersey account that paid the workers. It funneled through several accounts, but Garcia was, with a little less than legal hacking, able to trace it back to the corporation that Dwayne Stuart's Gentlemen's clubs were under. It wouldn't stand up in court, but it answered a lot of questions and helped to connect the dots.

They had not managed to hack into the BioDynamix network. There was robust firewalling. They still had no idea what was going on at the BioDynamix plant. They suspected drug manufacturing, but without shipments of anything going out and what appeared to only be food coming in twice a week, they couldn't prove it or even confirm it.

Besides the less than enthusiastic employees coming and going from work each day, two other suspicious things were identified. One was Sheriff Henderson's police cruiser pulling right into the warehouse of the plant every day. Even on the footage captured by Brielle's camera for the past two weeks, Sheriff Henderson made a visit and drove right in through the large garage door beside the dock that opened as he approached. He came at different times. There were no phone calls made to or from him arranging the visits on his phone they had tapped into.

Each day when he left, he went right back to the police station. No side trips, no stops, no phone calls.

The second suspicious occurrence was the housing in the trailers. The first row of five trailers had no Chinese in them, except one in the middle. It housed one Chinese man, who they identified as the man who had stepped out back during the rainstorm to have a smoke with Mike Spencer. The three gate guards lived in one of them. Mike Spencer in a third, two other white men they had no ID on in the fourth, three other men, two Hispanic and one black man, who they had no ID on were housed in the fifth. They assumed these men to be the management.

The remainder of the trailers housed Chinese men and women. Five of the trailers in the next row each housed four Chinese men, all who were armed. The ten remaining trailers housed who they assumed to be the workers, four to a trailer. Forty women in all. If the Parish workers appeared frightened or unenthusiastic, these women could only be described as zombies. How they entered and exited their trailers at shift change, accompanied by armed guards, could only be described as the movements of inmates in a maximum-security prison.

The team decided it was time to approach Tina Landry.

The SUV pulled up in front of Tina Landry's four room clapboard home. The front drapes were drawn, but it was obvious that she was home. Her car sat in her driveway, and her front door was open. Cooper turned in his seat to view Brielle, who sat in the middle of the backseat between Sherman and Sloan. Lambchop sat in the front passenger seat beside him. "Remember, don't tell her too much, just enough to get her to agree to help us."

Brielle nodded. "She needs to know that BioDynamix is under investigation by federal authorities. If she thinks she won't have a job much longer, I think she'll be more apt to cooperate."

"I doubt any of the Parish workers at that plant know what's going on there," Sherman said. "The most we can hope for is that she'll agree to plug in that flash drive for us."

"We'll see," Cooper said. He got out of the car.

The others followed. Brielle slid out behind Brian. Landon stayed in front of her, sandwiching her between the two men. She had the ballcap on, and even though it was dark out, her sunglasses. When they reached the front door, the men stepped back, allowing Brielle to be in the doorway.

Glancing in, she saw Tina's son, Toby, seated on the floor watching cartoons on the television. His hair had gotten longer since Brielle had seen him last. He had an adorable mop of curly black hair atop his head. Tina was in the kitchen area, which shared the front room of the house with the living room. She was at the stove, her back to the door.

Brielle removed her sunglasses. She tried the door handle. It was unlocked. She opened the door and went in. The men followed her and closed the front door once they were all inside. The small room was suddenly crowded.

"Bree-bree," Toby squealed in delight.

Tina turned, and a horrified expression fixed on her face. She rushed to her son and lifted him from the floor. She held him tightly to herself. "What are you doing here?"

The four men from Shepherd Security displayed their badges. "Federal authorities," Cooper said.

"You?" Tina Landry questioned, her eyes going between Cooper and Sherman. "You came into work."

"Tina, it's okay," Brielle said. "These men are here to protect us. We need to talk."

"I can't say anything," Tina said.

"Then just listen," Sherman said. "Tina, you know who I am, don't you?"

Tina nodded, still clutching her son in her arms.

"I'm from the Parish, a Cajun, and proud of it. I'm also a federal agent and we're down here investigating that BioDynamix facility you work at. We're convinced there is something very illegal going on inside that place."

"Your NDA isn't going to mean anything when these guys close that plant down," Brielle said. "I know you're afraid of getting fired, and that's why you won't talk to me about it."

Tina Landry closed her eyes and shook her head. "I'm legitimately afraid of them, not just of getting fired. We all are."

"Then why haven't you quit?" Brielle asked.

"I'm afraid to," Tina said. "Bradley Johnson quit and then he died in a car accident the next day. I don't think it was an accident."

The men from Shepherd Security exchanged glances. Brielle wasn't sure what that meant. Did they believe Tina?

"What's going on inside that plant?" Cooper asked.

Tina shook her head. "I don't know. They say we do cancer research there and that's why everything is hush-hush, but I don't believe that."

"What can you tell us about the Chinese living in those trailers?" Cooper asked.

"Nothing. We don't ever cross paths with them. They have their own entrance into the plant that they come and go through. They aren't in the lunchroom when any of us are. They even have their own bathrooms. There is one plant window I can look in once in a while when I'm near the lunchroom and I see them up in their workspace, what we call the tower, but I can't tell what they're doing. There's lab equipment, and it's a sterile room. They wear protective clothing. That's all I know."

"You're the front desk receptionist. What do the others do there who were hired from the Parish?" Sherman asked.

"Some maintain the grounds, cut the grass and such. Others are janitors, keep the inside clean. Jorie Newton and Chris Fischer are the only two who clean in the tower, but they're even more afraid than I am. They won't talk to you, so don't even try. About five others are the maintenance and HVAC mechanics. They employ another six in the food service area, got a full cafeteria going. I think it's to feed the Chinese workers from the trailers. The Halliday sisters and Bev Oakdie are in the accounting department, responsible for us getting paid."

"Do you fill out an on-line timecard?" Sherman asked.

Tina nodded.

He pulled the flash drive from his pocket. "We need you to insert this flash drive into a network computer."

"No, they'll know I did it."

"If you insert it right before you leave for the night, we won't activate it until you are out of that facility and in our protective custody. We'll keep you and your son safe," Sherman guaranteed her.

Tina's eyes darted to Brielle. "Please don't ask me to do this."

"There's no one else who can," Brielle said. "Tina, you know Sheriff Henderson has made my life hell since my first post on BioDynamix. He's helping them to do something illegal. I'm sure of it."

"They make us leave our stuff in lockers when we enter, even our phones. We have to use company phones, even for me to touch bases with my sitter. I know they are monitoring all our communications, probably even listening into our conversations in the lunchroom which are few and far between. Everyone is afraid to say anything. We go through what looks like an x-ray machine at the airport when we leave or enter the locker room. What if they find that flash drive on me?"

"Then you claim ignorance on how it got in your pocket. Let them suspect one of your coworkers of slipping it there, or even us," Lambchop said.

"Don't insert this into your own computer but find one that anyone would have access to and insert it into that one," Sherman said.

"What will it do?" Tina asked.

"Give us access to their network so we can see what they're really up to," Cooper said.

Tina took the flash drive from Sherman. She nodded. "Tomorrow?"

"Yes, at the end of your shift. We'll wait till we see your car drive out of the parking lot before we activate it. Go directly to your sitter and pick up your son. And then drive up to New Orleans." Sherman paused and produced a slip of paper from his pocket. "This is the address to the regional FBI office. They'll be expecting you. They will put you up in a hotel and keep you and your son protected until this is over."

Tina nodded. Her eyes went to Brielle. "You're sure about this?"

Brielle stepped forward and wrapped Tina in an embrace. "I trust these men, Tina. And I know that there is something very illegal going on at that plant. This is the only way for them to get the proof."

"We'll also look into Bradley Johnson's death," Cooper said. "The more charges against them, the better."

"Thank you," Tina said. "I think they killed him."

"One more thing," Cooper said. "Who are their IT guys? Do you have any names we can run?"

Tina shook her head. "I know there has to be someone who takes care of all the computers, but I've never seen or met anyone. If we have a technology problem, we open a ticket. We never actually speak to anyone. A few months ago, I accidently spilled a bottle of water on my keyboard. I dumped it, but the keys stopped working. I put a ticket in. It was Mike Spencer, the head of security, who brought me a new keyboard and told me not to drink anything at my desk ever again. He may have acted pleasant when you came to the office the other day, but he's not a nice man. I steer clear of him."

"Thank you, Tina," Cooper said.

"Be safe." Brielle gave her a final hug and stepped back.

"Keep your place locked up tonight and have your bags packed and in the trunk of your car when you leave for work tomorrow," Sherman said. "That phone number below the address is to our Operations Center, manned around the clock. If you feel threatened at any point, call it and identify yourself. They'll send help."

Oscar

ina had not slept well. She was not only nervous, but exhausted when she went to work the next morning. She'd packed a small bag with her and Toby's things and placed it in the trunk before she even woke Toby up to get him ready for daycare.

Her anxiety multiplied after she dropped him at the sitter and drove to work. She parked in the offsite lot ten minutes earlier than normal. There were only a few other cars in the lot, their drivers still seated within them. No one tended to get out of their cars until the bus was seen driving up the long driveway towards the gate. She fingered the flash drive in the deep pocket of her favorite black pants, praying the x-ray machine wouldn't detect it.

She had a hard time breathing as the bus neared the building. She followed the others off the bus and went right into the locker room, where she stowed her purse in her locker. Then she waited in line to go through the doorway that they all knew was an x-ray machine. No alarms ever went off, but she knew Mike Spencer had paid others a visit shortly after they arrived in their work area and questioned them about pocket contents. She'd heard he'd even physically searched a few people.

She went to her desk and got busy with her normal morning work, waiting, worrying that Mike Spencer would suddenly appear. Thankfully, he never did. The day went by without incident and she relaxed until the end of the day neared and she would have to plant the flash drive.

She'd already decided that she would put it into the freestanding PC within the locker room. She knew it was on the network as some people would use it to submit their timecard on the way out of the building. Others used it to surf the web over lunch. It was one of the few computers that could be used to access the outside internet.

After she'd shut her own PC down and tidied her desk, she walked into the locker room and grabbed her purse from her locker. She lingered by the PC, which sat in the far corner away from the door and figured she could lean against it and slip the flash drive in, unseen by her coworkers. Her hand shook as she grabbed it from her pocket. She took a deep breath and inserted the small flash drive into the computer.

Then she stepped away from the PC and made her way through the tangle of bodies in the room and exited into the hallway. People still lined the hallway, waiting for the bus. She gazed out the window and saw it hadn't arrived yet. It was late. It normally sat there right at five-thirty, when they all got off work. Of all days for it to be late! All she wanted to do was get out of that building and go get Toby.

The bus pulled up at five-thirty-five. She breathed out a sigh of relief and stepped towards the outer door. She was nearly out the door when she felt a hand grab her shoulder from behind. She turned her head to see Mike Spencer behind her.

"A word, please, Tina," he said pleasantly. He pulled her into the alcove near the door where another man waited, a man she'd never seen before. He had dark red hair and wore glasses. "We'll be taking these," Spencer said, taking her car keys from her hand. He handed them to the other man. "Pull her car around to the north access road and keep it hidden beneath the trees."

The man nodded and stepped away. He exited the building with the other employees and boarded the bus. Only a few of the employees were left in the hallway, filing out the door. Her eyes went to them, and she contemplated screaming out for help. It was as though Mike Spencer could read her mind.

"Don't do it," he warned. He showed her a gun he pulled from under his shirt, which had been stuck in the front of his pants. "No one, including you, has to get hurt. I just need some answers."

After the others were all gone, and the bus pulled away, Spencer led her back into the plant, through doors she'd never gone through. Before she knew it, he opened a door at the base of what she and the others called the tower, the three-story building within the building that was nestled against the old brick structure.

Those monitoring the satellite feed from both HQ and at the Coast Guard building at Port Fourchon, watched intently as the Parish workers filed out of the building and boarded the bus, as they did every day at five-thirty-five on the dot. They watched the bus drive down the long drive and through the gate which opened as they approached. It pulled into the small parking lot thirty feet past the gate guard's small structure. They watched the workers get into their cars and then the cars, one by one, pulled out of the lot.

"Okay, she's away. I'm activating the flash drive now," Garcia said. He clicked a few keys and navigated his way through several menus. "I'm in. They have a partitioned network, administration and finance is open." He clicked while remaining silent for two full minutes. "I'm copying the data now." He initiated the command to run the script to copy all the files. "Now I'm trying to gain access to the rest of their network. They have some robust firewalling, so give me a few minutes. I want to get access to their security cameras next."

Brielle's fascinated gaze was fixed on the monitor; a mirror image of what Garcia was working on. She saw one side of the screen showing file after file being copied, the names of each file flashing briefly as the program worked through each file on that portion of the network. The other side of the screen showed Garcia's attempts to breach the other half of the network.

They waited in silence and watched for nearly an hour while Garcia tried everything possible to gain access to the second side of the network. Finally, through a file on the admin side, which Garcia determined was accessible from the other firewalled side of the network, Garcia was able to hack his way in. He brought up the camera feeds, thirty in all. Ten were exterior views. He flipped right through them, concentrating on the interior feeds.

The cameras that showed hallways, showed empty hallways. The two cameras that were within the warehouse showed a vacant space. Another camera was focused on the empty lobby, Tina Landry's reception desk clearly and purposely in the camera's eye. The same held true for the cameras that monitored an office that they all assumed was where the finance people sat, the girls who ran payroll and entered purchase orders.

Two cameras covered the kitchen and cafeteria areas. They were placed to observe the people. There was no other possible motive for the way in which the cameras were positioned.

"I guess Tina was right. The workers were being observed every second," Brielle said.

Two cameras in the worker's locker room covered all of it. And those in the bathrooms were the most disturbing. The placement of the cameras in the ceiling gave the users of the bathrooms no privacy. Finally, Garcia accessed the camera feed within a room of workers cloaked in protective clothing. It was a lab of some sort.

"There has to be a dozen workers in that room," Madison said. There was equipment everyone from Shepherd Security recognized from the many drug busts they'd conducted on manufacturing labs.

"What are they doing?" Brielle asked.

"Making drugs. Legal or illegal is the question," Madison said.

"Can you zoom in closer on what they're doing, Garcia?" Cooper asked.

"Negative, not unless I want to alert someone to the fact that they've been hacked. Observing is one thing, taking control is another."

Just then, Brielle's phone rang. It was a local Parish number that she didn't recognize. She glanced at Madison. "That's odd. I don't know this number."

"Answer it," Madison prompted. She leaned with her ear near the phone as Brielle hit accept call and brought the phone to her own ear.

"Hello."

"Brielle? This is Darcy Sanders, Toby Landry's babysitter."

"Yes, this is Brielle."

"I hate to bother you, but Tina is over an hour late to pick him up and she's not answering her phone."

"She didn't?" Brielle asked, her eyes going to Madison and then Cooper.

"It normally wouldn't be a problem for me to keep Toby longer, but I have to leave in a half hour. I have an appointment I can't postpone."

"Tell her you'll pick Toby up before she has to leave," Madison whispered. She turned to Cooper, who barely heard the call from where he sat. "Tina never picked her son up from the sitter."

Immediately, Cooper transmitted this information to Garcia and whoever else was listening in at Ops. He brought the feed back up of the workers leaving the BioDynamix facility and reviewed it.

"I know where you live. I'll be there to get Toby before you have to leave. Thanks for calling me," Brielle said into the phone.

"I hope everything is alright with Tina."

"I'm sure it is," Brielle said, knowing she was lying. She disconnected the call and her eyes locked with Madison's.

"We'll have Burke bring you to get the child," Cooper said. "You'll bring him back here and we'll find Tina." He called Burke, who he knew was in the galley. "We need you back in the lounge."

Cooper advanced the filmed footage of the employees leaving, frame by frame. Garcia did the same at HQ. "That wasn't Tina Landry driving her car out of the lot. It was a man."

"A man with dark red hair," Garcia added. "Sounds familiar, doesn't it?"

Burke entered the lounge and came up to see what was on the monitor that everyone in the room was clustered around. After he was brought up to speed on the developments, he and Brielle left to go get Toby from his babysitter.

It took only seconds to secure the babysitter's spare car seat into the rental car. They were only back on the road, pointed south for five minutes when Toby fell asleep. "This can't be good," Burke said.

"What is it?" Brielle asked. She saw Rich's eyes fixed on the rearview mirror. She turned in her seat and looked out the back of the car. It was a sight she was familiar with, police lights. "You've got to be freaking kidding me!"

"I wasn't going over the speed limit, have done nothing illegal."

"That's been the story of my life for months," Brielle complained as she watched Rich pull the car over to the side of the road.

The police cruiser pulled up behind them. She watched in the side mirror as Sheriff Henderson and Deputy Downey both got out. The Sheriff had his hand on his gun as he walked up to the driver's side. Brielle's eyes locked with Deputy Downey when he reached her side of the car.

Burke hit the button and lowered his window. "Is there a problem, Sheriff? I'm sure I wasn't speeding."

Sheriff Henderson peered into the car, as did Downey on the other side. Downey saw Burke's sidearm. "Gun! On his right hip."

"Let me see your hands, boy!" The Sheriff yelled at Burke as he drew his own weapon.

Burke raised his hands. "Let me show you my credentials. I'm FBI."

"Slowly, get out of the car," the Sheriff ordered.

Burke stuck his hands out of the window and opened the car door from the outside. He moved very slowly. Sheriff Henderson turned him to face the car, body slammed him into the back-passenger door, and took the gun from its holster at his waist.

"Badge and creds are in the wallet, back left pocket," Burke said.

The Sheriff took the wallet from his pocket. He flipped it open and saw the badge. "What the fuck are you doing in my jurisdiction?"

"Sorry, Sheriff, that's classified."

"Oh hell," Henderson swore. He nodded to Downey.

"Out of the car, Brielle," Downey ordered.

She glanced behind her at Toby, sitting in his car seat in the middle of the backseat. "You do see the baby in the backseat? Right?"

Downey opened her car door. "Out of the car."

Brielle released her seatbelt and came to her feet. Deputy Downey took her by the arm and turned her, so she faced the car. She faced Rich.

"Hands on the car."

She placed them on the roof. She knew what was coming, an intimate pat down. Downey had stopped her dozens of times since she wrote that first article on BioDynamix. A fondling always followed him pulling her from the car.

"You got a gun on you? Any knives, needles, or other sharp objects?"

"You know I don't, asshole!"

A small grin curved Downey's lips. "Keep your hands on the car," he ordered, and then he began the pat down. He started up at her shoulders, felt over her back and sides. Then his hands slid to the front, and he groped over her breasts, slid his hands down her abdomen and over the front of her jeans. His touch moved to her hips, around to her lower back, and then lingered for too long on her ass. One hand then slid down between her legs. He ended his inspection by groping both hands over each leg, ending with his hand wrapped around to the front of her, and reaching between her legs. As always, he gave her pussy a squeeze.

"Hope you enjoyed that," Brielle said. "It's the last time you'll ever get to do it."

"Why is that?" Henderson asked.

"Because I'm moving up north," Brielle said. "Just down here to pack up my stuff."

"The baby is your stuff?" Downey asked.

"No, his momma didn't pick him up from the babysitter after work and I'm an emergency contact. I think something happened to her. You wouldn't know anything about that, would you, Sheriff?" Brielle said accusingly.

A smirk formed on Henderson's face. His eyes shifted to Burke. "And you need an FBI Agent on a classified assignment to help pack your stuff and pick up Tina's baby?"

"So, you know he's Tina's?" Burke questioned.

"I know everyone in my Parish," the Sheriff insisted.

"Would you know where Tina Landry is?" Burke asked, not expecting a reply.

"I'm done dealing with you and your shit, Brielle," Henderson said. He nodded to Downey. "Put her in the backseat and keep your gun on her. You want to know more about that BioDynamix facility? Let me show you." He pulled Burke from the car and pushed him towards the driver's door. Then he opened the back door, keeping his gun in Burke's back. After Brielle was seated in the backseat and the door was closed, he motioned for Burke to get in. "Real easy, and I'm keeping this gun on you. My deputy is covering pain-in-the-ass-Brielle and neither of us will hesitate to shoot."

Burke considered his options. He didn't have many with Brielle and the baby in the line of fire. As he eased his way into the car, he turned his head and tapped his comms, stuck in his ear canal, activating the two-way mode so he would transmit. "There's no reason to shoot anyone, Sheriff. We're cooperating."

"Good boy," the Sheriff said.

Burke wanted to shoot this jackass, just for calling him 'boy'. "You do realize I am a federal agent and you're stepping way outside the law, Sheriff."

"Shut the fuck up and drive," Henderson ordered.

"You want me to drive to the BioDynamix facility?" Burke said for the benefit of whoever at the Coast Guard command center would be listening.

Henderson glanced at Downey. "Follow us." Then he locked his eyes with Burke's, in the rearview mirror. "My gun is on Brielle. I've shot others for being less of a pain in my ass than she's been. Don't try anything. Do exactly what I tell you or I'll off her, then my gun goes on the baby."

"No need for any of that Sheriff. So, BioDynamix, is it?"

"Yes."

At the Coast Guard facility, Sherman was woken by the door bursting open and the overhead lights switching on. He opened his eyes and sat straight up in bed. Cooper didn't even need to speak. The look on his face told Sherman something was very wrong.

"The Sheriff has Burke and Brielle. He's taking them to BioDynamix. Full tactical gear, ARs, flash-bangs, we go in with everything."

Sherman jumped out of bed. "How the fuck did that happen?"

"Don't know. Burke activated his comms after they'd already been stopped, and things had transpired. The first words we heard was Burke telling the Sheriff there was no reason to shoot anyone."

"What the hell were they doing outside of this facility?"

"Tina Landry didn't pick her son up from daycare. Brielle is the emergency contact," Cooper reported.

Sherman immediately began dressing in his black fatigues. "You should have woken me to go out with her." He guessed it was Burke's inexperience that caused him to not activate his comms sooner. Son-of-a-bitch! "Did HQ come through with the building schematics on that facility yet?"

"Not yet, but Garcia is now hacking into the architect's network, hoping they're on file there, since they aren't in the Parish's building and inspection department files where they should be. We hope to have something before we go in."

Then Cooper left the open doorway, and he repeated his waking and alert in Lambchop and Mother's room, followed by Doc's. Within the door to Sloan's room, he saw he was changing into his fatigues and gearing up.

Madison appeared in the hallway. "All monitoring has transferred to Ops at HQ and they are watching Burke's tracker. I've notified the Coast Guard we'll need a chopper. They will have a pilot on standby. I have an aerial map of the BioDynamix facility and the vicinity up for our briefing. Shepherd and HQ is analyzing it as well and will be on while we plan our mission."

Cooper nodded. "Good, thanks for handling all that." Then he joined Madison in their room. The two of them also dressed in their tactical gear.

When both the vehicles arrived at the guarded gate to BioDynamix, the Sheriff rolled his window down to talk with the gate guard, who waved them through after a brief discussion. The Sheriff then ordered Burke to pull up to the big garage door at the shipping and receiving dock. The second door held no dock, just an entrance into the garage area.

The massive garage door opened, and Burke drove in, followed by Downey in the Sheriff's car, which had remained behind them. Burke hoped like hell that the satellite feed was being monitored at HQ and this entrance into the building was seen. In the very least, with his broadcast over his comms, his tracker should be watched, so HQ would know where they were.

Burke had a spare weapon in his boot, his little snub-nose .38. The Sheriff had not thoroughly searched him, not like Downey had searched Brielle, which bordered on criminal, the way he groped her. When this was over, he personally would punch the Deputy for his treatment of her. He wouldn't tell Sherman about it, as he believed Sherman would probably kill the man.

Deputy Downey came up to Brielle's door, weapon drawn, and ordered her to take the toddler out of his car seat and exit the vehicle. He was asleep and didn't wake when Brielle picked him up. She cradled him over her shoulder. He was dead weight in her arms, but she was glad he was asleep.

"You stay still, boy, till I tell you to get out," the Sheriff said. He opened his door and got out; weapon trained on Burke. "Okay, now nice and easy."

Burke got out of the car, his eyes scanning his surroundings. He was careful to keep the ear with his comms in it angled away from the two men. They were alone in the garage. If they remained alone and he could somehow get the drop on the Sheriff and the Deputy, he and Brielle could make a break for it. The gate hadn't looked that strong. They could ram it. The one thing he did not want to happen was for them to be brought deeper within the facility.

Just then, the man both Brielle and Burke recognized from his photo as Mike Spencer, though they knew that to be a stolen identity, exploded through the doorway into the room. Three armed Chinese men were behind him.

"Why the hell did you bring them here?" Spencer demanded.

"We deal with them here and now and end this," Sheriff Henderson said. He handed Burke's badge and creds to Spencer. "We have ourselves another fed. First Brian Sherman and his girlfriend, now this asshole."

Spencer's eyes scanned Burke's identification and then him. Then his eyes went back to Henderson. "A fed? You propose we kill a fucking fed? The Landry woman and this so-called reporter," he said, pointing at Brielle, "is one thing. We can make their death's look like an accident, drunk driving right into the bayou, but a fed? How the fuck do you suggest we cover that up?"

"The gators have to eat, don't they? And the poor FBI Agent wandering around in the bayou who didn't know the dangers. What a shame!" The Sheriff said.

"At the same time the ladies have their little accident? That's a hell of a coincidence to sell," Spencer said.

"I'm the Sheriff. I can sell anything."

Brielle clutched Toby more tightly to her chest. "No one will ever believe it, any of it. Do you think he's down here without his partner? And that his partner doesn't know that the two of us went to get Toby?"

"QBZ-95-1 assault rifles in the hands of three Chinese men. I find that fucking interesting," Burke said for the benefit of the team listening in. "Once it's noticed I'm missing, you're going to be swarmed by federal authorities. It's over. If I were you, I'd pack up and hightail it to a country with no extradition to the U.S."

"Shut the fuck up!" The Sheriff leaned into Burke's face as he spoke.

"Did you search them?" Spencer asked, ignoring both Brielle and Burke.

The Sheriff nodded. "Took this off the fed." He handed Spencer Burke's .9 mm.

"Where are their phones?"

"Brielle's is in her back pocket, right side," Downey said.

"His is in the cup holder in the car," the Sheriff added.

"They're on? You left their phones on to ping off the closest tower near here?" Spencer demanded.

He crossed to the car and pulled Burke's phone from inside. Downey took Brielle's from her pocket and handed it to Spencer too.

Spencer held them both up. "Does it strike anyone else as odd that they have identical phones?" His head snapped to Brielle. "I know you had an iPhone and I know the damn thing is still pinging off towers near Chicago." He turned both their phones off and slid them into his pants pockets.

Brielle didn't answer. She stared at him, fear surging through her. Brian had been right. Her phone was being tracked. She wondered how long they'd been watching her. Did they know about the camera she had on the building? And her late-night visit to break into this facility?

"The west coast batch is ready," Spencer said to the Sheriff. He pointed to two large suitcases that were parked near the door Spencer had entered through.

Downey went to them and rolled them over to the Sheriff's car. He popped the trunk open and placed the two suitcases into it.

"We're all going to walk to a special interrogation room I have set up, that you're not going to like. You have the next few minutes to think about how cooperative you're going to be when we get there. You're going to die today, but how much pain you feel before and during it, is up to you. I can make it easy on you, or I can make it crueler than your worst nightmare. The choice is yours."

Brielle's grasp tightened on Toby. She gazed at his head full of black curls. "Where's Tina?"

"She's there. She hasn't been very cooperative, either that or she really doesn't know much besides a couple of federal agents asked her to place the flash drive into one of our computers." He paused and shook his head. "It doesn't matter much." He pointed to the door he'd come through. "Now move."

Brielle glanced back at Rich. He nodded. She followed one of the Chinese men, armed with an assault rifle.

"We're leaving now. Notify me when it's done," Sheriff Henderson said.

"Fucking coward," Spencer spat. "I'll notify you all right." Then his gaze landed on Burke. "You too, move." When Burke passed Spencer, he was stopped by him. "What the fuck?" Spencer said. He pulled the earbud out of Burke's ear, examined it, dropped it, and stomped on it.

"The FBI will bill you for that," Burke said.

"Move," Spencer repeated.

Sherman knew he had to be cool and professional. He reigned in his emotions, which wanted to demand they leave with no plan, bust in there and kill everyone but Brielle, Burke, the baby and his momma, if she was still alive. He reaffixed his eyes to Shepherd on the monitor.

"The FBI out of New Orleans have been called in to go after Sheriff Henderson and Deputy Downey. They have left the facility. They're not our mission. Getting inside, acquiring the location of Burke, Brielle Jarboe, and Tina Landry and her son, is our mission. Neutralize all threats. We still have no schematics. If we get any before you get onsite, we'll transmit them," Shepherd said.

"Will we have any backup onsite?" Lambchop asked.

"Yes. There are a dozen agents with the DEA in the port area. They will drive up to the BioDynamix facility. We time our assault, waiting until after they arrive in the area. They will hold position on the road a quarter mile from the facility. After we are onsite, they will remain outside of the building after you breach it as backup if you need them. They aren't trained for what you'll be doing, so I don't want them to enter the building when you do," Shepherd advised.

"We have a Coast Guard chopper on standby," Cooper said. "We'll drop a small inflatable boat and Lambchop, Mother, and Sherman from the chopper into the bayou here." He pointed out the wide spot in the channel about a mile from the BioDynamix building that would easily accommodate the width of the rotors. "Then we drop the Undertaker here," he pointed out on the map. "He makes his way as close to the gate guard as he can, to take him out. Once he's neutralized, the chopper will fly in over the top of the building and drop Doc here, on the southwest corner of the roof, near the trailers to provide us cover. Then it will briefly land here, to drop Madison and me. By that time, the Undertaker makes his way up to the chopper and the three of us breach the front of the building as the rest of Delta Team breaches it from the back. Doc, you're Overwatch for this mission."

Doc nodded. "Forty trailers, probably one hundred sixty people max."

"Yeah, but don't forget, we believe the majority of the workers are slave-labor. Probably not armed," Cooper reminded him.

"I've been monitoring Burke's transmissions over his comms and the camera feed from inside the target building," Garcia's voice broke in. "The Sheriff turned Burke and Brielle over to Spencer and three, armed Chinese males. Spencer discovered Burke's comms, and it is no longer transmitting. I can give you an approximate location within the building where they are at based on Burke's tracker signal. There is no camera footage I can find from inside to tell me where they were brought to."

"Mission plan approved," Shepherd said. "Ops will direct. Go get our people!"

With every step Brielle took, her panic intensified. When the man in front of her opened the door into what she saw was a small room, she froze, unable to step forward.

"Inside," Spencer's voice said sharply. He was still behind them. When she didn't move, he came up beside her and grabbed her by the arm. He pulled her into the room.

To the right of the door sat Tina, who looked horrified to see them, especially her little boy, still asleep in Brielle's arms. She had several bruises on her face. She came to her feet. Brielle rushed over and Tina took Toby from her arms. "Are you okay?" Brielle whispered. The look on Tina's face and her nonresponse told Brielle she wasn't. She saw terror in Tina's eyes.

Two of the Chinese men pushed Burke into a chair where they wrestled with him and shackled his hands to the table.

Spencer pulled a second chair out. "This seat is for you, Ms. Jarboe."

Brielle watched him. His face was cold, unemotional.

"What happens in this room is up to you. If you cooperate, I won't hurt you, too much."

"But you're planning to kill us all." Brielle heard Tina's sharp intake of air accompanied by a whimper. She glanced at Tina, who held Toby in a fierce hug.

The unmistakable sound of someone getting punched brought Brielle's attention back to Spencer. Burke was just bringing his head back forward, his lip now split and bleeding. "Each time you fail to cooperate someone gets hurt, the degree of the wounds increasing with each occurrence," Spencer said.

Brielle forced herself to cross the room and take a seat in the chair. "I'll cooperate. What do you want to know?"

"Good choice," Spencer said. "Now, where's his partner?"

Brielle's eyes flickered to Rich. He shook his head no. "Port Fourchon. There is a DEA office there."

"How'd you know?"

"Know what?" Brielle asked.

"About the heroin stickers?"

"We didn't know for sure this was drug related. It was a guess. I just knew something was off and the more I looked into it and wrote posts about this place, which caused the Sheriff to harass me more with each article, the more convinced I became. I watched this place for weeks. I saw no real supplies coming in or out of here. No one would talk to me about their job here, except Brad Johnson, the day before he quit. When you killed him, that's when I approached the feds for help. I met with the FBI in New Orleans." No, she had never spoken with Bradley Johnson about BioDynamix, nor had she approached anyone for help.

The corners of Spencer's lips tugged into a scowl. "You seem to know a lot more than we thought you did."

With that statement, Brielle knew they had killed Brad Johnson. She hadn't known him well, but none-the-less, Spencer's confirmation angered her and increased her fear. She prayed to God that someone from either Port Fourchon or the Shepherd Security office in Chicago had been watching the camera feeds and saw that they had been brought here. She prayed someone was on their way to rescue them. If she could stall Spencer long enough for them to get there, just maybe, they would be rescued before they were killed.

"Where does Bobby and Brian Sherman fit in?"

"The FBI listened to my story and said they would investigate, but I didn't have a smoking gun, no real proof. That was when I decided to break in here and try to get that proof for them. The Sherman brothers really didn't have much to do with any of it. When I broke into this place last week, Bobby was a decoy to throw the Sheriff off, so I could get away. That was the extent of his involvement and I didn't know his brother was an ATF Agent, didn't meet him till he found me hiding on Bobby's boat."

"But they helped you to get out of the area."

"Yes," Brielle confirmed. "I flew up to Chicago with them and was put in touch with Burke and the FBI up there."

Spencer looked pissed. "What else do they know?"

"The FBI knows Michael Spencer died as a child at a summer camp, drowned. They also know that his mother, Maribel Spencer, died in Florida a number of years ago. She's not in an assisted living facility in Trenton," Brielle said bravely, an idea coming to her. "They've looked into all the names on BioDynamix's Articles of Incorporation. It's only a matter of time before they figure out who you really are, all of you. You thought you were opening up shop in an area with stupid hillbillies. You didn't count on how tight of a community the Cajun and Creole people are. If I don't make a check-in every twelve hours with a friend, an article with everything I know or suspect about this place will go viral around this community and it will also get sent to the FBI. I call it my safeguard."

"You're bluffing," Spencer said.

"I've felt in danger for months because of the articles I've been writing. I put this safeguard in place long before I broke in here last week. But if you don't believe me, let me miss my check-in and see what happens. And don't forget the locals at

Galliano Airport are my subscribers. No one is flying out of here after my safeguard goes live. It starts like this. If you're reading this article, something bad has happened to me. I'm either in danger or already dead. Take this seriously. This article was released by a friend who didn't hear from me at an agreed upon interval. Everyone at BioDynamix as well as Sheriff Henderson and Deputy Downey are suspects. Be suspicious of all outsiders to our community." She paused and stared at Spencer, who she could see was evaluating if she was being honest or not. "Would you like for me to continue? I have my entire article memorized. As more information came in, I updated the file. The last piece of information added was that the FBI suspected Mayor Stuart of stealing the identity of his brother from California and using it on the Articles of Incorporation for this company. They know Donald Stuart never lived above that strip club in Trenton that Stuart owns and Sheriff Henderson's cousin worked at."

The Coast Guard chopper took off into the dark night sky. It banked sharply and headed north following the Bayou Lafourche. Flight time was just under eight minutes for it to reach the first drop point in the bayou, a mile from the BioDynamix building.

Immediately, Sherman quickly ran through his pre-mission ritual. He kissed his dog tags three times and then tucked them away. He checked each of the three weapons he had with him, his M4-SBR, and his two semi-automatic handguns. Then he kissed his dog tags one last time, followed by making the sign of the cross. He prayed Brielle would be okay when they found them.

"A quick prayer," Lambchop said. The chopper was two minutes out. The team bowed their heads. "Father, bless and keep your sons and daughters safe during this mission. Protect the innocent in harm's way at the BioDynamix facility. Let us find our people unharmed. Forgive us for the lives we must take during this mission to ensure the innocent are safe. Judgement on their souls is yours. Have mercy on the redeemable. We are your servants dear Lord, guide us to do your work this evening. We pray this in the name of your son, Jesus Christ. Amen."

Amen echoed from the lips of the team members. The helicopter came up to the first drop zone. At the open doorway, Sherman and Lambchop lowered the small raft. They rappelled down and into it a second later, followed by Mother. The chopper pulled away heading to the second drop zone before they started the very quiet outboard motor. Sherman steered the raft just outside the channel marker to the left. They ran at a good clip up the bayou, NVGs giving them vision in the dark.

Sloan climbed onto the skid as the chopper lowered to his point of insertion. He jumped down when it was but a couple of feet from the ground. He immediately ran towards the edge of the trees for cover and then ran full-out in the direction of BioDynamix. It was an easy run. He didn't even have a combat pack on. Just his medical pack. He wasn't even winded when he took up position behind a thick tree trunk.

Papa

The Undertaker waited until he received confirmation the DEA were in position down the road. He was within fifty yards of the gate guard's small building. He could clearly see the guard sitting within. He had a clear shot. "Control, I'm in position." He was behind the tree. His eye was focused through his scope, the barrel of his gun trained on the target.

With a few keystrokes, Garcia took control of BioDynamix's network. He shut the camera feeds down to those in the building and blocked them from executing any commands but kept them up for himself. "Go!"

The Undertaker let out his breath and squeezed the trigger. One round shot out from his suppressed M4-SBR assault rifle, striking the gate guard in the forehead. He dropped from the Undertaker's sight. "Target neutralized." As he ran towards the guard's building, he heard the chopper coming in. It grew louder as it approached. He found the controls that opened the gate and activated it. He ran in, covering the distance between the fence and the building quickly.

Doc's dark form jumped onto the roof, landing in a crouching position as the chopper came in close and hovered. He moved to the edge of the building quickly, dropped to his belly, rifle aimed at the rows of trailers below him. The chopper landed beside the building for only a second for Cooper and Madison to jump out. Then it gained altitude and banked sharply, pulling away from the target building.

The trailer doors began to open. Doc didn't hesitate. He saw assault rifles. He fired with pinpoint accuracy, taking down the men, ten in all. He waited in the eerie silence which followed. No movement, no voices, no sounds except for the crickets and bullfrogs, a serenade calling from the bayou.

In the back of the building, once the cameras were cut, the three men pulled their small inflated raft with a powerful but quiet outboard motor up to the dock. In seconds, they were at the back door. "We are in position to breach Point Bravo," Lambchop broadcast.

The lock on the door clicked. "Point Bravo is unlocked. The immediate interior is clear," Garcia's voice came through their comms. "Killing the lights now."

"Roger that," Lambchop said, opening the door.

Sherman entered first, relieved to finally actively be doing something to rescue Brielle. He swore to God that if she'd been hurt, he'd kill whatever motherfucker had hurt her. Through his comms he and the other members of the team that were now within the BioDynamix building, heard Cooper's voice. He, Madison, and Sloan were entering through the front, Point Alpha. Game on!

Within the interrogation room, Spencer's phone sounded with an alert. He checked it, even though he knew what the tone meant. Their security system was down. Then he heard the unmistakable sound of a helicopter flying low over the building. It was so loud, it sounded like it was on top of them. A few seconds later he heard it move away, but he suspected it had not just flown over. He dialed his man, Keith Louis, who was in the security room manning the equipment. "Talk to me."

"We just lost cameras and all access to the network," Louis reported, pushing his glasses up the bridge of his nose.

"Sound the alarm. We're under attack." He turned to Burke. "How many are coming in?"

"I have no way of knowing."

"I'm assuming a DEA Assault Team. How many is that usually?"

Burke shook his head. "I'm FBI. I don't know. I can't even say if you're under attack."

"Come with me," Spencer said to the three, armed Chinese men in the room. They left, closing and locking the door. He left one of them stationed outside the door, and then he and the others hurried away.

"Quick, my right boot," Burke said to Brielle. "I have a gun in it."

Brielle dropped to the ground beside Rich. She pulled his pant leg up and slid her fingers into the boot. She pulled the small handgun free and placed it in his right hand.

He aimed it at the door. "Now get these cuffs open."

Brielle's shaking hand worked to free the bolt from the edge of the first cuff. She fumbled with it.

"Take a couple of deep breaths," Burke said. "Now try again."

This time she slid the bolt out and opened the cuff, releasing his right hand. Then she released his left.

"Get down in that rear corner. Stay low and don't move. The lights will go out as the team enters the building."

Sure enough, a minute later the bright overhead lights went out, and the room was dimly lit by the emergency light that came on in the corner of the room closest to the door.

Toby cried out when the lights cut. "Momma! Dark!"

Brielle wasn't sure when he'd woken.

"Shh baby, we're playing a game of hide and seek, just like we do under the blanket," Tina said, trying to soothe her little boy, even though she was terrified.

Brielle crowded in, using her own body to shield Tina and Toby. She glanced back. Rich had moved both chairs to the one side of the table and was crouched down behind them and the table, creating himself as much cover as possible.

It was quiet for several minutes. Then the sound of muffled gunfire filled the room, causing Brielle and Tina to both flinch. Next, they heard shouting in a language she couldn't understand. She assumed it to be Chinese. Brielle closed her eyes tight and recited every prayer she knew. The prayer, Hail Mary, full of grace came to mind, in the hour of our death, filled her thoughts. She banished that thought from her mind. Yeah, though I walk through the valley of the shadow of death, I shall fear no evil, Psalm 23:4, was the prayer she preferred to focus on.

The gunfire got louder. They were closer. Tina's voice joined hers. "For thou art with me. Thy rod and thy staff comfort me," she said.

Brielle didn't realize she had been saying her prayers aloud until that moment.

"He's in there," Mother said, pointing to the door in front of them, his eyes on the handheld tracker locator. Sherman figured this was the room because of the Chinese guard who had been standing there. He was now lying on the ground, six rounds in his chest, compliments of both Sherman and Lambchop.

Sherman examined the door. It was metal, a deadbolt lock engaged. He searched the dead man's body that lay in front of the door for the key. Nothing. He unzipped the small outer pocket of his backpack and grabbed a breaching charge of an appropriate size, and the accessories needed to detonate it. "Burke, we're blowing the door," Brian called from outside.

Mother and Lambchop kept their weapons trained behind them, into the expanse of the empty manufacturing floor.

"Understood," Burke called back. He moved in close and crouched down behind Brielle.

Sherman molded the small charge to the door between the keyhole and the door jamb. He pressed the remote detonator to it. He calculated the distance they needed to be back from the blast and moved to that point, three doors down from the target door. "Ready," he called to Lambchop and Mother.

They moved in close behind Sherman, Mother's weapon and gaze behind them, Lambchop's eyes peering through the darkness of the vacant manufacturing floor.

"Three, two, one. Fire in the hole, fire in the hole, fire in the hole," Sherman called in rapid succession and then he activated the detonator.

The charge exploded, shattering the silence and throwing a cloud of smoke and debris into the air. That would surely get the attention of any guards in the area. Sherman went to the door and kicked it open. Burke met him near the door. Crouched in the corner, he saw Brielle and Tina who cradled her crying son. They were just pulling themselves to their feet.

"Is everyone okay?"

"Yeah," Burke replied.

"All targets acquired," Mother broadcast from just inside the door.

Sherman gave Brielle a quick embrace.

"We need to move," Mother said.

"That asshole Spencer, took my primary weapon and our agency phones."

"I don't think he's been located yet," Sherman said. "Come on." He nodded towards the door.

Mother moved in close to cover Tina. "Stay close to me. I've got you and your son," he told her. He could see the terror in her eyes.

Lambchop was in position nearby. "We need to get out of the open and get out of here." A wide hallway lay to the left. "Does that lead back to the lobby?"

"I think so," Tina said with a shaky voice. The truth was, she really didn't know.

Lambchop covered their retreat from the open area. Sherman led the way into the hallway, keeping Brielle behind him. Burke was shadowing him, Mother leading Tina behind Burke. The shadowy hallway curved around what could only be a room and dead ended at two doors with no windows.

Sherman made a fist, stopping the advancement of his teammates. He listened at the first door. He heard a muffled male voice. He pointed to his ear and then the door, the signal to his team that he heard something from inside the room. He pointed at Brielle and then at Mother, hoping she understood that he wanted her to get behind him, where Tina was. She did and moved there right away.

He pointed at Burke and then the other door. Burke crept up to it and listened. He shook his head no. Just then the door Sherman had listened at, opened. He stood two feet away from it, his rifle aimed at it. He saw a gun in one of the man's hands, a phone in the other. He squeezed off three rounds. With a painfilled grunt, the man dropped where he stood. Sherman kicked his handgun away, a .45. He recognized the man, dark red hair with a receding hairline, glasses.

"Tango Keith Louis neutralized," he broadcast quietly. Then Sherman scanned the interior of the room. No one else was within. It was the building's security office, which was lined with monitors that were all down, thanks to Garcia.

He rejoined the others in the hall. Burke still covered the other door. Sherman came in and turned the door handle. It was unlocked. He threw the door open. He and Burke both hurled themselves into the space, their weapons leading the way. They found themselves in the shipping and receiving dock with the two large garage doors. This was not the door that Brielle and Burke had been brought through. Burke looked to his left and identified that door just as it opened.

Sherman and Burke were in the open, no cover nearby. They both opened fire on the man they knew as Mike Spencer. Spencer hesitated and didn't get off a shot. They hit him multiple times. His lifeless body crumpled to the ground.

"Tango Mike Spencer neutralized," Sherman broadcast through his comms.

"Two Tangos down, third floor of the tower," Cooper added. "Entering the cleanroom now."

Crouched in the hallway behind Danny, Brielle heard the gunfire and jumped. It was loud. Toby shrieked a shrill cry in response. Tina closed her eyes and fought to calm herself.

Relief washed over Brielle when Brian and Rich came back into the hall. Thank God!

Sherman pointed back towards the door. "The warehouse." He'd prefer not to go into another large, dark space with little cover.

A short burst of gunfire echoed down the hallway from the direction they'd come. "We've got company," Lambchop's voice came through the men's comms. "Alpha Team, we're in the south west area of the building."

Madison's voice replied. "We're in the tower in the cleanroom. Got a dozen Chinese women, making heroin laced stickers."

Before her, the women lay prone on the ground. On a shelf to her right that Cooper inspected, coils of heroin-laced stickers sat waiting distribution. At the door, Sloan covered the hallway, standing over the bodies of the two men they'd neutralized to gain access to the room.

"They've super concentrated it so that the small one-hit dose is potent," Madison added.

"Delta, we need to move, now," Lambchop's voice was heard. "Coop, we could use a hand."

"I'd prefer not to go through the warehouse, but we need to get these civilians out of here," Sherman said.

"Sorry, the warehouse it is," Lambchop said. "I've stopped two of them, know there are least three more back here."

"We're on our way, Lambchop," Cooper's voice came through their comms. "Razor do you have a count on the number of Tangos at Delta's location?"

"Negative," Garcia's voice replied.

Sherman locked eyes with Brielle. "Direct me, but stay behind me, in close."

She nodded. She watched as Rich went through the door first. She kept her hands pressed against Brian's back and moved with him. To her left, she saw Rich go over to the body on the floor. The motionless man's chest was soaked with blood. She didn't see his face. She watched Rich grab the gun that was near the body, and then he went through the man's pockets. He pulled their two phones free and stuffed them into his own pockets. She knew then that the dead man was the man they knew as Mike Spencer.

Brian prompted her to move towards the shelving racks. "Lead me to the door that you entered through."

"Around there," she said, pointing the way.

They crept around the corner of the shelves, stepping into a halo of the dim emergency lighting, and Brian pushed her to the floor. "Down!" He aimed his gun at the open area that ran the length of the warehouse between the shelves and the metal wall and sprayed the entire area with bullets.

And in the split second that Brian stood over her, she watched in horror as his body jerked backwards, once, twice. A splattering of moisture hit her face, and she heard his curse and loud moan. He dropped to his knees beside her, pain carved into his features, but he still aimed his weapon towards the threat in the back corner of the warehouse. He fired off another long burst of gunfire.

The loud sound of gunfire all around her became distant echoes in her brain as she processed what she saw. The shirt material on Brian's left side, on his arm and beside his bulletproof vest, was wet. Her eyes went to Danny, who was crouched low and firing his weapon through the racks, also aiming towards the back of the warehouse. How could she get his attention?

"I'm hit," Sherman broadcast through his comms. Then his eyes met Brielle's. He saw blood splattered on her face and his pain no longer mattered. His eyes searched over her. "Are you okay?"

"Yes," she said, her mind racing, every sense heightened. Was she okay? Yes, she had to be. She had no pain anywhere.

She realized that Danny was now huddled with them. She watched him fire his rifle at the two men who were across the room, partially hidden by the sturdy shelving racks. They fired back, the shots hitting the concrete floor just in front of them.

"Handsome, give us some cover!" Mother broadcast. Then he turned his attention to the bullet wound.

Brielle's eyes went to Rich, who now stood over Tina and Toby. He fired in the same direction Danny had, into the darkness towards the back of the warehouse.

"The Birdman has a GSW to the bicep," Mother broadcast.

Gunfire came from the other direction, from over by the dock. The sound of bullets hitting the shelving near them exploded in Brielle's ears. She tried to make herself smaller, hiding behind Brian.

"We're pinned down, south-west corner of the warehouse shelves," Danny said.

"Converging on your twenty now," Cooper's voice came through their comms.

The men near the dock fired again, moving into the open to advance on their position. The volley of bullets pinged and ricocheted off the shelves and struck the concrete all around them. Moving in behind them, Brielle saw Madison. She fired and hit the two men with multiple rounds. They dropped to the ground. Beside her was Cooper, firing back towards the door they had entered the warehouse through.

Brielle stared at the men, lying still on the cement. Pools of blood creeped out, inching away from their bodies. She heard more gunfire in the warehouse. It echoed. She couldn't tell from which direction the sounds came. It sounded like it came from all directions. It seemed to last forever.

"Press here," Danny told her, placing her hand over Brian's upper arm. "Hard." He paused, listening to the voices in his comms and then said, "roger." He glanced back at her. "Stay here."

She watched him fire more rounds towards the back of the warehouse. She panicked as he ran in that direction, still firing. *No, don't leave us!* She heard the sound of running feet and realized that Rich was running along the other side of the shelves, heading to the back corner as well. Only then did she realize that Madison, and Tina cradling Toby were beside her.

Brielle was in a mental fog when Sloan arrived. Sloan pulled her hand free after telling her twice to let go, which she didn't.

"I took one to the vest, too," Sherman told Sloan.

Sloan eyed the door. "We're going through that door," Sloan said to Madison.

Brielle didn't realize they were just ten feet from the outer door. Madison stood and pointed her weapon towards the dock area as Sloan pulled on Sherman's vest, bringing him to his feet. Sherman emitted a loud, painfilled screech. Not only did his arm hurt like a sonofabitch, his chest was on fire. He probably had cracked a rib or two. He was pretty sure the round hadn't penetrated the vest. He hoped so, anyway.

"Move," Sloan yelled at Sherman, pushing him towards the door. He grabbed Brielle by the forearm and pulled her to her feet as well. "Stay close." He held onto her and shielded her with his own body.

Once at the door, Sherman collapsed against the wall, willing himself to remain on his feet as Sloan fired at the lock until it gave way. Sherman fought to catch his breath. The pain in his chest was intense. The continuing sounds of gunfire echoed through the warehouse.

"Three targets neutralized, south-east corner of the warehouse," Lambchop's voice came through their comms.

"Three more down, north-east corner," Cooper added.

Sloan pulled Sherman through the door and pressed him against the metal wall, keeping him on his feet. Once outside, Madison took up position, standing in front of Brielle and Tina, with a still crying Toby, who were crouched down. She broadcast their position to the DEA. The outside of the building was secure, but she stayed on alert.

Sloan examined the wound to Sherman's bicep. There was a lot of blood saturating the entire area. He lifted Sherman's arm up a few inches, to which Sherman cursed out a long string of expletives describing how much that hurt. Sloan found what he was looking for, a secondary source of blood. The fabric of his shirt, just above the vest, in the armpit area had the telltale marking of a bullet hole. "Sonofabitch!" Sherman could have substantial internal injuries.

He pulled his shears from their location in his medical kit and sliced into Sherman's shirt, pulling it away from the injured arm and armpit area. He pressed a large gauze patch to the underarm area to absorb some of the blood. He'd need better light. He couldn't tell the extent of the injury. He handed his flashlight to Brielle. "Shine this under his arm for me."

She was horrified by the amount of blood she saw rapidly staining the gauze pad. Her gaze left the wound and went to Gary. "Is he going to be okay?"

Sloan nodded stiffly. He sure hoped so. There was a lot of blood under Sherman's arm, and he hadn't yet determined if it was a graze or a penetration. Of course, he hadn't yet taken the vest off. He hoped the blood was not coming from beneath it. If a round penetrated his vest, there would be substantial internal injuries.

When he pulled the gauze pad away, the tissue beneath, for the brief second it was free of blood, showed a jagged, long wound in the meaty flesh. It stretched from the front of his vest to the rear of it, about a half inch above it. Probably just a flesh wound, but they'd know for sure when they got him to a hospital.

Next, he checked the back of Sherman's arm. There was an exit wound. Looked like a through and through. This was good news, too.

"Stay with me, Brielle," Sherman said, grabbing onto her arm.

"I'm here, Brian," she said.

"No, up north, when this is over. Stay with me and Bobby up in Chicago, Brielle. Promise me you will."

"You didn't have to get shot to get me to stay with you," she said with tears in her eyes. She watched Gary inject him with a syringe. "What did you give him?"

"Painkillers." He locked eyes with Sherman. "It doesn't look too bad. I'll get your vest off once we're on the chopper."

He grabbed three packages of Quick Clot. He pressed one to the front of his bicep, a second to the exit wound at the back. Then pressed a fresh gauze pad to the wound under his arm. It was instantly saturated with blood. He pressed the third Quick Clot pack to it, hoping it would help to get the bleeding under control. He let Sherman slide down the wall so that he was seated on the ground. Then Sloan called in the order for the chopper to land at their location. There was just enough clearance on the lawn.

As the sound of the approaching chopper became louder, men clad in DEA bullet-proof vests swarmed in. "We'll take over from here," one of them said. He led Tina and a still screaming Toby away.

Next thing Brielle knew, Doc appeared. A Coast Guard helicopter landed, and she watched Gary and Doc muscle Brian onto the chopper. Danny helped her to climb inside and she knelt at Brian's head. She watched them take his bullet-proof vest off. Doc cut his shirt away. He had a nasty dark purple bruise the size of a softball over his ribs. There was no penetration into his skin from the two rounds that struck his vest on his middle left quadrant.

Sherman was drifting in painful bliss, the painkillers more whacking him out than killing the pain. He was aware he was lifted onto the chopper. He saw Sloan and Doc working on him as he lay gazing at the ceiling. Through his comms he was vaguely aware of the dialog between his team members. He did hear Cooper report that they got them all and that he and Xena were staying onsite to hand off to the DEA. They'd meet them at the hospital.

"Brielle?" Sherman muttered. Where was Brielle? She had to come with them.

"I'm right here," she said, her voice floating into his recognition as her face appeared over his like an angel hovering over him.

"She stays with us," Sherman mumbled before losing consciousness.

"Brian?"

"He's sleeping," Sloan said. "The painkillers."

She sat back and stared at him, watching the activity as Gary and Doc checked his blood pressure, palpated his abdomen, and examined the area around the gunshots to be sure the Quick Clot was holding. She felt a hand to her shoulder. Turning her head, she saw Danny.

"I can't believe this happened," Brielle said. "How could Brian be shot?" Tears streamed down her face.

"This job we do, it's dangerous and there is always the chance someone will take a bullet when there are that many flying around," Mother said, sliding his arm around her. "He's in the best hands right now, though. He's going to be fine, Brielle."

Sloan glanced up at them. "Yeah, he's going to be fine. We've got the bleeding under control. The bullet went clean through his arm, which means it probably didn't hit and fuck up any bones. We'll get him into surgery as soon as we get to the hospital. Ops has already called ahead. They know our ETA."

Lambchop came over and sat beside Brielle. He took her hand. "Pray with me," he said to Brielle. "Heavenly Father, wrap your son, Brian Sherman, in your protective embrace. Bring peace to Brielle's heart and mind, for you have Brian and will bring him through with the help of your servants, Sloan and Doc, and the capable hands of the surgical staff who will care for him. We put our faith in you and turn our worries over to you in the name of your son, Jesus Christ. Amen."

"Amen," Brielle echoed. She wiped her tears. "Thank you."

A few minutes later, they arrived at the Lady of the Sea Hospital in Cut Off, the chopper landing on the grassy expanse in front of the door to the emergency room at the rear of the hospital. Lambchop and Burke carried Sherman from the bird and into the hospital.

"Federal agents," Sloan said, holding his badge and credentials up. "I believe the Coast Guard Operations Center at Port Fourchon notified you of our arrival."

Two women in scrubs rushed forward with a gurney. "They did. Our surgery suite is ready and waiting for your GSW."

Brielle watched as they laid Brian onto the gurney. His face looked as pale as the white sheet beneath him.

Doc pointed to himself and Sloan. "We're both medics. We'll accompany you. And these two men will stand guard outside the OR." He pointed to Burke and Lambchop.

The nurses knew those decisions were above their paygrade. "Come with us," one of them said. "And we'll show you where the OR waiting room is."

Mother guided Brielle to follow them down the corridor, the gurney with Sherman lying on it, leading the way. After several turns into passageways that led them deeper within the inner hallways of the hospital, the nurses stopped at the door that read Operating Room One.

"Medical personnel and the patient only beyond this point," one of the nurses said. She pointed across the hallway to a door. "That door leads to the surgical waiting room. It's empty as there are no other surgeries going on right now. Your group can have it."

"Get me the doctor or your chief administrator," Doc demanded. "Now!"

The nurse pulled a phone from her pocket. "The GSW is at the OR. I need an administrator to interface with the federal authorities." She listened for a few moments. "Thank you." She disconnected the call. "Wait here. Dr. Champlain will be out soon." Then she and the other nurse pushed the gurney with Sherman on it through the automatic doors into the operating room.

"Champlain is French, most likely Cajun descent," Brielle said. "Let me talk with him."

"I've got this," Doc said.

A man in blue scrubs and a white lab coat approached, eyeing the armed men cautiously. "I'm Dr. Champlain, I'm told you needed to see me."

All the members of Shepherd Security presented their badges. Doc motioned to Sloan. "The two of us are the unit's medics. We treated him on-site and need to be in the OR with him. We're both level one trauma certified and can assist in the OR."

"And our protocols direct that while any threat still exists, that we will stand guard outside a treatment room when one of our own is incapacitated," Lambchop added.

Dr. Champlain sighed out loud.

"Dr. Champlain, please," Brielle said, stepping forward. "That's my man in there and he trusts these men." She pointed to Doc and Gary.

"Brielle Jarboe?" He asked.

"Yes, sir."

"I read your Parish Blog."

"Well stay tuned to see what went down that got my man shot. Now please, let these men into the operating room and let the others stand guard."

Dr. Champlain nodded. "No guns in the OR."

Doc and Sloan handed their weapons over to the others. Dr. Champlain ushered them into the operating room.

Quebec

*D*anny handed a coffee cup to Brielle. She hadn't asked for it, and she didn't recall him asking if she wanted one either. Though she would admit that her thoughts were a blur. And the longer she sat, waiting for Brian to get out of surgery, the more clouded her mind became. The moment Brian was shot replayed through her mind like a bad movie on an endless, repeating loop.

She took the cup from him. "Thank you."

She glanced at the clock on the wall. Three hours had passed. If Brian's wounds weren't serious, why was it taking so long? She wanted an update from Gary or Doc. Why wasn't someone coming to tell them what was going on?

Madison and Cooper were in the room. They'd arrived only twenty minutes before. They updated her and Danny on the activity at the BioDynamix plant after they'd left. The DEA took control of the scene. The FBI had arrested Sheriff Henderson and Deputy Downey.

So far, there was no concrete proof of any wrongdoing that led them to Stuart, the Mayor of Galliano. Madison was hopeful that there would be some evidence at either BioDynamix or at the Sheriff's residence or his office that would implicate Stuart. Until then, he was under surveillance by the FBI. They didn't want to approach him without evidence.

ICE was called in, as the Chinese who were housed in the trailers had no proof of citizenship or legal entry into the country. Madison had conversed with a few of the women and learned they had been abducted from various locations and forced to work here, producing the heroin laced stickers. She also learned that there had been a Chinese woman who freely came and went from the facility, who trained them. They referred to her as Madame Butterfly, because she had a butterfly tattoo on the back of her neck. They identified the driver's license photo of Jennifer Brubaker as that woman.

It was over. After months of wondering what was really going on out at the BioDynamix facility, Brielle had her answers. Drugs, the research and development, and the mass production of heroin on stickers for easy distribution that they hoped would evade law enforcement's detection.

Gary came through the door into the lounge, and Brielle shot to her feet when he entered. "Brian?"

"He's fine, stable. The surgery went well. I stayed with him in recovery until he was conscious."

"How much damage was done to his arm?" Mother asked.

"It was a through and through, didn't hit the bone. Took out a good portion of his bicep, good thing his was so well developed. And it's his left, shouldn't impede him too much. Physical Therapy and then weightlifting in the gym should get him back to nearly seventy-five percent in time. He was lucky. Under his arm was just a graze. This wasn't a career ending injury."

Gary's frank reporting of the bullet wound was sobering. "When can I see him?" Brielle asked.

"He'll be brought to a room shortly. You can go in as soon as they get him settled," Gary said. "As soon as he can be moved, we'll bring him back to HQ and care for him there, should be less than a day."

Brielle nodded. She still felt numb, the events of the past few hours unreal. "He wants me to stay with him."

Mother's lips tipped into a grin. "Don't worry, we won't take him anywhere without you."

Less than an hour later, Gary and Danny brought her to the third-floor room where Brian was. Rich and Landon stood in the hall outside his door. Landon gave her a sympathetic smile and reached his hand to her shoulder. "How are you holding up?"

"I'll be better after I can see him." She felt new tears flood her eyes.

Doc was with Brian when they entered. Brian was propped up in a half-sitting position. He was unconscious. He still looked ghostly white. His arm was bandaged, as was the armpit area. A deep purple bruise the size of a large grapefruit was on the left side of his torso, over his ribs. Brielle couldn't help but stare at the wounds.

"He was lucky," Gary whispered to her. "None of the wounds were serious. He's going to be in some pain for a few weeks, but he'll recover fully."

Brielle nodded again, her thoughts overwhelmed and racing. "When will he wake up?"

"He was conscious in recovery. The pain killers knocked him back out," Gary said. "Sleep is best for him right now."

"Can I stay with him?"

Doc pulled the recliner in close beside the head of the bed. "Get comfortable."

"Give me a call when he wakes up and I'll be back," Gary said.

Doc handed her phone to her. "Don't contact anyone but the team."

She nodded. Who did he think she'd contact?

"And let us know if you need anything," Doc added. "Lambchop and Handsome will remain on guard in the hall."

Brielle watched the two men pass through the door, leaving her alone with Brian. She took a seat in the recliner and held Brian's hand. Soon, though, she got antsy and stood. She wanted to hold him. It would be a tight squeeze, but she would fit on the edge of the mattress on the right side of the bed, far from his wounds.

Carefully, she crawled up into the bed with Brian. She wrapped her arm around his waist and gently rested her head on his chest. Her eyes scanned his resting face. His eyes were still closed. He looked peaceful. Then her eyes went to his bandaged bicep. She still couldn't believe he'd been shot. If he hadn't pushed her down, it could have been her. That thought made her shudder.

"I like waking up to find you in bed with me," Brian's weak voice said.

She angled her head up to look into his face. "How do you feel?"

"Like I've been shot a couple of times."

"You were."

Sherman saw the moisture in Brielle's eyes. "Hey, no tears. I'm okay."

"Do you hurt?"

"No, they have me on some good pain killers." He glanced at his bandaged left bicep. "How bad is the damage to my arm?"

"Gary said it was not a career ending injury."

"Crawl up here and give me a kiss."

Even though Brielle moved very carefully, her shifting the bed caused him to wince. "I'm sorry," she apologized, her head hovering over his.

"Don't be, just kiss me, baby."

Brielle pressed a kiss to his lips. When she pulled her lips away, she beamed a beautiful smile at him that filled his heart.

"That's my girl," Sherman said.

"I was so afraid, watching Gary and Doc work on you, and while you were in surgery."

"I'm fine," he said.

"I was afraid I was going to lose you."

A smile tugged at Sherman's lips. "You mean a lot to me too. Can you live with this?"

"With you doing this job?"

"Yeah."

"It's what you do, who you are, Brian." She nodded her head. "Yeah, I can live with this." She embraced him and held him.

"Good, because I've fallen in love with you, Miss Brielle Jarboe, and I don't ever want for you to not be in my life."

Her tears spilled onto her cheeks. "I feel the same. I don't want to ever lose you."

"Did the team get them?"

"Yes, and the regular DEA moved in and took over. Sheriff Henderson and Deputy Downey were arrested by the FBI."

Sherman nodded. "Good. Almost makes getting shot worth it."

Brielle shook her head. "You're crazy." She pressed her lips against his, gifting him with another passionate kiss.

"Crazy about you, momma," Sherman said when she pulled her lips away. He stared into her eyes and was thoughtful for a few moments. "I am, you know, crazy about you." A smile came to Brielle's face that made her glow. Sherman was pleased that his words brought about that reaction. "Have you started to write your piece on it yet?"

"No, I've been too worried about you."

"I'm fine. Have Mother or Lambchop get you into my tablet and use it to write your story. This is your big chance."

"Brian, you could have died. I had to be sure you were okay, couldn't even think about writing anything while you were in surgery. And I've been here with you since they brought you to your room."

"You agreed to move north with me."

A smile spread over Brielle's face that made Sherman smile too. She had a beautiful smile and all he wanted was to see it on her face every day for the rest of his life.

"I did," she agreed.

"Don't you renege on that."

She giggled. "I don't plan to. You're stuck with me."

"I like that," Sherman said.

Twelve hours later, Brielle watched as Landon helped Brian mount the stairs into the Lear. Brian was very stiff, very sore. Thanks to the bulletproof vest, he suffered only two bruised ribs beneath, but he ached with every movement he made, with every breath he drew in.

"He's going to be just fine, or he wouldn't be out of the hospital," Doc said.

Brielle made eye contact with him. "Did I look worried?"

Doc shook his head. "Honey, we all know you are, but don't be. We've got him. We take care of our own."

"His ribs hurt bad," she remarked aloud.

"I know and they will for about a week or two," Doc agreed.

"Taking a bullet to the vest feels like getting kicked by a horse," Madison said, appearing beside them. "I took one to the vest last year. Besides the big, angry purple bruise, that hurt just to have clothing touch it, the pain every time I sucked in a breath was crazy."

Brielle's eyes met hers. "You've been shot?"

Madison nodded. "Last year. Hurt like a bitch and it didn't even hit my ribs." She massaged her stomach, dead center, about an inch or two above her navel. "Sherman will hurt for a few weeks, but then he'll be fine," she said dismissively.

Brielle nodded. Madison motioned for her to board the plane. She climbed the few stairs, still numb from it all. She made her way aft, to the seat where Gary was helping Brian get settled.

"You'll be more comfortable reclined," Sloan said.

"Let me just catch my breath before you move me again," Sherman argued. He sat rigid, with his head pressed against the headrest.

Brielle watched as Gary fastened Brian's seat belt. It was obvious to her that Brian hated him fussing over him.

"I'll help you recline when you want to," Gary said. "And remember, try to suck in some deep breaths every minute or two or we'll be treating you for pneumonia."

"I got it," Sherman moaned.

Gary moved away and Brielle took the seat beside Brian. She took hold of his hand. "I hope this flight won't cause you too much pain."

"I'll be fine," he said dismissively.

Brielle leaned up and placed a kiss on his cheek. Then she fastened her own seat belt. She took hold of his hand again and didn't let go of it for the length of the flight. The flight went fast with little turbulence, which meant little jostling of Brian. Soon, the plane descended through the cloudy fall sky above the Chicago Executive Airport.

The landing brought about winces and groans from Brian. She could see the pain across his face. She couldn't wait to get him home and help him into bed. She'd take good care of him.

Once parked within the Shepherd Security Hangar, Lambchop pulled Sherman to his feet and then helped him off the plane. He led him over to one of the SUV's and assisted him to ease into the backseat. Brielle joined him, sliding in from the other side of the vehicle.

They drove to the Shepherd Security Building. Brielle got onto the elevator with Brian while the others unloaded the vehicles. Landon and Danny guaranteed Brian that they'd stow his gear for him. They rode the elevator to the fifth floor.

Shepherd's office door was open. They entered. Shepherd, Garcia, and Jackson were there. She watched the men greet Brian with handshakes, gentle shoulder bumps, and hugs. Shepherd presented his hand to Brian, a frown curving his lips. "I'm glad it wasn't worse."

"Thanks, Shep. I'll be fine." He shook Shepherd's hand.

"Take as long as you need to recover. You'll be on limited duty in the office when you feel up to it. Don't push it. Your recovery comes first," Shepherd said.

"Let me help you take a seat," Garcia said. "I know how much those ribs hurt. You need to take it easy for a week or two."

Brielle watched Garcia gently lower Brian into a chair. "Should I stay?" She asked Shepherd. He still intimidated her.

Shepherd nodded.

She took a seat beside Brian. Fifteen minutes later, the remainder of the team that had been in Louisiana entered the room. They all took seats at the table. Brielle glanced around, taking in the sight of them all. She held great appreciation for each of them. She wouldn't be alive if it weren't for them. And Brian may not be either, if it weren't for Gary and Doc. This was a very special group of people. She felt herself becoming emotional as she thought about it. She had to purposefully suppress her feelings, or she would have cried.

"Good job in Louisiana, team," Shepherd said. "To bring you up to date, neither Sheriff Henderson nor Deputy Downey are talking. They are in FBI custody. The charges will be many against them. There is no doubt bail is off the table. The FBI is still digging into all the evidence that was collected at the BioDynamix plant as well as at Sheriff Henderson's residence and his office. A search of Deputy Downey's residence, yielded nothing."

"Were the two suitcases recovered from the back of the police car?" Burke asked.

"Negative. We believe he dropped them at Galliano Airport as soon as he left the BioDynamix facility," Garcia said. "The flight plans of all the aircraft that departed that airport after the Sheriff picked those two bags up are being scrutinized," Garcia answered.

"So far there is no evidence implicating Mayor Stuart concrete enough for a judge to issue a warrant. The FBI will stay on it. They have him under surveillance but have decided not to interview him at this time until there is more evidence and an arrest warrant can be obtained. There are no leads on Madam Butterfly. Garcia, the FBI, and the DEA will continue to look into her. We all agree she is the link between the New Jersey crew and the Chinese."

"What about the captive workers?" Madison asked. "The women I spoke with were kidnapped from several different countries, as well as from here in the U.S."

"Their statements were all taken from them and they are safely in a government facility, segregated from other detainees. It's one of the nicer ones, more like a college dormitory than an ICE detention facility. It is realized their testimony may be needed to convict those who were running the operation," Garcia advised. "So, they won't be deported anytime soon. They're safe, and I'm told, very relieved they were liberated."

"This was a win for the agency," Shepherd said. "We did good work. The DEA sends their thanks. Those heroin laced stickers had just been identified in New York, New Jersey, and several other east coast cities, but no one knew where they'd come from. Now that they know about them, closer scrutiny has found that they have been distributed to all major cities."

"When do we resume the DEA Partner Mission in New York?" Lambchop asked.

"Tomorrow. We'll have a briefing at eleven hundred and the team will leave shortly thereafter. All of Delta team minus Sherman, plus Jackson, Burke, and Cooper are slotted for this mission. You're all dismissed until then."

"What about Bobby? Can you do anything to get him out of that rehab facility? He doesn't have a drug problem and doesn't belong there," Brielle insisted.

Shepherd's eyes focused on Sherman. "Do you agree with that assessment?"

"Yeah. He was stupid to set himself up, but according to both him and Brielle, he doesn't have an addiction problem and I'll be around to observe him. If he uses, I'll put him right back into that facility."

"I'll reach out to the appropriate federal authorities to assist with influencing that judge in Louisiana. He has to approve the vacating of that plea bargain," Shepherd said.

"Thank you," Brielle said, her eyes locked with Shepherd's dark eyes.

Shepherd nodded. Then his gaze went to Sherman. "You have a meeting with Lassiter."

"I want Sherman in bed, lying down," Sloan said. "He's been upright way too long. I'm going to settle him and Brielle in the apartment for a few days. It'll make it easier for Doc and me to check in on him."

Shepherd nodded. "I'll let Lassiter know to see you there," he said to Sherman.

"I'll bring your bags up before I head out," Lambchop said.

"Thanks." Sherman struggled to stand even with Gary's help.

Brielle followed behind Brian as Gary led him to the elevator. He moved very slowly. She wasn't sure who Lassiter was or why Brian was meeting with him. The other members of the team were heading home, dismissed. She didn't understand why Brian wasn't. She could take care of him at his place. Certainly, he'd be more comfortable at home.

At the bed within the apartment, Brielle watched as Brian set his phone onto the bedside table. Then he put his wallet into the drawer. He reached his hand to his hip and then around to the small of his back. "That's right, no weapon while on painkillers."

"Do you have to hit the head before I help you lay down?" Sloan asked.

"Probably a good idea," Sherman agreed.

"I'll be around all night in case he needs to get up," Sloan told Brielle after Sherman was closed within the bathroom. "You won't be able to help him, so don't try."

Brielle was about to argue that she could when Brian came back into the room. He inched his way to the bed with small steps.

"Drop your pants and I'll help take them and your shoes off after you sit," Sloan said, pulling the bedcovers back.

"You can take my shoes off, but I'd rather have the visual of Brielle depantsing me," Sherman said with a cocky grin.

Brielle watched as Gary helped Brian sit on the edge of the bed. They moved slowly, and it was obvious that Gary supported Brian's weight. Gary took his shoes off and then stepped back to allow space for Brielle to come in close. She smiled in a flirty way at Brian as she slid his jeans from his knees and off his feet. Next came pain-filled moans that coincided with the smallest of movements as Gary helped Brian to recline on the bed.

"Help swing his feet up, will you, Brielle?"

She came in and lifted his feet, swinging them onto the bed as Gary painstakingly lowered Brian to the mattress with small, deliberate movements. When he was finally reclined, Brian let out one last moan. And Gary had piled pillows three high, so he wasn't lying flat. Now she understood why they stayed here and didn't go to Brian's place.

Sloan pulled the blankets over Sherman's lower body. "If you need anything, you let Brielle get it or call me. Don't even try to get up without my help tonight."

A scowl set on Sherman's face. "You know I hate this."

"Let us take care of you. You'll be moving around better in a few days," Sloan said.

Just then the door opened and Lambchop and Mother came through, carrying several bags, including Brielle's backpack. They sat them on the floor near the foot of the bed. "Let us know if you need anything," Lambchop offered.

"Thanks," Sherman acknowledged. He wished everyone would stop fussing over him.

The room cleared out. Brielle crawled into bed and laid on Brian's right side. She held him.

Fifteen minutes later, two sharp raps on the door got both Brielle and Sherman's attention. "That's probably Lassiter," Sherman said. "Come on in, the door is open."

Brielle watched as a man with scars on his face and neck came into the room. He walked with a slight limp. He had dark blonde hair, worn cropped short. Brielle sat up.

"Hi Joe," Sherman greeted.

"Hi," he replied as he approached the bed. His eyes met hers. "And you must be Brielle."

"This is Joe Lassiter, our team shrink, here to evaluate my mental state because I was shot."

Lassiter chuckled. "I'll be evaluating the mental state of the entire team that was on the ground, so don't think you're special."

Sherman chuckled just a little and then winced from the pain from it.

"I should give you two the room," Brielle said, moving to get up.

"Stay," Lassiter said. "And you don't need to get up. You both look pretty comfortable." His eyes went to Sherman. "Or as comfortable as you can be."

"Yeah," Sherman agreed. "The bruised ribs suck. I can deal with the arm and the graze by my armpit, but man, every time I move or breathe, the ribs scream."

"That should calm down in a few days. Rest is what's best right now, so don't be stupid and push it," Lassiter said. Then he turned more serious. "I read the mission report. There were a lot of bullets flying around. The team was very lucky that only one of you got hit."

Sherman nodded. He took Brielle's hand in his. "I'm glad it was me who got hit and not Brielle or Tina Landry or her baby, the other civilians."

Lassiter nodded. "If it was your girl that got hit instead of you, we'd be having a different conversation right now and I'd be more worried about you." He wouldn't mention how messed up in the head the entire team would have been had it been the baby that got shot.

Sherman chuckled again, followed by another wince. "This is the third time I've been shot Joe. It ain't no thing. My mind is fine, and this won't impact me doing my job when I do go back on active."

"We'll talk about that over the next month while you're on limited duty, but I'm sure you're right."

Sherman glanced at Brielle and smiled. "At least I'm guaranteed I'll be home the next month. Sucky way to accomplish that, but I won't complain that I'll get to go to sleep beside my girl every night."

"Most nights," Lassiter corrected him. "Shepherd plans to train you in Ops and some of those will be overnight shifts, I'm sure."

"I suppose Madison, Garcia, and Jackson will have to go out in my place while I'm laid up, it's only fair I pick up the slack in Ops."

"So, you're good, nothing to talk about?" Lassiter prompted.

"Nope, it's the reality of the job, Joe, the possibility of getting shot."

Lassiter nodded. He knew Sherman would have to be pushed to admit how he felt. Then his gaze slid to Brielle. "What about you? Welcome to the reality of this job. Are you prepared to deal with this?"

Brielle forced a small smile. "I have no other choice. I want to be with Brian, and this is what he does. Does it scare me? Yes, it sure does but the thought of not being with him, is worse."

"That's a good way to look at it. You had a scary ordeal yourself, and that was before you saw Sherman get shot."

"It's funny. I spent months in danger, but I guess I didn't really realize it. Since Brian found me hiding on his boat, I was the safest I'd been in months, but when Cooper and Madison came down to the bayou and Mr. Shepherd took this seriously enough to send others down, that was when I really got afraid."

Sherman raised her hand to his lips and kissed her knuckles. "Oh, baby, I didn't know you felt that way. Why didn't you tell me?"

"I didn't want to admit it and I wanted to be able to stay involved. I was worried that if you knew I was afraid, you'd keep me away from it."

"And you wanted to see it through to the end?" Lassiter posed.

"Yeah. It was my story. I'm the one who called attention to that BioDynamics facility. I investigated it and just knew that something wasn't right. I wanted to see it through to the end."

"And you did. From what I hear, you have an exclusive to write the story on it. How's that coming?" Lassiter asked.

"I haven't started it yet. I need to do that," Brielle said.

"Is there something interfering with you writing the story?"

"Besides the fact that Brian was shot?" Brielle shook her head. "There just hasn't been time for me to write it yet."

"Work on it tonight. If you can't get the words down, there might be more to it. More you may want to talk with me about," Lassiter offered. He handed Brielle one of his cards. "Program my number into your phone and contact me if you want to talk with me. I have an office in this building."

Brielle took the card from him, but doubted she'd call him. "Thank you."

Lassiter stood. "Get some rest, Sherman, and take it easy for a few days. I'll be in touch."

"Thanks, Joe," Sherman said.

"It was nice to meet you, Brielle. Call me if you need me."

"Thank you, Dr. Lassiter," she said.

While Sherman slept, Brielle worked on her article. As she reflected on what had happened, her mind focused more on the brave actions of the Shepherd Security Team, than on the illegal activities of the Sheriff and the people at the BioDynamix facility. She knew she couldn't mention too much about them, and any reference to the DEA agents who investigated and brought down the bad guys had to be generic, naming no names, and not specifying what technology or tactics they used to investigate what was going on.

It was late when she finished typing the article. She'd given it a lot of thought. She'd given many things a lot of thought as she worked on it. As she closed the lid to her laptop, her eyes went back to Brian's sleeping form. She knew what she had done, and what she was planning to do was the right path for her. This man had become very important to her.

Romeo

oth Brielle and Sherman were awakened the next morning by a couple of knocks to the door. Then Sherman's phone vibrated with a new text message. Brielle got up and handed his phone to him. It was a message from Sloan. He was in the hall.

"Come in, it's open," Sherman called as Brielle turned the light on. She'd slept in her clothes, not knowing if anyone would be coming into the room during the night.

"Is everybody decent in here?" Sloan asked as he entered.

"Not even close," Sherman remarked.

Sloan chuckled. "No, you, my friend, are not."

Brielle smiled at the black-haired woman who entered behind Gary. She was pretty. She had a heart-shaped face, big brown eyes, and a genuine smile. She carried a tray with food.

"Brielle, this is Angel, our Office Manager, Shepherd's Executive Assistant, and Jackson's wife," Sloan introduced.

Brielle approached her as she placed the tray on the small kitchen table. She presented her hand. "It's nice to finally meet you. I've heard a lot about you."

Angel shook her hand. "Same. If there is anything you need, let me know. Garcia is going to push everyone's contact information to your agency phone, so you'll have my number."

"Thank you for bringing us breakfast," Brielle said.

"I'm ordering lunch out today. I'll shoot you a text when it's here and you can get plates for both you and Sherman. Garcia's also going to set you up with temporary access to move around the building."

"I'm going to get Sherman up and let them have breakfast," Sloan said. "Angel, can you come back in about a half hour and get Brielle while I change Sherman's bandages? You can show her how to access the panels to move around the building and maybe have a cup of tea down in the kitchen." His eyes shifted to Brielle. "A change of scenery will do you good while I'm tending his wounds."

"Sounds good," Angel said.

Brielle nodded, even though she didn't want to step away from Brian. She watched as Gary helped Brian up, another pain-filled maneuver.

Brian used the bathroom.

"How'd he do last night?" Gary asked.

"Good. Whatever you gave him let him sleep comfortably."

Sloan smiled a crooked grin. "My best friend deserves only the best pain meds."

"How long before we can go to Brian's place?"

"A few days, when Sherman can get himself up and down."

Brielle nodded. She was eager to get on with what would be their normal life, even though she was unsure what that normal life would look like for her. Brian rejoined them and Brielle watched the twisted grimace on his face as Gary helped to sit him at the table. Then they enjoyed breakfast, Gary promising to be back in a half hour.

"Thanks for arranging for Brielle to spend some time with Angel," Sherman said to Sloan as he removed the dressing around his bicep.

"I figured you'd want Brielle to, and she doesn't need to see your wounds, up close and personal."

"Yeah," Sherman agreed, studying the open wound.

"You were damned lucky, you know," Sloan said. "The bullet hit your arm in the best possible way. And under your arm, had your body been turned at all, instead of a graze you'd have serious internal damage, ribs, lungs, possibly even damage to your heart."

"Yeah, God was really looking out for me," Sherman agreed.

"How's Brielle dealing with all of this?"

"Better than I think most would," Sherman said. "She's a perfect fit."

"It's an adjustment, suddenly having a woman live with you. No longer being an I and suddenly being a we, is a lot to take in. I can attest to that."

"I'm sure the reality of it will hit me more when we go back to my place, even more so when Bobby is out of rehab and joins us."

"You're pretty relaxed about taking on two dependents."

"Family, it's all about family. I've got enough money put away, so it won't break me," Sherman said. "I do need to get a bigger place though. My place is too small for three people."

Sloan shook his head.

"What?" Sherman asked.

"Just like that?"

"Yeah, it's the right thing to do, for Bobby, for Brielle, hell, for me too. I don't have to tell you what it's like to have a woman you know is yours. I love going to sleep holding her and love it even more that I wake up to her too."

Sloan nodded. "Yeah, I got that the very first mission we went away on after Kaylee was living with me. I sure as hell missed her while we were gone and when we came home, it was like something I never knew was lacking in my life was suddenly there."

Sherman understood what he meant. He'd never wanted that with any woman, did everything he could to avoid it, but he craved it with Brielle. "Brielle is special. She just fits."

Sloan smiled. "I'm happy for you. We need to get her and Kaylee together soon."

"I need to get Brielle hooked up with the other girls too. I'm glad she and Angel are spending time together so they can get to know each other." He knew that Angel was the mamma bear not only to all of them, but to the other wives too. As far as he could see, the wives were all tight. He wanted Brielle to be included in that group. She'd need the support when he went back on active duty.

In the kitchen on the fifth floor, Brielle sipped her tea. Her laptop was in front of her. She wanted to proof her article one more time before she sent it to Shepherd, but she was enjoying getting to know Angel. She was a warm and genuine person. She understood why Brian had such an affection for her.

Angel's phone, which sat on the table, vibrated. Angel checked her text message. "Gary just gave Brian more pain killers. He suggests you hang out here for a while and let Brian rest." She nodded to Brielle's laptop. "Did you finish your article?"

"Yes, last night. I need to proof it one more time before I send it to Mr. Shepherd." She was a bit surprised. She didn't know that Angel knew anything about the article. She guessed that since Angel did, she probably knew about the NDA she'd been forced to sign too.

Angel stood. "I should probably leave you to it then. I know Shepherd is anxious to get it."

"No, please stay and talk a little while longer. I'm not ready to send it yet." She knew once she did, her path would be cemented.

Angel smiled and retook her seat. "This is a special group of people. Wait till you meet the other wives. We all support each other, especially when the guys are away on a mission."

"I met Kaylee. She seems really nice." Brielle smiled. "She and Gary are really cute together."

"Yes, they are. I've never seen Gary happier." Angel was thoughtful for a few moments. "It's not easy though, being with a man that does what our men do. You've seen firsthand how bad it can go with little warning."

"Yes," Brielle agreed. "It was really scary, seeing him get shot."

"Yes, it's something that doesn't easily get out of your head. Make sure you reach out to Dr. Lassiter if you need to. He can help."

"Why do I get the feeling you know that firsthand?"

Angel frowned. "Because I do. I was with Shepherd when he was shot. It was horrible. It was a blur. The team swarmed in from nowhere, saving us both. The gunfire was so loud, deafening. I watched Doc and Gary work on him. There was so much blood. He almost didn't make it."

Brielle stared at her in disbelief. "I had no idea."

"He was protecting me, but they got us," Angel said. "I had a normal life, didn't do anything wrong, but life took a horrible turn for me."

Brielle shook her head. "I'm sorry. Brian didn't tell me. I didn't know."

"No, I'm sure he didn't. We all have our stories, and I know the guys would never tell anyone what's ours to share. You can be confident in that, that no one will share your story, not even with their wives. I only know your story because I see all mission reports." She paused. "I can't wait to read your article."

"It will be heavily censored in what I am allowed to report on."

"There is a good reason for that," Angel said. "This organization wouldn't accomplish a fraction of what we do if we had to color inside the lines. Operating the way we do, is the only reason we accomplish what other units can't. And a lot of people are alive because of that."

Brielle nodded, believing her. After a few silent minutes, Angel excused herself.

Sierra

rielle hit send and closed the lid to her laptop. Her news article was sent. She felt good about it, even though she knew only a few people would ever read it. She stood and carried her laptop with her back to Angel's desk, exiting the kitchen with purpose.

"I sent Shepherd the article I wrote. I expect he'll be calling me into his office shortly."

Angel glanced up from her monitor. "That doesn't sound very promising."

Brielle's lips curved into a sad smile. "In life you make choices and hope for the best. Hindsight is twenty-twenty. I can only hope in hindsight I'll see that this was a good choice."

"What did you do, Brielle?" Angel asked.

"I wrote the very best article I could about what went down on the Bayou Lafourche."

She stood there by Angel's desk and waited, making small talk with her. Sure enough, ten minutes later, Angel's phone rang. Shepherd.

"Yes, Brielle is right here with me." Angel's eyes flickered to her. "I'll send her right in."

Brielle forced a smile. "Thanks, Angel."

"Good luck," Angel said to Brielle's back as she walked down the hall towards Shepherd's office.

The door was closed when Brielle reached it. She knocked.

"Come," Shepherd's voice came from behind the door.

She took a deep breath and opened it. She stepped in.

"Close it," Shepherd said, the two words clipped. He sat behind his big desk in the corner of the floor to ceiling windows. He motioned to the guest chairs in front of his desk.

She crossed the room and perched on the edge of the chair. This man still intimidated her. She didn't think anything would ever change that, not even the knowledge that he was human and had nearly died in front of Angel.

Shepherd shook his head. "I don't understand. You had to know I'd never okay this article."

"It's not meant for anyone's eyes but yours. I wrote the story that mattered. The story of a group of brave men and women, who no one knows about, who no one will *ever* know about. A group who do an important job and never take the credit for their courageous and valiant acts. They put their lives on the line, get shot," her eyes flashed to his wheelchair, "get paralyzed protecting other people. They're the story, not the drug dealers pretending to do cancer research in the bayou."

"I still don't understand. You have the exclusive on the takedown at the BioDynamix facility, the arrests of the corrupt Sheriff and his deputy. Why aren't you writing the story?"

"Mr. Shepherd, your team is the story, a story that I know can never be told, but I wanted you to know what I saw, what I experienced." She paused and opened her laptop. She read from her text. "This group, Shepherd Security, is the front line between us and the evil that threaten the civilized, the law abiding, the ordinary citizens who don't know vile people exist in the world. These outlaws are merciless, corrupt, have no value for human life. The members of Shepherd Security equalize the playing field to protect the unknowing, the innocent. They go in armed to the teeth to meet those who threaten the weak on a level playing field." She glanced up from her laptop. "This reporter wouldn't be here right now if it was not for the job these fearless men and women do, expecting no recognition, no thanks. Well, this reporter says thank you."

Shepherd gazed at her, a confused look on his face. "You have the exclusive on the DEA takedown of that plant. This story can make your journalism career take off."

"No longer interested," Brielle said with tears coming to her eyes. "I can't have that job, that life, and still have Brian. Believe me, sir, I have always dreamt of being a reporter, of travel, of writing articles that matter. But I'd never see Brian then. Between that schedule and his, we wouldn't last. He's more important to me than anything."

Shepherd nodded stiffly. "I will share this article up the chain of command, if that's all right with you. There are people in D.C. who will appreciate this piece. And it never hurts to toot our own horns when I'm looking for additional funding."

"It's yours. Do with it what you like," Brielle said.

"Thank you, Ms. Jarboe," Shepherd said in a dismissive tone.

Brielle rose and left, closing the door behind her. She walked half-way down the hallway before she allowed the tears to roll down her cheeks. Inside, she felt a crushing loss, but she knew it would feel worse to lose Brian. And he didn't even know what she had done. She pulled her phone from her back pocket and dialed Dr. Lassiter. She was grateful he answered on the second ring.

"I need to talk with you," she said.

"Are you crying, Brielle?" Lassiter asked.

She wiped the tears. "Yep, that's exactly what I'm doing."

"Are you still in the building?"

She nodded her head, like Dr. Lassiter could see her!

"Come right to my office," he said. "It's down on the fourth floor through the public access."

"Okay," she murmured.

She exited out of the inner office area into the outer office by Angel and left the suite without saying a word to her. She took the public stairs down one flight to the fourth floor. Joe Lassiter stood at the door to his inner office when she entered his suite.

He held his arms open to her, and she immediately went into them. She sobbed.

"Brielle, what is it?" He led her into his office and sat beside her on the couch.

She told him of her decision and the article she wrote.

"Does Brian know?" Lassiter asked.

Brielle shook her head no. "He is confident we could make it work, but I know we can't if we're not together as much as his job will allow."

"He wouldn't want you to sacrifice your happiness for him," Lassiter said. "This is a decision you should have made together. There is no I in we, Brielle."

"I love him, Dr. Lassiter. He's more important to me than anything else."

"Then why the tears?"

"Because now, I have no idea what I'm going to do. Ever since college, all I focused on was what it would take for me to get a job in the big leagues of journalism. I have no other dreams."

"You feel lost?" Lassiter said.

She nodded.

"Give yourself some time for your new dream to take shape. What you are feeling right now is loss because you have no focus, no driving force behind your being. Your new goals will take shape. You just need to give it some time." Plus, he knew that the events of the past week had taken an emotional toll on her. She needed some time to decompress.

Brielle wiped her tears. "I'm sure you're right. This has just been a really emotional time. It was so scary seeing Brian shot."

Lassiter nodded. He knew it would have been. Her previous bravado, he was sure, was either a front or her not facing what she felt. No one could see someone they care about shot and not have it phase them. "I'm sure it was. How did you sleep last night?"

"I had a hard time falling asleep. Every time I was close to drifting off, I saw it again, the moment Brian was shot."

"That's perfectly normal. The more you talk about your feelings, the faster that loop will stop playing."

"It just still all seems surreal, him being shot, watching Gary and Doc work on him, all the blood."

"And when you could see that he was okay?"

"It was a relief, but it didn't make it any less surreal."

"The reality of what you've signed up for by being with him probably hasn't completely dawned on you yet, either."

Brielle shrugged. "Angel told me she was with Mr. Shepherd when he was shot, that something happened to her. I didn't ask what because honestly, I don't think I could have handled knowing right now."

She was quiet for a few moments. Lassiter let her be with her thoughts. He knew she had to decide to share her feelings without prompting from him, and he wanted to see where they would go on their own.

"I guess I've always known that there are evil people in the world, but I've never been around them. Knowing what Sheriff Henderson was capable of," she paused and shook her head, a deep frown cutting across her face. "He brought me and Toby to that plant, knowing we would be killed. Toby is an innocent two-year-old boy? Who could do that?"

"And you too. Don't underestimate how jarring it is to know that someone would have been okay causing your death," Lassiter said.

Brielle nodded. "I've tried not to think about that."

"That's the wrong approach. You need to think about it, need to talk about it. That's what I'm here for. You need to face it. Brielle," he said, taking her hand in his. "You're human and human emotions come with that. Also, you could have lost Brian, and you witnessed a military operation that few others are ever a part of. It's sobering seeing all that."

"Yeah, it was. You know, I spent time with those people, but seeing them in action was shocking. I was really intimidated by all of them at first. But after I talked with them and got to know them, I saw them as regular people, but they're not. Even Madison, seeing her with that assault rifle shooting those men in the BioDynamix plant," she paused and shook her head again. "She didn't even hesitate."

"No, she wouldn't. She's an experienced professional who knows the enemy won't hesitate, so she can't either. If she were to, either she or one of her teammates would be dead."

"How does a person get on with living a normal life with this knowledge?"

Lassiter smiled. "With a lot of gratitude that there are people out there, like those who work for Shepherd Security."

Brielle's lips curved into a smile. "I know you're right. Maybe I just need a little more time."

"I'm sure you do. And you need to give yourself that time. None of this is anything you need to figure out today."

"Thank you, Dr. Lassiter. I know."

"But over the next month or so, it's stuff we need to talk about, until you can honestly say that you're okay living with the knowledge you have and living with the danger that Sherman will be in every day when he goes to work."

Brielle glanced away, unable to maintain eye contact with Dr. Lassiter while she considered that. "And if I can't, Brian and I don't stand a chance."

A small grin curved Lassiter's lips. "It's my job to make sure you can. I've got you, Brielle."

She returned her gaze to him. "Thank you."

Lassiter nodded. "You are welcome. I'm here for you both. Even though Sherman assures me he's okay with being shot again, I know that isn't the case. I'll work with him a lot, sometimes meeting with the two of you together. Just remember it's a process, recovering from what the two of you have been through."

"I will," she promised him.

When she left Dr. Lassiter's office, she returned to Angel's desk. "Do you have a few minutes?"

"Sure," Angel said with a smile. "Sammy is just getting up from his nap. I'm very lucky that I get to have him here at work. Let me just grab him and we can have another cup of tea while I give him a snack. He usually wakes up hungry."

Brielle went back into the kitchen. She realized she'd left her laptop in Dr. Lassiter's office. She brewed the two cups of tea while she waited for Angel, and she sent Lassiter a text message about her laptop. He guaranteed he'd get it to her within a few hours.

Angel came back into the kitchen carrying the most adorable dark-haired toddler, bringing a smile to Brielle's face. He rubbed his sleepy eyes. He was clearly the combination of Angel and Jackson. She immediately thought of Toby and wondered how he and Tina were. She hadn't even said goodbye to Tina when the DEA Agent led her and Toby away. She'd have to reach out to Tina and see how they were.

"Oh, thank you for making me a cup of tea," Angel said. She got a sippy cup out of the refrigerator and grabbed a banana from the fruit bowl on the counter. Then she sat with her little boy on her lap. "Sammy, this is Miss Brielle, a friend of Mommy and Daddy's."

The little boy smiled at Brielle and acted shy.

"Hi Sammy," Brielle said. "I've heard a lot about you."

Angel laughed. "He's still waking up. He's usually not so shy."

"Brian has a genuine affection for him," Brielle said. "Can I talk in front of him?"

Angel's gaze grew more serious. She nodded. "We spell certain things, but for the most part, he doesn't understand a lot."

Brielle nodded. She'd never say anything inappropriate in front of the child. "I just left Dr. Lassiter's office. I was really upset when I left Mr. Shepherd's office. I chose not to write the article on what went on down in the bayou."

"How come?"

"I wrote a different article, on what you guys do here."

A worried expression came to Angel's face.

"It wasn't for anyone but Mr. Shepherd to read. I decided I couldn't have the life I always dreamed about, as a reporter. I can't work the hours and travel as I would need to because if I did, Brian and I wouldn't last."

"Brielle, you don't know that," Angel argued.

"Yes, I do. Brian told me he is usually away for work at least eighty percent of the time. If I'm working that twenty percent when he's home, we'll never see each other. That kind of relationship will never work, and Brian is more important to me than anything else."

"Then why were you upset?"

"Because I'm not sure I can be okay with his job and not worry to death every time he goes to work. How do you do it?"

Angel glanced at her son. "Because it's who he is and what he does. If it wasn't for people like him and the others here, I wouldn't be a-l-i-v-e." She spelled out the word alive. "Also, because I know how competent everyone else is. I trust them with his l-i-f-e, just as he does."

"I know it's who Brian is too, and I could never ask him to give up who he is. I hope at some point I can have that same faith and truly accept that."

"Give it some time," Angel advised. "This is all very new. The more experience you get with it, and the more you understand what we do, the easier it will be to accept that and have the same faith in the team that I have."

Shortly thereafter, Brielle received a text message from Shepherd, asking her to come to his office. She approached his door with apprehension. Why did he want to see her now? This time it was open. She was surprised when she stepped into the room and both Brian and Cooper were seated at the conference room table with Shepherd.

"Thank you for coming so promptly," Shepherd said to her. "Please close the door and join us."

She closed the door quietly, as though it was the door to a nursery with a sleeping baby within. Then she approached the table and took a seat beside Brian, her eyes silently questioning him. Brian flashed her a smile and gave her a small nod which helped to put her at ease.

"Brielle Jarboe meet Jason Manning, Deputy Director of the DEA," Shepherd said, bringing her attention to the man on the large monitor on the wall.

"Ms. Jarboe, it's nice to meet you," Manning said.

Her eyes studied the man on the monitor. Jason Manning was in his early sixties. He was a white man with a full head of salt and pepper hair. He looked serious, an all business expression across his thin face. "You too, sir," she replied.

"I read your piece on Shepherd Security. It's good. I'm told you have declined the exclusive to report on the takedown of the BioDynamix facility."

"That's correct," Brielle replied.

"Why Brielle?" Sherman asked. "This story is yours."

"I don't want the attention that will go along with it." Her gaze shifted to Brian. "I know you think we can work it out if I get a good journalism job, but I know that would be the end of us and you're what's important to me, Brian."

"Then write the article and let us release it with a fictitious reporter byline," Manning said. "You make up a name."

"The story has to be told and we want you to tell it," Shepherd interjected.

"Can you submit it to me by first thing tomorrow morning?" Manning asked.

Brielle nodded. "Yeah, I should be able to. I had it half written when I realized the Shepherd Security story was the real one that I wanted to write."

"Brielle, Shepherd Security has a contract with the DEA to partner with them on missions to get intel on and take down suspected drug labs and distribution centers in various cities in the United States. Those too are stories that need to be reported on," Shepherd said.

"And we need to carefully control what information is reported. This fictitious staff reporter we are creating could be very valuable at writing those stories too," Manning said. "We want you to be that reporter."

"You would officially be employed by Shepherd Security," Shepherd said. "To have the full picture, you'll sit in on mission briefings, be in Ops to see how surveillance is carried out, be there if you can stomach it when the team goes in, and during the take down."

Brielle was stunned. She merely nodded her head yes. Were they really offering her this job? And an exclusive on many more stories to come?

"And since there would not be enough of the DEA writing work to make this a full-time job for you, and since we could use your writing skills with various reports, we would have other agency work that would be assigned to you," Cooper piped up.

"It is not general knowledge, yet, but Angel is pregnant again so we could use some additional front-desk help. Doc's wife Elizabeth is her backup, but that baby of theirs is keeping her awake more nights than not and she's not available as much as I think we will need her to be, at least not right now," Shepherd added. "So, that is another need we have that you could fill if you take the job."

"You're offering me a job?" Brielle asked after a lengthy silence. Then her eyes went to Brian. He nodded and smiled. She could tell that he was as pleased by this as she was.

"We'll draw up the employment contract if you agree. The position will officially be Special Projects Coordinator," Shepherd said. "We'll give you an office up on seven near Sherman's."

A proud smile curved Brielle's lips. "I'd love to take this job."

"Is there a but coming?" Cooper asked after a few quiet moments that the men waited, thinking more was coming from her.

A big grin spread over her face. "There's no but. Yes, thank you. I accept your offer." Though she had no idea what the offer was. She didn't know the salary or benefits, the expectations or the work schedule, and it didn't matter either. She'd get to write stories that mattered and be with Brian.

"Very good," Shepherd said. "We'll get into particulars later. Have that article submitted to me by zero seven-thirty tomorrow and after I review it, I will forward it on to you, Manning."

"Meet with me tomorrow at zero eight hundred," Cooper said. "We'll get you set up with the access you'll need."

Brielle nodded. "Thank you."

Cooper came to his feet. He came up to Sherman. "Come on, I'll help you up and get you back to bed like I promised the Undertaker I would, don't want to piss him off." He reached his hand out to Sherman and pulled him to his feet.

Brielle could tell the movement hurt Brian's ribs. She hoped he'd heal quickly. She knew they couldn't go back to his place until he could get up and down on his own. She followed them out of the room and onto the elevator.

"I read the article you wrote," Cooper said to Brielle. "Shepherd was impressed by your insights and by how you worded it, and not much impresses him."

A smile formed on Brielle's lips. "Is that right? Wow. I would not have thought that."

"What, that not much impresses Shepherd?" Cooper asked.

"No, that he was impressed by it. I pretty much guessed that not much impresses him. He seems like a tough and demanding man."

"You have no idea," Sherman said with a chuckle.

The doors opened and the three of them stepped off on nine.

"Let's get you settled in bed," Cooper said.

"I'm already fed up with taking it easy and lying around," Sherman complained as they reached the door to the apartment. He opened it and stepped inside.

Cooper chuckled. "You are not a pleasant patient." His eyes went to Brielle. "Come hang out on five whenever you want a break from Mr. Pain-in-the-ass."

Brielle laughed. "No, right here with Brian is exactly where I want to be."

"Lunch should be here soon. I'll prop you up in more of a sitting position, but after he eats, Brielle, he has to lie further reclined. You'll have to pull a few pillows out from behind him. Don't you dare try to raise yourself up for her to do it, Sherman,"

"I'll call Doc if she can't," Sherman said. "I won't try to get up by myself yet."

"Hold him to that, Brielle," Cooper said half-jokingly. Then he left.

Brielle took a seat next to him on the bed. She learned that Angel ordered out lunch five days a week, with Shepherd picking up the tab. She ordered from fifteen different places, rotating the restaurant and the food in the catering sized order. There were always leftovers in the refrigerator in the kitchen on five. Brielle would have to make plates from there for their dinner tonight.

"That's quite a perk, lunch provided every day."

"Shepherd applies common sense to everything. It makes sense for him to provide meals because Ops is manned twenty-four-by-seven. Sometimes, they end up being on twelve hours or more. They need to have food available. Plus, we get back from missions at all hours. We need to eat too, and it isn't always convenient to run to the store or through a fast-food drive-thru, and it takes more time away from our work to do so. Plus, fast-food is not healthy."

Brielle laughed that sexy sound that Sherman loved. "I wouldn't have pegged you as health-conscious," she said.

"I do try to be healthy, not that I don't love a good burger and a beer, or a pizza, but you have to fuel your body properly for it to perform well. Doc is our senior medic, and he is all about healthy foods. He's actually taught me a lot about healthy eating."

"I guess I never thought about things as normal as having meals available for people working long hours, or for us just flying in and staying here in the apartment. I was surprised at that Coast Guard base that they stocked the galley for us. Otherwise, someone would have had to go shopping or go pick up fast-food for every meal. When we went to sleep last night, I was wondering if there was a place walking-distance I could go get us breakfast."

"I'm sure Angel will have breakfast for us tomorrow in the fridge right now too. We'll bring it up with us later so that we have it when we wake up."

The text came from Angel that lunch was set up in the kitchen. Brielle went down to get plates for Brian and herself. She entered into a room full of people, half she didn't know. A woman with short, spikey red hair came up to her. "Hi Brielle. I'm Yvette, also known as Control on comms."

"It's nice to meet you," Brielle said.

"How's Sherman feeling?"

"He's sore, but he'll be fine," Brielle replied.

"Good. I hate it when one of ours is injured. I worry about them all while they're in the field."

"We love you too, Yvette," Doc said with a laugh from near the large tin trays of food that smelled incredible. There was a young, tiny woman standing beside him with her dish-water blond hair in a ponytail. "Brielle, my wife, Elizabeth."

"It's nice to meet you," Elizabeth said, stepping forward.

Brielle was surprised by Doc's wife. She wasn't sure what she envisioned his wife would look like, but this young woman was not it. "It's great to meet you too," Brielle replied. "Don't you have a little baby?"

Elizabeth giggled. "Yes, Olivia." She pointed towards the room Brielle knew was the nursery. "She's in the crib taking a nap. She's a great sleeper during the day, it's the nights that I can't get her to stay asleep."

"I think she was born to work overnights," Doc said.

"Train her for Ops so the rest of us can work fewer overnight shifts," Yvette said. "Three months old is old enough," she added with a laugh.

Brielle giggled. "So, Brian told me that you also work here at the office."

"Yes, I'm in to man the front desk and public phone line for a few hours while Angel works on some budget stuff for Shepherd. I'll also help take care of Sammy until he goes down for his afternoon nap. Angel is so lucky that he has a schedule she can count on."

Just then Angel entered the kitchen, holding Sammy's hand. "That's because he isn't three months old. You'll get there, Elizabeth. She'll settle into a routine."

"She already has, keeping us awake all night," Doc complained.

Brielle smiled at the thought of how normal this conversation was compared to what this group did. Just the day before, Doc was firing his weapon at who they guessed were Chinese gang members and he was working alongside Gary to save Brian's life. Today he was moaning about his baby, keeping them awake at night and introducing her to his wife.

"I'll see you later, I'm sure," Yvette said to Brielle. She had two containers of food in her hands. "I have to get back up to Ops."

"Is that for Garcia?" Doc asked.

"Yeah, he's covering for Smith. Smith was on for twenty-four hours. He's sacked out in his office right now." She left the room.

Doc shook his head. "I'm sure Garcia was on for that long too. Angel, get me on Shepherd's calendar this afternoon, will you?"

"Will do, Doc," Angel said. Brielle still stood back, watching the others serve themselves from the containers that were lined up on the counter. "Brielle, get in here and make plates for you both." She opened the cabinet. "Here are the containers to take it in. Just bring them back down and wash them at some point."

"I will, thank you." She wanted to congratulate Angel, knowing that she was pregnant, but Mr. Shepherd had said it wasn't common knowledge yet. She loaded the container for Brian with a serving of each of the dishes, garden salad, roast chicken, mashed potatoes, gravy, and green beans. She had no idea what he liked or disliked. She ate everything, so she could always finish his uneaten portions for dinner. Then she placed portions of each in her container.

She rode the elevator back up with a man named Ryan. She vaguely recalled seeing him when they were here before. He said he maintained all the supplies from toilet paper to weapons and ammo. He got off on the eighth floor.

The rest of the day flew by. After Brielle finished the article she promised to write, and she sent it to Shepherd that afternoon, she snuggled with Brian in bed. They watched a movie, took a nap, and then Brielle went back to the kitchen and got their dinner portions and the breakfast foods for them for the next morning too. She felt relaxed when they turned the light out, but the same thing happened every time she was about to drift off. The moment Brian was shot flashed through her mind.

Tango

rielle made her way to Cooper's office at eight a.m. the next morning. She was surprised that he already had an employment contract for her to sign, with a salary more generous than she expected. There were also medical and dental enrollment forms for her to sign. The premiums were covered one hundred percent by Shepherd Security, with great coverage. They provided life insurance, though she couldn't decide who to list as beneficiary. After Cooper guaranteed her that she could change it any time, she put down her sister, Dahlia.

Cooper advised her that she needed to go see Garcia when they were done regarding porting her personal cell phone number over to the Shepherd Security profile. The agency phone would be all she carried, but Garcia would explain it to her. He also gave her an agency issued, secure laptop like everyone else had. Garcia would help her out with that too, but it was set up and ready to go for her.

"Brielle, one more thing," Cooper said. "Do you remember how the team all has trackers in our shoulders?"

"Yes. I remember, and Brian told me about them too. He said I'd probably have one."

Cooper was happy Brian had already told her. "That's correct. All agency personnel do, as do all the wives. So, you have no problem with having one?"

"No," Brielle said. "It's part of the job, an expectation of employment, right?" At least that was how Brian had explained it.

"That's correct. I'll set the appointment up with Doc to inject it into you."

"Sure," Brielle agreed. "Just someone let me know when and where."

Cooper knew he shouldn't be surprised by her, but he was. Shepherd had asked a lot of questions about her throughout her involvement in the mission. He wasn't surprised that Shepherd suggested the DEA offer her the position they did, nor that Shepherd wanted her to also work for the agency. Cooper agreed it would be a good fit and help alleviate a staffing shortage they had. Hell, he hoped Shepherd would shift over some of the administrative crap that was on him, monthly reports, mission report formatting and proofing, and the hundreds of other monthly reports he was responsible for.

Then, he took her to the seventh floor and showed her the office assigned to her. It was just down the hall from Brian's. He called Garcia to be sure he was ready for her. He was in his workroom. Cooper brought her there and then left. As she stood awkwardly just within the door, she tried to remind herself he was just a normal guy, like Brian had said. She also reminded herself that his wife was pregnant with their first child, a son, and he had sounded genuinely thrilled about it.

"So, you need to authorize your existing phone number with your carrier to be ported over to us so you can keep that number. We'll keep your agency phone set up as it is now, so you can get calls and text messages to both phone numbers, unless you'd rather notify all your contacts on your personal number of this new number."

"No, I'd rather keep my old number too," Brielle replied.

"I figured you would. Let's take care of that call right now."

She placed the call to her carrier's customer service number, authorized them to speak with Garcia, and he took care of the rest. She stood there and waited while he was on the call. It only took five minutes, and it was done.

"What about the bill for my personal line?"

"There isn't one. Shepherd's budget takes care of all phones. Now, let's talk about your agency issued laptop."

Brielle took in all the information, the dos and don'ts regarding the laptop computer.

"And remember, never ever override the settings and access a Wi-Fi network. Never," Garcia warned. "You have a satellite card. Use it."

Brielle nodded. "Got it. Never."

"Okay, you're all set," Garcia said.

"Thank you." Brielle turned to leave.

"And Brielle," Garcia said, stopping her after she'd stepped into the hallway. "Welcome to the team. As soon as possible, I want to introduce you to my wife, Sienna. She is excited to meet you. I know you can't leave Sherman alone yet, but as soon as you can, the girls all want to have a lunch or a dinner with you."

"That would be really nice." Brielle's smile was genuine. She was very excited about this new life she was starting.

"I pushed the phone numbers of all the wives to your phone, and yours to theirs this morning. Don't be surprised if you get text messages from them."

"I appreciate that. Thank you for everything." She walked away feeling grateful and with a much different opinion of Garcia.

At eleven hundred, Brielle and Sherman entered Shepherd's office. They were the first to arrive.

"During the briefing, I'm going to ask you not to ask any questions. Write them out and we'll go over them after. And you do need to take notes for yourself regarding the mission," Shepherd said to Brielle.

Brielle held her new agency issued laptop up. She was planning on it.

Brian was breathing easier, however, he still needed assistance to get up or down, and forget rolling over in bed. Brielle thought he was doing very well considering the trauma his body had suffered, but she also thought it was way too soon for him to be returning to work, even on limited duty. She'd feel better if he just laid in bed for a few more days. She suspected he was the one who insisted on returning to work. She'd have to talk with Gary about that.

The others came in and quickly took their seats.

"For those of you who don't know," Shepherd began, "Brielle has accepted a position with us. She will be writing news reports for the DEA to release regarding the arrests made around our DEA Partner Missions, amongst other things. What this means is she will be present during our mission briefings, watch mission feed in Ops and then submit her articles, which both I and Manning will edit prior to release. The DEA has been looking for someone to write these articles from their perspective for a while. Brielle will also write other reports for us as well as man the front desk whenever Angel or Elizabeth cannot be in."

Congratulations and welcomes were offered from everyone around the table.

"As you all know as well, Sherman is on limited duty for probably the next month. With this mission he will begin training to man Ops," Cooper said.

"The DEA hasn't made much headway with the suspected meth lab in New York since we pulled out due to the priority mission in Louisiana. Pretty much expect to pick up where you left off, gentlemen. Lambchop, bring us up to speed on what transpired before your team was pulled," Shepherd said.

Lambchop nodded. "We were only on the ground for two days. We didn't get too far into it. We took over surveillance on the suspected meth lab and ran the people who we observed coming and going from the property through facial recognition if the DEA didn't already have an ID on them. It was mostly low to mid-level dealers that were identified, which we didn't expect. Normally, it's the higher-level dealers who pick up product to then pass it to their mid or low-level street dealers. We observed a couple of guys on their corners selling after they left the suspected meth-lab." His eyes shifted to Brielle. "Normally, only one or two guys know the location of where the meth is being cooked to protect the location. Where it's cooked and distributed from are normally two separate locations. So, we have to wonder if this is just a distribution location and not where it's being produced."

Brielle typed her questions into her laptop. She had many, beginning with why these low-level dealers weren't arrested. She found it very hard to remain quiet.

"The security they have on that house screams something illegal is going on," Jackson said. "They have lookouts two blocks away in all directions. When a squad car rolls through, they phone ahead, and everyone moves. All the guards within a block of the house go into hiding, but they are all still nearby and watching with their guns drawn. The front and back doors appear to be heavily fortified; not sure a battering ram will even be able to crack them open. That too makes us wonder if this is just a distribution location. When we pulled out, we suggested to the DEA that they need to tail anyone coming to the location with bags or boxes large enough to transport product in."

"Even if this is a meth lab, the raw material needs to be brought in. The source of the supplies needs to be an initial focus," Lambchop added.

"Okay, that's it. Pack up, gentlemen. You leave within the hour," Shepherd said, dismissing them. "Brielle and Sherman, stay."

After the team going on the mission except for Cooper left the room, Shepherd turned to Brielle. "I saw a lot of typing going on. Besides your notes on the mission, I'm assuming you have questions."

"Yes, sir."

"And once we're done here, I'm getting you back to bed for a few hours rest," Cooper said to Sherman.

"I thought I was going to begin training in Ops?"

"Later this afternoon. Doc and the Undertaker have ordered that for the next week you are up for no more than four hours, followed by at least three hours in bed," Cooper said.

Sherman grumbled, but Brielle was relieved. Gary was going on the mission, but Doc would be here to change Brian's bandages, check in on him, and make sure he rested. She was grateful for that.

She read her many questions off, and Shepherd, Cooper, or Brian answered them all to her satisfaction. She got a much better understanding of what they did and why. If the house they were watching was just a distribution center, they wanted to trace the drugs back to where it was produced. Close down the manufacturing facility first, then the distribution center. Then scoop up all the dealers they observed too.

"During this mission you'll be on call to go into Ops whenever there is something to observe, since you'll be staying in the apartment for the foreseeable future. We'll figure it out after you're no longer there," Cooper said. "Maybe we'll just have you watch taped mission feed."

"And since you're on the payroll as of today, I want you to start training with Angel for the front desk coverage," Shepherd said. "I'll also have her acquaint you with our standard report formats."

"Should I report to her when we are done?"

The corner of Shepherd's lip pulled up. He liked her enthusiasm and her willingness to do whatever job they asked of her. He was already considering what other reports she could help out with. "After lunch is fine."

Cooper stood. "Let me help you up," he said to Sherman.

Brielle's eyes went back to Shepherd. "One more thing, sir. Do you have any news on Bobby's release yet?"

"The DEA is waiting for a reply from the judge in Louisiana. He has to agree to dismiss the case and authorize Bobby's release from the rehab facility. Then the order must be executed through official channels with the rehab staff. It shouldn't take more than a week."

Brielle frowned. A week? She wanted him out of there now. He didn't belong there. In the very least, she wanted to go see Bobby at the facility. She and Brian spoke with him on the phone earlier that morning and told him it was over, arrests were made, and that they were working on his release. They didn't tell him about Brian getting shot, though. Brian insisted that was something they would tell him only in person once he was released.

Brielle followed them to the elevator. Once in the apartment, Cooper got Brian settled in bed. Doc was in his office to call when Brian needed to get up. Brielle crawled onto the bed and sat beside Brian, facing him.

Sherman took in her beaming smile. "You look happy."

"I am. I still can't believe Mr. Shepherd and Director Manning offered me a job. I'll get to write stories that matter, just like I've always wanted. And I get to be with you." She leaned down and kissed him. It was passionate, lengthy, and left them both wanting more.

"I bet I could lay nearly still and not hurt my ribs if you were on top." He unbuttoned his jeans. "Help me get my pants off."

"No, Brian Sherman. Gary said no physical activity at all for you, and that includes sex. We need to wait a few more days till your ribs don't hurt so bad."

"Ugh! Brielle, come on." He wrapped his hand around the back of her neck and pulled her in for another of those electrifying kisses.

When Brian's hand moved under her shirt and pushed her bra up, she pulled away. "I promise, as soon as you can get up and down by yourself, we'll make love. I do need to get to a doctor before then and get some birth control. I plan to ask Angel who her doctor is."

"Or we could go by your cycles and let God decide."

"You know what they call people who use the rhythm method of birth control, don't you? Parents!"

Sherman laughed, then he winced. Man, the ribs still hurt. He thought they had gotten better. Well, they had a little. Deep breathing didn't hurt quite as bad as it had even the day before. "I know I have fallen in love with you, Brielle. And that's not going to change."

This was only the second time he'd said I love you. It felt just as exhilarating to hear those words as it did the first time. "I feel the same. There is no place I'd rather be, than here with you."

"Would it be the worst thing in the world to have my kid?" Sherman chuckled. He could picture her pregnant and it was a mental image that, surprisingly, brought a smile to his face.

"I think we should wait more than a week to talk about that."

"It feels like I've known you and loved you a lot longer than that," Sherman said. He kissed her again. He couldn't get enough of her lips on his.

After a lengthy kiss, Brielle sat back and smiled at him. "I love you Brian Sherman. I don't want a kid yet though. So, I will be talking with Angel to get her doctor's name."

"But you do want to have kids, don't you? I never really thought about it before, but it's something now I want," he confessed.

"Yes. I've always wanted to be a mom. I always thought I'd have kids, but just not yet."

Sherman lifted her hand to his lips and pressed a kiss to her knuckles. "When we're both ready, or God decides."

"Agreed."

Uniform

*B*rielle received a text from Angel that lunch was set out in the kitchen, Italian. "I'll text you what there is, and you can let me know what you want," she said.

"I like just about everything. Just like yesterday, please get me a little of it all." He gazed at her with appreciation. "And thank you for taking such good care of me."

"You don't have to thank me." She gave him a kiss and then left.

As she took the stairs down to the fifth floor, it occurred to her how comfortable she was with Brian, with moving around this secure building, and with the others who worked here. She already felt like she belonged. And taking care of Brian felt perfectly natural. She recalled the days she spent with his momma. She talked about Brian often, the pride she had in her oldest son obvious. Of course, back then, Brielle still held a grudge against him for breaking Dahlia's heart. She believed that Helene Sherman would be very happy that they were together.

She entered the kitchen. She greeted a few of the others who she knew, and Kaylee was there, sitting at the table with another woman she didn't know. She was a beautiful woman. She had shoulder-length light brown hair, a warm smile, and soft blue eyes.

Kaylee got up from her chair. "Hi Brielle!" She wrapped her in a hug. "I was shocked about you and Brian, when Gary told me. I thought you had a thing going with Bobby."

Brielle laughed. "Bobby and I are just good friends. Besides, Bobby's gay."

"Really? I didn't catch that vibe at all," Kaylee said. By this time the other woman stood beside her. "Brielle, this is Sienna, Anthony's wife."

"Hi Sienna, it's nice to meet you," Brielle greeted. She remembered the name Sienna and figured out that Anthony must be Garcia's first name. Wow! She was not at all what Brielle had thought Garcia's wife would look like. She looked very normal, sweet even, with her girl-next-door look. She'd expected maybe a biker chick, or a female WWF wrestler look-alike. She just assumed Garcia's wife would look as rough as he did.

"It's great to meet you too," Sienna said. "I've heard a lot about you."

Brielle wondered from who and what she'd heard. "Aren't you both teachers?"

The two ladies nodded.

"What are you doing here during the day? Was there no school today?"

Kaylee looked confused. "It's Saturday."

Brielle realized she hadn't known what day it was for several days. She smiled an embarrassed smile. "Wow, we've been so busy, I guess I lost track of the days."

"That's perfectly normal," Sienna said. "I don't know what happened, but I know you were part of a case the team worked. I was too. I understand. You lose track of things like what day it is."

Brielle stared at her and said nothing.

"I was too," Kaylee added. "As was Elizabeth. We all understand. That's why we're here. To welcome you to our group and have lunch with you."

Brielle wasn't sure what to say. "Brian is in the room we're staying in. I have to bring him lunch."

"Anthony's going to bring it to him and have lunch with him in the apartment," Sienna said. "Make his plate and I'll text Anthony." She pulled her phone from her back pocket and typed out a text message.

Brielle recognized Sienna's phone. It was the same as hers. Sienna had an agency phone too.

"And then we'll stay here. Michaela and Angel are going to join us too," Kaylee said.

"Who's Michaela?" She hadn't met her yet, wasn't sure if she'd heard her name.

"Michaela works upstairs in the tech lab," Kaylee replied. "She invented the trackers and a lot of the other cool tech they have that isn't bought off a shelf someplace."

Brielle was even more surprised. "She invented the trackers?"

Both the ladies nodded. "There are even ankle charm bracelets with trackers in them on the babies," Sienna said.

Brielle knew the look on her face was one of surprise or disbelief.

"I know, right?" Kaylee said. "That's what I thought when I first heard about them. Putting trackers on the babies. And I didn't like that Gary's office was going to track my every move, but once I realized it was for my protection and why I might need protection because of what they do, I relaxed about it."

"Anthony said Doc would be injecting yours in later today. Just a warning. It hurts like a bitch at first," Sienna said. "Make sure you ice it all night."

"Thanks," Brielle said. She turned and grabbed one of the to-go containers from the cabinet. "I better make Brian's plate."

"How is Brian feeling today?" Sienna asked.

As Brielle used the spatula to take out a small piece of lasagna from the tray, she answered. "He's breathing a bit easier, but he still isn't moving too well."

"That'll take a little longer," Garcia said from behind the women as he entered the room.

Brielle watched him greet his wife with a quick embrace and a kiss. She softened his rough appearance, Brielle thought. They were as unlikely a couple as Elizabeth and Doc were, appearance wise, but she saw the tenderness in Garcia's actions and the affection he had for his wife.

Garcia grabbed a to-go container too, filled it, and then Brielle watched him take his and Brian's and leave the room. Brielle filled a plate for herself and joined the two ladies at the table. Angel and another woman entered the kitchen. The other woman was stunning. She had smooth, long, dark hair framing a flawless complexion of light mocha skin. She wore a white lab coat over a pink top and a pair of blue jeans.

Angel pointed to Brielle. "Michaela, this is our new coworker, Brielle. Brielle, this is Michaela."

"Welcome," Michaela said with a perfect smile. "It's nice there's another one of us."

"What do you mean?" Brielle asked. She wasn't sure what nationality Michaela was, but Brielle didn't think she was part Indian, Caribbean, African, and a host of other ethnicities, like she was.

"Another woman. We are definitely a minority here."

Angel and Michaela got their plates and joined the other women at the table. It was over an hour later when Garcia returned with the two empty containers. Brielle didn't realize they sat, talked, and laughed that long. Angel announced her pregnancy to everyone, though Brielle was sure several of the women already knew. Brielle was happy she could congratulate her.

"Angel, it's Saturday. Do you always work Saturdays?" Brielle asked. She knew her schedule would vary.

"Only when Shepherd has something special, he needs me to do. Today I worked on some financial reports he needed finished from yesterday."

"Where is Sammy?" Brielle asked.

"I needed to concentrate. He's with my aunt today. I'll take a couple afternoons off as comp time this week, when Elizabeth can come in and cover."

"We help her out with Sammy on weekends too," Kaylee said, pointing to herself and Sienna. "But we obviously couldn't help today because we wanted to have lunch with you."

Brielle smiled, happy that they had. It had been a pleasant and comfortable lunch. They were all nice ladies, welcoming, and she could see that they were all good friends. No one had asked her what she had been involved in that was a Shepherd Security case, and none of them offered up any information on themselves in that regard either, but it was okay. It didn't matter. They told her they often had movie nights or dinners out when the guys were away. They guaranteed her she would receive invitations.

"I better get back up to the lab," Michaela said, coming to her feet.

"Yes, I need to finish this spreadsheet for Shepherd, then I can get Sammy and go home. I have tons of laundry to get done," Angel said, standing as well.

"Shepherd told me I'd start training with you for front desk duty after lunch," Brielle said.

Angel shook her head. "He probably forgot it was Saturday. We'll start Monday morning. I'll text you when I get to the office."

"We're going to the mall to do some shopping. Baby things," Kaylee said. "Do you want to come, Brielle?"

"Thank you, next time, okay? I need to get back upstairs to be with Brian."

"Understood," Kaylee said. "I'd feel the same way if it was Gary. Is there anything you need, that we can pick up for you?"

"That is so nice of you to offer," Brielle said, truly appreciative. "I'm good though."

Over the next few days, both Brielle and Sherman spent time in Ops while the team was conducting surveillance. Sherman found it difficult to watch his team, and not be there with them, but he did find this side of it fascinating. To see what the analysts in Ops did and what they saw while the team operated in the field gave him a whole new perspective. He believed it would make him a better Operator.

For Brielle, watching what the team did and how they did it in an urban environment was very different from observing them in the bayou. And listening to the conversation inside of Ops, understanding what the analysts were doing to support the team, was enlightening and would make her reports more three dimensional. She made notes, not sure exactly what would be allowed to be reported on and what wouldn't.

Brielle also spent time training with Angel on the front desk duties. It was usually pretty quiet at the front entrance. They didn't even receive packages through the front of the office. There were two phone lines, the public, published phone line and the private, secure line. There were different greetings and different protocols for each line. Another big part of the job was making travel arrangements for the team and ensuring meals were provided. Brielle had never had a desk job, but she knew she could adjust to the inside, sedentary environment.

On the sixth day the team was onsite in New York, they were ready to move on the suspected meth lab and distribution house. Brielle and Sherman were both in

Ops. She watched camera feed from each of their men's vests, fascinated by the process. The team was inside a large warehouse. They were geared up in black tactical clothing. It was eleven p.m., twenty-three hundred hours. Dozens of DEA Agents were there, similarly dressed. Several armored vehicles sat waiting. The local police were poised to arrest the dealers and any customers who would be unlucky enough to be making purchases when the operation commenced.

Even though Brielle knew that Brian was right beside her, she couldn't help but think about his future safety as she watched the feed on the monitor of the team getting ready to enter the suspected meth lab. Very soon, he would rejoin his team and take up position outside of a house or a warehouse in some American city. He'd be dressed in tactical gear like he had been when he was shot. He'd be armed like he was in a war zone.

It did not escape her that the dark figures she watched were men she knew, husbands, a father. Madison stood in front of her. Brielle glanced at the monitor with the text designating Coop, her husband. Madison herself would be out there in future missions. Her eyes swept to Garcia. He would be as well.

She watched the team load up in vehicles and drive to the suspected meth lab. She heard and watched Landon's short prayer with the team as they arrived onsite. Short, clipped words rang through the armored transport. "Go! Go! Go!"

Following the events on the monitors, through the team's camera feeds, she watched the six men from Shepherd Security along with a dozen other agents all rush from the vehicles, assault rifles grasped in their hands. They ran along the side of the building, kept their bodies pressed to it. A large man wearing a bullet-proof vest with the letters DEA stepped forward with a large, hand-held battering ram. He stepped up to the door, swung the heavy metal weight, hurtling it into the door. The door splintered open with a loud crashing sound, which made Brielle flinch.

That man stepped back, and the line of men rushed in, one by one. She heard shouts, "Federal Agents, we have a warrant!" Seconds later she watched the feed from Cooper's vest, who was the first of their people to enter the building. She saw several people running from the authorities. "Freeze, federal agents!" She recognized Cooper's voice. "Hands, let me see your hands!" Several men yelled.

One of the men in Cooper's line of sight raised a gun. She saw the muzzle flash from Cooper's weapon and the man dropped to the floor. By this time, the camera feeds from the others showed they were in the house. They were searching rooms. Danny's feed showed him enter the garage to where an entire lab was set up. The back door was open. Danny went to it. In his camera feed, Brielle saw a half dozen agents standing around at least five people who were face-down on the ground.

"Clear!" Danny yelled to them.

She watched Jackson's feed. He followed Gary up a narrow staircase. At the top, a man fired an assault rifle at them. They both leaned against the wall, out of his sight. She watched hand signals between the two of them, and then they leaned into sight and both squeezed off multiple rounds, striking the man at the top of the stairs. He fell, face first down the stairs, his body stopping before he reached Gary, who then kicked his weapon away from him before checking for a pulse. There wasn't one.

Through the speakers in the room, Brielle heard Cooper's and Lambchop's voices repeating "Clear!" as their video feeds showed them search rooms, behind doors, in closets, under beds. The raid lasted less than three minutes for the team and the other agents to have everyone in custody and the whole place searched.

Then they got confirmation that all the lookouts near the suspected distribution house had been taken down. The local SWAT Team with another team of DEA Agents had completed a similar successful raid on that distribution house. At the same time, local police moved in with warrants on all the dealers who they'd observed coming and going from the distribution house. Warrants had been issued on all of them.

They also executed warrants at the same time on the three people who had been identified bringing the raw materials to make the meth into the cook house. One of them was a teacher at a local grade school. Brielle found that shocking.

In all, over sixty arrests were made, six people had resisted and were shot, four of them killed. The large meth lab was seized, over twenty-two million in product was recovered at both locations. At the distribution house, over fifteen thousand in cash was recovered as well as a thousand pounds of marijuana and several dozen handguns.

It had been a very successful operation. Brielle feverishly jotted down thoughts on it once it was all over. During the operation, her eyes had remained on the monitors. She didn't even look to see what Yvette and Garcia were doing, though she did hear clicking of keys at different times.

She and Brian made their way back to the apartment. She was way too keyed up to sleep. She helped Brian sit on the edge of the bed and then helped him to recline. He was using his own abdominal muscles, bearing much of his own weight. She knew this meant they would get to go home to his place soon.

"Watching the raid was incredible," she said, sitting cross legged on the bed, facing him. "What does it feel like to you when you're there, doing it?"

"A lot different from watching it in Ops," Sherman replied. "You're pumped up, your adrenalin really cursing through you all the way to the mission site and while you're holding in position. Once the go command is given, everything moves so fast. Training and instincts take over."

"Do you think about the danger at all?"

"No, not until the shooting starts, then you just focus on getting them before they get you."

"But it's a rush, while you're doing it, isn't it?"

Brian looked disturbed by her question. He ran his hand over his scruffy chin and then glanced away. "Look, I'd be lying if I told you it wasn't. And anyone who does this job, yeah, they've got to be an adrenalin junky. But it's more than that. There is also a pride, knowing you're doing it to protect the United States and the innocent civilians. There is also pride in knowing that there is a very small percentage of people out there that have the skills we do, the training, and the grit to go into these situations and handle them."

"Yeah, I get that," she said. "Do you get used to it? Does it ever seem routine?"

"No and the second it does is the moment a person needs to stop doing this job. That's the kind of thinking that will get you killed. There is nothing ever routine about these kinds of operations, be them civilian or military."

"And that rush? Has it changed over time?"

Sherman shook his head no. "It's the same today as it was when we kicked in doors and cleared houses in Afghanistan."

Brielle was again surprised to get a meeting invitation from Dr. Lassiter. It was nine a.m., zero nine hundred. Brielle sat her phone back to the small table in the apartment and then she gazed at Brian, who sat across from her sipping his coffee. She'd managed to help pull him out of bed that morning. His pain was significantly less, and he was moving a bit easier. She hoped that meant they would be able to go to his place today.

"Dr. Lassiter. He sent me a meeting invitation for this morning."

"He wants to check in on you because last night's mission was the first you've witnessed since I was shot. It's protocol that we all have regular check-ins with him, especially after a mission."

"But I wasn't there, with the team," Brielle argued.

"You witnessed it. That's enough. I watched you closely when the gunfire started. I was worried about you too." Sherman took her hand in his. He kissed her knuckles. "We're lucky to have Lassiter. Lucky Shepherd understands we are human beings and they need to be sure we're handling everything okay. Trust me, all units aren't like this. Go talk with Lassiter and be honest. It'll save you a lot of grief in the long run."

"I'm okay, Brian," Brielle insisted, even though the sound of the gunfire had caused her to replay the moment Brian was shot in her head last night. She expected it would just take longer for that to go away.

Later that morning when she sat in Lassiter's kitchen sipping a cup of tea, she remembered what Brian had said. She didn't plan to tell Dr. Lassiter about the recurring visions of Brian getting shot, nor did she plan to tell him that she did dread when Brian would be released to full duty. She didn't want to be banned from watching the mission feed. But just a few minutes into the meeting, she let it all tumble out.

"When that happens, I want you to take a deep breath and let it out slowly. Focus your thoughts instead on Gary and Doc's expertise in treating him. That memory hit as you were in bed with him last night, and it may tonight too. If it happens, try to concentrate on how it feels to hold him, to drive away the memory of him being shot. It's going to take some time and focus on your part to drive that image away," Dr. Lassiter said.

"I was okay watching the team last night."

Lassiter nodded. "It was perfectly natural that you flinched when the shooting started."

She wondered how he knew she had. This man seemed to know everything. "I don't want anyone to think I shouldn't be in there. I want to do this job."

"I'm not going to recommend you be pulled from duty," Lassiter said. "Brielle, that isn't what this is about."

"Then what is it about?"

"It's just a check in to be sure you are okay. The more interactions we have, the more likely you are to trust me and open up to me when you need to. And, I need to know every member of this team, so I will know when something is wrong."

Brielle chuckled. "I'd imagine you have a hard job with all these macho guys not wanting to admit that things bother them."

"It's actually you ladies who put on a stronger front, like you think vulnerability will get you relieved from duty." He shook his head. "Not expressing your emotions is what will get you pulled right away but admitting what you feel and owning your emotions show me you're not covering anything up."

Brielle nodded. "I'll remember that."

She went back to the apartment and wrote her article on the raid she had witnessed the night before. Later that afternoon she got the heavily redacted copy back from Shepherd. He'd sent it along to Director Manning after he'd removed the parts that he deemed classified. She was quite upset he'd deleted as much as he had. She went back to her original copy and compared the two, trying to analyze why he removed what he had so she understood and would not include anything like it in the future.

It was the next day that Doc gave them the okay to go back to Sherman's condo. Sherman was off the pain killers, so he had weapons privileges back. Sherman knew he could not get in and out of either of his own cars. They were both sports cars and sat way too low to the ground. Shepherd agreed to let him borrow one of the agency's SUVs as it would be more comfortable.

As Sherman and Brielle walked off the elevator and into the garage, he pointed out his little red baby to Brielle. Doc walked beside them, carrying Sherman's bags. He too was heading home. "Now remember, take it easy. Let Brielle get you drinks and food, so you don't get up any more than you need to. You're off work for two days. Take them to rest."

"I promise you Doc, he'll rest. I'm going to do everything the next two days," Brielle promised.

"Oh, I like the sound of that," Sherman said with a big smile.

"I said take it easy, no exertion," Doc said.

Sherman laughed. He wouldn't be the one exerting himself.

"And I'll be over tomorrow afternoon to take a look at the wounds and change the bandages," Doc said as Sherman eased behind the wheel. "But call me if you need anything before then."

"We will," Brielle said, and then got into the front passenger seat.

She was genuinely excited that they could leave the building. It meant Brian's injuries were substantially healed. They were beginning their new life together, and she'd figure out what the new normal would be. Already, she'd met several women who she believed would be good friends. She had a new job, full of potential. She had Brian in her life, an unexpected relationship she hadn't been looking for, but one that already proved to be the most significant relationship she'd ever been in.

Through the steady rainfall, she watched the route he took carefully, knowing she'd have to drive it alone soon. By the time he pulled into the driveway of his condo, a hard rain was driven sideways by the strong wind. They stepped out of the car and were soaked in the few seconds it took to get inside.

Sherman showed Brielle how to disarm the alarm system and set the mode for occupancy rather than vacancy, as it was set. He gave her his four-digit code and explained the panic code again, even though he knew Garcia would have when setting her up with building access.

"I've got it." Brielle shivered in her wet clothing. "Damn, I thought it could rain hard in the bayou. I really need a warmer coat. I know it's going to get a lot colder than this here and nothing I have back home will be warm enough."

"Get your wet clothes off," Sherman said, pulling at the waistband of the wet hoodie.

She didn't argue. She pealed it over her head.

"Your jeans too," Sherman said. He stepped towards the bathroom. "I'll get you a towel. He dropped his wet clothes to the bathroom floor while he was in there. He came back out with a towel draped around his own shoulders, and one in his hand for her.

She took it and toweled off and then wrapped it around herself.

"Let's go snuggle in bed. That'll warm us both up." He took her by the hand and led her to the bedroom. He set his gun and phone to the nightstand. "Where's your phone? You need to have it here too."

"It's in my bag. I'm going to have to get used to keeping it near me." She rushed back to the front room and grabbed her backpack. Brian pulled the covers back and sat on the bed when she returned. She placed her phone beside his on the nightstand.

"Can you help swing my legs up as I recline?"

After she helped him, she unzipped her bag and pulled her oversized, sleeping t-shirt from inside. With her back turned to Brian, she unfastened her bra and dropped it to the floor before putting the t-shirt on.

Sherman watched Brielle's back as she removed her dark blue bra. The matching dark blue panties hugged her ass so well. Damn, if his woman wasn't the sexiest thing he'd ever seen. He was one lucky sonofabitch! He groaned when she slid that big t-shirt on.

"What?" She asked, turning back to face him.

"Lose the shirt. Come to bed naked."

"Brian, Doc said no exertion."

"Come on, skin to skin will warm us fast."

Brielle crawled up beside him, into the middle of the bed from the foot of it. She pulled the covers over them both and settled in close to him. She watched him reach to the bedside light. He turned it off, casting them in darkness. She ran her hand over his bare chest.

"You promised me when I was well enough to come home, that you'd be on top and make love with me."

"I don't recall it being a promise," Brielle said.

"At least lean up here and kiss me goodnight."

He heard her sultry chuckle as the mattress shifted and she cautiously moved up beside him. This was the first time she was lying on his left side, closest to his injuries, and he could tell she was being careful not to even bump him.

Brielle pressed her lips to his, keeping the rest of her body off him. She was surprised when his hand grasped her by the back of her neck and pulled her down onto his chest. Even in the dark, she was alert as to the location of his ribs.

"Straddle me," he moaned. As she began to move on top of him, he added, "and lose the shirt."

"Brian," she began to protest.

"Baby, I've been waiting to hold you and feel all of you. I won't exert myself; I promise."

Brielle could feel the heat radiating from him and she was still chilled. She stripped her shirt away and then slowly lowered herself onto him. He pulled her head in for another lengthy kiss. Before she knew it, she was grinding herself against his shaft of steel, that was only kept out of her by their underwear, still in place.

"Let me inside you," he whispered. "You're not hurting me, and I'll lay as still as I can."

"If I hurt you, you have to tell me."

"Baby, you're hurting me by not taking our underclothing off. I want you so bad it's killing me."

Brielle laughed again. She climbed off him. "Can you raise your hips a little and I'll slide your shorts off?"

"I'll raise mountains if it means we'll make love."

"Your hips are enough."

The actual action of him raising his hips from the mattress was a monumental effort for him. He wouldn't let on to her how hard it had been or how painful it was. He was rewarded when she came back atop him sans panties. His right hand took in the smooth skin of her ass as her breasts pressed against his chest and her lips pressed an opened mouth kiss to his lips. Their tongues danced and dueled, and he enjoyed the lengthy kiss, knowing nothing was between them.

When she grabbed his cock and pushed herself around it, the sensation of the hot, wet, vise, was heaven. All the pain of his injuries no longer mattered. He moaned his pleasure. "God, I love you, Brielle."

Brielle kissed him more ferociously as she moved on him. He fit perfectly inside her, filling her completely and rubbing her in all the right places. They'd only made love once, but the level of trust she had in him was something unlike she'd had in anyone ever before. He gave her his word that he'd never hurt her, and she had faith in him that he never would. It was freeing to be with him and not worry he'd cheat. It allowed her to fully enjoy the moment, to fully enjoy him.

As she neared her peak, she sat up on him, her hands gripping his pecs. She used her strong leg muscles to ride him, raising almost completely off him with each thrust. When she felt him throbbing inside her, his breath coming in deep draws, her own thighs quivered as an intense wave overtook her and she screamed out an incredible release.

When she recovered from it, she laid atop Brian's chest. "Oh shit, we didn't use birth control."

Sherman chuckled. "What? You didn't get to a doctor in the past few days?"

"You know I didn't."

He laughed again. "Is it your fertile time?"

"No. Next week will be. You don't go on the pill till the Sunday after your period starts, so there's no use in my rushing to the doctor. It'll be three weeks before I start the pill pack."

Sherman ran his hand over her bare back. He loved naked snuggling with her.

"So, we'll have to use some kind of birth control next week or abstain."

Sherman acted horrified. "Abstain? I can't lay in a bed any longer with you and not make love to you."

"Then you better be prepared to use a condom, or I better get to the drug store and get something else."

Sherman cupped her chin and raised her lips to his. "I love you. I'll do anything for you but wear a condom. What we have is special. I won't let it be like any other time for me." And the truth was, the sensation of being inside her with nothing between them was too incredible to compromise on.

Brielle had wondered before how many women Brian had been with, but she didn't want to ask. She didn't want to know. She assumed it was more than the four other males she'd been with. There was her college boyfriend, her first. She thought they'd get married, but life had other plans for them when he got a job out of state after graduation and their relationship didn't last.

Then there was the man from New Orleans who she met when he brought his out-of-state family on a bayou tour. He was a lot of fun. The year and a half that they went out, she spent several days a week in New Orleans at his place. When she wouldn't move in with him when he asked, that relationship fizzled. She realized later that the entire relationship had been on his terms.

Two years later she got involved with a local boy. He was a few years older than she was, and she didn't know him well. Had she known he wasn't capable of being faithful, she never would have dated him. She rushed into another relationship with another man who turned out to be a worse snake in the grass. She found out he was cheating on his fiancé by dating her. And he was cheating on them both with two other women. That one, she knew, shook her self-confidence. How she hadn't known or suspected made her doubt her instincts. She hadn't let anyone get close in over a year, until now.

She felt him gently caress her back. It felt good, connecting. "I love you, Brian."

Sherman waited. "Is there a but coming?"

"No. I love you and won't ask you to do anything that would make this feel like anything else for you. I'll get to a drug store and get something else until I can start the pill."

"Thank you," he whispered.

Brielle woke wrapped in Brian's warmth and his arms. The room was dark, room darkening shades. Brian still slept. She listened to his even breaths and his heartbeat, then realized that she snuggled up against his injured side, his left arm was beneath her and held her at the small of her back.

"Oh, my God, Brian! Have I hurt you?"

"No, but you woke me," he mumbled in a sleepy voice.

"I'm on your left side."

"You're fine. Go back to sleep."

She floated, appreciating the closeness, the warmth, the feeling of safety his arms brought. Her heart was filled. But then the moment he was shot flashed through her mind again. She was jolted wide awake in that second.

She remembered Doctor Lassiter's advice. She took a deep breath and let it out slowly. She focused on the memory of Gary and Doc's expertise in treating him. She focused on the here and now. Brian held her. He was healing and would make a full recovery. Brian was the man who rescued her from that BioDynamix plant. The job wasn't just what he did, it's who he was.

Victor

rielle was done with her work for the day. She packed up her tablet and walked the short distance down the hall to Brian's office. He was just finishing up an on-line training module for working in Ops. She lounged on his couch and waited. It was fifteen hundred hours. They'd gotten in at zero six hundred. She was learning her job, their jargon, and their way of doing things. She was proud of herself and so far, loved her new life.

Just as Sherman finished the training module, his phone rang. It was Shepherd. He listened to the two sentences that his boss spoke. "That's great news, Shep, thank you." He repeated them to Brielle. "Bobby's release from rehab has been approved and communicated to the facility. We have an appointment at sixteen hundred to go get him."

Brielle jumped up and came around the desk, engulfing Brian in a big hug. "Thank God!"

Brian moaned and winced. "Not so tight, please."

"Sorry, baby," she apologized as she loosened her hold. She pressed a quick kiss to his lips. "I'm just so happy and relieved. There is so much for us to tell him. I hope he agrees to stay up here with us."

"I'm sure he will. We can convince him, I'm sure. I do really think it will be better for him to be out of the bayou. And I want to watch him and be sure he stays clean."

"He's not addicted, Brian. I'm telling you; he went months without using anything or even drinking beer."

Brian held his hands up in a stopping motion. "Okay, okay."

Sherman drove to the rehab facility. He was still driving one of the Shepherd Security SUVs. He parked and eased out. Brielle was waiting at the back of the vehicle when he joined her. She gave him a big hug. The smile on her face was telling of how happy she was.

They walked into the building and advised the front desk receptionist who they were there to see. They were expected and were ushered to the manager's office.

"I understand the court has vacated the mandatory in-patient rehabilitation services; however, I truly think you may want to consider Bobby staying for at least another week," she said. "He's made tremendous progress, but I believe another week would solidify the behavior change needed for him to be successful."

"Bobby doesn't have an addiction problem," Brielle said. "I've been with him and I can verify that up until the night he was arrested, he'd been sober for months."

The manager clicked a few keys on her computer. "That isn't what the drug testing showed. And Bobby himself confessed to the usage of marijuana as well as the cocaine he snorted the night of his arrest. He has an addictive personality which only requires triggers for use."

Brielle seethed beneath the surface. "Can we please just see Bobby?"

The manager affixed her eyes on Brian. "You at least need to enforce out-patient visits. I'm telling you, Agent Sherman, your brother is not ready to be out of treatment."

Sherman nodded. "Does Bobby know we are here?"

"Yes. His things are packed, and he is waiting in the in-patient lobby."

"Let's go there and see him."

Brielle held Brian's hand as they followed the manager. Bobby sat reading a book beside a fountain in the beautiful atrium. He put the book aside and stood as they approached. His backpack was on the bench beside him.

"Brian, Brielle, I'm so glad to see you!"

Brielle bolted ahead and wrapped Bobby in a big hug. She held him tightly for a few seconds. When she released him, he went to hug Brian. "Easy, don't hug him too tight. He was injured."

"Brian, are you okay?" He stood still and let Brian embrace him. Only then did he gently fold his arms around him.

Brian released him and stepped back. "I'm fine. How are you?" He pointed at the manager. "She doesn't think you're ready to leave yet. What do you think?"

"Oh, I'm ready to go," Bobby insisted. He faced the manager. "I learned a lot about myself these past few weeks. I understand I have an addictive personality, and I understand why I've used in the past. I know my triggers."

"You have no court order to follow up with any treatment," she said. "But I think you should commit to a few out-patient visits, just to reinforce what you've learned. Please consider it."

"I think it's a good idea," Sherman said. "I have your card. Let me get my brother home and we'll look at schedules and I'll be in touch."

The manager nodded. "It is important. Please do get back in touch with me."

Once the three of them passed through the outer doors, Bobby breathed a sigh of relief! "I can't tell you how happy I am to be out of there."

"Was it that bad?" Brielle asked.

"No, it was fine. The food was good. I worked out in the gym and swam every day. I really did figure out that I did abuse drugs in the past, but it's the past, not now. I was clean for months before I helped Brielle."

"I want you to stay up here with us, Bobby," Brian said as they reached the SUV.

"With us?" Bobby repeated.

Brielle embraced Brian. "We're together, Bobby. And I'm moving up here, in with Brian."

"What?" He demanded. His outraged and accusatory stare on his brother.

A grin curved Sherman's lips. "You told me not to go there unless I could offer her a relationship. I listened." Sherman opened the car door for Brielle, closing it once she slid in.

Bobby followed Brian around to the driver's side. "She's moving in with you? Already?"

Sherman smiled wide, proud to tell his brother. "I'm in love with her, Bobby. I'm going to marry her. And I want you to be up here with us. You'll have an easier time getting a job up here. And it will be best if you are away from the triggers to use, down in the bayou."

"What in the hell happened in the last few weeks?" Bobby asked.

Sherman didn't answer. He opened his car door and slowly deposited himself behind the wheel. Bobby was in the backseat with the door shut before Sherman was able to pull the door shut, moaning in pain as he did. He was supposed to use his left arm for normal activities like closing the car door, but damn did it hurt!

"Brian, are you okay? How were you injured?"

Brielle turned in her seat to look at him.

Sherman's eyes went to the rearview mirror and locked with his brother's. "We'll talk about that when we get to my place."

"Damn it, Brian, Brielle, someone tell me what happened!"

"There's a lot about my job you don't know," Sherman said. "We'll be at my place in ten minutes. Please, you need to wait till we get there." He put the car in reverse and backed out of the parking spot. Then he drove them straight to his condo.

Sherman parked the SUV in the driveway. He unlocked the front door and led them in, entering his code into the security system. "It's only a one bedroom, but the couch is very comfortable." He went to his refrigerator and grabbed three water bottles. But damn did he want a beer. "Sit." He pointed to the sofa.

Brielle watched Brian lower himself to the couch. She could tell he was sore. He cradled his left arm against his chest, holding it by the wrist with his right hand. She sat between the two brothers. She held her hand out to Brian. He dropped his hand into hers. Then she turned her head to gaze at Bobby. His questioning stare was fixed on Brian.

"I'm not just an ATF Agent. I'm part of a multi-agency special task force. We investigate, but we're also an assault team. We went into that BioDynamix facility and were met with heavy resistance. There was a fire fight, and I took a couple of rounds."

"Rounds, as in bullets? You were shot?" Bobby questioned, shocked and worried at the same time.

"Yeah, one to my bicep, another grazed the skin just above my vest, and I took a couple rounds to the vest. My ribs were just bruised." Sherman pointed out each spot as he talked. "I was lucky. I'll heal completely and none of them were career ending injuries."

"Lucky, holy shit, Brian! You were shot."

"It's not the first time," Sherman admitted.

Brielle squeezed his hand. "But I hope it's the last."

Sherman kissed her. Then he proceeded to tell Bobby everything that went down. Bobby sat and listened, stunned. When Sherman got to the part that Brielle had been taken, Bobby looked angry. Sherman wasn't sure if he was angry with him for not protecting her. Bobby's gaze softened when Sherman told him that he'd rescued her.

"The thing is, you can't ever tell anyone what I really do. It's top secret. The regular DEA took the credit for the bust and as far as anyone knows, it was one of their strike teams that raided that plant. Not my team."

"You were there when he was shot?" He questioned Brielle.

"Yes." That moment still played through her mind when she closed her eyes at night.

"Oh my God! You're quitting that job, aren't you, Brian?" Bobby asked.

Sherman's laugh was sarcastic. "Sure, just quit on my team and kiss my career goodbye." He shook his head in disbelief. "No, Bobby, I'm not quitting my job. This is what I do."

"And it's who he is," Brielle added. "I wouldn't be alive if it weren't for him and his team. I think a lot of people can say that. What they do, is important."

"Let someone else do it. It's dangerous."

"I appreciate your concern," Sherman said, taking a drink of his water. Yeah, a beer would taste better, but even he knew it was not cool to have a drink in front of someone working on their sobriety. "But I'll be keeping my job." He rose and stepped away from the couch.

"Brielle, are you really okay with this?" Bobby whispered as soon as Brian was behind the closed bathroom door.

"I'm getting used to it. He won't be going back out on any missions for three to four weeks. He's on limited duty because of the wounds."

"Yes, and next time it could be worse. Well, I'm not okay with it. He could get killed doing this job, then where will you be?"

"Here with you," she replied, taking his hand. "You were never worried about him doing his job before. Nothing has changed as far as Brian's job goes, just what you know about it."

"What about your journalism career? Did you get to write an article about what was really going on? And did you sell it to any big news outlets?"

"Yes and no," she replied.

Sherman emerged from the bathroom and came back over, taking his seat beside Brielle on the couch. He took her hand back into his. "Brielle had the exclusive inside story on the arrests and what went down, but she couldn't mention my team. The DEA took credit for all of it, which is the way it works."

Bobby's eyes focused on Brielle. She looked nervous. "So, what happened with the story?"

"I wrote it under a fictitious name, someone who was supposedly embedded with the DEA Strike Team that investigated and raided the BioDynamix facility."

"Why?" Then his eyes went to Brian. "Did your team make her do it that way? This sucks! Brielle Jarboe should have had the byline on the story. She did all the work!"

"Bobby, calm down. It was my choice. And there will be a lot more articles. I got a full-time job with Brian's employer to write these articles and help out with other reports." She thought this would make him as happy as she and Brian were about it. It only made him angrier.

"Are you fucking kidding me?" He exploded; his eyes trained on Brian. "You're dragging her into your dangerous job? No fucking way! If you care about her."

Sherman cut Bobby off, matching his tone of voice and volume. "I do care about her! And she will be in no danger. She'll watch mission feed from our Operations Center. She'll never be in the field."

"Great, so she'll get to see you shot again!"

"Stop it!" Brielle cut in. "Bobby, this was my choice. I don't want to work for a regular news outlet or network. I want to work with Brian, writing stories that really matter. And the work they do matters more than any other job out there. I don't care if the byline goes to me or to Jane Doe. What matters is I get to be with Brian, here when he's home. His team just got back from a mission and they brought down an entire drug network in New York. They raided where the meth was manufactured and also where it was distributed from. And they arrested sixty people connected to it. And I got to write the news release about it, a story that mattered. I sat in on the mission briefing before they left, was in on the surveillance they did, and watched the raid and arrests, all from right here in Chicago. I was perfectly safe the whole time."

"Drugs? I thought you were with the ATF?"

"We're a multi-agency task force, DEA, ATF, CIA, FBI, ICE, we even have a couple of guys that carry creds from Homeland and the NSA. Drugs are a huge problem, taking a lot of American lives, cause a lot of the crime in this country. We work a lot of cases related to illegal drugs. But Bobby, you cannot tell anyone anything about me or my team ever. Living here, you're bound to meet my friends, my team. We're tight, spend a lot of time together when we're not working. You have to, oh hell, I don't know. You have to be cool with all of this and realize that they're just normal guys who do a job most people don't understand and cannot ever know about."

"That Madison and Cooper guy who were on your boat, they're both on this team?"

"Yes, and my buddy Sloan who you met on the plane."

"Gary is one of their medics, saved Brian's life. He and another one of the medics took care of him the last week that we were back, changed the dressings on his wounds, gave him painkillers. They're incredible, all of them. When Brian was shot, the way they all took care of him and me too, was," she paused, tearing up. "It was amazing. One of his teammates stayed with me from the second Gary and Doc started to work on his injuries, and the whole time he was in surgery. When Brian was transferred to a room after, they brought me to him."

"Mother?" Sherman asked.

Brielle smiled fondly. "Yeah. He really is a mother hen. He took care of me and made sure I wasn't alone during any of it. They're special people, Bobby, and Brian is lucky to have them in his life. If anything ever happens to Brian, I know they'll be there for me."

Sherman raised her hand to his lips and kissed her knuckles. "I pray you never have to go through anything like this again. But you're right. Shepherd and the whole team will always be there for you."

Bobby rubbed his forehead. "Damn, Brian, it's just that you're the only family I got. With Momma gone, and Daddy God knows where, maybe even dead by now and we'd never know, you're it, and I don't want to lose you too."

Brielle hugged him. "You have me, and I consider you family."

"Oh, damn, Brielle, you know I feel the same way about you. I love you, girl." Bobby shook his head. Then his eyes went back to his brother. "I promise. I'll never tell anyone about what you really do."

"And you'll stay up here with us? With your trade school certificates, you'll be able to get a job real easy."

"Please, Bobby, stay," Brielle seconded.

"Okay," Bobby agreed. "It might be time for a change for me."

"And after you get a job and can handle the payments on this place, I may let you have it and Brielle and I will get a bigger place. But if you'd prefer, I'll get a place big enough for the three of us and you can move with us. Think about it. I won't be thinking of making that move for a few months."

"If I'm staying up here, I need to go home and get more of my stuff." His gaze shifted to Brielle. "You probably do too."

"Not necessary. I'm having it all shipped up here," Sherman said. "I'm hiring packers to go to Brielle's place and to my boat and pack it all up. Is any of your shit stored anywhere else?"

"I have some stuff in a storage shed, but nothing I need," Bobby said. "I just need to send them a payment next month. It's only paid through the end of the year."

Sherman nodded. "I'll help you with whatever you need. I have the name of a recruiter who places workers in local trade and manufacturing jobs. With all the trade school certificates you have, I'm sure he can help you find a job. But you have to call him, follow up on it, and present yourself well at the interviews."

"I will," Bobby promised.

"And you have to stay off the drugs. I'm serious about that. If I even suspect you're using, I'm putting you right back into that rehab facility. That includes weed."

Whiskey

One week later, Brielle stepped out of the front door to Brian's condo into a snow globe. The swirling, large snowflakes were beautiful for about a half a minute before the frigid air invaded her. She wore her new black wool coat that hung down to her knees, her new green hat, scarf, and glove set. She had on blue jeans and her new winter boots. And she froze within a minute of being outside.

The big black SUV pulled up, and she climbed in. "My God is it cold out there!" She said as she closed the door. Thankfully, the air inside the car was warm.

Sherman pointed to his lips as he leaned in to kiss her. "Welcome to Chicago in the winter. Just wait till the real cold hits in January and February."

"I'm liking this city less by the day," Brielle complained. "But you're here and that's all that matters."

"Should I be worried?" Sherman asked.

Brielle smiled and settled back against the heated seat. "No, I'm just whining about the cold."

Sherman chuckled. "It sure is pretty outside though, isn't it?"

Brielle glanced back out the window as Brian backed the car out of the driveway. Pretty, no, it was stunning, a perfect winter wonderland. The snow came down heavy, blanketing everything in a lush layer of pure white. It coated the trees and the leaves that still held on. It looked magical.

"Just wait till the sun comes out, and the snow sparkles like diamonds. This is early for a big snowfall. It won't last long."

"Thank you for coming to get me before the briefing. I didn't want to drive one of your expensive cars and wreck it."

"We should go car shopping for you soon and get you something that handles well in the snow."

"You know I don't have a down payment saved for a car and my junker back home would never make the drive up here."

"Brielle, I've got the down payment for you."

"You just helped Bobby buy a car. Don't you think you should get another paycheck before helping me too?"

"I don't need to. I've got it in the bank." He raised her hand to his lips and kissed her knuckles through her gloves. "I love you Brielle. I don't care if you drive one of my cars, but I'd prefer you don't wreck it, so let's get you a car before I go back on active next week and go on the next mission."

Brielle gazed out at the swirling snow. The flakes coming down were huge. "I'm really going to miss you. I've gotten used to us being together."

Sherman squeezed her hand. He had too, and he would miss her more than she'd ever know. "Me too. I'll call, and we can text. And you'll have Bobby at the condo, so you won't be alone. Plus, I'm sure Angel and the other wives will check in on you."

She smiled. "I really like them, Angel and the other women. I really feel like I belong here, Brian."

Warmth filled Sherman. "That's because you do."

Her smile was beautiful. He never tired of seeing it.

"Did Bobby get going okay this morning?"

"Yes. He was excited to start his new job. He was ready a good hour before he had to leave."

"This is just the fresh start he needs," Sherman said. He was very proud of his brother. He'd pointed Bobby to the recruiter, but Bobby called him right away, set up the interview, and then aced it.

His pride in his brother spiked off the charts just over a week later. It was Thursday, Thanksgiving Day. All three of them were invited to Jackson and Angel's house for a late afternoon dinner. All of Alpha and Delta Teams were there. It was a rarity that Delta was not away on a mission over a holiday.

Brielle made both a pecan and a pumpkin pie from scratch. Everyone brought something to contribute to the meal. Furniture was moved to accommodate the many tables that were lined up across the length of their living room to seat sixteen adults and Sammy's highchair. The house was full of people. It was a loud atmosphere with many voices and laughter overlapping.

Sherman introduced his brother to each of his teammates and their wives, impressed by how respectful and friendly Bobby was as he met each. Sherman had warned him before that the Operators would all be armed. He only noticed Bobby openly staring at someone's sidearm once. He knew this would be an adjustment for Bobby, but he handled it well.

Brielle watched as Brian took baby Olivia from Doc's hands. "She's grown so much since I saw her last," Brian said. "I can't believe she's three months old already." He pressed a kiss to the top of the baby's head. Brielle was amazed at how comfortable he was handling the baby.

Brielle watched Sammy make the rounds to all the guests. He climbed right up on Brian's lap and handed him a book. Brian was animated as he read the toddler the short story, roaring like a tiger, and laughing like a hyena where appropriate. Her heart swelled as she watched him. She sat beside them. When they got to the last page of the book, Sammy took the book from him and handed it to her. She read the last page.

Then Sammy took the book, climbed down and brought it over to Lambchop, who sat at the table, talking with Michaela. Brielle chuckled. "That little boy is something."

Sherman's eyes met Lambchop's. His gaze flickered to Michaela and then back to his team leader. A part of him felt bad for what he'd said to Lambchop about her when he was called out for sleeping with Brielle at the Coast Guard facility. But he knew that the big man had feelings for Michaela. And he knew those feelings were reciprocated. He wished the two of them would just get together already. Knowing the happiness that he felt with Brielle in his life, he wanted that for his friend too.

They took their places at the long table. As Brielle listened to Landon's prayer of thanksgiving, she realized that this team was really a big family. She was grateful to be accepted by them. She did truly feel like she belonged. She glanced at Bobby. She hoped that he understood that this was a family that Brian was a part of. She hoped he sensed the closeness these people shared. She knew that Bobby still didn't like the job Brian did, and Brian hadn't even been released to go back on active duty yet.

The team would be leaving the next day on another mission. The pre-mission briefing was at ten hundred hours. Brielle wasn't sure who else would accompany Delta Team on it. Six people was standard for a DEA Partner Mission. She knew that Brian was anxious to get back to active duty. He was nearly ready. He had been working out in the gym in the subbasement level of the Shepherd Security Building for two weeks now. Doc monitored him closely.

A week and a half after Thanksgiving, the snow fell from the gray sky again. Brielle sat behind the wheel of her new car, a silver Jeep Cherokee. She gazed at Brian as he got into the passenger seat, after stowing his gear in the backseat. After the briefing, Brian would fly out with the team to Atlanta, the site of their next DEA Partner Mission. Doc had released him back to active duty the day before. Later in the afternoon, Brielle would drive herself home without Brian. She knew that she was going to miss him. She would also worry about him.

The briefing went as all the others. Mexican heroin was the drug that they were going after this time. The DEA had a lead, but no proof, and so far, their surveillance had not brought any results. Cooper and Madison both were going on this mission, as was Garcia, with all of Delta Team. This mission was slightly different from the others Brielle had been a part of. In order to get leads, several of the team members, including Brian, would go in undercover as buyers at a dive bar in a seedy part of Atlanta. By the sounds of it, this wasn't the first time they had done it this way.

She felt edgy all afternoon. That edginess turned to anxiety as she drove home. Shortly after she entered the empty condo, her phone rang, startling her. Bobby was working the second shift that day. He wouldn't be home till midnight.

"Hello," Brielle answered, seeing it was a call from Kaylee.

"Hi. I'm heading over to Sienna's for the night. We thought you might want to join us. We're going to make some pasta for dinner and watch a movie or two."

"That's nice of you," Brielle replied.

"With all three of our guys away on this mission, we might as well keep each other company."

"Yes, I'd like that," Brielle said. "Give me the address and I'll plug it into my maps app. And what can I bring? I can throw together a quick salad."

"Sounds good. Make it fast and come over. I'm just getting to her place now."

Brielle prepared a quick salad and then left the condo. Sienna lived just fifteen minutes away. She pulled into the driveway and shivered against the cool evening air as she walked up the sidewalk to the door. Kaylee peeked out of the blinds and then opened the door, relocking it behind Brielle. She took the salad from her.

A chocolate lab greeted her with a wagging tail.

"Her name is Bailey," Sienna called from the kitchen. "She's very friendly."

Brielle smiled. "She looks it." She stroked over the soft fur on her head.

"I'm glad you could come over," Sienna said.

"Thank you for the invitation." Brielle glanced around. "You have a beautiful and inviting home." The fireplace was lit, warming the room and casting reflections on the wall.

"Thank you. Anthony and I are very comfortable here. It's a three bedroom, so we shouldn't outgrow it anytime soon. And I'll tell you, with as much as Anthony works, the maintenance-free exterior is great. My first husband and I had a house, and he worked and traveled a lot too and I had to do it all, mow the lawn, shovel the snow. Let me tell you, I don't miss that at all!"

"Gary and I hope a unit will come on the market in this subdivision. I'd love to move into this neighborhood," Kaylee said. "But until then, I'm very happy in Gary's condo. It's small, but that's less to clean." She smiled at Brielle. "I just started teaching this year and I will admit I spend a lot of time every night on my lesson plans. I want to do a great job and be invited back next year. I really love this job."

"You are doing a great job," Sienna told her. "You're a natural and the kids love you."

"Oh, thanks," Kaylee said. She made eye contact with Brielle. "My life has changed a lot in the past few months. I'm a much different person now and I can honestly say I am really happy; in a way I haven't been in a very long time."

"And you absolutely deserve that happiness," Sienna said, giving Kaylee a hug.

"Everyone deserves to be happy," Brielle added. "I'm glad you love teaching. Kids need teachers who feel that way."

"And you have a new job too," Sienna said to Brielle. "Do you like it?"

"Yes, I love working at Shepherd Security. Of course, this is the first mission Brian is gone on. I'll admit that makes me nervous."

"I remember that first mission Anthony went on after we were together," Sienna said as she rounded the counter and returned to the kitchen. "You will get used to it."

"At least you work there and get to know where they're going and how dangerous the mission is," Kaylee said. "We don't usually find out where they've been until after they're home."

"Angel does tell us a little bit about their missions, most of the time. It's usually just enough so we don't worry too much," Sienna cut in.

Brielle knew she couldn't say where they were or what the mission was. She was surprised that Angel would tell them. She doubted Mr. Shepherd knew that.

"Can you at least tell us if they're in the United States?" Kaylee pressed.

Brielle considered it for a moment.

"Gary hasn't gone out of the country yet, since we've been together, but Sienna and Angel have both told me that they do go to the Middle East, South America, or to Africa once in a while."

"They do?" Brielle asked. This was news to her. "No, they're not out of the country."

"Thank you." Kaylee pointed at the barstools that lined the counter. Brielle took a seat. Kaylee held up a bottle of red wine. A poured glass was on the counter.

"Yes, thank you," Brielle said.

"I'm making spaghetti with meat sauce. I hope you like it," Sienna said.

"It smells wonderful. I'm sure I will."

Kaylee handed her glass over. Then she held her own up. "To new beginnings at new jobs and new lives."

Brielle smiled. That toast was so appropriate.

Brielle had a great time with the girls. Angel and Elizabeth even stopped over for dessert. She learned that Angel lived across the street and Elizabeth just up the block. They never got to a movie as the conversation flowed effortlessly. Brielle was surprised when Angel did tell them that the mission was in Atlanta.

It was nearly midnight when Brielle left to go home. Bobby would be home from work soon, and she was looking forward to talking with him about her night. She really liked the other women. She felt accepted by them and felt like she belonged here. She wouldn't admit to Bobby how worried about Brian she was. She knew he was, too.

The next morning when she went to the office, she was informed the team had gone into one of the dive-bars the previous evening. Mission footage was recorded, waiting for her to watch. Seated in her office, she pulled the feed up on her computer. The quality wasn't the best. Between the dark bar and the fact that the cameras were small and concealed in clothing, some of what was going on was hard to make out.

What she did see was Garcia and Brian going into a bar. There was no way they wore bullet-proof vests under their clothes. They sat at the bar, ordered beers and shots, and then very quietly Garcia asked the bartender, a rough looking man, about buying some H. Garcia flashed the bartender cash. The bartender reached for it. Garcia grabbed his hand and twisted it until the bartender screamed out. A menacing look was on Garcia's face. Jeez, he was scary!

"Not till you hook us up," Garcia warned in a low, threatening voice.

"Don't fuck with us, and it better be some quality shit," she heard Brian add.

"Okay, okay," the bartender agreed.

Garcia downed his shot, seen in the camera worn by Brian. Then he took a pull from the beer bottle. Through the camera mounted on Garcia, Brielle saw that Brian watched the bartender. He raised his shot glass to his lips and slowly downed it, his eyes never leaving the bartender who was now at the far end of the bar on his cell phone.

The bartender came back over. "Good quality in the amount you want is going to cost you two bills."

Garcia nodded. He motioned to his shot glass. The bartender refilled both his and Brian's. Then Garcia laid money onto the bar. A few minutes later another man came in close, filling the small space between Brian and Garcia. The exchange went down. Cash for drugs. Brielle was shocked. It took less than thirty seconds. The seller moved away, a fresh beer in hand, placed there by the bartender.

Through Brian's camera, Brielle watched the seller move away and disappear through a door at the back of the bar. Garcia and Brian finished their drinks, left cash on the bar to cover them, and then left through the front door. They immediately went across the street and into a little motel. The team was set up there in two connecting rooms. Madison was inside the room they entered, watching monitors that were set up on the desk.

Garcia tested the drugs. It tested positive for an opiate. Then the recorded camera feed cut over to cameras worn by Danny and Gary. They had been in the bar at the pool tables. Brielle was relieved that they were in there. The entire exchange was caught on their camera feeds. It struck her how smooth it was, nearly undetectable. The seller looked like he had just poked his way between the two men to get a beer.

Another camera feed queued up. It was from the camera worn by Landon. He was in a dark corner of the bar. She saw that he followed the seller through the door which led outside into the alley. The man got into a black pickup truck, which Landon walked past. He kept walking down the alley. When he was far enough, he spoke, reciting the license plate number.

"Running it now," Yvette's voice came over the recording.

"Returning to home base," Landon's voice was heard. The visual feed showed him exit the alleyway and enter the same motel room.

Cooper was the last to enter the motel. His camera feed showed that he had been in position in a car across the street from the bar. Brielle was very relieved that they all had been nearby, covering Brian and Garcia. She listened in, intrigued as they discussed tailing the dealer to follow the drug trail upstream. Danny and Gary would return to the bar; they'd be the next to buy. While the dealer was inside, Brian would plant a tracker on his truck. Landon and Cooper would be inside. Garcia would be in the car in front of the motel. Then she watched them carry it out. It went just as planned.

She made notes on what she'd just watched. Then she sent Brian a text message telling him she'd just watched the feed from their operation the night before. She received a text back right away. They were surveilling the dealer from the night before. He'd already led them to where he slept, to a diner where he made early morning sales, and now they were trailing him to where they hoped he picked up his product.

Brielle was notified later that morning by Jackson in Ops that the team had made progress and she should come observe. The young guy, Caleb Smith, was with Jackson in Ops when she entered. "So, what are they doing?"

"Following suspects," Smith replied.

"We've identified the dealer from the bar last night as Tyrone Adams," Jackson said, displaying a picture of him on the monitor. "He has one bust for possession from a year ago. He isn't on anyone's radar as a dealer," Jackson advised.

"He is now," Smith added.

"The team tailed him all night. He met up with this guy early this morning." The picture of a second black man displayed on the monitor next to the first. "We ran his picture through the Atlanta DEA. They don't have anything on him. They believe this new guy is Tyrone Adams' supplier based on what they observed during the meeting, backpacks were exchanged," Jackson said. "We've got that surveillance feed saved for you to review. I know you just got done with the feed from last night's mission."

"He led them back to a unit in an upscale apartment building, that we believe he is living in. He was inside for just long enough to change clothes and come back out carrying what appeared to be a very full backpack, a different one than he'd gone in with. I traced the lease info on the apartment, and it came back to Dennis Leahy, a sixty-eight-year-old white guy." Smith paused as he pointed back at the picture of the black man. "And he obviously isn't that white guy. I'm still trying to find Dennis Leahy. There's no death certificate filed, and his mail is still going to that apartment."

"The team got a tracker on his car while he was in the apartment," Jackson said.

"Why did our team get called in? Why couldn't the local cops or DEA run this operation?" Brielle asked.

"Two reasons," Jackson said. "We're unknown to everyone in this area. Just like the cops keep track of the bad guys, the bad guys keep track of their local cops and agents, many times, have moles inside the police department if they're a big enough organization. The DEA went into that same bar and tried to buy drugs on multiple occasions. The bartender shut them down, no sales. It was like they knew who they were before they walked into the joint."

"Secondly, we're good at this and don't have to get warrants or follow the rules while we are getting the lay of the land and compiling our list of the players," Caleb said.

"There had been about a dozen raids in this area by a task force a few months ago. The local DEA believe these guys were newly recruited to fill the void," Jackson said. "The top dog was never identified."

On the monitor, Brielle saw Garcia and Danny approach an apartment building. "What are they doing?"

"They're going to enter and snoop around mystery man's place," Jackson said.

Brielle watched Garcia pick the lock in less than a minute. He was a lot better at that than she had been. Obviously, they didn't have a warrant to enter the apartment. That was why their unit was conducting this operation. As Angel had said before, this unit didn't color inside the lines. They used whatever methods were needed to get the job done.

Inside, the apartment was filled with expensive furniture, professionally decorated, no doubt. She watched the monitors as both men conducted a methodical search of the premises. They found what they were looking for behind the locked door to the second bedroom. A six-foot-long table was littered with drugs, some packing materials, and a scale. Along one of the walls was a shelving unit, stacked with backpacks full of either money or drugs. There were no large quantities of drugs in bulk, awaiting packaging. The team suspected this man was a middleman between the major distributor and the street dealers.

Over the next few days, the team tailed the middleman, investigating everyone he came in contact with. They identified a network of street dealers he traded backpacks with. But they didn't get a break in who was supplying him until the afternoon of the fifth day on the ground.

A delivery truck from a discount furniture store showed up outside of the apartment building. The delivery men wrestled the box onto a dolly and brought the large box to Mr. Mystery Man's apartment door. The team could see that box was the only thing in the truck. Everyone agreed, there was no way that a professionally decorated apartment would also house another piece of furniture, especially from a discount furniture store. Cooper sent Madison in for a closer look.

Brielle watched as Madison went into the building like she belonged there. She walked down the hallway, checking each apartment number. Mr. Mystery Man stood in his doorway talking with the two delivery men who still had the box out in the hall.

"Can I help you?" He asked her.

"I can't remember the apartment number but I'm looking for a Gil Haigh."

"Gil's a lucky man," he remarked. "I don't know the neighbor's names, but what does he look like?"

"I don't know, never met the man."

A smile spread over Mr. Mystery Man's face. "You have now." He presented his hand.

"You were messing with me," she said in a flirty voice as she shook his hand. "Maddie Hayes. It's nice to meet you."

"It is nice to meet you too, Miss Maddie Hayes." He nodded at the two delivery men and then stepped back into the apartment, swinging the door wide, inviting Madison in.

"Nice place," Madison said, smiling and flirting as she entered.

He closed the door behind her.

"Shit, that can't be good," Brielle said. "What is Madison doing?"

"Distracting him and getting intel," Jackson said. "Don't worry. You can believe that Cooper is right outside of that door. She's on comms and he'll bust in if he even suspects she's in trouble." Camera feed did indeed show Cooper and Danny in the hallway outside of the apartment.

The rest of the team followed the delivery truck. Once it was several blocks away, they moved on it as it was stopped at a red light. Brielle watched the feed from Landon, Gary, and Brian's cameras. Landon jumped up on the running board step beside the driver as Brian did the same on the passenger side. They both opened the doors, and they grabbed the two occupants from their seats, throwing them out into the street. Gary waited by the passenger side. Two men in jackets that said DEA waited by the driver's door. They had the men handcuffed and pulled to their feet in seconds. Then Landon drove the truck around the block and into a parking garage.

Gary followed in the car they'd been in after turning the two suspects over to the DEA.

In the parking garage were several more DEA Agents. They opened the box. It was filled with cash in perfect stacks, packaged by denomination from singles to hundred-dollar bills. Residue in the box tested positive for opiates. They transmitted this information to the rest of the team.

Outside of the man's apartment, Cooper and Danny unholstered their weapons. Madison was making small talk with her host, leading him to believe that she was a real estate agent who was there to give a market appraisal on the unit. She kept the tone of her voice flirty. "Now Gil, this kitchen is beautiful. And as I'm sure you know the kitchen and the bathrooms are the biggest selling points to any property besides location."

"I happen to believe the master bedroom is one of the most important rooms. I'd love to show you mine, Ms. Hayes," he flirted back.

"We'll get to that room in due time," she said with a laugh.

On the monitor, Brielle watched as the man stepped in very close to Madison. "Or we can cut to the chase and go to my bedroom."

Madison stepped back and drew her gun. "Or we can just take you to jail. Get them up!"

At that same moment, Cooper and Danny burst in. The man was just reaching for his gun at the small of his back, doubting she would shoot him. "Don't!" Cooper yelled. Danny went behind him and took the gun. Then he secured his hands behind his back in zip ties.

As expected, the delivery box had been filled with drugs, which was on a tarp on the floor in the second bedroom. Also as expected, when they offered the man a deal to give up his supplier, he declined. The DEA arrived and took the man and the drugs into custody.

After the operation wrapped up, Brielle met again with Dr. Lassiter. He was quickly assured that she was indeed okay watching Brian operate in the field. She admitted to him her nervousness watching it, but she also relayed to him her pride in Brian and in the team for the work they did.

"I'm really happy with this new life, working here and being with Brian."

"So, your new goals have taken shape?"

Brielle nodded. "I want to do the best job I can. I've been paying attention to what Mr. Shepherd has edited out of my articles. My first goal is to not have anything that needs to be edited out."

Lassiter smiled. "I'm sure he will appreciate that."

"And I want to help Angel as much as I can. She works so hard to take care of everyone." The truth was, everyone who worked here worked harder than anyone she ever knew. She was in awe of all of them.

$\mathcal{X}$-ray

$\mathcal{B}$ rielle was in her office working on collating the various sections of the mission report from the DEA Partner Mission the team had just concluded. This was a new assignment for her that Mr. Shepherd thought would help with her articles. She found it fascinating, the reports from each person who had been a part of the mission, those in Ops as well as the team on the ground. She was mostly copying and pasting their accounts into the report format, but in reading them, she did gain a different perspective on events than merely her own observations brought.

She was told that Cooper was responsible for the final review and edits on the report before he submitted it to Mr. Shepherd. Once she was through with the report, she would write her article. She would admit, though, that she was distracted. The team was in the air, due back in just over an hour. She couldn't wait to see Brian. She had missed him more over the past week than she thought she would.

The mission had concluded the night before, but the team stayed overnight as the company Lear jet was unable to get them until this morning. It was being used the previous evening to transport Charlie and Echo Teams to their next worksite in Nevada. She had just learned that week of the Power Grid Protection Project those teams worked on. It was another government contract Shepherd Security had. She was amazed what all the agency was involved in.

There was also a Bravo Team that was hired out providing personal protection services. They were currently safeguarding a Saudi prince and his family that was in New York City on a shopping and sightseeing trip. They provided protection to celebrities, foreign dignitaries, and even high-ranking U.S. officials when there was a threat.

As she read the accounts from each of the team members that made up the report, she was impressed with how official sounding each of them wrote their parts. It was the facts, the timeline, the operational particulars. No thoughts, feelings, or emotions were present in their reports. She knew those who wrote these sections, but none of their personalities were present in their accounts. Even Brian's spoke of mission objectives and suspects substantiated. She was impressed by the professionalism displayed in each person's statement.

She kept an eye on the time, knowing the team was due to land at zero-nine-forty. As she began her article, her mind returned to different aspects of what she'd observed during the mission. Seeing each of them in the bars and the characters they portrayed, she was impressed by their bravery and poise. They went in without bullet-proof vests, with no protection but their instincts and their confidence in the team who was nearby, covering them. They had all slipped into those roles so easily, and they played them very convincingly. Even Madison, cozying up to that man they'd identified as the main distributor of the drugs, her performance was believable. Brielle knew she could never do what Madison had. Her respect for Madison increased.

Thirty arrests were made, drugs with a street value over four million were seized, and not a single person had been injured or killed. Mr. Shepherd had already proclaimed this a very successful operation. She couldn't agree more. She looked forward to the debriefing after the team arrived back. The team would be dismissed after it. Unfortunately, she wouldn't be able to leave right away and go home with Brian like she wanted to.

She was assigned to cover the front desk for Angel from twelve hundred hours through seventeen hundred as Angel had the afternoon off. Angel had a prenatal doctor's appointment for herself and then a visit for Sammy for shots at the pediatrician that afternoon. Brielle knew she shouldn't complain, after all, she was being paid a generous salary, more than she had ever made, and she had to earn it. But she'd missed Brian, and all she could think about was going home with him and making love to him.

Finally, the text message from Brian notified her that they landed. Euphoria washed through her. You would think he'd been gone months. It was only a week. She messaged him back that she was in her office. He would come there after they arrived, and he stowed his gear.

From that moment on, she couldn't concentrate on her article. Collating and formatting the mission report was complete and she really should have been working on the article, but all she could think about was wrapping her arms around Brian and holding him. She never felt this way about another man. Of course, none of her previous boyfriends had a dangerous job. She was sure that had a lot to do with her scattered thoughts.

Forty minutes later he appeared in the open doorway. She jumped out of her chair and rushed around the desk to greet him. He stepped within her office and shut the door. She flung herself at him, squeezing him fiercely as her lips pressed to his.

She felt his hand wrap behind her neck, and he held her in place as his kiss deepened.

Sherman had never had a woman hurl herself at him the way that Brielle did. He loved it. And her wild kisses instantly hardened him. He turned her, pressing her back against the door, pressing her to it with his own body. He craved the closeness. He ground his pelvis into hers. The clothes had to go. They had fifteen minutes till the debrief. It wouldn't take that long, he was sure.

He unbuttoned and unzipped her jeans and pushed them and her panties down her legs while his mouth devoured hers. He only broke the kiss to remove one of her feet from its pants leg. Then he dropped his own pants. He lifted one of her legs, and then sank his throbbing cock into her, letting out a quiet moan in response to the incredible sensation that surrounded him.

He made love to her against that door with a hunger that wouldn't be satisfied by this short tryst. His ache to simmer inside her for hours would not be satisfied by a few minutes of ecstasy. He wanted to hold her naked flesh against his, caress over every inch of her, hear her scream through several releases. And then he wanted to keep her wrapped in his protective embrace as they both fell asleep only to wake and repeat it with a renewed vigor.

Brielle felt him throb inside her and then the convulsing of his body told her he was coming. She was close, but not there yet.

Once he recovered, he kissed her deeply. He pulled his lips just an inch away and opened his eyes. "I missed you," he whispered. "I love you."

"I love you," she whispered back. "And I missed you more than you know."

Sherman realized she had not come. He reached a hand between them and strummed her swollen and sensitive clit while circling his hips, his cock still inside her. She gasped out, throwing her head back. Her fingernails dug into his shoulders. She was close. How he wished they had more time. He'd love to keep her there for hours, hovering on the brink until she begged him to let her come.

He felt her vise grip tighten around his cock. Her whole body convulsed as her orgasm tore through her. She emitted a low moan of pure ecstasy. He smiled, delighted. He'd satisfied his woman. His woman. She was his woman. He'd never been as excited and eager to get home from a mission as he had this one.

They quickly redressed and made their way to the debrief. Shepherd recapped the wins from this mission. Since turning the middleman and the two delivery drivers over to the DEA, the next higher up in the food chain was identified. A warrant was issued, and he was arrested that morning. Shepherd congratulated the team and dismissed them, giving them the next forty-eight hours off until Delta team plus Jackson and Burke would report for the briefing before the next mission.

Brielle's article was due that evening. She worked on it as she manned the front desk. Brian went home. She was surprised when she walked in to find he made dinner, steaks. A bouquet of flowers, roses, waited on the table for her.

"They're beautiful, thank you." She kissed him, wrapping her arms around his neck. "You didn't have to do all this."

"I wanted you to know how much I love you and how much I appreciate you." He embraced her, and then kissed her again. "I missed you while I was gone."

"I missed you too," she whispered.

Two days later, they were back in Shepherds office for the next briefing. "Okay, that's it, people," Shepherd said. "Report tomorrow morning at zero six hundred. You'll pack up and leave for the airport by zero seven hundred."

Brielle watched everyone rise. Delta Team plus Rich and Jackson were going on this mission. This time, Houston, Texas was their destination. She was distracted though. She'd realized the previous day that her period was late. She'd bought a pregnancy test and hid it beneath the bathroom counter. Brian came in the bathroom with her that morning to get a shower while she got ready. She would have peed on the stick had he not been in there. She doubted she was pregnant. She had no other symptoms. Her friend Tina had all the classic symptoms before she took her test, and she too was only a week late when she took her test.

Brielle locked the front door behind Bobby as he left for work and then watched him through the front window as he backed his car out of the driveway, and then out of sight. She rushed to the bathroom, not bothering to close the door. She had to pee bad. She took the box with the pregnancy kit from below the sink where she'd hidden it after buying it. She knew the HCG hormone was strongest in first of the morning pee. She needed a definitive answer if she was pregnant or not.

She pulled the sweatpants down and sat on the toilet, maneuvering the stick between her legs so it would be directly in the line of her urine. As she finished peeing, she heard the front door open. Shit, Brian or Bobby were back. She set the stick to the counter and quickly pulled her pants up.

"Did you forget something?" She called as she stepped into the main room. Inside the house were two men. One of them she recognized, blond-boy from the bayou. She'd never seen the other man. She froze for a moment, her breath sucked from her chest. They closed the distance quickly. She finally got her legs to move, and she ran to the alarm panel just steps away, near the door that led out to the garage. She pressed one-two-three-four as one of the men grabbed her from behind. He yanked her away from the panel.

She let out a scream, went on the offensive, turning into blond-boy and throwing punches at him with all her strength. The other man grabbed her wrists and stopped her attack. He pulled her in close to him, sneering in her face. Blond-boy grabbed her hair and yanked her head back. Her terror-filled eyes gazed into his eyes. He looked amused.

They wrestled her over to the front door, her hair feeling like it was being yanked out of her head. Once there, the other man picked her up. She curled her hands around his neck and squeezed. He swung her, crashing her head into the wall. She saw stars and was just a hair this side of consciousness.

In Ops, Madison cursed aloud as her eyes read the display. Immediately, she typed into the communications system, an alert to both Alpha and Delta Teams. Shepherd and Cooper would automatically get copied. Protocol called for team members to insert their comms for direction when a Panic Code Activation was broadcast. A verbal alert with any additional information available would follow within two minutes, per protocol. "Yvette, pull up Brielle's tracker and watch it." She heard Yvette's fingers clicking on the keyboard. "I've got a Panic Code Activation at Sherman's residence." She read the address, broadcasting it to the copied in team members.

"Brielle's tracker is moving away from the residence."

"Hold for a location. Brielle's tracker is on the move," Madison updated.

"I'm three minutes out from Sherman's place," Doc's voice came through.

"Proceed to the residence with caution, Doc," Madison acknowledged.

"Razor and I just left HQ," Cooper advised.

"Roger that, Coop. The tracker shows her heading north, move to intercept."

Cooper drove in the general direction of north of Sherman's condo.

In the back seat of the SUV he was in, Sherman didn't want to hold for any reason. "Turn this car around! We've got to go back towards my place."

"We need to be sure that's where Brielle is first," Lambchop said. He did pull off into a strip mall parking lot. The second Shepherd Security SUV followed. They were less than a mile away from Chicago Executive Airport, preparing to fly out for their mission to Houston.

"Garcia, Doc, and Cooper are on their way to your place," Yvette said. "Hold at your location for directions."

Brielle was dazed from her head's impact with the wall. It was through the equivalent of drunken eyes that she watched the living room give way to the outside sky. She was also aware of her hands being bound together in front of her body.

She felt the cold breeze wrap around her, and although she wanted to fight what was happening to her, she couldn't quite get her limbs to obey. She recognized the back end of a car, a silver one. She watched the trunk pop open. Through the fog in her brain, she realized she was put into it. Then the trunk was closed, and she was sealed within, alone and in the dark. A chill invaded her, yet her mind was still not alert.

The car started, and she knew it was moving. She bounced along, slid, and shifted with the car as it made turns. She wasn't sure how long she was in the car when she finally broke through the haze in her head, but when the fog cleared it was replaced with panic.

Tears flooded her eyes as the thoughts ran through her head in rapid succession. She'd been attacked. She was in the trunk of a car, kidnapped. "Calm down," she told herself aloud. She'd entered the panic code. They'd know she was in danger. She had the tracker in her shoulder. They'd know where she was and come get her, that's if the two men didn't kill her before they could get to her. "As long as this car is moving, I'm safe." And she knew that had they just wanted to kill her; they would have at the condo. She was alive for a reason. She had to remain calm and be smart.

She pulled at her hands. They were secured tightly. She brought them up to her face. In the darkness she couldn't see how they were bound. Pulling on them, she had the sensation of a single, thin wire or rope keeping them together. She brought them to her mouth. It was a zip tie. She couldn't even try to chew it off. She dropped them back to her abdomen as the car took a sharp curve, suddenly jostling her. Then she remembered that there must be a trunk release. She raised her hands and reached towards the side, feeling for it.

In her head she repeated the words, *they will find me, they will rescue me,* over and over while she concentrated on steadying her breathing. She felt along the walls where her hands could reach, trying to locate the trunk release. She rolled on her side, but couldn't reach high enough to where she thought it should be. She reached up while doing a partial sit-up. She held it as long as she could while feeling for the release. Finally, her hand found it, but a sharp turn rolled her and slid her along the carpeted floor.

Sloan hung his torso over the back seat and reached to grab his backpack where the handheld tracker locator was stored. He pulled it out and then re-sat himself in his seat. "So, we can identify right where she is when we catch the bastard who took her."

Sherman nodded, grateful. He watched the traffic on the highway pass, frustrated that they sat there, doing nothing. Through his comms, he listened to Yvette give orders to Cooper and Garcia on the changing direction they should head to intercept Brielle's tracker.

"Sounds like she's heading right towards us," Lambchop said.

"That general direction, anyway," Yvette agreed. "Coop, continue north. She's maybe two miles ahead of you." The seconds dragged into minutes. Finally, Yvette spoke again. "Target vehicle just exited fifty-three onto Palatine Road, heading east."

"Shit, she is heading this direction," Lambchop said. "Control, do we have any idea the make and model of the vehicle?"

"Negative, Lambchop."

Yvette continued calling her location out. Cooper and Garcia were a few miles back. They'd hit every stoplight.

Lambchop pulled the car up to the exit from the strip mall and waited. Brielle was within a mile. Mother, driving the other SUV, pulled up behind him. They waited. Sloan handed the tracker locator to Burke, who sat in the front passenger seat. He aimed it at the cars.

"She's approaching your location, Lambchop, one block back, half a block," Yvette said.

Lambchop eased the vehicle out onto the right lane of the four-lane road.

"She just passed you," Yvette broadcast.

Mother pulled his car out with that notification. There were only three vehicles between him and the other Shepherd Security car. Jackson had his tracker locator out too. He was scanning the cars in front of him. Unfortunately, he also picked up the trackers from the other team in the car ahead of them. His money was on the white cargo van in front of them.

They all stopped for a red light. He swept the tracker locator between the three cars ahead. "I think I have something! The silver Ford Taurus in the left lane," Jackson broadcast.

Burke handed the tracker locator to Sherman in the backseat. He aimed towards that same vehicle, nearly beside them. "Positive identification," he said. "The tracker is pinging from that car." The target car was back a half a car length. Looking through the windows, he could only see the two men in the front seats. "I have what looks to be two Caucasian males in the front seats. I do not have a view of the backseat from my location."

"Neither do we," Mother reported.

Lambchop let the target vehicle pass him. Easier to tail a car from behind it. "I'll be damned," he swore as the target car pulled into Chicago Executive Airport. "Do you have this Control? Do you see her tracker entering the airport grounds?"

"Affirmative," Yvette replied. "Go get them. You're in a more controlled space. You are cleared to proceed."

The target car veered off, heading towards the private hangars. Just their luck. The two Shepherd Security SUV's converged on the target car, which had slowed as it approached the first hangar. One cut it off from the front, the other pinned it in place in the back. Before either SUV was in park, the men jumped out, weapons trained on the two occupants of the car as they swarmed it.

"Hands! Let me see your hands!" The men shouted, the many voices overlapping each other.

"Stick your hands out the windows," Lambchop yelled as he joined the others after he had put the SUV in park.

Outmanned and outgunned, both car's occupants complied.

"Where is she?" Sherman demanded. He pulled the car door open and was shocked to see blond-boy from Louisiana. The man didn't answer. Sherman pulled him from the driver's seat and threw him against the side panel of the car. He kicked his legs apart and covered him as Sloan came in and searched him.

"I've got a nine," Sloan announced, pulling it from inside the man's coat.

"Got a .45 on the seat," Mother announced from the other side of the car after he had pulled the passenger from his seat. Burke searched the man while Mother kept his weapon on him. He pulled a fifty caliber from a holster at the small of the man's back. Then he secured his hands behind his back.

"Where the fuck is she?" Sherman growled in blond-boys face; the barrel of his weapon pressed into the man's stomach. Blond-boy's hands too were secured in cuffs behind his back.

Brielle heard voices she recognized. "Help! I'm here, in the trunk."

Sherman pushed blond-boy against the car, his knee delivering a sharp blow to the man's groin. "Fucker!" Then he released him to crumple to the ground. He leaned into the car and hit the trunk release. He rushed to the rear of the car as the trunk raised, revealing Brielle lying within. "Fuck," he cursed aloud, his anger at the two men who put her there increasing. "Brielle, God! Are you okay?"

Brielle couldn't stop the tears at the sight of Brian. She'd held them till now, knowing she had to keep her thoughts focused if she was going to survive. She reached her bound hands up towards him. He reached beneath her and cradled her in his arms as he lifted her from the trunk.

Sherman sat her to her feet and swallowed her up in an embrace. "Baby, are you okay?"

Brielle nodded against him. She felt her hands being gently pulled from between them. Her eyes met Jackson's, and she watched him snip the zip tie, freeing her hands. She immediately wrapped her arms around Brian and leaned into him. A chill invaded her, and she shook uncontrollably.

"Baby, you're freezing," Sherman said, feeling Brielle tremble against him. She wore only her pajamas. He took his coat off and draped it around her shoulders. He looked her in the eyes. "Did they hurt you?"

"I don't know," Brielle admitted.

Sherman passed her to Jackson, who still stood beside them. He closed the gap between him and blond-boy in two large strides. Anger surged through him. He threw two rapid punches, connecting his fist with the man's stomach. He put all his weight and muscle into it. Blond-boy moaned as each punch made contact. He doubled over.

"That's enough," Lambchop said, pulling Sherman off. His gaze burned through blond-boy. "Who sent you?"

As expected, blond-boy remained quiet.

Sherman drew his weapon and pointed it at blond-boy's head. "You heard the man. Who the fuck sent you?"

"Go fuck yourself!"

Sherman's gaze was serious. "Answer the question or I'm going to shoot you in the head."

"You aren't going to kill me. You'll never get your answers if you do."

"I'm not going to shoot you in *that* head." He dropped his aim to the man's crotch. "I'm going to shoot you in this one. Then my buddy over there, our medic, is going to crowd in here and save your life, getting that bleeding under control because there will be a lot of blood when I blow your dick and nuts away. There always is. And then you'll live the rest of your life with one bag at your waist collecting your piss and another that you'll shit into because the bullet will also obliterate your asshole. Now who the fuck sent you?"

"I want a deal, and protection," Blond-boy proclaimed. "And keep this psycho away from me!"

"You hurt my woman. You damned well better believe I'll go psycho on your ass!" Sherman shouted.

Lambchop laid his hand to Sherman's shoulder. "Bring it down a notch. He's going to roll on who sent them, and you really don't want to do him real harm in front of Brielle."

Sherman's eyes flashed to Brielle. She stood beside Jackson, shivering. She had a traumatized look on her face. "She's freezing out here. I'm going to get her into a car and blast the heat."

"I'll come check her out as soon as we have these two secured," Sloan said.

Just then, the car with Cooper and Garcia pulled up close beside them. The two men were out of the car seconds later.

"Big Bear wants Razor and Jax to take the lead. We're to take them to the DEA office on South Dearborn, turn them over to the DEA, one to a car," Cooper said.

Jackson nodded. He figured as much. He and Razor were the two team members onsite who carried DEA credentials.

Lambchop led blond-boy over to the SUV he'd driven. He sat him in the rear passenger seat behind the driver's seat. He pulled the floormat aside, revealing a metal ring securely bolted to the frame of the car. "So, here's the deal. You get one chance to ride comfortably. You blow this and your wrists will be chained to the floorboards." He pulled a reinforced strap from the side of the car and threaded it through the man's arms, still secured behind his back. The end snapped into a buckle at the base of the seat. Then he fastened the lap and shoulder strap over the man. He reached in his back pocket and produced a set of ankle cuffs. "Don't kick me," he warned the man. He secured one of the cuffs on his right ankle, threaded the other open end of the cuffs through the metal floor ring and then fastened it onto his other ankle. When he was through, he looked the man in the eyes. "Thank you."

Mother led the other detainee over to Cooper's car and mirrored Lambchop's actions. This man struggled against Mother as he tried to thread the back of the arms restraining strap through his arms. "Sit the fuck still or you're riding on the floor," Mother growled in his face. "I'd prefer to treat you like a human being, but it's up to you. Your friend is cooperating, will get a deal. That's an option for you too."

"Fuck you, man. I'm as good as dead if I do that."

"Your choice," Mother said to him. The man continued to struggle.

Garcia stood behind Mother. "Enough of this shit, you ride like an animal." He unthreaded the tether, and pulled the man to the floor, wrists first. He took hold of the ankle restraint cuffs and secured it to the cuffs around his wrists at the man's back, pulling it tightly so the man had no wiggle room. He was pinned to the floor. Then he went to the opposite side of the car and opened the back door. He secured the man's ankles in another set of cuffs and also secured those to the bolt under the floormat.

Cooper went to the door of the SUV where Sherman and Brielle sat. "Birdman, Shepherd wants you to go pack up some of her things. She'll stay in the apartment on nine until this is sorted out. We're pretty sure your place is safe for the moment but be on alert. The mission will be postponed for twelve hours. There'll be a briefing this afternoon."

Sherman appreciated that Shepherd had already thought that far ahead. "I've got to warn my brother and find a place for him to stay."

"He can stay with Madison and me, if you want," Cooper offered.

"Thanks, Coop. I'll let you know."

Cooper nodded and then closed the door.

Brielle watched numbly as Cooper and Garcia got back into their car. They drove away, followed by the other SUV. Danny slid into the driver's seat as Rich entered the front passenger side of their SUV.

Gary got into the back beside her. He dropped his medical backpack on the floor between them. "Now, let's take a look at you. Are you hurt anywhere?"

Brielle shrugged. "I don't know. I know my head hit the wall when I was struggling with them." She raised her hand and grasped her forehead. "Yes, my head hurts."

Brian held her hand as Gary shined a penlight into each eye. He took her pulse and her blood pressure and checked over her head as Mother drove the SUV to Sherman's condo. Gary produced a water bottle from inside his pack and prompted her to drink.

Sherman watched Sloan check Brielle over. Sloan was being thorough. He appreciated that.

Sloan made eye contact with him. "I think she's fine, just shook up."

"Thanks," Sherman said. He looped his arm around her. "We'll get you packed up and settled in at HQ before we head out."

Brielle had forgotten they were heading out of town on a mission. She didn't want Brian to go. Even though she would be at HQ and safe, the thought of Brian not being with her frightened her. "I know it's your job, but I wish you didn't have to go."

Sherman wished he didn't have to go either. He kissed the top of her head. "I'm sorry, babe. You'll be safe at HQ."

"I know I will," Brielle said bravely. "I'll be fine, don't worry about me."

Sherman pressed another kiss to her head. "I know you'll be fine. I'll still worry about you though."

As the SUV pulled into Sherman's subdivision, all four men's phones pinged with a new voicemail. It was from Shepherd. That was odd.

"Begin message. I'm sending this message out to all Shepherd Security personnel and their family members who carry agency phones. At zero seven hundred this morning, there was an attack against our agency. The Birdman's residence was broken into and our new agency Special Projects Manager, Brielle Jarboe, was taken by two assailants, who are now in custody. Brielle entered the panic code into the security system, which alerted Ops. Our personnel intercepted and recovered Brielle promptly. She is unharmed. We are investigating how his residence was compromised. I expect that this was an isolated incident, but I urge you to all be more cautious than normal until we confirm if any further threat exists. As soon as we have information, I will share it with you. Contact me or Cooper with any questions or concerns. End message."

Immediately, Sherman's phone came to life with text message after text message pinging it, Sienna, Kaylee, and Elizabeth sending group text messages to check on Brielle. Then it rang. It was Ops. "Sherman," he answered.

"Did Cooper tell you that Big Bear wants you to move yourself and Brielle into the apartment here at HQ until further notice?" Yvette asked.

"He did. We're just arriving at my residence now."

"He's pushing off the mission until tomorrow and replacing you with Cooper. There is a new briefing scheduled for Alpha and Delta Teams at fourteen hundred this afternoon. Both you and Brielle will receive invitations."

"Thank you for letting me know, Yvette."

"No problem. Take care of your girl. She has to be shaken up."

"Yeah. We'll pack up and be back to HQ within the hour, I'm sure." He filled the others in on what Yvette had just told him.

Then they all exited the car and went to his front door. Doc opened it from the inside when they reached it. "It's clear." He stepped back and let the others pass into the house. "How are you doing, honey?" He asked Brielle as she passed him.

"I'm okay," she replied.

"What hit the wall here?" Doc asked, pointing out the spot near the security panel where the drywall was dented.

"That would be where my head hit."

"Oh, baby," Sherman said, pulling her more tightly against himself. "Come on, let's go pack a few things." He led her to the bedroom. "Where's your phone?"

"I think I left it in the bathroom."

"I'll get it," Sloan volunteered. On the bathroom counter beside the phone, he immediately recognized what was there. It was the wand to a pregnancy kit and the plus sign was blue. He knew what that meant. "Sherman," he called.

Within the bedroom, Sherman had just grabbed a couple of empty backpacks from the closet when he heard Sloan call. "Start packing a few essentials, mostly tops and underclothing. You'll get away with one or two pairs of jeans. I'll be right back." He joined Sloan at the doorway to the bathroom.

"You're going to want to see this," Sloan said, lifting the test stick into view. "Blue plus sign, positive."

Shock hit Sherman. "Shit man, is that for real?" He took the stick from Sloan. A smile spread over his face.

"Congrats, man," Sloan said. He embraced his friend.

"Do you two need a minute?" Mother asked, now standing beside them.

Sloan held the stick up. "It's blue."

Mother embraced him as well. "Congrats. Does Brielle know?"

"Brielle," Sherman muttered. He rushed back into their bedroom. He came up beside her and held the stick up. "Brielle?"

"Oh, my God. I forgot I took it. I was peeing on it when I heard the front door open. I thought it was you or Bobby coming back."

"You're pregnant. We're pregnant, Brielle," Sherman exclaimed. He grabbed her up in a hug. "Oh, baby, thank God you hit the panic code."

"Hate to interrupt, but let's get packed up and out of here," Mother called from the door.

Brielle hurried and dressed in jeans and a sweater. She packed the backpack full of clothes. She knew there was shampoo, conditioner, and a blow dryer in the apartment, so she didn't have to pack those things. She just added her moisturizer, brush, comb, and toothbrush into the backpack in the bathroom. Then she donned her warm winter coat and followed the others from the house. Brian was the last to leave, setting the alarm system and locking the door.

Gary handed her phone to her. She immediately began replying to the many text messages from the other wives, her friends, assuring them that she was okay. She was surprised when she got a text message from Dr. Lassiter, summoning her to his office as soon as they arrived at HQ. She was even more surprised when Brian told her that her complying was mandatory. Dr. Lassiter would bar her from duty if she didn't go see him.

Yankee

*B*rielle stared at her coffee cup. Sitting here, talking with Dr. Lassiter was the last thing she wanted to do. She wanted to go take a nice hot shower and lie in Brian's arms. That was all. She just wanted to feel safe in his arms.

"Brielle the sooner we talk, the sooner you can go do whatever it is that you feel you need to," Lassiter said. Her eyes were focused on the door out of the kitchen, like she was trying to will herself out of this room.

"I'm okay," she insisted.

"No, you're not, or you wouldn't be saying you are. You were kidnapped and thrown in the trunk of a car. No one can experience that and not be phased."

"I hit the panic code on the alarm system. I knew someone would know I was in danger. And I have the tracker in my shoulder, so I knew they'd find me."

"Doesn't mean it wasn't a scary ordeal."

"I never said it wasn't scary. I tried to keep calm, prayed like hell while I was in that trunk, and kept faith in the team."

"You know it's going to come back to you, while you sleep, or when you're alone in the house again. That fear, memories, or even visions of the moment when those men broke into the house will replay through your mind. That's what traumas do. Just like the moment that Sherman was shot. You saw that moment for a few nights when you closed your eyes."

Brielle nodded stiffly. "I know. Can we talk about it tomorrow? It's over for today and I know I'm safe here in this building and I know those two men are in custody."

"It looks like it will be learned who sent them. After that person is in custody, it will be over. That's why you're staying here. And, the team needs to discover how they found you. One of the team's residences being located is a huge security breach."

"And as soon as that's determined, we'll be able to leave the apartment?"

"As long as you're ready to," Lassiter said. "If you're mentally not up to being there, you need to speak up. There is nothing wrong with being afraid, Brielle. But it is wrong to not face that fear, or worse yet, fail to admit it."

"I'm used to just pressing on, no matter what."

Lassiter smiled. "An admirable trait, but not the healthiest, mentally or emotionally. You have to promise me that if you're replaying it in your head or if you're feeling anxiety or fear because of it, that you'll tell me. I can't help you if you're not honest with me."

"I promise," she agreed. Her eyes went back to the door. "Can I go now? I really want to get a shower and just lie with Brian for a bit."

"I plan on speaking with Sherman next."

"Please, can it wait?"

"How did you feel about him threatening to kill that man?"

Brielle shrugged. "It was effective. I knew he wouldn't shoot him, and I knew Landon wouldn't let him, either."

Lassiter was impressed that she understood all three of those things. "I'll talk with Sherman after the briefing. You can have time with him now."

Sherman was stretched out on the bed, sitting with his back against two propped up pillows when Brielle emerged from the bathroom. The humid air from the hot shower and the heat from the blow dryer followed her into the room, rapidly elevating the room's air temperature by five degrees.

"You feel any better, babe?" Sherman held his hand out towards her, an invitation to join him.

She crawled onto the bed, dropping her behind between his spread legs and draping her torso over his, taking him in an embrace. Sherman was instantly engulfed in the fresh, clean scent that clung to her. He felt her shrug against him.

"Today has just been surreal. I've never been that afraid in my life. And I knew that I hit the panic code, so I knew someone would know I was in trouble and be looking for me. I knew I had the tracker in me, that you would find me, but I just kept praying that they wouldn't kill me before you got there."

Sherman wrapped his arms around her and held her snuggly. "When Madison broadcast the panic code activation and said it was for you, I think my heart stopped beating. I've never been that afraid in my life either."

"I want to learn how to defend myself better and I want to get my conceal carry license, like Shepherd talked about. And I always want to have a gun near me. I want to do those things right away. I don't ever want to feel so helpless again."

"Shepherd has already assigned Cooper to teach you the hand to hand self-defense skills. He's the best and can teach you everything you need to know. And I can teach you to shoot better and get you qualified for your CCW. You and I'll both be

here for at least the next week. We'll spend some time down in the range every day."
He knew she needed to actively do something to feel more empowered, to feel safe.
He'd do whatever he could to help her.

He felt her nod against him. His hand found its way to her abdomen. They hadn't
talked about the positive pregnancy test. He didn't realize that he was caressing
softly over her belly until she spoke.

"How do you feel about that?"

Sherman felt the grin spread over his face. "Momma, I'm gonna be the best
damn daddy to our kid. You have to know I'm the happiest man in the world. The
question is, how do *you* feel about it?"

"Well, we said we'd leave it up to God and I guess He decided for us."

Sherman chuckled. "You said not too long ago that a kid at this point didn't fit
into your plan."

"That was the old plan. I think I can be a mom and still do this job for Shepherd
Security and the DEA. I honestly haven't had the chance to process it yet."

"You suspected it and bought that test kit. Why didn't you tell me?"

Brielle rolled over just enough to look him in the eyes. "I didn't want to say
anything till I knew, because I didn't want you to be disappointed if I wasn't. I've
watched you with Sammy and little Olivia. You're great with them and I knew you
wanted one of your own."

Sherman leaned up. He gently grasped her face between his two hands, and he
took her lips in a kiss. "Let's get one thing straight. You could never disappoint me. I
love you, Brielle." His gaze penetrated her eyes down to her very soul.

Tears filled her eyes. She tried to blink them back. "I love you too," she said in a
whisper.

"And secondly, I only want a kid with you, never thought about it before I fell in
love with you."

"I've always wanted to have kids," she admitted.

"You will marry me, won't you?" His fingers held her face in place.

A smile radiated from her. "Yes." The emotion in the one word was
overwhelming.

Sherman kissed her again. A long, passionate, melt your clothes off type of kiss.
If they didn't have the briefing in fifteen minutes, he'd make love to her. Their lips
parted, and they just stared affectionately into each other's eyes for a few quiet
moments.

"Will you want your daddy to give you away at our wedding?" He watched her
gaze shift away from his and a scowl etched itself on her face.

"No and I don't want him there."

"And Dahlia?"

"If it can work out that she can be there, great, if not, that's fine. I'm okay if we just elope."

"I don't want to elope. This agency is my family. I want to marry you in front of my team."

"As long as Bobby is there, that's all I care about," Brielle said.

"Are you ready to tell me why you had a falling out with your daddy and Dahlia?" Sherman would press this time. She didn't answer. "What does it have to do with your momma's drunk driving accident?"

"It wasn't my momma's accident. It was his. My daddy was driving drunk and killed her. Not that she was sober either. But he was driving."

"He didn't get charged?"

"It happened on the reservation, Indian police department, Indian courts had jurisdiction. They wanted Dahlia to train with the old shaman. She agreed to move onto the reservation and train in exchange for their protection of our daddy. As long as he lives on the reservation, he's safe. I don't think Dahlia really wanted to, but she wanted to save our daddy from jail time, so she agreed."

"I'm sure your daddy had to feel terrible for your momma's death, knowing it was his fault. I'm not sure him going to jail would have punished him anymore than he probably punishes himself."

"He crawled into a bottle and has been there ever since," Brielle said in disgust. "He ruined his own life and Dahlia's."

"Dahlia had freedom of choice, still does."

"I know. I think a part of her wanted to hide out on the reservation and pursue everything spiritual. Old Rainbow Bear, the shaman, that man was nearly one hundred years old! He believed Dahlia had some power. I think it was the ravings of an old man suffering from dementia. He passed a few years ago."

"You ever hear the saying, not your monkey, not your circus?"

"Yeah," she admitted.

"It's not you know. Dahlia's life is her own. Her decisions are her own to make and live with."

"I know."

"We better head to Shepherd's office for the briefing," Sherman said.

They were the last to arrive. They took their seats. The men who escorted her two abductors to the DEA office downtown were back and seated at the table. "Please tell me you got a full statement from blond-boy," Sherman said, his eyes on Lambchop.

Lambchop nodded. "Troy didn't shut up. That's his name, Troy Farwell. His statement needs to be substantiated, but I'd bet my prized Sig .9mm P226 that it all verifies."

"Who sent them to my house and how the hell did they know where we lived?" Sherman asked, his voice tense, his emotions reigned in.

"Dwayne Stuart, Galliano's Mayor and Jennifer Brubaker, also known to the slave-labor at BioDynamix as Madam Butterfly. Farwell rolled on them as the masterminds of the heroin stickers," Lambchop said.

"They could have made them anywhere. Why in Louisiana?" Brielle asked.

"When they first set about forming their corporation, they were going to set up shop in Trenton, but things had gotten hot for them there. There had been several large busts by the DEA in the past few years, and they figured their luck was probably due to run out. Stuart had gone to the Louisiana area on a fishing trip and the plan came together for him there, fresh start, fresh opportunity," Lambchop answered.

"My address?" Sherman asked again.

Lambchop and Jackson's eyes went to Brielle. But it was Shepherd who spoke. "Brielle, did you send your sister a package?"

"Yes, a Christmas gift."

"And you put Sherman's address on the package."

"Yes, but I told Dahlia to destroy it, burn the address label."

Shepherd shook his head. "She didn't, threw the intact label in the trash. Blond-boy was watching her, pulled it out of her trashcan."

"Oh, baby, you were told not to give our address out," Sherman said. "I told you I'd get you a secure mailing address to use."

"You were gone on a mission and it is only a few weeks till Christmas. I didn't want it to be late. I thought it would be okay," she said, but her voice trailed off, realizing she had put herself in danger. "I didn't know," she added nervously.

"It's okay, at least we know how the breach happened," Shepherd said.

"I'm sorry," Brielle said. "I won't do it again. I promise." She felt Brian's hand take hold of hers under the table. Her eyes remained focused on Shepherd. "So, now what?"

"Farwell swears that no one else knows the address, just him and his partner, Dave Garver, another New Jersey native who works for Stuart," Jackson answered.

"So, it's safe then? We can go back to the condo?" Brielle asked.

"Not yet, babe," Sherman answered.

Lambchop nodded. "Garver lawyered up. He could pass the address on. You can believe the attorney has ties right back to the crime network run by Stuart."

"But won't they all be arrested?" Brielle asked.

"If everything Farwell gave us pans out, yes. But we won't discount their reach. Brielle, you have to understand, this network is going to be pissed off and want revenge," Cooper said.

"Against me," she murmured.

"Yes," Shepherd confirmed.

"So, what do we do?" Brielle asked.

"We make them believe you're gone, into WitSec," Cooper answered.

"The witness protection program?" Brielle questioned.

"Yes. Sherman is going to hire a moving company to move all your things, we'll have a couple of Marshals oversee it. We'll let it slip in front of the right audience that you have been moved to a secret location," Shepherd said.

"I don't want to leave," Brielle argued.

A small grin pulled at Shepherd's lips. "You're not going anywhere, but Sherman's condo is burned. Your place has to go up for sale and you'll have to buy a new place."

Sherman nodded. "I needed to get a bigger place with Brielle and Bobby living with me."

"I'm sorry, Brian. I know you weren't ready to do that yet," Brielle said.

He squeezed her hand. "Baby, it's okay. We'll find us a nice three-bedroom place." He locked eyes with Shepherd. He could see in his eyes that Shepherd knew about the pregnancy. His eyes scanned his teammates. Based on the grins on each of their faces, they all knew. "Isn't anyone gonna congratulate us? Yes, Brielle's pregnant."

Shepherd's lips pulled into a smile. "Congratulations. I wasn't sure if you wanted it to be public knowledge."

"It seems like it already is," Sherman said, glancing around the table.

"I'm not very far along," Brielle said.

"There are several nice units in my complex for sale," Mother spoke up. "I was just telling Sloan about them yesterday. There's even three-bedroom units with full, finished basements. That would make a nice private place for Bobby."

"I wish there were a few units in our area, but there aren't any on the market right now," Jackson added.

"My house isn't too far from yours," Mother remarked. He glanced back at Sherman and Brielle. "I have a three-bedroom place. Both of you and Bobby are welcome to stay at my place till you move."

"We've gotten off track," Shepherd said. "You three discuss that offline. Regardless, you don't go back to his condo, Brielle. You got that?"

"Yes, sir," she replied.

"We're holding off on the Houston mission. If Farwell's statement pans out, we'll be in on the raids to round up the crime network in Trenton. It's big, by the sounds of it. That's where he says Madam Butterfly is operating out of. The FBI will arrest Dwayne Stuart in Louisiana," Shepherd said. "Okay, dismissed, but keep your gear packed. You're all on a thirty-minute standby. All members of both Alpha and Delta will be on this one." He said, his eyes going to Sherman.

"What about me, sir," Burke asked.

"You're on with Alpha and Delta."

Brielle felt a pang of disappointment that Brian was back on active. She was looking forward to the week they'd have together. She also felt terribly guilty that it was her actions that led to the two men finding her, which now necessitated Brian selling his place and them moving. She didn't bother to get mad at Dahlia. Even though she didn't burn the address label as she was supposed to, it wasn't Dahlia's fault. It was hers for mailing that package with the return address on it.

She realized that everyone else stood and were filing out of the room. Her eyes landed on Shepherd. "I'm very sorry I caused this."

"Without this happening, we'd never have gotten Farwell and his statement, which undoubtedly will bring down an entire crime network, lead to proof to arrest Stuart, and locate Jennifer Brubaker, aka Madam Butterfly. Don't break any protocols again. They are all in place for a reason, but this time, the effects aren't too catastrophic. You got the panic code in and are okay. Be sure to follow up with Lassiter though."

Brielle came to her feet beside Sherman. "I will, sir, thank you."

Zulu

rielle and Sherman, as well as Bobby, stayed at Mother's townhouse. It was spacious, with an open floor plan. The garage was accessed from a drive at the back of the unit. The door from the garage led into the kitchen, which was open to the family room. It had a lofted ceiling. A second family room type space was in the loft overlooking the first floor. Over the large kitchen and the two-car garage were the three bedrooms and bathrooms.

Brielle fell in love with the layout and they put a bid in on the unit across the street with the finished basement. They only looked at two of the four available units, didn't need to look any further. They knew they wanted that one. And it was a plus that it was so close to Mother's place. Plus, it was vacant. They could close in under thirty days.

"I still feel guilty that I caused this to happen," Brielle said. "I am sorry, Brian."

"Babe, please stop apologizing. We needed a bigger place. Bobby will love his suite in the basement." It even had a bathroom and a bedroom in addition to the main area that Bobby could use as his own living room. All it lacked to be considered an apartment was its own kitchen.

"This is a good family neighborhood, lots of little ones and a park down the street," Mother added. "You'll like living here, I'm sure. Now we just have to get Sloan to move over here too."

The alert they'd been waiting two days for, came. Even though Brielle knew it would come, her heart sank. She watched Brian and Danny grab their backpacks, which were near the door.

Sherman wrapped his arms around her. "If you don't want to be here alone while Bobby's at work, go back to the apartment at HQ or over to one of the other women's houses. Be careful and stay alert." He felt her tremble in his arms. "Baby, you're safe here."

"I know," she agreed. "Bobby will be home in a few hours. I'll be fine." She reached up on tippy-toes and kissed his lips. "I love you. Be safe."

"I've got his six, don't worry," Mother said.

Later that evening, Brielle and Bobby had just finished dinner when she got a text message. It was Yvette in Ops. The team was with other federal authorities. They would be conducting raids on suspects beginning in thirty minutes. Brielle had time to make it to HQ before it began.

"I'll be right there," she tapped out her reply.

When she got to HQ, she entered Ops to find a full house. Besides Yvette, she was surprised that Shepherd was there. Tony 'Wang' Miraldi and Caleb 'Hound dog' Smith were there too. She glanced up at the monitors. As she suspected, both Delta Team and Alpha Team were onsite. They were in full tactical gear with cameras transmitting. They were with what looked to be several dozen other agents also in tactical clothing, with a variety of agency abbreviations on their bullet-proof vests. They were inside a garage. A map was displayed on a large monitor, city blocks with several buildings circled in red.

"That's the mission map," Yvette said. "Stuart's strip club will be raided simultaneously with three other properties that have been validated as targets. One is where the woman going as Jennifer Brubaker is confirmed to be right now."

"We also believe that one of the locations is now producing the heroin laced stickers with slave labor," Caleb Smith added.

"A third building, a warehouse in Camden, very well could be a major human trafficking hub," Shepherd added.

"What's the fourth target?" Brielle asked.

"A takeout pizza joint. The DEA believes the product is being distributed from it," Shepherd replied.

Brielle sat at one of the desks and typed this information into her tablet. She assumed she'd be writing the DEA news release on the raid. She listened to the briefing, taking notes throughout. The Shepherd Security Team along with FBI would be executing the warrant on Jennifer Brubaker.

She watched the team get into two SUVs. She heard the chatter between them, all mission related. Then, through Gary's camera, she watched Brian run through his pre-mission ritual. The corners of her lips tipped up. He kissed his dog tags, believing that in doing so they would never need to be used to identify his body. He made the sign of the cross, his faith strong. She loved this man, loved who he was, was proud of what he believed in, was proud of the job he did.

Then Landon said his pre-mission prayer to keep all the teams from the different agencies safe, for those they targeted to cooperate, so no one got hurt or killed. For the raids to be successful, for dangerous drugs to be confiscated so they would not make it to the streets. He prayed for any victims of human trafficking to be rescued and set free. He finished his prayer as they rolled up on the target location, a large home in the West End neighborhood.

Brielle watched as the team and the FBI Agents swiftly and silently exited their vehicles. They fanned out, Alpha Team heading around back, the FBI Agents leading Delta Team up to the front door. The wait seemed to last hours. It was three minutes until Alpha Team came up beside the two French doors at the back of the house.

"Alpha Team in position," Cooper broadcast.

"Go! Go! Go!" Was heard.

Through Delta Team's cameras Brielle saw one of the regular FBI Agents swing a battering ram at the beautiful front door. The lead crystal window shattered as the door splintered open with a deafening bang, the light from inside spilling out into the dark night.

"Federal agents executing a warrant!"

Then they all rushed through the front door, fanning out in different directions. All four members of Delta Team went up the lavish, arcing staircase. At the top, Brian and Gary went left, the others went right. Through Alpha Team's cameras, Brielle saw Cooper and Madison enter the house through one of the French doors that led into a beautifully decorated family room. Doc, Jackson, and Garcia went through the other that brought them into the designer kitchen.

As they cleared room by room, "clear!" was heard resounding through the house. In the master bedroom suite, Brian and Gary came upon a locked door, the bathroom.

"Lambchop, got a locked door in the master," Brian broadcast.

"Hold your position. We'll be there in a few. Clearing the last few rooms on this floor."

Brielle's eyes went back and forth from each of Delta Team's feeds. She, as always, barely breathed as she watched, praying that no gunfire would shatter the silence. Then the sound of gunfire made her flinch. Scanning Delta Team's cameras, it was not from their locations.

"Federal agents, we have a warrant," she heard Cooper yell.

Her eyes went to Alpha Team's feeds. They were going down the stairs to the basement. She watched as they covered each other, taking turns advancing on those who fired at them from behind furniture around the room. There was a half-dozen muzzle flashes from behind a pool table.

"Fuck this," Garcia's voice was heard. She watched as in Jackson's feed, Garcia pulled a device from one of the compartments on the front of his bullet-proof vest. He pulled the pin out. "Standby, standby, go!"

Then he tossed it at the pool table. A loud explosion and a blinding bright light engulfed the room. Pieces of the ceiling fell; a cloud of dust and smoke engulfed the area. The team immediately swarmed in, neutralizing the few threats that remained.

Gunfire sounded from the southwest corner of the room. Jackson and Garcia converged on that location, firing at the two men who were concealed behind a tipped over poker table.

"Federal agents, we have a warrant," Jackson repeated.

Gunfire answered. Jackson fired, keeping the two assailants pinned down as Garcia circled to the left. Through his camera, he had a clear view of the two men. "Freeze!"

The men turned their guns in his direction. Garcia didn't hesitate.

On the second floor, Danny and Landon came into the master suite. The four men got into position. With a powerful thrust of his leg, Landon kicked the door open. Brian rushed past him and into the room first, followed by Gary, then Danny, and finally Landon. The bathroom was huge, with two more closed doors within. Through Gary's camera feed, Brielle saw Landon and Danny by one of the doors. Landon counted down on his fingers, three, two, one. Then Brian raised his leg and kicked the door open in front of him. Landon did the same on the other door. Both doors burst open.

A Chinese woman sat crouched beside the toilet, a pistol in her grip.

"Drop it!" Brian commanded.

Brielle's breath caught in her chest as she watched the woman hold the gun on Brian.

"You don't have to die here today," Brian said. "Real easy, put the gun down."

The woman laid the gun to the floor in front of her. Brian reached in and pulled her to her feet. Brielle recognized her from her photos. She was the woman known as Jennifer Brubaker and Madam Butterfly. Brian brought her into the larger main bathroom area and then pressed her to the wall, spread-eagle. A beautiful butterfly tattoo was on the back of her neck.

"Target acquired," Brian broadcast.

"Basement secure," Cooper reported.

"First floor secure," another voice stated.

"Second floor secure," Landon added.

Brielle glanced at the mission timer. Less than four minutes had elapsed. It always surprised her how little time an assault such as this took. The Shepherd Security Team always interfaced with other federal authorities seamlessly. The methodical manner in which they operated was smooth and expedient. And when gunfire erupted, they never hesitated. She typed her notes, the facts and her observations.

Shepherd's phone chirped, bringing her attention away from her computer.

He raised his phone to his ear. "Shepherd." He listened. "Very good. Thank you for the notification." When he brought the phone down, his eyes went to Brielle.

"The New Orleans FBI executed a warrant for the arrest of Dwayne Stuart. He's in custody."

Her lips curved into a satisfied smile. With his arrest, it was finally over. She would write one last blog post as Brielle Jarboe. Hopefully, outsiders would never again gain positions of power in the bayou. They thought the residents were backwards, uneducated hillbillies. They were wrong, and it was their downfall. Yes, Brielle was very satisfied.

Once statements were made, deals were struck, and the full picture formed, Shepherd shared it with the team. Madam Butterfly, AKA Jennifer Brubaker, AKA Fei Yue was in fact the link between the Trenton Syndicate and the Chinese. Her brother was in the top ranks of one of the worst and most powerful Chinese Triads in the United States. They ran drugs, human trafficking, committed fraud and extortion, engaged in money laundering and the smuggling of counterfeit goods. Unfortunately, he was not scooped up in the raids. His whereabouts were unknown.

Fei Yue was also Dwayne Stuart's lover. She claimed Stuart and her brother were the masterminds of the entire plan, but the authorities didn't buy that. Per the statements from the Chinese women who were liberated from their forced labor at the BioDynamix facility, they knew that Fei Yue was the engineer behind the potent heroin laced stickers. Statements from the women rescued from the warehouse in Camden that was raided at the same time that she was arrested, put her smack dab in the middle of the human trafficking and forced prostitution ring.

The raid on the pizza place netted the DEA over three million in heroin laced stickers packaged for distribution. The raid on Dwayne Stuart's strip club liberated ten women forced into the sex trade and at least a dozen customers engaged in sex with prostitutes when the feds entered the premises. A back room illegal gambling operation was shut down and drugs worth just over a million were confiscated.

In the end, fourteen suspects were killed, twenty-three were arrested, and just over fifty women and teens were rescued from the human trafficking ring that had kidnapped them from many locations. New information regarding the Triad was obtained, several new investigations would commence based on what they learned. It had been a successful operation. Brielle wrote a comprehensive story about it as well as her final blog post on the happenings in Lafourche Parish. Shepherd approved both with nothing redacted.

Three Days Later

Sherman set the six-pack on Sloan's coffee table. He took two from it, popping the caps off. He handed one to Sloan. "I talked with Shepherd. As soon as it will work operationally, Brielle and I are going to get married. You'll be my best man, won't you?"

Sloan held his bottle out to Sherman. "Absolutely. Congrats, man. You're going to be a hell of a daddy."

"And a husband," Sherman added after he took a long pull from his bottle. "I know I haven't known Brielle that long, but I love her, never felt this way about any woman. She helped Bobby take care of my momma when she was sick. It's weird, she's like already a part of the family, has been for a long time before now."

"I'm happy for you," Sloan said.

"What about you? When are you going to marry Kaylee?"

Sloan ran his hand through his hair. "We're in no hurry. She's settling into her new life. Likes working at the school."

"Let's make it a double ceremony. Who knows when operationally it will work again? Let's make it easier on Shepherd."

Sloan grinned at him and brought his beer bottle to his mouth. He didn't answer. "Will Brielle's family be there?"

Sherman shook his head. "She had a bad falling out with her daddy, won't even tell him. And she says she doesn't care if her sister is there or not."

"She says?"

"Yeah, I don't want her to have any regrets. She sent Christmas gifts to her sister. I know there is still a relationship there."

"I'm glad Kaylee resolved things with her folks but having them and my brother and his family at our wedding will add a lot of complication to it."

"So, are we doing this or what?" Sherman asked.

"I don't know."

"Shit or get off the head, man. You gonna marry your girl or not? Shepherd will make it work for both your families to be there."

"Fuck, man, look at you, eager to marry Brielle and be a daddy. I never thought I'd see the day."

Sherman chuckled. "She's pregnant with my kid. You know the saying, step up and be a man or sit the fuck down so she can see the real man standing behind you. And there ain't no way in hell I'm gonna let any other man take my place. I owe her and my kid that and more, so yeah, I'm ready to marry her and be a daddy."

A grin spread over Sloan's face. "Man, I couldn't be prouder of you."

"So, what about you?" Sherman again asked.

"I love Kaylee, I really do. And right now, everything is perfect."

Sherman waited a few quiet moments. When Sloan didn't continue, he prompted him. "But?"

"But it was before too, and then everything went to shit in a second."

"And you're afraid lightning will strike twice."

"Something like that."

"Yeah it could, and you could be the one to take the bullet next time out, or a dump truck could hit Kaylee."

"I know," Sloan agreed. "There are no guarantees."

"Kaylee loves you. She's wearing your ring, expecting to marry you. Don't let your girl down and don't leave her wondering when it's going to happen, or even worse, if it is. Marry her when I marry Brielle. Come on, we'll do this together. We're partners."

Sloan laughed. "That would be appropriate. Okay, I'll ask Kaylee what she thinks of the idea."

"Tonight," Sherman pressed. "You ask her tonight."

"Okay, okay," Sloan agreed as the sound of the garage door opening was heard. "Sounds like the girls are back."

A few minutes later Kaylee and Brielle came into the room. Both of them carried at least six shopping bags each. The corners of Sherman's lips tipped up. "Looks like a successful shopping trip."

Brielle set her bags near the front door and then approached him, placing a kiss on his lips. "Very. I'm officially done with my Christmas shopping."

"And we looked at some baby stuff," Kaylee added. She rummaged through one of her bags. She pulled a tiny sleeper in camouflage colors from it. "I bought you your first baby thing." She had a big smile on her face.

Sherman laughed. "Oh man," he remarked taking the newborn sized sleeper from her. "It is so small." He examined it closely. "I love it. Thanks Kaylee."

"You're welcome. You have to know that Gary and I are so happy for you both," Kaylee said, her arm wrapped around Sloan.

Just then, Both Sherman and Sloan's phones sounded with the alert tone. That tone meant only one thing, and their team wasn't even on an active standby, Charlie Team was. Sherman and Sloan both checked their displays.

"This can't be good," Sherman remarked.

"What is it?" Kaylee asked.

"We just got scrambled, have to report to HQ immediately," Sloan said.

Brielle checked her phone. Nothing.

"It's not a DEA Mission if Brielle didn't get the alert," Sherman said.

"I thought Charlie Team was on standby this weekend?" Brielle asked.

"They are, so this means it's big enough that both teams are getting launched," Sherman said. He downed his beer. Then he pulled his car keys from his pocket. He hit the button, popping his trunk. He'd have to grab his go-bag. Then he handed his car keys to Brielle. "I'll catch a ride to the office with Sloan."

Brielle wrapped her arms around Brian and held him tightly. "I love you. Be safe," she whispered in his ear.

Sherman held the back of her neck and kissed her like he'd never kissed anyone. He heard the sound of kisses from behind him, where Sloan and Kaylee stood. "I love you too. You also be safe. I'll be in touch when I can."

Brielle heard a similar conversation taking place between Kaylee and Gary. Then the men grabbed their bags and were gone. She watched Kaylee finish Gary's beer and then she stared at her engagement ring. "I guess we're eating the pizza by ourselves."

Brielle wrapped Kaylee in a hug. "They're going to be fine. This team is the best. And this is what we signed up for, being with them."

Kaylee nodded her head. "I know. And I wouldn't be anywhere but here, with Gary."

Brielle smiled. She felt exactly the same way. Even though she had to live with the uncertainty of Brian's job, she wouldn't change a thing. Her life was perfect in every way. She loved Brian with a ferocity she didn't know existed. Shopping for baby things that afternoon had amped up her excitement over the pregnancy. She couldn't wait to meet their baby. She had a job writing articles that mattered, what she'd wanted for as long as she could remember, and Bobby, her best friend was with them and he was happy. He'd make an amazing uncle and was just as thrilled about the baby as they were.

On the drive to HQ, Sherman glanced out the window. Flurries were just starting to fall. His thoughts jumped from the white snowflakes to Brielle in a white gown. They'd be married as soon as possible, not that he needed a ceremony or a piece of paper to validate their relationship. He'd committed his heart to her before the first time he'd made love to her, but he couldn't wait to see her walk down the aisle in a long, flowing wedding dress. She'd be stunning in it.

His momma had once told him that when he met the girl who would forever hold his heart, he'd know it. A smile cracked his lips as he recalled his feisty woman refusing to come out from the storage panel where she hid on his boat just a few months earlier. His momma hadn't been wrong. She was unlike any woman he'd ever met, and she intrigued him from that first moment, made him want a forever with her, children with her, things he'd never wanted with any other woman. She understood and accepted his job. She was a perfect fit in his life. He was one lucky man.

Sloan interrupted his thoughts. "All of Alpha Team got scrambled too. This can't be good."

Sherman's thoughts immediately snapped into work mode, mentally reviewing the gear he'd be packing up very soon. Three teams meant they'd be flying out on the C-9 from the cargo hangar at O'Hare. Their destination could be any hot zone in the world. He and his brothers would do what they did best. They would protect the innocent and eradicate the evil, be it domestically or in some third world shithole.

He glanced at Sloan's profile. He and his partner would handle this together as they always did. Yeah, they absolutely would have to marry their girls together when they got back. Nothing in his life for the last decade had been done without Sloan by his side. His marriage to Brielle would be no different.

"You and Kaylee will be Godparents to our kid, won't you?"

He watched a smile curve over Sloan's face. "It's about time you asked." Then he chuckled. "And Kaylee and I put an offer in on that unit three down from the one you and Brielle bought. Kaylee wants to try to get pregnant in May, when the school year is almost over. That way she'll have the summer off during her first trimester in case the morning sickness is bad."

"Well look at you, all ready to buy a bigger place and become a daddy. You know what that means, don't you? You have to marry Kaylee when I marry Brielle."

Sloan laughed. He turned into the Shepherd Security Garage and followed the long line of cars deep into the second subbasement level. In the side mirror, Sherman saw Mother's pickup truck behind them. Lambchop's car was two in front of them. One of the Shepherd Security SUVs was between them. He couldn't tell who was driving it. He suspected it was Cooper.

The vehicles parked in the private area and the team members all exited their vehicles. "Coop, you know what this is about?" Sherman yelled to Cooper as he pulled himself from behind the wheel of the SUV.

Cooper shook his head. "No, but all three teams got scrambled. It's big."

Yeah, tell him something he didn't know. Sherman grabbed his backpack and followed his brothers into the stairwell. It was time to go to work.

The End

The Shepherd Security Series
Book 1: Operation Protected Angel
Book 2: Operation Recruited Angel
Book 3: Operation Dark Angel
Book 4: Operation Fallen Angel
Book 5: Operation Departed Angel
Book 6: Operation Bayou Angel
Book 7: Operation Unknown Angel – Coming Soon

Acknowledgements

I truly say thank you, to you, the reader, for choosing this book. If you enjoyed it, would you please leave a review, so others might find this book to enjoy, as well? As an Independent Author, without a publishing house to help advertise my work, I rely on reviews from readers such as you and followers on social media to promote me. Thank you! I would greatly appreciate it.

Thank you to my sisters, RK Cary and Charlie Roberts, who are writing their own Romance books. RK has finished up her Destined & Redeemed series and has several other Science Fiction/Fantasy stories in the works. Charlie is working on a contemporary romance series, the Stevens Street Gym Series. Both have been wonderful friends with the honesty and encouragement that only a sister can give. Check out their work on Amazon! Links directly to all our books on Amazon can be found on our website. The link is below.

Thank you to my wonderful and supportive husband for his patience and love while I spend hours upon hours to research and write this story. Also, for advising me on any parts of this story requiring knowledge of the military or weapons that I did not have.

Thank you to my mother who shared with me her love of books. As a child, the wonderful example my mother set for me as an avid reader led my sisters and me to write our stories. She has encouraged me to publish and I thank her for her support.

My friend, photographer, and graphic artist, Harry R., shot all the covers for this series. Thank you, Harry!

A big thank you to my girlfriends who have encouraged me and made me feel that I could do this at the times I felt insecure in my ability to accomplish this. You know who you are ladies! You hold a special place in my heart.

Thank you to my editors, a special callout to Evelin, who gave of her time selflessly to help me with the grammar, not my strongpoint.

The models for this cover, are husband and wife. Thank you Gina and Kirby for posing for this cover!

About the Author

Hello! I am Margaret Kay. They say being a Military wife is the toughest job in the Armed Forces even though there is no MOS for the position. As the veteran of more than a few deployments, I have to agree. My husband proudly served eight years in the United States Navy in the 80s. That was before cell phones and the internet.

For anyone who's never had a loved one who's served, being associated with the military is being part of a special community of people who support each other, who understand what the day to day is like when your loved one is deployed half-way around the world.

Saying goodbye to your loved one as they leave on a lengthy deployment is unlike saying goodbye to someone for any other reason. It's not like dropping a son or daughter at college or hugging an aging parent after a visit. Your military member is being deployed, part of a mission. You cannot go visit when you miss them too much. You know it's different. You plan for it differently. They may be getting deployed into harm's way. And even if they are not, you know what their purpose is and that they could be in harm's way at any time.

The emotions you feel when you stand with other families, when the unit, boat, or flight returns after many months of separation cannot be described in words that bring adequate justice to it, but I will try. There is a level of excitement equaled only by a child's wonder on Christmas morning. A pride in your country, in the unit, and in your loved one that surges through your vein's as you, your children, and all around you hold American flags and signs welcoming them home, waiting all together sometimes for hours before they appear and make their way towards you. As a spouse, you're hungering for your partner's touch, for their lips to meet yours, and for the reunion that will occur later, when you're alone. With that excitement also comes nervousness because it has been so long since you've been together as a couple, sharing your bed.

My husband honorably separated from the Navy and easily transitioned to civilian life, but I never forgot what it was like while he served. Many of our returning servicemen and women have not had it so easy. Please keep them in your thoughts and prayers as they recover from physical and emotional injuries. Many struggle to find employment. If you have the ability in your work to encourage the hiring of a Vet, please do.

Our military members are special! I honor all past, present, and future members of our military with my stories. Salute the flag, stand for the national anthem, and thank a Vet for their service. Freedom is not free, a lot of people sacrificed for the freedoms we enjoy.

Don't ever forget!

Margaret

Please stay in touch. I have more books in the Shepherd Security series in process plus two more, separate stories I think you will enjoy. And remember to check out my sister's books. You can be kept abreast of my sister's work and mine at our website:

Visit our website at: www.sistersromance.com

Email me at: MargaretKay@sistersromance.com

Follow me on Facebook at: @MargaretKayAuthor

Subscribe to my Newsletter to be kept informed of when my next books are due out at the top of my page on our website.

Manufactured by Amazon.ca
Bolton, ON

18839879R00162